When the militia's platoon leader saw the enemy's vehicles, fifteen of them, fill the circle of his Owl fourth-generation low-light-sensitive pocket scope, he fired the flare. As soon as its loud pop was heard by the two fifteen-man squads, one on either side of the road, the thirty militiamen opened up with AK-47s, pouring a hail of 7.6mm into the Hummer, the first three and last two troop-laden trucks. There was a splintering of glass and the Hummer went into the S-shape defensive driving pattern but to no avail. The vehicle, its driver hit, slammed into the side of the cutting, its rear wheels still spinning on the road, burning rubber with nowhere to go. The trucks behind screeched to a stop, and several smashed into the vehicle in front of them. Soldiers jumped out over the tailboards onto the I-5 as the second truck in the convoy errupted in flame. The third truck's cooling fans exploded like so many airborne coins, reflecting the descending light of the parachute flare, and the stink of burning gas and oil filled the air.

By Ian Slater:

FIRESPILL
SEA GOLD
AIR GLOW RED
ORWELL: THE ROAD TO AIRSTRIP ONE
STORM
DEEP CHILL
FORBIDDEN ZONE*
WWIII*
WWIII: RAGE OF BATTLE*
WWIII: WORLD IN FLAMES*
WWIII: ARCTIC FRONT*
WWIII: WARSHOT*
WWIII: ASIAN FRONT*
WWIII: FORCE OF ARMS*
WWIII: SOUTH CHINA SEA*
SHOWDOWN: USA vs. MILITIA*

*Published by Fawcett Books

Books published by The Ballantine Publishing Group are available at quantity discounts on bulk purchases for premium, educational, fundraising, and special sales use. For details, please call 1-800-733-3000.

SHOWDOWN

USA vs. MILITIA

Ian Slater

FAWCETT GOLD MEDAL • NEW YORK

A Fawcett Gold Medal Book
Published by Ballantine Books
Copyright © 1997 by Bunyip Enterprises, Inc.

Library of Congress Catalog Card Number: 96-90775

ISBN 0-449-14933-1

Manufactured in the United States of America

First Edition: March 1997

10 9 8 7 6 5 4 3 2 1

The Cleaver

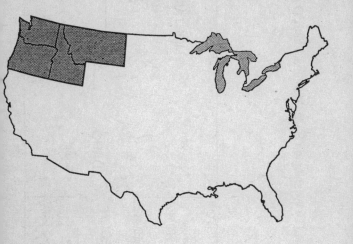

The Cleaver (shape formed by Washington State, Montana, Idaho, Oregon)

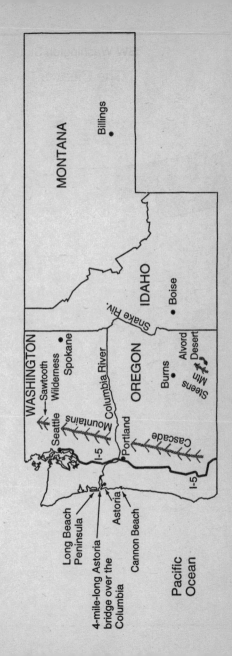

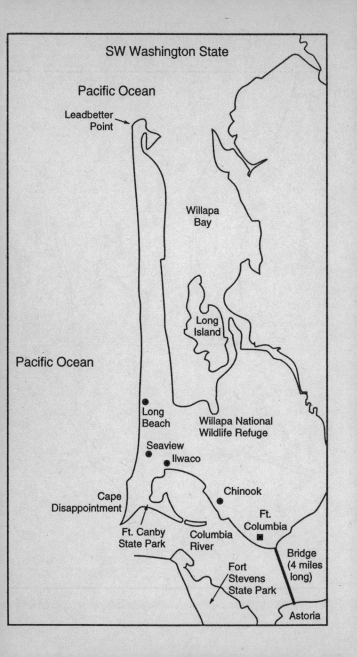

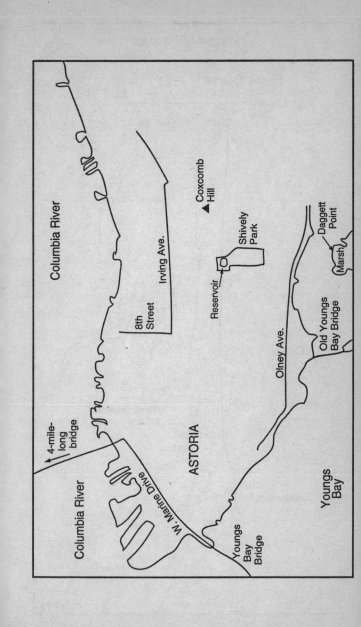

For Marian, Serena, and Blair

I am indebted to my wife, Marian, whose patience, typing, and editorial skills continue to give me invaluable support in my work.

MILITIAS AIM TO LURE ELITE ARMY TROOPS, U.S. GENERALS FEAR

Washington, March 21—Senior Army commanders believe that members of the Special Operations Forces, the elite fighting units that include the Green Berets, have been selected for recruitment by extremist militias . . .

—*The New York Times*, March 22, 1996

Two days after the bombing, 550 patriot Christians gathered in Branson, Missouri, for the International Coalition of Covenant Congregations Conference. "I mingled with a lot of people there, and there was not a shred of sympathy for what happened in Oklahoma. . . ." A father of three is girding for guerilla-style warfare against his own government. He's got a 9-mm semiautomatic pistol strapped on his hip, a wad of emergency cash and enough ammunition to fight a small battle. In the back of his battered Chevy Silverado, he packs a green .223-cal. Sporter assault rifle, a $200 Kevlar helmet, a CB radio, walkie-talkies, camouflage uniforms and 15 days of provisions . . . if you include all the people in as many as 40 states who respond to the patriotic rhetoric about a sinister, out-of-control federal bureaucracy—all the ranchers fed up with land- and water-use policies, all the loggers who feel besieged by environmentalists, all the underemployed who blame their plight on NAFTA and GATT—then the count soars upwards of *12 million*. [Italics added]

—*Time*, May 8, 1995

PROLOGUE

Washington State

"DON'T MOVE!" YELLED McBride. "We're in a minefield. Don't anybody—"

Another charge popped.

"Thought I told you guys not to move!" McBride shouted at the militia platoon.

Lucky McBride, ex–Special Forces sergeant, was, as a rule, an easygoing instructor, but at the moment he had a serious job to do. He'd seen men blown apart in 'Nam because they'd panicked—couldn't wait for a sapper to come up with a detector and work them through it. It was the only way. Slow but sure. If it came to a showdown between the militias and the government, his militiamen of first platoon A Company, First Washington State Regiment, might be under fire *and* in a minefield at the same time. No matter what the temptation, you had to freeze. Otherwise you'd lose a leg or an arm or both. And if that had been a real antitank mine that had popped, you wouldn't even find the pieces.

"How we gonna mark 'em?" one of the platoon's machine gunners called out as the sapper moved cautiously forward, sweeping the ground.

McBride grinned. "Now pay attention, boys and girls. I learned this one from Norman."

"Yeah, yeah, we know, Sarge. You served under Schwarzkopf. Big deal. How we gonna mark the god-damn mines?"

Still grinning, McBride reached for his vest-load pack and took out a small can. Gillette shaving cream—odorless. Following the sapper, he squirted a white blob on the position of every mine. After fifteen minutes he announced, bowing slightly, hands out welcomingly like some kind of butler, "Walk right on through, gentlemen."

"Very fucking clever," said the machine gunner.

"Yeah, well," McBride returned nonchalantly, "come a showdown, Morph, it might save your sorry ass."

The story swept through the militias like a Montana wildfire, so that even as the clouds of civil war were gathering over America, Lucky McBride had become something of a legend in the militias, from Washington State to the Florida Everglades, from Maine to Texas.

CHAPTER ONE

Arlington, Virginia

HE COULD SEE the attorney general's panties—pink—as the breeze lifted her skirt on the third green. She was bent over, intent on sinking a two-foot putt for a possible birdie. Sheila Courtland, a divorcée in her late thirties with two young children, was the most beautiful and, by general agreement, the most compassionate AG ever to grace Washington, let alone the fairways of Arlington's exclusive Army and Navy Golf Club.

Her partner for today's round was retired General Douglas Freeman, a widower at fifty-six, a man known more for his prowess in war than in love. He couldn't take his eyes off her. He envied the job of the male agent who, along with a female counterpart, accompanied the AG wherever she went. Sheila Courtland was a strong advocate of gun control and topped the Internet's USMC—United States Militia Corps—"enemies" list. The general was still mentally undressing her when he heard her cellular ringing. It was attached to her golf cart. Both agents, about twenty yards from the green, were watching the rough by the fairway.

"I'll get it," he said quietly so as not to break her concentration.

"Hello. General Freeman here."

"Oh . . ." There was a tone of disappointment. "Is Sheila there?"

"Yes. She'll just be a second."

"Thanks."

Freeman watched her sink the putt. "Nice shot."

"Thank you, Douglas. How about ten dollars on the next hole?"

"Feeling cocky, are we?" he said, handing her the phone and moving off to his own putt.

"I feel lucky," she said, smiling. "Hello. Sheila Courtland."

"Attorney General Courtland?"

"Yes."

The phone exploded.

Blood streaming from her head, only part of her right hand remaining, the attorney general of the United States staggered a few paces, an acrid black smoke wreathing her body, then collapsed like a rag doll.

She was rushed to Alexandria Hospital in a coma.

Freeman and the two agents, Tracy Albright, FBI, and Tony Beck, Bureau of Alcohol, Tobacco and Firearms, were released from Emergency with cuts and abrasions from the phone's shrapnel. General Freeman's left eye was still bloodied, its cornea lacerated by a sliver from the remote-detonated C-4 plastique bomb, the same kind that had been put into a cellular by Israel's Shin Bet to kill Arab terrorist Yehya Ayyash, known as "the Engineer," in January 1996.

As Tony Beck and Tracy Albright questioned him about what exactly had transpired on the green—exactly what had been said on the phone—the normally good-humored Freeman, who bore a striking resemblance to George C. Scott, was in no mood, as he indelicately put it, "to fart around. Hell, there's no mystery about who did it. It's the damned militias! Sheila's been telling—" He paused. "How is she? Any progress?"

"No," said Beck. "She's still critical—in a coma."

"Well, she's been telling me for weeks of her concern about those people—how their numbers have increased tenfold in the past few years. She's been especially worried about this giant convention they're having up in Spokane and the joint maneuvers they've got scheduled up there. Thousands of 'em apparently. Like a goddamned jamboree!"

"Except," said Tony Beck wryly, "there're no Boy Scouts or Campfire Girls."

"Maybe," said Freeman, "but nevertheless, their motto is 'Be Prepared.' Sons-of-bitches' organization is superb. Lot of 'em might still live in rural areas, but they get e-mail out faster than the NRA."

"We know the AG's been concerned about them," responded Tracy Albright, who until now had said nothing.

"Have your people traced the call?" the general asked them.

"Yes," said Tony Beck. "All incoming calls to the AG are automatically recorded. We know the call was a landline feed from a place called Well Springs, Idaho. Public phone. The remote detonation would have had to be made locally, though—within cell range."

"So," said Freeman, "the landline call was the setup to get her on the cellular?"

"That's right. Landline's a lot harder to intercept than a cellular signal. But whoever pushed the button had to be within remote range—a mile or two."

Before Freeman could ask the next question, Tracy Albright was answering it. "We didn't get anyone. We flooded a two-square-mile area with agents within twenty minutes of learning what had happened."

"Golf-club parking lot?" the general suggested.

"Nothing," Tracy assured him. "Could've been on foot—though I doubt it."

"How about BATF?" Freeman asked Tony Beck.

"Ditto. We've carried out normal procedures—had the highway patrol with a fake speed trap taking videos on all roads leading out of the area. No computer license match with anything yet."

Freeman shook his head with impatience. "Prick could be in Canada by now."

Tony Beck glanced at his watch. "Not unless they took a plane, General."

"Near enough," Freeman responded sharply. He paused. "Look, I'm sorry if I sound . . . impatient. It's because I am. Sheila Courtland and I are close—"

"We understand," said Tracy. At a certain angle, Freeman, with the eye patch, looked menacing.

"How in hell," he asked, "did they get to Sheila's cellular in the first place—to pack the bomb?"

Tracy shrugged. She felt embarrassed for the FBI. "We don't know. We infiltrate them, they infiltrate us. But in any case that's a cold trail by now. The explosive could have been planted or cellulars switched weeks ago—we've no idea. We stand a much better chance of getting the person who pushed the button."

"Tracy and I," said Beck, "have been asked to work on it as a team. Assumption is we might recall something from being near the green. That's why we're questioning you."

Freeman was exasperated. "I've been telling General Limet up at Fort Lewis and the joint chiefs for months—they should carry out a preemptive strike on the militias. Least we should do is go up there and arrest the ringleaders." He paused, his tone now one of unabashed sarcasm. " 'Course, he couldn't do that—might violate somebody's *civil rights*!"

Neither Beck nor Albright said anything. It wasn't that they disagreed with the general in principle. All federal agents believed something had to be done about the alarming growth of militias, but in Washington, D.C., the official word was out about Douglas Freeman. A good man, loyal, brave, a hell of a fighter in 'Nam, the Gulf, and in half a dozen other wars, and a general who was always up front and out front with his men. If he was afraid of anything, it was of growing old gracefully. But his biggest enemy, in his case as in Patton's, was his mouth. He had an open contempt for bureaucrats of any description—those in the state department in particular— and didn't care who knew it. "Eased out" of the army because of "policy differences" with the joint chiefs, the general was still giving free and unsolicited advice, to colleagues and anyone else who'd listen, about what they ought to be doing to "save America." If you were seen or heard espousing Freeman's philosophy of "Love your enemy but keep the son-of-a-bitch in your sights!" it could have deleterious effects on your career. It was said that back in his California home near Monterey—unlike most retired generals' abodes, a modest bungalow— Freeman had a contingency list of officers and other enlisted personnel all over the country—specialists— who were still serving and whom, via his computer, he could call together within hours to form a one-thousand-man battalion-size SOF—special operations force.

"What for?" army C-in-C Les Limet had asked.

"For any contingency," Freeman had told him.

Later, Limet told friends, "Douglas is looking for a fight. He can't stand being out of the action."

"Oh, he'll settle down."

"No, he won't."

CHAPTER TWO

TRACY ALBRIGHT AND Tony Beck took Sheila Courtland's two children, Melinda, age ten, and Robert, five, to see their mother at the hospital. It was a mistake. Young Robert was so terrified of the hospital smell and of all the tubes sticking in his mom, it was all he could do to touch her. She felt cold and sticky.

Back at the office they were sharing, Tracy and Tony found the attorney general's department in turmoil. Assistant AG Patricia Wyeth had taken over for the time being and had stressed to all agents "the need," which she said she was sure Sheila Courtland would agree with, "to keep focused—to do your job."

Thus, a few days later, Tracy Albright, down in Quantico, was trying to do just that. Her shoulder-length auburn hair out of the way in a ponytail, legs apart in the crouch position, she held the Sig Sauer P239, its grip specially designed for a woman's smaller hand, its mag capacity reduced from ten to seven rounds of 9mm Parabellum. She inhaled, let half the air escape, felt the first pressure of the trigger, then squeezed it on the second. Her shot wasn't dead center but was on the edge of the bull's-eye. She was among the FBI's best and brightest and one of the few women to have passed the bureau's required trigger-pressure test—twenty-nine pulls in thirty seconds. Tony Beck in the next stall nodded approvingly at Tracy's shot. Struck again by her figure, silken red hair, and blue eyes that seemed unafraid of anything, Beck looked on as if waiting to admire her next shot when all he was doing was watching her breath. You had to be careful these days—a woman only had to utter the term "sexual harassment" and you were guilty until proven innocent, instead of the other way around. Besides, the FBI and BATF were very leery of "relation-ships" among male and female agents. She inhaled again, began to exhale, held it, then fired. A bull's-eye.

"Good shooting, Agent Albright!"

She made a little bow. "Thank you, Agent Tony."

He had a fantasy of him rescuing her from a hostage situation. She would be so grateful, so moved and excited by his courage that—

"Feel like a coffee?" she asked.

"Sure." He held the firing-range door open for her and watched her walk ahead of him. Her white blouse and navy-blue derriere moved symphonically with the tempo of his sudden lust, and he wondered what it was that had attracted her to the FBI. Beck was still old-fashioned enough to think it a little odd that women should be packing guns, except when he actually met a woman who did. Then he didn't mind, especially in the case of Tracy. Her trick was that she'd managed to retain a certain femi-nine mystique about her, even though those blue eyes expressed a Thatcher-like determination to get things done, no matter who or what stood in her way. No engagement ring, not even a whitish mark where a recent ring might have been. Maybe she was gay?

They walked over to Starbucks. He said he'd get the coffee if she grabbed two of the window seats, which she did, rearranging a mess of morning papers. Beck knew the type well enough—a place for everything and everything in its place. Below *The New York Times*' update about Sheila Courtland—no change—there was a report under the heading SAGEBRUSH REBELLION. It was about an armed confrontation out west between the militia and ranchers on one side and the federal Environmental Protection Agency on the other.

"Too much whipped milk," said Beck as he put down the caffe latte. She took a spoon to the froth and licked. "You've got a white mustache," he said. "Like those stupid milk commercials."

"I know," and her tongue slid slowly over her top lip. She caught him looking at her with more than coffee on his mind.

"How you enjoying the job so far?" Tony asked.

She gave him such a generous smile he felt instantly closer to her. She wasn't wasting time on trite openers. "Well," she said, "I must confess I don't enjoy the early-morning workout. It's what I'd call . . . a little excessive. Don't quote me on that."

"I won't." He smiled back at her. "You'll like it better in the field." She sipped the coffee and pressed the napkin to her lips. There was an awkward silence. To fill it she pointed to the story about the trouble out west. It recapped the bombing of the Reno land-management office in '94, the Carson City forest office in '95, and the '96 confrontation between the FBI and the Montana Freemen. The Freemen refused to pay taxes, gave seminars to militias on how to evade them, refused to recognize federal or local laws, and advocated independence from the United States. They even had their own courts and system of "Just-us," and threatened to hang the local sheriff.

"Pretty testy lot!" said Tony. "You think there's any connection to the attempt on the AG?"

Tracy shrugged. "They all hate gun control, and Courtland's determined to push it through. You see any new intelligence on the Freemen? Internal stuff?"

"Not much," Beck answered. "There's so many of them around the country I've lost track of . . ."

She looked surprised.

Suddenly Tony Beck felt irrationally guilty, as if he'd failed some kind of IQ test, and badly. "Like you," he said, "we keep a watch out for them, but we can't be monitoring every crackpot in America."

"Who said they're crackpots?"

"You don't think they are?" Now it was his turn to be surprised.

"Some of them, yes." She was holding the coffee mug with both hands, as if they were near a fireplace in the dead of winter instead of spring. Cozy. "But even among the crackpots there's often an element of truth—I mean a legitimate beef—that's got out of hand. Know what I mean?"

"They don't see themselves as political."

" 'Course not," said Tracy. "They say they hate politics and politicians, but they're as political as any lobby group. 'Cept they seem to put more trust in bullets than ballots."

"True."

They'd recall this conversation a week later, on a cold day in April, as they marched in a drizzling rain to pay their last respects to Sheila Courtland.

As the funeral cortege made its slow and solemn way up the hill in Arlington National Cemetery, where early-spring blossoms were dulled by the rain, the late attorney general's two children, Melinda holding her little brother's hand, walked, out of step, behind the flag-draped coffin. An honor guard of marines marched in slow time to the mournful beat of a lone drum. Behind the children and relatives came a very angry Douglas Freeman in full-dress army uniform, his rows of ribbons hidden by his topcoat, the left side of his face still freckled by the small cuts and abrasions from the blast, the black patch still over his left eye.

As the burial proceeded Freeman's anger grew to quiet rage.

CHAPTER THREE

Spokane, Washington

"SO NEXT TIME the government tries to do what they did to Randy Weaver at Ruby Ridge—the next time they try to 'Waco' us—we'll whack them good and proper!"

There was thunderous applause from the First Idaho Regiment, five thousand strong. The speaker, Colonel Vance, in immaculate uniform, was the USMC—United States Militia Corps—liaison officer for the Northwest: Washington, Oregon, Idaho, and Montana. A lean man around five-foot-eight, a hundred and forty-five pounds, damn near all of it muscle, Vance wasn't here to waste time. He held up his hands for silence.

"Now, I can tell you," he continued, "the showdown is

coming. Everybody in the media, led by *The New York Lies*, are hollerin' for investigation of, and action against, the militias. The showdown's coming 'tween each one of us and the federals. State troopers ain't a problem—they know us and know better. And the sheriffs—we elect the sons-o'-bitches. They aren't going to mess with us."

This got the room clapping and the colonel going. "But the *federals*, my friends, the *federals* are the liberal hound dogs. They ain't never gonna give up till we show 'em that we aren't to be messed with and that they can't subvert the Constitution of these here United States by trying to disarm its citizenry, a citizenry empowered by God through the Founding Fathers."

"Amen!" Now there was cheering and stomping. "You tell 'em, boy, you tell 'em!"

The colonel's arms rose again like a preacher before his flock. "After seeing you boys and your young'uns firing on your range, I'm not about to question your marksmanship. 'Tain't nothing wrong with that. If I was a federal and saw that—" He started strutting across the stage. "Mama, I'm goin' home fast as I can."

This got a standing ovation and just plain hooting and hollering. The speaker held up his hands like Moses and they sat, God-hungry for more, for Idaho's First Regiment were "legalists," in the jargon of the militia, men who believed the Holy Bible was the literal word of God.

The colonel paused to acknowledge the response and went on: "After Oklahoma City, which we had nothing to do with, and the media blitz which the ponytailed liberals thought would shake us, we've received more applications than ever before—*and*—hold it, now! Hold it!" He paused for effect. "We now have the financial resources to act should the federals attack."

"Ya mean *when* the federals attack!"

"Ah stand corrected," the speaker acknowledged in

his strange, happy accent, somewhat Southern but then sounding Northern too. "*When* the federals attack." He waited till they simmered down.

"Gentlemen." He was speaking more slowly now. "You are among the finest-trained militia I have ever had the honor to be associated with. You're well trained, well supplied, and well led." Vance turned half left, acknowledging the other militia leaders, including Commander-in-Chief General Mant, all in combat fatigues, on the dais. He turned back to face the sea of white faces—not a black one among them. "You're better prepared than your militia forebears who fought against the British. But I have to impress on you the need to follow orders—no matter how difficult or crazy they might seem at the time. After this conference we're going to be on maneuvers all across the country. Now, I know you've been on maneuvers before, but never on this scale. This means that sometimes you're going to be in uniform a lot longer than you expected to be. And you'll be getting orders you think are crazy or don't make sense to you at the *local* level. But rest assured, it's all part of the strategic planning, and sometimes GHQ won't have time for detailed explanations. You'll know why soon enough." He looked about the room. "Questions?"

"Colonel, is it in the strategic planning that we'll be reimbursed for any extra time we have to spend away from our jobs?"

"Yes—you'll be fully compensated, all billing to be approved verbally by local militia commanders—no bills, no receipts, no *taxes*!"

"Right on!"

Another hand rose in the air. "That's all fine and dandy, but what if we can't get more time off?"

"You will."

"How d'you know? Somebody's boss is likely to refuse."

"We'll reimburse *him*."

"What if he doesn't want to help?"

"Then," said the colonel somberly, "he will be classified as a hostile."

One militiaman told another, "If this isn't all bullshit, Henry, he's talking about a river of money."

"Well, Sam, there's one hell of a lot of Americans out there who don't like ethnic pollution, the U.N., affirmative action, no school prayer, welfare for bums, and being taxed blind for handouts to Third World dictators. But most folks can't say anything—otherwise they'd be out of a job. Only way they can tell us how strongly they agree with us is to send us a few bucks. You got a lotta people out there fed up with the federal government wastin' our taxes on damn-fool liberal programs. Republicans, Democrats—all of 'em piggin' out at the tax trough."

Sam nodded right enough, but something was tugging at him. "Come the showdown, I hope there ain't no children involved. That was a bad business in Oklahoma."

"Yes, Sam, I know. 'Course, McVeigh said he never knew there was a nursery or whatever in the building. Still, fact is you gotta be realistic. Hell, more kids than that die every day in motor-vehicle accidents. My granddaddy—he flew with the Eight Air Force in 'forty-four—says he must've killed hundreds of people—men, women, and children. If push comes to shove, it's either you or them, Sam, that's what it'll come down to. Like the colonel says, we've gotta turn this country around. 'Member what they say—you can't make an omelette without breaking eggs. Hell, that Reno bitch killed twice as many young'uns at Waco than that bomb did in Oklahoma."

* * *

Colonel Vance shook hands with new members, including Bob Brisco, a rancher from the Yakima Valley who was fed up with federals making him herd his cattle on a fifteen-mile detour around the northern shore of a lake rather than let the herd go in a straight line through an acre or two of federal land at the southern end. Made absolutely no sense. Finally Colonel Vance shook hands with Colonel Rawlins, CO of Idaho's First. " 'Course, I didn't want to say anything to the men," Vance told him, "but one of our problems at the moment, especially after Oklahoma and the Amtrak derailment in Arizona, et cetera, is infiltration by FBI and Alcohol, Tobacco and Firearms agents. Remember the drill, same for every militia in the country—find out who they are by selective leaks. It's extra work, I know, but it's got to be done. Root the bastards out. Goddamn traitors."

Rawlins winced. His Idaho militia being religiously based, he didn't hold with blasphemy.

"Root 'em out," Vance repeated.

"With extreme prejudice?" Rawlins asked hesitantly.

Vance sensed his reticence. "There's no other way, Colonel." He was pulling his gloves on tightly, his voice a whisper now. "They're sellin' us out for thirty pieces of silver. Do what you have to."

"I understand," said Rawlins. "I don't like it, but I guess—"

"That's right," Vance cut in sharply. "Has to be done! Now!"

CHAPTER FOUR

Sawtooth Wilderness, Washington State

THE MILITIAMAN SAID a short prayer of thanks and steadied his aim. The shot, soon to be heard all across America, reverberated through the mountain pass, the hot wash from the M-16 causing snow to plop, like lumps of confectioner's sugar, from a nearby pine. The wolf two hundred yards away became a momentary blur, then crumpled, the whiteness of the spring crust about the body turning red.

"Murderer!" A woman's voice. The militiaman spun around, surprised to see a figure—no, two of them—emerging from a clump of trees. One of the figures disappeared momentarily. There was the roar of a skidoo and the next instant the vehicle appeared from behind the trees carrying both of them toward him. The militiaman was disgusted with himself for not having sensed their presence earlier, even though they had been downwind. As the skidoo, a white-and-red Arctic Cat, approached, its feral roar at thirty mph shattering the silence of the mountain wilderness, the militiaman, dressed in arctic combat fatigues, recognized one of the figures as a park ranger, a level 4. Armed. The other person was a woman. The militiaman, a fit forty-year-old of above-average

build, with intense blue eyes, turned his back on them, trudging in the deep snow past his cabin off to his left, heading toward the dead wolf. Glancing up at the cabin, he saw his wife and two children peering out in alarm. He could hear the skidoo behind him.

"You bloody murderer!" the woman shouted at him, her voice quavering in her furious attempt to overcome the deafening noise of the skidoo. "What kind of animal are you?" she screamed.

"A human animal," the militiaman answered, and kept walking. "B'sides, it's none of your damned business."

"It's everybody's business, Ames," the ranger cut in. "Don't you feel any responsibility at all for preserving the wildlife?"

"No," Ames said sullenly. "Wolves kill the deer I need to eat. I kill the wolves. Evens out."

"No, it doesn't!" yelled the woman, so mad she was shaking. "It does *not* even out, you moron! The wolves are an endangered species."

"Endangered, my ass," said Ames, stopping and looking over his shoulder at her. "*I'm* the endangered species, lady. You and all your goddamned government regulations smother a man."

"A man!" shouted the woman. "Is that what you call yourself?"

"A free man. Least I was when I came up here. I left civilization to get away from the likes of you and all your stupid regulations."

"They're not so stupid, Ames," said the ranger, turning off the motor, holding his hand up, signaling the woman to cool it. "Regulations are designed to protect endangered species. B'sides, you know it's illegal to hunt wolves. Any culling that has to be done has to be done by park rangers."

Ames, his face tanned and weather-beaten, smiled malevolently. "So you goin' to arrest me—is that it?"

"Yes," said the woman, out of breath from trying to keep up with him.

"Daisy," said the ranger, "let me handle it here on in."

"Yeah," Ames snorted contemptuously. "Let *him* handle it, *Daisy*."

"Mrs. Buchan to you," she snapped.

Ames was still smiling.

"Going to have to take you in, Ames," said the ranger, whose name was Carter.

"Yeah, right," said Ames, his left hand pulling back the rifle's bolt, the empty brass casing catching a glint of sun as it was flicked into the air, then tinkling on the icy snow. "You and what army?" He bent down and picked up the casing—a lot of militiamen packed their own ammo.

"You threatening me?" the ranger said.

Still smiling, Ames said nothing.

"You militia guys," the ranger told him, "are gettin' way too big for your boots."

" 'S'at a fact?" said Ames.

Mrs. Buchan told the ranger, "Arrest him."

Ames's stare was fixed on the ranger, waiting for a move.

"You come with me now, Ames, or there'll be trouble."

Ames remained silent, but his eyes said it all. They told the ranger that if he went for his sidearm, Ames would kill him where he stood. Finally, through her rage, Daisy understood this, too.

"Let's go," she told Carter. "We can come back later."

Carter looked relieved. "I guess you're right," he said, and was about to add something else but thought better of it. Ames's smile widened and the ranger's face turned beet red. "You're not getting away with this, Ames. Man that comes next time'll be a federal marshal."

"What was that about, Charlie?" Ames's wife asked him.

"What'd it look like?" retorted Ames, placing his M-16 in its rack by the stove. He didn't keep it loaded with the twins about, but if he ever had to use it quickly, the heat from the wood fire meant there'd be no cold-sticking of the bolt, that he could get off the first shot in the blink of an eye. Next to the rifle rack was a small hinged table that they pulled out for meals, and on a shelf above it was a Bible—King James Version—Charlie wouldn't have one of those modern editions where God was a He/She. God was God and His son was Jesus Christ and God told you plain and simple that the fowl of the air and beasts of the land were yours. You said a prayer of thanks and you slew the wolf, skinning it for warmth. And to hell with bureaucrats in peaked hats comin' around telling you what you could and couldn't do. What'd that French guy say: "Man was born free and everywhere he is in chains." You better believe it, he told his wife, Laura. And he'd told his eleven-year-old twins Luke and Rebecca that "God's given us all the rules we need—ten of them." Then Luke had asked him how come so many people get to killing one another in wars. "God told us 'bout that too, Luke. Sometimes you can't do anything about a bully but slay him—like it says in the Bible. And like a famous American writer called Papa Hemingway once said, Luke, 'Only way to treat a bully is to give him a thrashing he'll never forget.' " Ames had taken out the rifle's bolt and was now feeding the pull-through weight down the barrel.

"Was Hitler a bully, Dad?" Luke had asked.

"Sure was. So was Mussolini. Both had to be thrashed."

"That ranger a bully, Dad?" asked Rebecca.

"Yeah," said Ames. "He—"

"Charlie!" It was Laura, sounding reproachful. She was ten years younger than Charlie but still a good looker at thirty despite a few wrinkles. Wasn't easy living up here. Hardest thing of all was no running water—creek down back of them through the windbreak of pine and fir froze solid early in the winter and you had to use so much of the wood piled high outside to keep warm. Kids loved it, though, and that kept Charlie going. He'd seen a kid in Seattle, seven-year-old girl, shot to death "accidentally" in a drive-by shooting, right by the day-care where he'd normally pick up Becky and Luke after school. Laura had collected them earlier—both running a temperature in a "shared" cold—and hadn't been able to get Charlie on his cellular at the used-car lot. But the drive-by murder, that's what did it for Charlie. Saw it as plain as day as a sign from the Almighty to get out of the pit of the city.

Laura remembered that day, too. Charlie had said he was like the guy in that movie *Network*—mad as hell, fearful for his kids, and he wasn't going to take it anymore. Besides, he told Laura as they had lain hand in hand in bed that night, he was heavy "with guilt," having to lie all the time to sell damn cars so he could put bread on the table and keep up the damn mortgage payments. Whole damn society was built on lies. After a day's work he'd come home and tell his kids the bedtime Bible stories about trying to be good, to be honest, how no one else might know but God always knows. Tell the kids one way and you live your life another. Put pepper in a leaky radiator to seal it for a few days, long enough to sell the car. Tell a widow—all the men died younger from the stress of business, of lying—tell her she could take the used car to a test garage for an "electronic diagnosis." Then phone the garage and tell Bill there's a fifty in it if the printout looks good. Find some little piddling thing—a dash bulb that the dealer needed to replace— just to make the diagnosis look really convincing. Top it off—tell her it's best to pay cash. "Save on bank charges." Skim Bill's fee off the top—maybe a little for the mortgage. Bit of a fiddle on the tax form. Who's to know?

God knew, that's who.

Charlie and Laura had a garage sale, not that they had much to sell, transferred the mortgage, got all the correspondence-school stuff for kids grade six to eight, and headed north toward the Cascade Mountains, where Charlie would build the cabin himself. "Lookit," he told Laura, "we don't have to live like vegetarian 'eco freaks.' We'll stock up with staples first, then we'll live off the land. You ever eaten venison, Laura? Fresh venison? Order that in a restaurant. *If* they have it you'll pay top dollar—and I'll bet it's been frozen."

First breath of mountain air and they knew they'd made the right decision. They built the cabin in the Sawtooth Wilderness ten miles in from the Cascades Highway. It made Charlie feel good, working with his hands. Made him feel like the old pioneers he so admired. And, something neither he nor Laura had expected, other settlers from around the small towns such as Winthrop and Twisp that nestled in the Cascades came to help them get set up. They were people like Laura and Charlie, people who were fed up with life in the city, fed up with big banks and big government running people's lives. Pretty soon they'd tax the air you breathed.

At first Charlie had joined the militia more as a social thing. He liked guns. The militia liked guns. It was like a meeting of car enthusiasts, each one passionately arguing the merits of his collection and believing with equally passionate conviction that the government slowly but surely was seeking to rob them of the right to bear arms that their forefathers had given them.

Oh sure, Rebecca and Luke missed playmates for a while, but before long they'd discovered they were living in one great enormous playground with snowcapped mountains and sky and forest—far as you could see—and they saw how it became a new playground every three months. They were learning all about the seasons, the natural cycle of nature in God's world, and they learned the names of the stars because through the unpolluted air you could see them, as Becky said, like sparklers at night.

"You shouldn't tell them the ranger's a bully."

"I didn't," said Charlie, hauling on the pull-through in one unbroken movement. "Told 'em the ranger was just a tool of the federals. Government's the bully—Washington tryin' to tell us what to do from over two thousand miles away."

"What are you gonna do when that ranger comes back?"

Charlie didn't answer.

"Charlie?"

"Don't worry."

"What if they do?"

"I told you—don't worry."

Laura wouldn't let it rest. "What if the ranger comes back with a marshal?"

"I'm not worried about the lawmen," said Charlie. "It's that damn woman frightens me. Old battle-ax!" He grunted good-humoredly. "She'd frighten Mant." Charlie saw no irony in the fact that the militias were becoming as rule-bound as the federals.

"You can joke all you want," said Laura. "But what if he does come back with a marshal?"

Charlie had the bolt out, eyes focused on the firing pin, blowing hard on it to make sure there were no dust particles. He had thought of getting Laura and the kids out—send 'em to Winthrop. "Trouble is," he told Laura, "you'd have to hike out."

"Kids couldn't do that," she said. "Not in this snow."

"I know." He pulled out the table for lunch and set the places, something his militia buddies had ribbed him about: "Where's your apron, Charlie?" He'd shucked it off.

For several minutes neither he nor Laura spoke. Looking outside, Laura could see Becky and Luke building a fort in the snow. She and Charlie had gotten used to one another's silences. They were still in love after twelve years, and their silences could be eloquent. But finally, as Laura put in another block of wood, jabbing worriedly at it with the poker till it caught fire, she could contain herself no longer. "What'll you do, Charlie?"

"What I have to."

Ames's wolf kill was the fifth recorded that week but the first CNN reported on its "environmental watch" segment of *Headline News*. Within ten minutes the station's phone lines were jammed, not only by calls from the lower forty-eight, Alaska, and Hawaii, but from around the world. There was no middle ground. People were either dead set against killing any endangered animal or argued that because wolves were the "natural" predators of other species, it was all right for men to hunt wolves. Hunters said that if you saw a big gray tearing the guts out of a fawn while it was still alive you'd soon change your mind. And how about the meat you get at a super-market? they asked indignantly. We humans, they said, don't have any compunction about killing beef cattle for hamburgers or bleeding baby calves to death for veal, but now "everybody's yellin' about a few wolves in areas where there are probably more damn wolves than people."

"Well, we've got to start somewhere, haven't we?" said one caller.

"Look," cautioned a biologist, an expert on wolves, "both sides in this debate are coming in loaded with too much emotion and too little science. If we're to preserve a species, sometimes we've got to cull the wolf stock."

"Cull?" the caller challenged. "You mean *kill*."

CHAPTER FIVE

Atlanta

THE HEAD OF CNN news called in Marte Price, a resourceful and highly competent correspondent who, using her red-haired beauty along with her journalistic talents, had provided CNN with some of the worldwide network's most memorable scoops and who had just fin-ished a story on the lingering tension between China and Vietnam over the oil-rich islands off Vietnam's coast.

"Well, Marte," said her boss, Jack Wilde, smiling, "you had enough of the South China Sea?"

"Depends." She smiled back. "What's up?"

"A wolf kill," he told her. "Seems that animal rights is one hot topic, and not just here in the States. We've got faxes, phone calls, e-mail pouring in from around the world. The Internet has become a war zone. There's been nothing else discussed on the phone-in shows."

Marte Price nodded. "I saw our snippet on it."

"Yeah, but that's all it was—a snippet. Local guy—freelancer in Seattle—gave us that, but we need an in-depth on this. Do a hookup with you and Larry King and a few local people up in Washington State, pro and con. When can you leave?"

"This afternoon."

"Atta girl! Oops, sorry. Patronizing male. I mean 'Good for you, Marte,' or something like that."

"Atta boy!" she riposted, her hand sweeping back a cascade of shining auburn hair.

He handed her a piece of paper with *Ames*, *Buchan*, and the freelancer's name written on it. "Ames—that's the name of the guy who killed the wolf. Couldn't find out a heck of a lot about him except that he's going to be arrested and flown to Seattle to face the music."

As the cab made its way to her home in Druid Hills, one of Atlanta's wealthier suburbs, Marte used her cellular to call Seattle and track down Mrs. Buchan, who was "delighted" that CNN was sending up a correspondent. Everybody watched Marte Price.

Was there anything Mrs. Buchan could tell her about this Mr. Ames? Marte asked her.

"He's a hunter," Buchan replied, her tone oozing contempt, "and he's one of those militia guys."

"Oh," said Marte Price. "What militia is that?" She

suddenly saw another angle to the story. A "two-in-one." A right-wing crazy—à la Randy Weaver, *and* one who shoots endangered species as well. Christ, it could be a CNN special report.

"You're not gonna believe it," said Mrs. Buchan.

"Believe what?"

"What they call themselves, this militia. The Wolverines! Don't you just love it?"

"Ironic," said Marte, making a note that turned to scribble as the cabbie swerved to avoid a Rollerblader. "Asshole!"

"Pardon?" asked Mrs. Buchan.

"I said it's ironic."

"You could call it that," said Mrs. Buchan. "I call it sick. They say they admire the wolves' independence. Lone wolves, Jack London, and all that crapola and then they go and kill them."

Marte made arrangements to meet her in Sedro Woolley, sixty-eight driving miles north of Seattle on the highway leading into the Cascades. Next Marte called the national park rangers' office in the Cascades. The ranger she wanted was someone called Carter, but he was at lunch. Marte glanced at her watch. It was four-fifteen; a quarter past one in the North Cascades. The West was always behind New York.

CHAPTER SIX

Oregon

FOR MICHAEL HEARN, eighteen, skinhead, drifter, jack-of-all-trades and master of none, sitting on Oregon's Cannon Beach, looking out at the Haystack and other rock monoliths that dotted the coastline, this was the best it had been since he left San Diego. The ocean here was too cold to swim in, but the stark contrast afforded by the huge, dark rocks, the pounding creamy surf, along with the tangy smell of the sea, made him happy. It created in him an especially receptive mood for his favorite pastime: listening to and seeing on his Walkman virtual-reality headset the speeches of the Führer.

Nothing else in Hearn's life so far had given him such an emotional high. In the same way that the majestic scenery of the Oregon coast inspired in him the feeling of being as one with the vastness of the earth, sea, and sky, and it with him, the Führer's speeches made him feel at once akin to a single grain of sand in the enormity of the universe and yet part of something much larger than the self. The only feeling like it was the deliberately drawn-out unbearable tension of a vast audience waiting for a rock star—hard rock—to appear. Waiting—every nerve in your body taut as a violin string. He could see an ocean of faces, the enormous imperial eagle clasping the swastika, and all about, long bloodred banners with the black swastika on their pure white circles.

And then the Führer himself, plainly dressed, the eyes—always the fierce beauty of the cold blue eyes—and the lick of hair on the forehead. No medals, not even his Iron Cross won for bravery in the trenches of World War I, and with each step he took toward the rostrum that seemed a mile away, the excitement of the crowd, like some huge animal in the thrall of an impending kill, an exhausted prey waiting for the blow.

The Führer began speaking slowly, his body farther back from the lectern than the speakers who preceded him, hands folded calmly in front, almost desultory in his presentation, one hand now and then wiping back the slick of hair. But then gradually the timbre of his voice increased, the hands more expressive, the pauses more dramatic. Hearn felt himself holding his breath as the Führer told his audience that they and the party were one, for what is the self in the life of the nation, when all of one's problems and doubts are subsumed by the nation, when in the nation there is no doubt, no fear, only the promise of transcendental glory?

So moved was Hearn that by the end of Hitler's speech his heart was pounding to be let out, to be set free, like a lover in orgasmic flight, in a frenzied rush of life and death, of affirmation and negation. Swept away.

And now he could see Rudolf Hess, arm outstretched, affirming to the ecstatic thousands that "*Hitler ist Deutschland and Deutschland ist—*"

"Hey, I'm talking to you." The highway patrolman's foot nudged the drifter.

Hearn sat up abruptly, pushed the stop button, and the feral roar of the Nuremburg masses was gone.

"You can't sleep on the beach."

"What?" said Hearn, taking off the VR and phone headset. "Not even during the day?"

The patrolman's finger pointed at the drifter. "Don't be a smart-ass or I'll run you in. You know damn well what I mean—you can't camp down here. Period."

"Don't intend to." Hearn was still sitting down.

"Mind your mouth or I'll run you in. And get up when I'm talkin' to you."

Hearn got up slowly, brushing sand off his backside.

"What's this shit?" The cop was fingering the beaded swastika on Hearn's backpack.

"Old Indian sign—for good luck."

"The shit it is. This here's a swastika."

"You're looking at it the wrong way 'round."

"You're full o' shit. Let's see some identification."

Hearn showed him his California driver's license.

"You got any money?"

Hearn showed him two twenties, a ten, and change.

"Where you stayin' tonight?"

"I'm not. Moving on."

"Moving on where?"

Hearn shrugged. "North."

"How far north?"

Hearn shrugged again. "Washington State."

"Long walk," said the trooper, eyes invisible behind the mirror shades. "Seeing it's illegal to hitchhike." He walked back to the patrol car.

Hearn, squinting in the sun, gave him a wave. The trooper acknowledged gruffly with a nod.

"Pig!" said Hearn under his breath, his squinting making it look as if he was smiling. "Bastards are all the same."

Hearn wanted the cop down on his knees and then he'd kick the prick right in the face. Smashed bone and blood.

Hearn snatched up his pack and started walking. Something told the skinhead he'd see the cop again.

Hearn walked past the shops of Cannon Beach and the religious conference center up toward Interstate 101. Before he reached it a green Jeep Cherokee with Washington plates pulled up and the passenger door opened. "Want a ride?"

"Heading north?" asked Hearn.

"You betcha! Hop in."

As Hearn got in he saw a pump-action shotgun in the back with a box of .00 cartridges, some thigh-high wader boots and fishing rods.

"Outdoorsman, huh?" he remarked.

"Eh—oh yeah." The man, wearing a sweat-stained hat and blue coveralls, had a tall, wiry build, and was in his late forties, possibly early fifties. Rough hands. "How far you goin'?" he asked Hearn.

"I dunno. Far north as I can get."

"Free and easy, eh?"

"Yeah," Hearn answered. He liked the other man's description of him. "Yeah—free an' easy. Name's Michael Hearn."

"Fred Latrell. Glad to know yer, Mike. Yessiree, that's the way to live. Free and easy. I take it you're not married."

"Nope."

"Better stay that way. Women, kids, tie ya down. Not free then."

"Guess so."

"I know so, son. Been married twenty years."

"Don't like it much, huh?"

"Hell, yes. Betsy an' me're—well, she's stuck with me through good times an' bad and I love my kids." He pulled out his wallet and showed the hitchhiker a photo. "Rhonda and Ben—that's 'em. Good Aryan stock."

Hearn was excited. "Aryan?" Latrell had said a magic word.

"Yeah—you got a problem with that?"

"No—hell, no. I . . . like stuff about the Aryan race."

"Yeah?"

"Yeah."

"Thought you might," said Latrell, watching a car coming up in his rearview and side mirrors. "Asshole's tailgatin'." He pumped the brakes. "Get back, you nigger. Go on now. . . ." He turned to Hearn. "Huh, you must think I'm some kinda fool, pickin' up a hitchhiker, showin' him my wallet, eh?"

"No—I—well, now you come to mention it. What I mean is—"

"I know what you mean, but I had you tagged. Moment I saw your swastika dangling from your pack, an' that cop givin' you a hard time. They don't want a man to be free, Michael—you remember that."

"Hey!" yelled Latrell, braking hard. Hearn felt his body lunge forward and stop abruptly against the strap.

"You black turd!" Latrell shouted, looking angrily at his side mirror. "Get off my ass. Go on, boy, git!" The car's blinkers were indicating a left swing into the fast lane. Latrell immediately swung the Cherokee left to block it. "Holy shit, look at this!" He was laughing. "We're gonna have some fun with this nigger."

Hearn happily joined in. "Hell," he said, "the Cherokee's got more weight than him."

"You betcha!" said Latrell gleefully. "Higher, too." He smiled across at Hearn. "Closer to God, too, right?"

"Right."

"Geez, look at him steamin'. Man, he's gonna have a stroke—praise be to God."

"Amen," said Hearn excitedly. The black driver

behind in a beat-up Cutlass Supreme was leaning on the horn.

Latrell laughed. "That's it, you li'l black turd. Blow your stack! Ain't gonna let you pass, nigger. I'm enjoyin' this."

A sharp bang like a blowout and the Cherokee's rear window cracked and went milky like one huge spiderweb.

"Jesus!" shouted Hearn. "He's shootin' at us."

"Right," said Latrell, the laughter gone, Hearn looking on in fright as Latrell pulled a handgun from the glove box. "Here, son, give 'im a taste of this."

"Wha—no, I—"

"C'mon!" Latrell shouted angrily. "He's tryin' to kill us! Just aim and pull the trigger. She's ready to go."

"Let 'im pass!" Hearn shouted back, but the Cherokee was speeding till it was a good fifty yards ahead of the Cutlass. Steering with his left hand, Latrell reached over, straining slightly, until his right hand felt the butt of the Remington. On the hill's summit a half mile ahead there was the blip of an oncoming vehicle.

"Holy shit!" said Hearn, excitement evaporating in fear.

There was another sharp sound like the snap of a twig—another hole in the rear window, the bullet smashing high into the windshield, another spiderweb. Suddenly, his vehicle swinging dangerously, Latrell cut into the slow lane. The Cutlass came abreast, passing, and Latrell fired. The black man's head exploded like a melon. Latrell braked hard as the Cutlass went wild over the center line. What had been an approaching dot a few moments before was now a huge white semi loaded with logs. Its driver, risking a jackknife, tried to brake, but it was hopeless, the huge semi, like a fist against a paper cup, slamming into the Cutlass, sending the crumpled wreck somersaulting off the highway, smashing into a clump of pine trees.

As he increased speed Latrell was pushing the shotgun's butt into Hearn's side. "Here, grab it, put it in the back."

Still in shock, the skinhead did as he was told, telling himself there was nothing he could have done in time. To have tried to wrestle control of the Cherokee from Latrell would almost certainly have caused the Jeep to sway and flip out of control.

"Don't worry about it, son," said Latrell. "Nigger was asking for it." He paused. He was sweating but his eyes were bright with thought. "Who fired the first shot?" he asked Hearn.

"He did."

"That's right. Well then, when a monkey messes with an Aryan, who wins?"

"Huh?"

"Who wins, dammit?"

"Oh, the Aryan."

"Bet your ass."

Though badly shaken, the driver of the semi had enough presence of mind to call the state patrol on his CB and tell them about the accident. He told the patrolman that he'd seen the white Cutlass crossing the line but there was just "nothin' I could do."

"Uh-huh," said the officer, quickly moving off down the embankment toward the wrecked car.

"Just one guy . . ." the truck driver began, but he could barely speak, his throat dry from shock. "I already seen 'im," he said. "He's dead." The patrolman nodded but kept moving through the passpalum grass and fireweed until he reached the pile of metal that had been the Cutlass. There was blood and tiny sparkling cubes of glass everywhere, most of it over the front seat. The driver was slumped over the wheel. The patrolman could smell excrement and leaking gas, and slipping on a pair of surgical gloves, he felt for a pulse. None. Gently he eased the dead man back from the wheel.

"Jesus Christ . . ." What had been the man's face was nothing more than a raw mush of blood and bone. It was only then, as the officer stepped back, that he noticed the right shoulder of the man's suit was peppered with small holes.

Though telling himself not to speed, Latrell was finding it almost impossible to keep under fifty-five miles per hour. He was rambling on to Hearn about how, thank God, since the Republicans "got the majority in that toilet" they'd left it up to the states to set their own speed limits. Trouble was that in Oregon the "damned egghead authorities in Salem" had stayed with fifty-five as you approached the four-and-a-half-mile-long bridge at Astoria where you crossed the Columbia and from which you could see the infamously dangerous bar where the big river ran "slam bang" into the ocean.

The more Latrell talked, the quieter Hearn became. He'd experienced a sudden rush when the "nigger" had bought it, but now he was afraid of being caught. He was sweating, watching the rear vision. He closed his eyes.

"What the heck you doin'?" asked Latrell, adjusting his CB radio. "Goin' asleep?"

Hearn opened his eyes but didn't look at Latrell. "I'm prayin' we don't get caught."

Latrell approved. "You go right ahead, son. The good Lord'll help a good man. You pray and He'll answer you. An' don't you worry, you'll get over your trigger fright. Hell, first nigger I shot I was tremblin' all over. Soldier's always a bit gun-shy first time out. I'll tell you somethin' else, son. First time the Aryan cleansing squads had to shoot Jews, some of 'em felt so strung out after coupla hours they had to have a bottle of schnapps to finish. 'Course, they gassed most of 'em. Men get too tired shooting all day—wear your trigger finger out an' waste one hell of a lot of ammo." Latrell squirted the windshield with cleanser and put the wipers on "fast." "That's better—couldn't see for bug shit." He turned to Hearn, whose eyes were still fixed on the sideview mirror. A white blob he had seen disappear into a dip in the road now reappeared, larger and getting bigger.

"I seen 'im," said Latrell. "Isn't a cop car."

"How do you know?" responded Hearn, his face creased with doubt. "Could be unmarked."

"It ain't a cop car, Mikey." Latrell nodded toward his CB radio. "I'm on the police band here, son. No traffic on us yet, or haven't you been listening?"

"Haven't been listening." Before Latrell could say anything, Hearn was asking him about the semi-trailer. The driver must have seen the Cutlass go off the road.

"So?" said Latrell.

"So he saw us keep going. Maybe he heard the shot."

"Horsepiss—over the noise of his semi?"

"Well," pressed Hearn. "He sure as hell must've seen us go by."

"Sure he did, but you don't think he was busy with the air brakes? You heard 'em squealin' like a cut pig. He had his hands full just tryin' to stop that sucker. Probably didn't even notice we was in a Jeep, and I'll bet you a dollar to peanuts he didn't get our number. Hell, we were past him in a shot." He saw Hearn wasn't convinced. "You want to get out?"

The skinhead had already thought about it but was more afraid of being alone and being questioned by a cop again. He didn't think he'd be able to hide his nervousness. He'd stay with Latrell. "When are we going to get off this highway?"

"Soon as we cross the bridge, Mike." Latrell smiled. " 'Less you want to swim across."

Once on the bridge that stretched beyond them forever, Hearn noticed a sudden change in Latrell, who was now sitting forward, hunched up, hands tightly gripping the wheel. As the Jeep began the long run along the web-steel matting of the bridge, its tires began to hum.

"Don't like bridges," announced Latrell. "Only one way on, one way off. Too easily trapped."

"Yeah," agreed Hearn, glancing in the sideview. The white car was starting across the bridge about three hundred yards behind them.

Having turned east off Interstate 101 after crossing the Oregon-Washington bridge on the road to Kelso, Latrell felt more relaxed, welcoming the darkness as a huge canopy that would camouflage him on his journey to the sparsely populated area of eastern Washington.

"Used to be a Democrat, right?"

"Who?" asked Hearn, nervous that they only had till daylight, then they'd have to get off the main roads.

"You," Latrell answered. "Bet you used to be a Democrat."

"No."

"Republican?"

"No."

"Well, I used to be a Democrat 'cause my granddaddy and his daddy was. Granddaddy thought Franklin Delano Roosevelt was sent by God 'imself."

Hearn said nothing. He didn't know where the hell this conversation was going and was starting to think that Latrell wasn't the full dollar. He didn't care about the nigger getting shot either, but Latrell seemed totally unafraid of the police. It struck Hearn that maybe Latrell had cancer or something—one of those diseases that left you only a year or so, so that you didn't give a shit. Maybe that was why he was so thin.

"Know what I think?" said Latrell. "Roosevelt was bringin' us communism. You're too young to remember what he done, but he started bringing in all this damned government we got. Can't spit without some government stooge tellin' you ya can't."

Hearn was still watching the rear vision. Headlights about half a mile back. "Where are we goin'?" he asked Latrell.

"Where it's safe."

Hearn reconsidered his position, but it was the same as it was before and it made more sense to stay with Latrell because the truth was he didn't trust himself not to break under pressure. There, he'd finally admitted it to himself. He was afraid of the police. He'd been arrested one time for being a public nuisance, pissed out of his mind, could hardly walk. Cops put him in jail overnight, took away his belt and laces, and left the naked lightbulb on all night. Next morning all his supposed toughness was gone, vanished. Awful—he was ready to confess to anything. Nobody had come down to help him. He'd pleaded guilty, paid the fine, and hit the road. "Where's it safe?"

"Spokane. Big militia convention."

For a few minutes they said nothing, but Hearn was feeling more comfortable, safer by the second. Inside the Cherokee's warm cab the subdued lights of the dashboard in the night gave him a sense of security, of a safe, warm place in from the cold and the vast loneliness of the outside world, a world of blackness broken only by the wink of a distant farmhouse now and then. Wild America, far away from the glitz of big cities.

"Stop!" he yelled, but it was too late. The Cherokee,

braking, slammed into the deer, the Jeep's radiator punched in, the injured animal kicking spasmodically with one of its hind legs, blood gushing, looking like black velvet on the blacktop.

"Damn!" said Latrell. "There goes my deductible. Damn!" He reached into the glove box, opened the door, then paused, thrusting the gun at Hearn. "Here, you do it."

Hearn hesitated.

"C'mon, Mikey, just aim it at his head an' pull the trigger. Nothin' to it." Latrell paused. "You ain't never done it before, have you?"

"No . . ."

"Better get used to it, boy. Showdown's coming."

"Show . . ."

"Against the federals," said Latrell irritably. "Haven't you bin listenin' to anything I been sayin'? Go on—ain't got all night."

Hearn got out, held the handgun the way he'd seen in the movies. He'd been brought up in hunting country and knew something about rifles and shotguns, but handguns? He pulled the trigger. There were sparks on the highway and the sound of the bullet whistling into the woods.

"Shit." Latrell laughed, calling out, "Hold it steady. Go on."

This time the bullet tore into the childlike eye and the deer stopped moving.

"Take 'im off the road. Heavy bastard, eh? That's it, pull 'im off."

When Hearn got back in the cabin he held on to the gun for a few seconds.

"Like the feel of 'er?" said Latrell.

"Yeah."

"She's a beauty, eh?"

"Sure is."

"Browning, nine millimeter," said Latrell. "You got eleven left—thirteen-round clip. Never forget how many you got left. It's hard to keep that straight in your head when you're firin'—noise and everything—but you've gotta do it. You don't—it could cost you your—" Latrell started to pull off the road's shoulder, right hand on his forehead. He was grimacing in pain.

"What's the matter?" asked Hearn.

"Fuckin' headache," said Latrell. He reached into the glove box, took out a vial of pills, threw a couple into his mouth, and began chewing them.

"Jesus!" said Hearn. "How can you do that?"

"What?"

"Take pills dry."

"I can't. Gimme a Coke. They're in the backseat down by the box of lures. Have one yourself. Christ, feels like a knife in my head."

Latrell and Hearn had passed up through the Indian reservation on Interstate 97 and on through Yakima. Hearn, though tired, offered to drive awhile in hopes that once Latrell got into the passenger seat, he might shut up. But Latrell, despite his tall, emaciated-looking frame, exhibited an almost ceaseless energy and happily refused Hearn's offer.

"Glad we're outta that reservation," he said. "Trouble is, Mike, you got your whining Indians—ain't never got enough of anythin', always cryin' in those toilets they call home. Then come your niggers gettin' uppity all 'cross the country—affirmative-action crap—and then your Jewish bankers, politicians, an' liberals, all suckin' up to the niggers, the freakin' Apaches, and the queers. Suddenly you an' me is to blame 'cause we're white—like everything's been all our fault."

Hearn wound down the window, ready to toss out his gum wrapper.

"Hey, don't do that," said Latrell. "Don't hold with litterin'."

"Sorry."

"You're in white man's country now. Any of the boys see you doin' that they'd skin you alive."

"What boys?"

"Militia. Yep. We got militia all over this state. Gonna have our own country pretty soon. 'Course, we have close liaison with Idaho and Montana units too." He paused to spit out the window. "You know in Germany, Uncle 'Dolf started with private militias."

"I know," said Hearn. He'd found a home.

CHAPTER SEVEN

IT WAS THE beginning of a new day, and as Laura rustled up breakfast Ames stood outside his cabin admiring the spectacular vista of the mountains, snow clouds closing in. He'd made it a point that having escaped the pit of the city, he'd never take his newfound freedom for granted. He heard the cry of a Steller's jay and then another sound, the far-off, angry growling of snowmobiles invading the great white silence. Probably

Carter and the bitch. And a marshal? Ames's dog, Blue, normally licking the children awake at this time of day, stood by his side, tail wagging furiously, her eyes fixed on Ames, the dog's impatient barking punctuated here and there with a plaintive and impatient whine for action. It was then that Ames heard the sharp chopping of a helicopter in the pristine air. All senses alert, he could smell gas fumes in the wind.

He saw the chopper appear above the snow-covered pines about a mile to the west like some huge, insolent bug hovering for several seconds, beginning its descent. Ames went into the cabin, grabbed his gun, and with Blue at his heels, barking furiously at the invasion, he started his skidoo and headed into the woods east of the cabin.

Ames was no coward, but he wasn't anyone's fool, either, and within thirty seconds he had vanished into the forest, Blue riding in the specially constructed pinion seat, her warm breath on his neck.

By the time the helo's snow-filled wind had subsided around the cabin and Marte Price had alighted from the helo, Ames was nowhere in sight. And when Park Ranger Carter arrived with U.S. Marshal Brian Rolston and the anti-wolf kill, Mrs. Buchan, on their respective snowmobiles, Carter lost his cool. For the first time, at least in Marshal Rolston's memory, Carter began shouting, the object of his wrath being CNN's Marte Price. "You were so damn eager for hot copy you landed before we arrived!"

Marte Price glared at the pilot, who held up his hands. "Hey, far as I was told, Miz, these guys were already here."

Part of Carter's chagrin was caused by the fact that while CNN could afford to send its reporters by helo, he and Rolston had been ordered to go arrest Ames by skidoo. "And now," said the ranger, "he's gone."

"No sweat," said the pilot accommodatingly. "I'll take you up for a look-see if you like—if Miz Price here will give up her seat."

"Glad to," said Marte.

Somewhat placated by the offer, Carter accepted, and in two minutes he was aloft, the figures of Marte Price, Mrs. Buchan, and the marshal quickly receding as the chopper banked hard southward from the toy log cabin that now seemed to be sliding downhill as Carter took his eyes off the sweeping vista of pine, lake, and mountains, and instead looked for the telltale snail track of Ames's skidoo. He saw it for a second as a scratch across the snowy landscape, but then it disappeared again into the forest of pine that spilled down toward the lake.

"Damn woman!" Carter said, his exclamation lost to the noise of the rotor blades. "Now we'll have to go down and wait the bastard out." He told the pilot to take her down.

"Down where?"

"Next to his cabin. We're moving in. His family's movin' out."

"Can you do that?"

"Damn right we can. Take 'em into protective custody. That'll flush the son-of-a-bitch out of hiding. Yeller belly."

But by the time Carter landed and, head down, exited beneath the slowing blades, he knew he had a problem. He could hardly expect Mrs. Buchan to wait out in the snow, or the reporter for that matter, and yet he didn't have the authority to let anyone else other than himself and the marshal into Ames's log cabin. If he did, he was sure that some smart-ass lawyer would get Ames off because of the irregularity. He told Marte Price and Mrs.

Buchan that he and the marshal would stay but that they should go back, Marte Price in the two-seat helo and Mrs. Buchan on the skidoo. It wasn't going to be the quick snatch-and-grab he'd promised them. "Can you manage Twisp alone, Mrs. Buchan?"

She was incensed that any male would dare be so condescending. "Of course I can," she snapped. "I've lived in this state longer than you have and I—"

"Fine, Mrs. Buchan. Miz Price, I'd like you to go as well." He indicated the helo.

There was an awkward silence before Marte Price asked, "How can I be sure of getting the news first?"

"If something breaks," Carter assured her, "I'll give you a call on the cellular—when I get in range of Twisp."

"Thank you."

Within five minutes the helo was a dot in a sky that had turned to a sullen gray. It began snowing heavily.

"Shit!" It was Carter. He could no longer hear a skidoo in the direction Ames had taken off and any tracks left by the militiaman would be obliterated by the snow. He told Rolston he was impatient to get it over with.

"Listen, bucko," Rolston cautioned. "We'll wait him out. In this business impatience can get you killed. You go in that forest—well, these militia guys know their bushcraft."

"Yeah," Carter conceded gruffly. "Guess you're right."

The real problem, Rolston thought, would be the dog. He'd seen its paw prints all round the cabin. If it attacked, he'd use his shotgun, not his sidearm.

He walked with Carter to the cabin door. Two kids were peering out the frosty window, a boy and a girl— faces pressed up hard against the glass. Carter knocked and heard a chain being slipped in. Old city habits die hard, he thought—even up here in the mountains. The door opened a crack.

"What do you want?" Laura asked. Carter shook his head at Rolston. As if she didn't know.

"We want to talk to your husband."

"He's not here."

"We know that. We'd like to come in and wait."

"No."

Rolston stepped forward. "Ma'am, U.S. Marshal Rolston here." He was holding his ID up so she could see them through the narrow slit. Despite his shooter mittens, his hands were numb from the cold. "Ma'am?"

"You're not welcome."

Rolston sighed and could see his breath. He was a young man, still in his thirties, but he was getting too old for this bullshit. It was twenty below. Besides, Ames was a fugitive, for Christ's sake. "Ma'am, open this door or I'll bust it in."

"You do and I'll shoot."

Rolston looked at Carter.

"She's bluffing," Carter intoned in a low voice. Rolston looked through the slit between the edge of the door and the frame. He caught a glimpse of the woman's skirt and the woodstove at the far end of the cabin. "Mrs. Ames," he said, "you've got two children to think about, right?"

There was no answer.

"Mrs. Ames—you don't want to put the children at risk, do you?"

Still no answer.

"Isn't that why your husband left?"

"You come through the door, mister, I'll shoot."

"C'mon," Carter told the marshal. "Let's go." They backed off. Now it was Rolston who was steamed, and Carter was beginning to think that his decision not to request additional rangers to help in arresting Ames owed too much to his pride and not enough to common sense. He and the marshal would be enough if Ames decided to return to the cabin and give himself up; otherwise it'd take an army to track him down, air searches impossible in this weather. He could see Marte Price's report on CNN—flashed all around the world. He and Rolston, the two men outsmarted by a woman. And two kids. They'd be a laughingstock. Christ, he could see Jay Leno and Letterman: "You hear about this ranger and marshal up in Washington? Apparently . . ."

"Well, she asked for it," said Rolston. "Fucked if I'm gonna stand out here and freeze to death—and be a fucking target for Ames."

"Maybe he thinks we're gone," said Carter. "He would've heard the skidoo and helo heading back."

"Maybe," grunted Rolston. He was still thinking about the reception he'd get going back empty-handed. "We're goin' inside," he said, reaching inside his jacket to the ring clips on his Kevlar vest.

"How about the kids?" Carter asked nervously.

"Don't worry," Rolston told him. "I'll give her fair warning." And he did, reminding Laura that he was the law, and if she didn't open the door there was going to be "forcible entry."

She didn't answer, but they could hear movement inside—sounded like a coffeepot or something falling and a faint scurrying sound. Rolston moved back to the edge of the small clump of woods about forty feet from the cabin. "Tell her," Carter suggested, "exactly what you're going to do if she doesn't open—"

"Oh, fer Christ's sake," snapped the marshal. "I tell her that and she'll move away from the door, stand by the friggin' window. Soon as I chuck it in, she'll toss it out. We won't get anywhere playin' that game." He'd drawn his Smith & Wesson .38 and pointed it in the direction of their skidoo. "Now go get the masks."

Carter hesitated.

"Look," said Rolston, exasperated, "it'll only be for a second or two. One whiff of that tear gas and they'll be out the door like a shot. They'll be right as rain after a bit o' fresh air."

"I dunno," said Carter, having trouble putting on the mask, his voice sounding like he was inside an echo chamber instead of out in the wild. "These militia families—they're pretty stubborn."

"So's tear gas," said Rolston. "They'll come out. Now put your fuckin' mask on before I freeze to death."

Laura, holding the twelve-gauge, Becky and Luke huddled beside her, heard the window implode, glass flying everywhere, and saw thick smoke pouring from a grenade. She moved toward it, Becky screaming hysterically, calling her mom back, Luke holding his twin, both children coughing, and now Luke was yelling—they couldn't see. Unable to find the canister in a fog of gas, her throat burning, Laura drew back, twelve-gauge in hand, yelling for the twins to follow her. She flung the door open and ran out.

Rolston saw smoke, glimpsed the twelve-gauge pointing right at him, and fired before he knew it, blowing Luke and Becky back into the opaqueness of gas and snow, and flinging Luke hard against the cabin wall, his neck broken by the impact, Rebecca's face peeled off, screaming in agony, her mother dead by her side.

"Jesus, Jesus, Jesus . . ." Carter tore off his mask, his ears still ringing from the blast, unaware of the tortured howl of an approaching skidoo, not more than a hundred yards—fifty yards—from the cabin, and now coughing uncontrollably from the gas. Rolston stood there, grotesque in his mask, paralyzed.

On his hands and knees, scrabbling around frantically for his mask, which he'd discarded only seconds before, Carter was oblivious to the fact that the approaching skidoo had fallen silent.

"Laura!" Ames was running through the trees, his arctic camouflage a blur in the falling snow.

Rolston swung about—too late. Where was the dog? There was the crack of the shot and a whack, Ames's M-16 slug slamming into Kevlar, knocking the marshal down, the second shot splintering the lawman's mask, exiting from the top of his head.

Carter, only now fully realizing what was going on, went for his sidearm. Ames blew him away with a three-round burst. Everything had gone wrong.

Sobbing uncontrollably, Charlie Ames cursed himself for having left the cabin in what he now saw had been his futile hope of drawing off the federals—away from his family. If he had only been here. But here he would have fought. Or would he have gone meekly? Better that than this.

At first he had no strength in him, the life force drained from him, and he was barely able to carry out the jerrican of gasoline with which he would immolate his wife and the incredibly small, fragile figures that had been his children. The frozen ground precluded any thought of trying to dig graves.

The wolves could have the two murderers.

For several hours Charlie Ames was insane—just how long he couldn't remember—only that he must have sat by the pyre of his family all through the snow-filled night, wolves all around in the darkness howling their lament. And in the snowing dawn all he had left in him was a pitiless resolve.

He didn't know when it was that Blue had reached the cabin after having been thrown off the skidoo in deep snow as it hit a mogul during Charlie's dash for home. Perhaps the husky had arrived only seconds after the shooting—or an hour later. Ames could only remember her slowly approaching Laura's body, sniffing, then whimpering, and looking up at him inquiringly, and then the dog sitting by his side at the funeral pyre.

As Charlie Ames sat, eyes fixed on the glowing coals at the heart of the fire, blackened bone crashing in on them, sparks spitting and dying in the frigid air, he realized he had two choices. To walk away—or fight. What would God want? He began loading up his skidoo.

CHAPTER EIGHT

FROM ATLANTA VIA CNN's satellite feed, the CNN anchor was telling the world of the latest confrontation between a militiaman and the federal government: "In the remote Cascade Mountains of northwestern Washington, a hunter, accused by park officials of violating the wolf preservation ordinance, has been involved in a shoot-out with two federal officials. Our correspondent Marte Price has the story."

To lend her report an air of authenticity, Marte was dressed in a parka with fur trim and was on camera as snow was still falling at the tail end of the blizzard. "Yesterday a U.S. marshal and a ranger from the National Park Service went to arrest Charles Ames, a militiaman who park rangers said had illegally built a log cabin on federal land and who had refused to surrender to authorities several days before on charges of killing wolves. Only park rangers or park-authorized biologists are allowed to cull wolves. Ames refused to surrender a second time, and in a shoot-out, Ames, a member of the Wolverine militia, apparently murdered the two federal officials, a park ranger and a U.S. marshal, and then killed his wife and two children. The Washington National Guard has been called in, in an effort to capture Ames, who is said to be heavily armed. Air searches have been ruled out, because as you can see, it's snowing heavily here in the Cascades."

There was a close-in shot of Mrs. Buchan getting ten seconds' worth, saying that while it was a tragedy that five people had been killed, it was "high time" that these militia types were being held accountable for their "cold-blooded murder" of helpless animals.

CNN's switchboard lit up like a Christmas tree, the pro-and-con wolf debaters in gridlock. It was perfectly clear to both sides what had happened. For antimilitia groups and anti-wolf-kill ecologists, a wolf killer and murderer was on the loose and had to be apprehended. For the militia, hunters, and all gun owners it was obvious: Ruby Ridge. The federals were closing in.

In Spokane, where Tracy Albright and Tony Beck had been dispatched, the militia's "big guns" were readying for the largest militia convention the country had ever seen—over ten thousand already in the city. Crowds hadn't been this big since the city had hosted the World's Fair in 1974. They were all there, from the Freemen of Florida, Texas, Oklahoma, Idaho, and Oregon, to MOM—Militia of Montana—and Arizona's Police Against the New World Order, to Michigan's Militia Corps, the latter's 1995 membership of twelve thousand now grown to eighteen thousand. Watching CNN's report from his hotel room—he'd refused a suite—the USMC's (United States Militia Corps') C-in-C, General Mant, shook his head in disgust. "Ruby Ridge. Same tactics. Creep up on a guy and blow his family away."

"Wonder they didn't use tanks," put in Arizona's commander disgustedly. "Like they did at Waco."

"We'll never know," Mant commented. "Another cover-up already under way."

"Now," the Idaho commander told Mant, "the antigun lobbyists are gonna go ape and the federals move that much closer. Showdown's comin', General."

"It's *here*," said General Mant, rising from his chair. "Can't let this go unchallenged. Brother Ames has to be protected. Whole world is watching. If we don't make a stand now, we lose all credibility." He turned to his top aide. "Colonel Vance. Conference here—fourteen hundred hours. All state C-in-C's. Bug sweep of this room, thirteen hundred hours. Full security. *No absentees*."

"Yes, sir."

"And Vance."

"Sir?"

"Put Washington Wolverines and MOSBA One on ACON Three."

"Yes, sir."

Of all the militias' mobile strike battalions, MOSBA One, like McBride's Wolverines, was an elite force, made up exclusively of 'Nam and Gulf War vets like

Lucky McBride. "ACON Three"—Attack Condition Three—was one step from all-out war. If announced by Mant, "ACON Four" would mean general mobilization for all militias in the United States. Practically speaking, once announced, ACON Four would be impossible to countermand—the dogs of war unleashed.

CHAPTER NINE

IN WASHINGTON, D.C., the president, the head of the park service, and newly sworn in Attorney General Patricia Wyeth were under fire from the militias in general, the National Rifle Association, the American Civil Liberties Union, and by individuals all over the country who were angry—"outraged" was the most common word used—with the federal authorities for what many were claiming was the murder of Laura, Rebecca, and Luke Ames.

From Spokane, General Mant, via Marte Price's special CNN report, called for a day of "national mourning" for the three slain victims of the government's continuing "undeclared war" on the American people. He urged all Americans, all those who believed in freedom, to express "their collective outrage" at the government's action.

A famed defense attorney, attired in his fringed buckskin jacket and known the world over for his commentary during the O. J. Simpson trial in '95, made the observation that "even with the few facts available" the "Ames debacle is chillingly reminiscent of Ruby Ridge. Tear gas on children, for God's sake."

The Jeep Cherokee's tires were humming on the blacktop, Latrell playing a country disc that he referred to as "rebel music." On the flat country of the Columbia River basin, he'd heard Mant's call "loud and clear." Hearn had realized he was in over his head. He was drowning and didn't know how to get out. Latrell punched a button on the dash and the music stopped. "American Pie." "Thought a young feller like you had what it takes?"

"For what?" replied Hearn, trying for adult confidence in his tone but not getting it.

"For doin' what's necessary. For folks rise up—storm break loose!"

Hearn was silent, wondering just what the hell was going on.

"Storm break loose!" shouted Latrell, thumping the steering wheel. "Eee-liminate the bastards! Hey!"

Whatever was going on, Latrell was crazy, a certifiable loony.

"Eee-liminate the bastards. Right?"

"Listen," said Hearn, trying to sound strong, calm. "Let me out. I want to get out."

Latrell's face contorted, imitating the skinhead. " 'I want to get out. My mommy wants me to come home.' " Suddenly he was hysterical, talking to himself in two different voices. "Is Sheila Courtland there? Yes. She'll just be a second. Thanks. Hello. Sheila Courtland? Yes. *Boom!*" He turned to Hearn, eyes blazing. "Fuck you, George! You're in it—up to your balls."

"My name's not Geor—"

"You got balls, George? That swastika a Christmas decoration or what? Skinhead, my ass. You're a pretty boy. Queer—that it? Queerer'n a three-dollar bill? What?"

"I want out."

Latrell let out a string of obscenities. "Stand and be counted! Folk—" he screamed, then suddenly went quiet, shaking his head like a wet dog, the Cherokee veering dangerously, then he lapsed into silence.

The fit was over, and even in the dim cabin light Hearn could see Latrell was soaked with perspiration, his body giving off a strange odor, and instantly Hearn was taken back to his childhood, watching a boy—who, they said, wasn't "quite right"—blubbering by a water tank, his body emitting the same peculiar odor, some overactive chemical perhaps or some kind of chemical deficiency—he had never found out. The next moment Latrell was talking quietly, without histrionics, about the need to give the new FBI "bitch" a warning to back off.

Hearn didn't say a word, but he was seething. For Latrell's information the swastika wasn't a friggin' "Christmas decoration," it was the sign of an Aryan, a sane, purposeful Aryan, not an Aryan unhinged like Latrell. What if he waited till Latrell was on a long hill, the Cherokee in low gear, and he just suddenly hopped out? Latrell might turn around and try to find him, but maybe he'd get away in the dark. Maybe not—it was awfully flat out there. Besides, you might grow old waiting for a hill, one steep enough to slow the Cherokee. For that you'd have to turn west out of the valley and head into the Cascades. Hearn could still hear his heart thumping from the fright Latrell had given him—the blood coursing so loudly through his ears, he was sure Latrell must hear it, too.

"Sorry," said Latrell. "Sometimes I get these goddamn

headaches—think my head's gonna explode." In the darkness behind there were two pinpoints of lights coming toward them.

In the patrol car, heading east from Yakima on Interstate 90, Patrolman Ernesto Valdez, age forty-one, of Moxee City, Yakima County, was monitoring dispatch while listening to Mexican folklorico music to relieve the boredom. Traffic was light and on such a flat road there were not that many places where he could hide to watch speeders. Now and then he might see an out-of-state plate and punch it in the computer, just to see if anything came up.

Ernesto grew tired of the folklorico after a while, pushed eject, turned the inside light on, and fished around in a little wicker basket on the passenger seat that his wife had made for him to hold the tapes. Trouble was, he had more tapes than containers and was constantly getting them mixed up. He had Frank Sinatra in a Three Tenors—Pavarotti, Domingo, and Carreras—box and the three tenors in a Jim Reeves box. "Jesus, Ernie," the boys at the station kept ribbing him, "when the hell you gonna get this mess sorted out?"

"Mañana."

Ernesto smiled at his friends joshing him. It meant that being the son of onetime illegal immigrants didn't matter anymore. He was one of them, an American, and he praised the Lord for the day his parents had crossed the Rio Grande. But it meant when he came across a wetback working the fields in the valley, he couldn't show them any favoritism in front of his fellow officers. If he found someone without a green card he'd tell them that if he came 'round again and found them he'd have to take them in. Some would offer him bribes and he'd tell them they'd better put the damn money away pronto, otherwise he'd take them in right there and then.

He loved America and outside his bungalow in Moxee he flew the Stars and Stripes. Only time he absolutely lost his cool was when some punks—skinheads—took down the flag and replaced it with a swastika. Ernesto went ballistic and treated it like it was a serial murder. He suspected who it was, but it took a week to get one of the skinheads to confess and name the others: three of them in all. He let two go with a warning, some of it in Spanish, he was so worked up. After he'd spent a half hour with the ringleader, he drove him home to the outskirts of Yakima, where the boy, Gerald Freeth, lived. The father answered the doorbell dressed in ragtag shorts and a stained T-shirt—or maybe they made them like that?—and stank of bourbon. "Yeah," he asked Ernesto. "What d'ya want?"

"For you to get control of your son," Ernesto told him.

"He does what he wants," answered the father sullenly.

"That's not a good idea," Ernesto told him. The skinhead, about seventeen, was grimacing in pain. His father glanced at Valdez. "What happened to 'im?"

Valdez looked the father straight in the eye. "He fell down some stairs. He should watch where he's going. Especially near the Stars and Stripes."

"What?" asked the father. "What in hell you talking about?"

"Your son'll tell you, won't you?"

The kid was staring at the dusty ground. Valdez told the father.

"This the truth?" his father bellowed.

The youth mumbled. The father undid his belt and pulled it out. "Get inside!" The father glared at Valdez. "I fought in 'Nam. By Christ, I'll—next time just bring 'im to me."

"I hope there won't be a next time, Mr. Freeth."

"By Christ, no—there won't be."

Valdez felt bad because he thought the kid's old man might kill him.

Next thing he heard about young Freeth was that he'd joined the army. Just what had gone on inside that house that afternoon Ernesto didn't know—maybe it was the old man's belt, maybe he didn't touch the kid after Valdez had left, maybe he'd given the kid an ultimatum: join the army or else. Whatever, Ernesto was glad he'd caught the kid. Sometimes a whole life could turn on just one incident—a few words here, a kick in the butt there. Only God knew.

When Ernesto saw the Jeep in front of him, it was well within the speed limit. Bored, he turned down the volume on the three tenors and called Yakima dispatch. "Green Jeep—Cherokee—looks like a 'ninety-four. Washington plates XK—he's running for it!" Valdez finished calling in the license number and flicked on the siren.

"That's a computer match," said dispatch, "with the video of plates leaving the area of the AG's assassination in Arlington. Prime suspect."

"Get in the backseat," Latrell said. "Grab the shotgun." The siren was getting closer. No way the Jeep could outrun him. "Grab the shotgun!"

Instead, Hearn reached for the keys. Latrell smacked him away, holding the 9mm gun with his right hand. "What's the matter with you?"

The police car was about to overtake them.

"Too fast for us," said Latrell, pulling over toward the shoulder. "Sorry I hit you, Mikey. You're right, we gotta pull up. Let me do the talking. Get in back and get the shotgun," he said, pushing Hearn. "It's ready to go. We've been huntin', right?"

"Hunting," said Hearn, clambering into the seat behind, his throat dry as leather, barely able to speak.

"Yeah. Just be cool, eh—wait—hey, hey, there's only one of 'em, Mikey. He's alone."

"So?"

"When I stop 'er I'll go into a slide. You get out into the grass—fast. Fucker won't see you in all this dust. Come back 'round him."

"Pull over and stop!" came the voice booming through the rattle of the two vehicles on the rough dirt road.

"You remember, Mikey," yelled Latrell. "You're a young'un. You go to prison they're gonna gang-rape you—you hear me? They're gonna hold you down. You're gonna get raped—every day."

"Pull over and—"

Valdez saw the Cherokee's brake lights light up like two big red eyes in a dust storm, and he slammed on his brakes. It took a full thirty seconds for the thick dust to clear. By then Valdez was out of his car, lights still flashing, weapon drawn, his window down, crouching behind his open door, his arm held steady, arms supported by the door. "Don't move—stay in the car. Put your hands on your head and keep 'em there. Don't move. You hear me?"

Latrell had his window down. "I hear ya."

"Do not move!" Slowly, his gun held steady in both hands, heart thumping a deep bass in his chest, Ernesto approached the Cherokee, maintaining by-the-book caution, left hand opening the door. "Keep your hands on your head. Get out of the car. Slowly."

"Sorry about this, Off—"

"Shut up. Against the car, hands on the hood." Now Valdez's voice exploded with the pent-up tension. "Legs apart!" His gun in Latrell's back, Ernesto quickly frisked him, taking the 9mm out of Latrell's belt and cuffing him.

"Christ!" complained Latrell. "They're too tight."

"They're meant to be. C'mon." Valdez grabbed his prisoner by his shirt, pushing him toward the police car. "Get in the car." He opened the back door. "Listen, Officer, I can explain the—"

"Shut up and get in the car! You're gonna do all your explaining in a cell." Valdez pushed Latrell's head down to clear the roof as he put him in the backseat behind the mesh. Latrell looked through the wire mesh and flashing light, saw the cop, gun still drawn in his left hand now, walking back to the Cherokee—driver's side.

Valdez took out the keys in his right hand and felt the passenger seat. It was still warm. *Dios!* He turned, walking briskly to his car. There was a tremendous roar. Thrown against his car by the force of the shotgun blast, Valdez's back was a bloody mass, his gun gone, his body sliding down into the dust stirred up by the shot. Latrell was screaming, "Get the cuffs off me, Mikey!"

Hearn emerged from the night's shadows, shotgun still in hand, his whey-faced expression one of utter surprise, as if he didn't know what was happening. He'd had no idea of what a shotgun blast could do at near-point-blank range.

"Mikey—get the cuffs off me!"

Hearn was like a sleepwalker. Maybe he'd do Latrell as well. Why not? That'd shut him up.

"We'll look after you, Mikey. You don't have to worry."

Valdez was still alive, the skinhead looking down at him.

"Me an' the boys," said Latrell. "The militia. We'll look after you, Mikey. You did the right thing—believe me. Now let's get these stupid cuffs off, eh? Mikey?"

Hearn was still looking down at the cop, Valdez's barely conscious eyes looking up at the skinhead.

"I'll finish him off, Mikey."

Hearn stood back and fired. Valdez's head exploded. Latrell, showered in blood and flesh, started from fright. "Jesus—hey, Mikey, that's right. You done the right thing."

Latrell's voice was barely audible to Hearn, the skinhead's ears ringing like crazy. Hearn stooped to retrieve the cop's keys and got in the police car. "How far're we from Canada? Vancouver?"

"What—" Latrell began, his hands pins and needles, the cuffs were so tight. "I dunno, two hundred miles, why?"

" 'Cause that's where we're goin'."

"What?"

Hearn was in the driver's seat and he pointed down to the radio. It was still on and he put a finger against his lips. Latrell sat back, impressed with the skinhead's quick thinking.

"We'll go in the Cherokee," Hearn said. "Sure as hell don't want to be in a stolen police car."

"Good thinking," said Latrell, grinning despite the pain in his hands and now his shoulders. "All right, we head through the Cascades then up the coast."

Hearn turned the radio off, got a pair of pliers from the patrol car's tool kit, walked over to the dead patrolman, and bent down. Latrell, still locked in the backseat, couldn't see what he was doing. "Hey!" Latrell cried out. "Take these cuffs off."

Hearn came back to the police car, blood dripping from his right hand that held what had been Valdez's gold bridgework. "You be quiet," he told Latrell.

"What?"

Hearn stuffed a rag into the Jeep's gas tank, lit it, and

walked back to the police car. He slid in behind the
steering wheel, wiped his hands with a bunch of Kleenex,
shut the door, slipped the automatic into drive, and
made a U-turn, the left rear wheel bumping over
Valdez's body.

"I gotta think," said Hearn. "I need quiet."

Latrell wanted to scream, but now there was something dangerous, unpredictable, about this skinhead.
Something had gone wrong with his wiring. And killing
the cop like that. Christ, another six inches to the right
and Hearn would've taken *him* out!

CHAPTER TEN

Pennsylvania

IT USED TO be called "NECUMAD" by some press
types but the Pentagon logistic chiefs, sensitive to
"Strangelovian" analogies with MAD in the acronym,
renamed the New Cumberland Army Depot "DEDI"—
Defense Distribution in Region East. A hundred yards
from the perimeter of the enormous installation with its
"Deadly Force Authorized" signs on the Cyclone fences,
ex–Ranger commando Ray Nesmith adjusted his MP's
helmet, sitting in the backseat of the MP-marked Humvee, a soldier reeking of booze between him and another
MP, the driver slowing down before the checkpoint. One

of the two guards came out asking for ID. The three MPs showed him. "How about your friend?" asked the guard, indicating the boozehead. Ray Nesmith jabbed the boozehead in the side. "Show him your ID."

The soldier couldn't find it. "C'mon," Nesmith told him. "Show 'im your ID."

"Can't . . . find it."

"It's in your jacket," Nesmith said impatiently. "Inside pocket." He was losing his patience. "All right, asshole—outside—up against the Hummer. Right now."

As the soldier got out he was clearly unsteady on his feet.

"He's one of yours," said Nesmith.

"We don't want him, man. He's drunk."

Nesmith was spread-eagling the soldier across the back of the Hummer. "Here it is," he told the guard, holding out the ID card. The guard came around back of the Humvee. Nesmith and the other MP with the prisoner were now on either side of the guard. "Listen," said Nesmith, sticking the .38's barrel hard into the guard's side. "Call the other guy out."

The guard was so surprised he couldn't say anything. Nesmith jabbed the gun in farther. "You got three seconds or I'll blow your fuckin' kidney out. Get him around here—away from the fuckin' camera."

"Hey, Melville, come here a sec, will ya?"

The other guard poked his head out. "Just a mo. I'm on the phone," and turned back to the phone. "Three of them, sir, behind the Hummer. MP uniforms. Pretty sure they got a gun on him."

"Right," said the duty officer. "Lock yourself in. Go low, sit tight. We'll have an ERT there in two minutes. And Melville?"

"Yes, sir."

"Anyone tries to pass through that gate, hit your alarm siren and shoot to kill."

"Lieutenant, what if they try to use Kelly as a shield?"

"Shoot them, Melville. I'll back you all the way."

"Yes, sir." He put the phone down.

Fuck! He slipped his M-16 to semi, switched the door bolt to lock, and went down behind the desk to wait for the Emergency Response Team. Melville figured all that shit out west must have something to do with this. Probably militia wackos here after supplies. Well, the mothers had come to the right place. DEDI used to have everything from toothpicks to tires, but now they had weapons and ammo as well. Biggest damn warehouse in the world. Eight hundred and fifty acres of it.

"He's not comin' out," the other guard told Nesmith.

"All right," said Nesmith, jerking him away. "Get into the Hummer! Move!"

Melville, shaking by now, heard the ERT's sirens and saw the Hummer reverse, make a U-turn, and go like hell. The ERT Hummer, a .50 on the top, screeched to a stop and a lieutenant got out, .45 drawn, its white cord looking like a thin snake in the harsh glare of the arc lights.

"What happened?" he shouted.

"They're gone," Melville yelled.

"Damn!" said the lieutenant. "Get me the sheriff's office. Damn, I thought we had 'em. Now we'll have to hand it over to the goddamn civilians."

"Hey!" It was the lead driver in a convoy of six trucks heading out from the warehouses. "What's the holdup?"

"Hold your horses!" the lieutenant called out. "We had a situation here."

"How's that, Lieutenant?" the driver shouted over the noise of the truck.

"Aw, shit," said the lieutenant disgustedly, reholstering his .45. "We nearly had 'em."

"Can I let our guys through?" said Melville. "Papers are fine."

"What? Yeah. We nearly had 'em, Melville."

"Yes, sir."

The trucks rolled out, each one loaded with grenades, 81mm mortars, HE rounds, .50 machine guns and ammo, Basic, Interim, and Longbow Hellfire air-to-ground missiles with a half gross of Hellfire-II AGMs, Mark 19-3 40mm automatic grenade launchers, M16A2 5.56mm lightweight, air-cooled with improved muzzle compensator and three-round burst controls, fifty M249 16.3-pound lightweight SAW with 5.56mm rounds, maximum effective range nine hundred yards, thermal weapon sights, as well as helo- and ground-deliverable Volcano RADEM—rapidly deployed mines systems—which was stupid because the six drivers, all militia plants, knew they could have gotten the Volcano systems in Montana, that being one of the states, along with Florida and Illinois, where the Volcano system was deployed. It was taking coal to Newcastle. Subsequently the six militiamen were not amused by this criticism and said that if militia corps HQ wasn't satisfied then they should go and get the fucking stuff themselves. Besides, after all the hardware was transferred to moving trucks for delivery, half of it went to Michigan, which didn't have *any* Volcano RADEMs until this heist. To calm everybody down, Mant, via encoded e-mail, personally thanked the six drivers for a job well done.

CHAPTER ELEVEN

MICHAEL HEARN WAS a changed man. The feeling of pleasure he'd had earlier after shooting the "wetback" deputy had become more intense. He had experienced the ultimate thrill of absolute control, of total domination over his world, over his enemies. Never had he felt so virile, so powerful—so indestructible. Besides, even if he'd wanted to—and he didn't—there was no turning back. He knew that once innocence is lost it's gone forever. And there was a freedom in knowing he had done the worst and was still alive, more alive than ever before. Guts, that was it. No matter what all the timid, whining do-gooders said, you had to be brave to kill a man head-on, eye to eye, to let him see it was coming. Hearn knew it made him dangerous and he reveled in it.

"You guys leveling with me?" one of the militiamen at Mant's HQ asked them. "You never killed nobody?"

"Absolutely," said Hearn, looking at the earnest militiaman.

"No way," Latrell concurred. "I told ya. Cops pulled us up 'cause I didn't have a permit to hunt, so when the federals found this fucking deer with a bullet through its head and somebody tells 'em they saw a green Cherokee in the area, the cops say I been hunting—against the law—that there's a fucking moratorium on deer huntin'. So I guess when they found this kid—black kid, was it?"

"Yeah," said the militiaman.

"Yeah," said Latrell. "Well, I guess what the federals did was put one and one together and made it three. Christ, I told 'em, look at the grille. Deer cost me my deductible. Know what the cop says? He says, 'You could've bumped something a while ago.' A *while* ago. 'Gimme a break,' I told him. 'Have a look at the grille. Not a speck of rust on it. You'll find deer skin. It's a brand-new collision, fer Christ's sake.' Does he listen? Nooo, sir. Gives me a goddamn summons for illegal *hunting* instead."

"This," said Hearn, "is another Ruby Ridge. Give 'em a chance, the bastards'll make a big production out of anything. Trouble I reckon is the pricks don't have a clue about what's happenin', so who better to pin it on than a militiaman? They hate our guts."

"You a militiaman?" the man asked Hearn.

Latrell answered. "Aryan Nation—good as."

"Well," the militiaman said, "General Mant says you boys are victims of a media frenzy. 'Member the feds going ape after Oklahoma? Moved in their tactical thugs, hauled out and arrested two guys in the motel on their way home from a hunting trip? Federals in flak jackets and with shotguns running every which way, and the two guys turned out to be completely innocent. Going home after a hunting trip. General says the public didn't see what went on behind closed doors, didn't see what those two guys and their families went through when CNN was no longer there. General says you two guys should keep low. Best for you to go up in the Cascades. Up to Pateros. We'll tell the Wolverines you're comin'. That's Lucky McBride's outfit."

"Fine," said Latrell. "Meanwhile we stay in the hotel?"

"No. You go tonight." Before he left them, the militiaman said, "I'll make sure you boys get some fatigues. I got a coupla sets of tigers."

"Hey, hey," said Latrell. "Way to go—Mitch, is it?"

"Yeah."

"Thanks, Mitch," said Hearn.

The moment the militiaman closed the door, Hearn asked, "What the hell's *tigers*?"

"Combat—Vietnam issue. Top o' the line."

In his hotel room, General Mant had made a momentous decision in ordering the militia into ACON Three, and he asked the commanders of the states affected—indeed, everyone in the room—to bow their heads to seek God's guidance. "Dear Lord who art in heaven, give us strength to lead our troops in battle as we go forth to the aid of our brother in Christ. Help us to remember always that we are children of You who made us each in your image but not the same, who gave us our individuality, which we must protect against *all* oppressors at home and abroad. Grant that we may have the will and the courage to stand firm when all about us threatens us with satanic will." And then, calling upon the memory of the terrible events, the massacres at Waco and Ruby Ridge, and now the slaying of the Ames family, the general drew upon the passages from the Book of Revelation so beloved by Randy Weaver before Weaver had to unbuckle his Aryan Nation's belt and surrender to Gog—Satan. "Son of man, set Thy face against Gog. . . . And I will call for a sword against him throughout all my mountains, saith the Lord God. Amen."

In Spokane, an FBI mole in the militia, code name "Milthroat," had informed the FBI of an impending declaration of war and that the prime suspects in the AG's assassination were believed to have arrived in Spokane and joined the Wolverines militia in and around Pateros.

CHAPTER TWELVE

Morning

WHAT TONY BECK in the chopper he'd hired for surveillance of the militia's Pateros site wished he could do was have the helo scoot along the Methow River, peel off, and give the Wolverines' campsite a couple of shots overhead. Something for them to think about. But like the stakeout of the Freemen in Montana in '96, after Waco you couldn't do anything without clearance from Washington, D.C.—from the AG herself. Mustn't upset the militia.

Neither the chopper pilot nor Beck could see any tents in the open campground, and it was assumed that the militia had put them up and camouflaged them in the woods.

As the chopper swung about at the apogee of its search then went low, the pilot felt rather than heard a staccato vibration on the Huey's fuselage. He hauled hard on the stick, jinking hard left, hard right, right again, Tony Beck feeling his gut wrenched by each crazy swing. "What the hell—" he began, but now the pilot was yelling into his mike. "We've been hit. Bastards are shooting at us." It was only then that Beck glimpsed the flickering orange of automatic fire coming from the green blur of forest. "Let's get out of here!" he yelled.

"That's what I'm trying to do, goddammit!"

A few seconds later they were over the grass margin between the woods and the river, and beyond the river itself.

"Sons-of-bitches could've killed us!" shouted Beck. He felt sick.

"Yeah," the pilot conceded, his forehead glistening with sweat. "But I think they just meant to frighten us off. If they'd wanted to they could've gotten us at that range."

Tony Beck was incredulous. "They did get us! Didn't you feel the shots hitting us?"

"Yeah," replied the pilot. "Probably just a wild burst."

"Wild? Jesus, man, you're more charitable than I am."

"Well, you know," said the pilot, a local and a 'Nam vet, "militias are pretty touchy folks sometimes, especially when they're being blamed for things they didn't do." Despite their near miss, the pilot was grinning on their way back to the federals' field HQ outside Pateros. "Like I was back in 'Nam for a while there. Gets the adrenaline pumping, right?"

Tony didn't answer.

In the woods, militia squad leader Harold Rymann was, as he later reported to Company Commander Lucky McBride, farther down the line, "tearing a strip" off an overeager seventeen-year-old militiaman. Rymann, who sported an AK-47, had told the squad to discharge only warning tracer with their M-16s, but because of the unexpected recoil of the M-16, the young militiaman, Ovitz, got lucky and hit the federals' helo or "slick," as the Huey helo was called by the older militiamen, many of whom were Vietnam vets and who formed the hard, highly trained core of the militias.

"You stupid son-of-a-bitch," Rymann told him. "You could've killed one of those bastards. If you can't handle that weapon we'll take it off you—give you a fucking BB gun instead. Matter o' fact that's what I'm gonna do right now. Gimme that rifle."

The boy, sullen with injured pride, gave over the M-16, asking in a sulky tone, "What if I see a bear?"

"A bear? Jesus Christ! We've got a company, over two hundred men, holed up in these woods. You're gonna be lucky if you see a fuckin' mouse." Rymann was taking the mag out of the M-16, and in the primeval gloom of the moisture-dripping forest he heard footfalls behind him. He turned and saw it was McBride. Quickly he tossed the M-16 back to the youth.

"Rymann. Was that one of your squad who hit that chopper?"

"Yes, sir."

McBride was in his mid-forties but looked younger, ruddy-faced, tall, and as fit as a marathoner. "You know what kind of provocation that is? Just the thing the federals need to justify going tactical. You want another Waco here before we even get to Ames's cabin?"

"No, sir. It won't happen again, sir."

"Who was it?"

"One of my men."

Lucky McBride shot a glance at the youth. "This man here?"

"I'll deal with it, sir," said Rymann.

McBride was still looking at Ovitz, who, like most militiamen, didn't have his name sewn into his fatigues so as to deny the federals any means of identification.

"Where's the mag for your weapon, son?"

"I have it," said Rymann. "He couldn't fire—mag spring jammed."

"Rymann," said McBride, "in 'Nam I could smell Charlie's fish paste two hundred yards away, breeze or no breeze. And right here I smell cordite."

"Yes, sir," answered Rymann. "Guys all around fired warning shots."

McBride said nothing for a second or two. "I assume whoever did it, it *was* an accident." It was as much a suggestion as a question.

"Yes, sir."

McBride nodded and walked away.

After he was out of sight, only a matter of seconds in among the ferns and secondary growth, Ovitz turned to Rymann. He'd joined up only a week before the convention—a newcomer among veterans. "Thanks, Sarge. I owe you one."

"Well," said Rymann, waving aside the youngster's appreciation. "We'd better get the squad organized. General's orders to McBride are for our company to do a forced march eighteen miles west of Twisp, into the Sawtooth Wilderness—establish a cordon around Charlie Ames's cabin. But our squad'll stay here as a rear guard for a while. We'll join up with the main force later."

CHAPTER THIRTEEN

"THEY SHOT AT the helo?" Attorney General Patricia Wyeth's question on the phone was matter-of-fact, devoid of surprise. Quite frankly, after reading a six-inch-thick file on all the militias around the country, over a hundred thousand fully armed and trained, she believed the militias capable of anything. But she was careful not to inject any of the anger she felt into the already highly charged atmosphere. As attorney general, it was her job to stay calm, reject emotion, make sure she had all the facts, and to prepare, based on those facts, a cool rational explanation for any action she took. She had no desire to end up like Janet Reno, being grilled before a congressional committee. "Anyone wounded?" she asked agent Tony Beck.

"No, luckily. But I think it might be time to call in the HRT." She ignored his reference to the Hostage Rescue Team. "How sure are you that this Latrell and the skinhead are with the militia?"

Beck had to admit that all the evidence was circumstantial. No one on the government side, including "Milthroat," had actually seen Latrell or the skinhead, whom authorities in San Diego had identified from the fingerprints found all over Deputy Valdez's car as

Michael Eliot Hearn, an eighteen-year-old white-supremacist skinhead dropout. A loner.

"But *you* think this Latrell's hiding in the militia?" Patricia Wyeth pressed.

"Along with the skinhead—Hearn. Yes. 'Course, they'll tell their militia buddies that it's the federals' fault again—a setup. They can't get Waco or Ruby Ridge out of their heads."

Neither could the American public, thought Patricia Wyeth, her doodling on the blotter shifting from what had been hard, definite cubes and rectangles to more amorphous abstracts. As horrible as the murders of her predecessor, the black man, and Valdez had been, her agencies had to have more hard evidence. A good lawyer, by which she meant a shrewd, unscrupulous one, could beat these charges in half an hour.

"I think we should call in Tactical," Tony suggested, meaning the Hostage Rescue Team.

"Of course," said the AG, "you being in the helo tends to sway your judgment."

Sway, thought Tony. What in hell was the matter with her? How'd she like an M-16 burst up her skirt?

"Could it have been an accident?" she asked.

"An *accident*?"

"That's what I said, Mr. Beck, or is your hearing failing you? You said earlier that there was 'multiple firing' from the ground. If so many of them were shooting, wouldn't the helo have suffered more damage, or are they all bad shots in the militia—at close range?"

"Well, yes," replied Tony reluctantly. "It's possible I suppose. It could have been an accident."

"All right. Now assuming it was, do you expect me to risk a shoot-out à la Waco?"

"No." There was a long silence. He could have said, No, ma'am.

"Look, Mr. Beck, I appreciate your position. No one likes to be shot at. But the tension down here is so thick you could cut it with a knife. The president is under tremendous pressure to act, but with Waco and Ruby Ridge hanging over us we can't afford a misstep."

Misstep, noted Beck. Now there was a Washington word—a weasel word for "screwup." Why didn't she just admit she was afraid? He was on the verge of his what-the-hell-are-women-doing-heading-the-FBI? mood when he remembered Tracy back at the field HQ. She'd be taking the same risks as he.

"I understand, ma'am," Tony told the AG. "We'll try talking to them."

"Very good. Use HRT as backup only. I stress 'backup.' Don't put them in front of you. It'd be seen as a provocation. I'll get back to you."

CHAPTER FOURTEEN

WHILE THE MAIN body of Lucky McBride's company of two hundred men, including Latrell and Hearn, had already crossed the river road, heading into the Sawtooth Wilderness, McBride, promoted in the field to captain by order of General Mant, remained with and took command of Rymann's squad of ten men. Along with Ovitz, who'd hit the federals' chopper, they were digging in. Two-man foxholes, the two ends of the trench sloping to form a grenade sump either end. After his nearly disastrous mistake, Ovitz was eager to prove himself safety-conscious and able, especially in front of McBride. He was not, he told himself, going to be a screwup. After the chopper incident he understandably regarded his M-16 as a bad-luck weapon. What he wanted, psychologically at least, was to make a new start, and besides, he was keen to have the "sexier," as the boys called it, AK-47, folding-stock type, so that at close quarters you could use it like a machine pistol.

"Sarge," asked Ovitz, "you thought any more about that AK-47?"

Rymann unshouldered his AK-47 and traded it for Ovitz's M-16. "Know how to fire it?"

Ovitz grinned. "Just pull the trigger."

"Yeah, well, just so long as you don't point it at another—"

"Hey, Captain McBride!" called out the M-60 man whose foxhole had the best view of the grassy margin between the woods and the river and the black strip of road beyond that ran parallel to the river. "Look who's comin' to dinner." It was a federal, in a suit—both hands up, one holding a badge.

Tony Beck advanced unarmed through the wet and tall green river grass. He was backed up in plain sight by two black helos that seemed to descend from nowhere, touching down just beyond the Methow River on the road, and around which were a dozen or so "Ninjas," so called because of their flexi-armor of black Kevlar bulletproof vests, leggings, and knee guards along with black helmets and weapons.

Ovitz cocked the AK-47 and thumbed the selector switch to what he thought would be the semiautomatic or one-pull-one-shot position. Perhaps in another second or so Rymann or even McBride might have noticed his mistake and warned him, but if only rain was beer and if only you'd done this instead of that. Whatever, neither Rymann nor McBride, with the larger picture of what was happening in mind, had said anything, most likely taking Ovitz at his word, that he was already familiar with the AK-47.

As the federal agent approached the sodden river grass up to his waist, his hands high, showing his badge—shirt, no vest, making it clear he wasn't armed—McBride's squad was alternately sighting him and the Ninjas, a hundred yards or so back of him across the river.

"Agent Beck!" Tony called out to the woods. "BATF."

"Take me to your leader," said the M-60 man, and there were a couple of guffaws.

"Shut up!" said McBride. "Mark your man."

Ovitz, keen, excited, confident he'd put the safety selector switch on, let his finger unconsciously caress the hair trigger. The automatic burst was only three rounds duration, but it struck Tony Beck full in the chest, a nickel-sized hole in his throat ejaculating jets of frothy blood into the damp green grass as he fell. His right hand squeezed the jugular to stop the bleeding, his mind recalling in that instant how that English writer, way before he had written *1984*, had been shot through the throat in the Spanish Civil War, how he survived.

Ovitz was frozen in shock, the two black helos already airborne, each with four Ninjas aboard, three hundred yards apart, heading left and right of where the AK-47 had cut down the BATF agent.

The Ninjas knew the negotiators shouldn't have fucked around with the militia. Ninjas should've gone in first. It was the only language these militia freaks understood.

The six Ninjas who'd been left on the ground were now crossing the river as the two helos, four Ninjas apiece, went lower, using outgrowths of trees along the main wood line to hover, four Ninjas jumping from each chopper, moving quickly into the woods to "concertina" the militia squad, the six Ninjas now across the freezing-cold river and into the high grass, moving as fast as they dared toward where Beck had fallen.

Now Rymann's militia squad could hear Ninjas firing, Heckler & Koch 5.6mms and Ingram M-11 9mms ripping through the timber, and could see the purplish-red flames of HE grenades going off. Then more muffled explosions and screams. Someone yelling now, and then high, whistling sounds that were new to the Ninjas. More screaming and then movement in the woods . . . but by whom?

When one of the six Ninjas in the river grass reached him, Beck was dead. The Ninjas in the grass stayed low, not wanting to fire into the woods for fear of hitting their own men but ready to take out any militiaman who showed himself. They waited—no point in calling in one of the slicks to pick up the dead BATF agent. There was nothing anyone could do for him now and there was no sense in exposing a slick to fire from militia in the woods.

It was so quiet now the six Ninjas could hear their ears ringing from the sounds of the short, fierce battle. The rain grew in intensity and they waited ten minutes—which felt like an hour—in the sodden grass, most of the six still unable to hear the soft hiss of the rain. They knew that the other eight Ninjas were in the woods in front of them on the east and west flanks, probably doing the same thing, frozen in position, hardly daring to breathe, waiting for any of the enemy, perhaps wounded, to make a move.

The six Ninjas waiting in the grass were whispering into their throat mikes, using slang terms unknown to any civilian who might be listening in on their wavelength. But three miles back at Pateros HQ, BATF agents and now Tracy Albright knew what the Ninjas' "chitchat" was about. After seeing one of their own cut down before them in cold blood and remembering the militia's burst at the helo earlier, the six Ninjas in the grass had come to the decision, aided by the absence of any media, that there weren't going to be any militiamen taken prisoner. Any fucker in fatigues coming out of the forest would be shot "while attempting to evade arrest."

Now and then there were noises from the woods, the faint snap of a branch, a rush of wind in the trees. Then they saw a Ninja running, or rather stumbling, from the edge of the forest, his black helmet contrasting sharply against the green of the grass. Suddenly he fell to the watery ground. Four of the six Ninjas in the grass covered the remaining two as they ran toward their fallen comrade.

He was bleeding profusely from a gut wound, his pants shredded, his body hemorrhaging from several other wounds as well, the man trying to speak, "All—" then going into shock.

"The militia?" they asked him, but he'd lapsed into unconsciousness from which he did not recover. The leader of the six Ninjas, whose weapons were already cocked, dropped two purple smoke canisters where the body of the BATF agent and his slain comrade lay, and told the helos to come collect the bodies while they, the six Ninjas, advanced toward the woods.

Three miles eastward in the FBI's motor-home command center, Tracy Albright, as yet unaware of who was down, was in contact with the bureau's director, who in turn was hooked up to Patricia Wyeth's office. Via Tracy Albright's hookup, Wyeth contacted the six Ninjas just as they reached the forest's edge, telling them to proceed with utmost caution, as if they wouldn't, for even though she was over two thousand miles away, Wyeth said she had a bad feeling about this.

She had a much worse feeling twenty-seven minutes later as the six HRT Ninjas, examining every inch of their way into the woods, discovered the seven remaining Ninjas dead and found the fern-covered area just beyond where the militias had been dug in littered with ball bearings, some of them smeared with blood, pieces of flesh scattered about amid fern and trees like chicken innards. Only one of the investigating Ninjas, a Vietnam vet, knew immediately what had happened. The fast-moving tactical FBI force, the Ninjas, used to quick-action hostage taking, had blundered into a circle of claymore antipersonnel mines. Each crescent-shaped mine, standing on metal legs, released over seven hundred ball bearings through a sixty-degree horizontal arc and could be manually activated or set off by a trip wire, both methods having been used by the militia squad whose foxholes were now deserted, except one, where the M-60 gunner slumped forward, dead, his machine gun gone, and his ammo feeder, face blown away by a Ninja burst, thrown back against the lip of the foxhole, insects already buzzing and crawling around the edge of what had been his chest. Unlike the first wave of eight Ninjas who had had to move fast to get close enough to the militia to engage, the second wave of six had the luxury of time, and now, moving slowly, avoided two undetonated claymores, the Vietnam vet calling out to the others to freeze while he cut a fishing-line trip wire with his knife.

"Jesus Christ!" said one of the Ninjas, looking about at the carnage. "This is a fuckin' war!"

The Vietnam veteran nodded slowly. Three of his dead buddies were unrecognizable. He hadn't been part of the HRT at Waco and he hadn't seen a butcher shop like this since 'Nam. He knew now that this had been too big a job for the FBI's tactical squad. The HRT were highly trained specialists for hostage-taking episodes, but they weren't soldiers. They weren't ready for this. Who was?

One of the Ninjas, devastated as the rest by the sight of his dead comrades, knelt down beside one who had been his buddy at Quantico. Out of simple respect and sheer fright from the man's awful dead stare, he rolled the man over facedown.

"No!" shouted the Vietnam vet, but it was too late. A grenade exploded, and the wounded Ninja screamed in pain. He spun around, crashed into the ferns, and fell, doubled over, his face porcelain white, his hands cupping the bloody remains of his genitals.

A visibly shaken Patricia Wyeth called the president and told him what had happened, recommending that all civil police, FBI, BATF, and sheriffs be immediately reinforced by the National Guard. Her voice almost cracking with the knowledge that nine of her agents now lay dead in the wilderness of the Northwest, she told the president that such a flagrantly murderous challenge to federal authority could not be allowed to stand, that Washington could quite simply not let the two men wanted for murder flee under the canopy of the militia's maneuvers. She also added that in the opinion of her investigating agents, the brutal defense by the militia must have been engineered by an army type, someone who'd seen service in Vietnam. One of Mant's Washington State officers, a certain Lucky McBride, was suspected.

The president agreed with Wyeth about the necessity for firmer action but asked her if she thought that the militia leader, "General" Mant, was knowingly harboring the two "suspects."

"I don't know. The problem, however—the *fact*—is that Latrell and Hearn, the two fugitives, have disappeared. We know Latrell's a member of the Washington militia, and from identifications made from Identikit photos in the town of Pateros, the bet is that they're in the Cascade Mountains with the militia, with this Lucky McBride."

"Why 'Lucky'?" the president asked.

"Because," said the attorney general, "he's never been caught. FBI's been after him for years."

"Thank you, Patricia. Tell your people to back off until we can reinforce them. I'll get back to you shortly. And Patricia—"

"Mr. President?"

"We're all working on this. We'll get this McBride."

After the president had assembled his aides and chiefs of staff, he solicited advice.

"National Guard sounds like a good idea," his interior secretary opined.

"I disagree," said the army chief of staff, Shelbourne. "No offense to the Guard, but that's what they are, a national *guard*. That is their mandate. I know they've been trained for some offensive roles—used some of 'em in the Gulf War—and they're good men, but we're not dealing here with a riot in L.A. or Mississippi, gentlemen. We're dealing with sons-of-bitches who know how to use claymores, M60s, and God knows what else."

"So," cut in the president, "you think the army should step in?"

"I do."

"Objections?" asked the president.

"Mr. President," began the secretary of the treasury. "I don't want to appear too hard on this, but the use of the United States Army against its own citizens? I mean I can't predict what the market will do. I mean we don't use our army against civilians."

"President Hoover used it in 1932," said Army Chief Shelbourne. "Against the bonus marchers in Washington. Sent General MacArthur in."

"Well, perhaps in extreme—" began the treasury secretary.

"These *are* extreme circumstances," said the president. "We have nine people dead. Murdered. Federal law officials." He paused, his hand waving at the Oval Office's large computer screen. "Look at the terrain. This isn't open country we're talking about, this is some of the most rugged country in America. Point is, I don't want to send any Guard units up there and have them slaughtered and embarrassed. They're good people, but as General Shelbourne's already pointed out, they're essentially weekend soldiers. If we're going to go in, let's use full-time professionals."

The treasury secretary, Harry Strand, still didn't like it. "Can't we talk to them?"

"Jesus, Harry, what d'you think we've been doing?" asked General Shelbourne. "We tried talking to them and their answer was a goddamned firefight. Only language they understand is force. Period!"

"Does anyone know what the public's opinion is on this?"

An aide opened a manila folder. "Mr. President," said senior aide Delorme, "opinion's swung dramatically away from concern about possible federal overreaction in the Ames situation to concern about the size and ferocity of the militia response. Public now sees the two as one problem and they perceive it as a direct challenge to the White House. A law-and-order issue plain and simple."

"They know—I mean, the public knows about the militia moving to protect Ames?"

"Yes, sir. Marte Price of CNN has been updating everything right from the command site near Pateros. I should add that we've been monitoring all the important talk shows as well, Larry King, Limbaugh, et cetera, and the opinion that we should move quickly with overwhelming force against the militia crosses all income and racial lines. Especially with this Latrell and Hearn being suspected of killing the black motorist in Oregon and a white policeman in Washington State. Most everybody wants the militia brought to heel, except the ultraright cuckoos. It's the only time, since the Mark Fuhrman thing, that I've heard callers agree on the *Rush Limbaugh* and *Larry King* shows."

"Good Lord," said the president. With that piece of information alone he felt the decision to bring in a Special Forces contingent would be well received in most quarters.

"Bomb them!" It was the air-force chief. Everyone was aghast at the suggestion.

"General," the president replied, "there is no way that the American people would sanction Americans bombing fellow Americans. Besides, our stated aim must be to get these two bastards, Latrell and Hearn."

The treasury secretary was still in shock at the air force's suggestion. "I agree one hundred percent. Good God, General," he said to the air-force chief, "this is the United States, not Yugoslavia—or what used to be Yugoslavia."

"I'm not so sure," the air-force chief retorted. "These

Freemen, for example, want to secede from the union. Declare their own country, for God's sake."

"But," jumped in the interior secretary, "we have reports that women and perhaps children are up there as well."

"We don't know that for sure," said the air-force general.

"Yes, we do," replied the interior secretary. "We know there are women in the militia."

"Jesus," said the president, "even if we found there were no women and children, I will not give authority for any bombing or aircraft of any kind—except for surveillance—to be used in this operation. The electorate wouldn't stand for it—I'm certain of that."

There was clear agreement with him, except for the air-force general.

The president asked the army chief of staff how many men it would take, not simply to rout the militia force but to round them up.

"We'd need at least a ten-to-one advantage. One man dug in can hold off a much larger number before he's overrun. The public doesn't realize how difficult—"

"Yes, yes," cut in the secretary of the treasury. The polls were with the president to act and act quickly, but a large force was out of the question. He told all those assembled in the Oval Office that to send such a force against the militia, as suggested by the army chief of staff, was quite simply politically untenable. Not so much because of domestic reaction but because of the "enormous lack of confidence" it would engender abroad against the United States. Unstable, fiscally unreliable banana republics sent large forces into rebel redoubts in their *own* countries, not the United States of America. Look at what the Chechen militias did to Russia— embarrassed Moscow and shook investor confidence all over the world. Here the president knew the secretary of the treasury was right. The financial drain on the United States, investors dumping U.S. dollars for deutsche marks and yen, would be catastrophic with the U.S. already trying desperately to balance the budget.

"Whatever we do, General," the president told Army Chief Shelbourne, "we can't go sending in a mass of troops. Can you see that spread all over the world, courtesy of CNN, *The New York Times*, et al?" He paused. "Our friends would be dismayed and our enemies would gloat. No, what we need is a relatively small, highly efficient strike force that's worked before."

General Shelbourne thought for a few seconds. "There is such a force of specialists—a mix of Delta Force, Rangers, and SEALs we've used. They're spread over several corps but they can be ready to go in forty-eight hours, particularly as there'll be very little, if any, armor used. The Cascades aren't hospitable to tanks. We'll send some up at both ends of Highway 20 from Fort Lewis to provide mobile artillery should we need it."

The president told the general he didn't like the idea of using artillery against the militia.

"And what if the militia uses it, Mr. President?"

"Well, yes, then I suppose we'd have to react. But surely the militia doesn't have artillery?"

"We don't know exactly what they've got, Mr. President. Break-ins like the one in DEDI have been occurring all over the country."

"I think," said the president, "we might put out a few feelers about the tanks. You know the FBI used two in Waco and there was a lot of condemnation about that."

There were murmurs of concern.

"Look," said the president, "I think you'd better defer any use of tanks or anything like that until you get authorization from me through the secretary of defense."

"Yes, sir, but I can have them ready."

"Yes, but keep them parked at the two ends of the highway." He looked up at the map. "That'd be where? Around, ah—"

"Sedro Woolley, sir. Out of the mountains. And a few near Pateros—on the eastern side."

"Beyond the mountains?"

"More or less."

"What does that mean?" asked the president irritably. "Is it beyond the mountains or not?"

"Ah, in the foothills, sir."

"Who do we have in mind as the commander of this strike force?"

"General Limet. He's at the Pentagon now, but he's just come to us from Fort Lewis. He's a good man."

"Experience?"

"Fought in the Gulf War."

"Vietnam? South China Sea area, guerrilla warfare?"

"No."

"This is more like a guerrilla war, wouldn't you say? Given the mountainous terrain."

Well, thought General Shelbourne, give the president his due. He'd put his finger right on it, and without a poll. "Yes, Mr. President, I'd say it was more like 'Nam. Damn sight colder but thick country, yes."

"How about Foreman?"

"You mean Freeman."

"Yes, that's him."

"Retired."

"Uh-huh, all right, but ask Limet quickly. Give him an option. He'd be the first American since the Civil War to fight Americans. I'll want to announce this evening at the press conference that a force is going in. After that, let's keep the whole thing on low profile." He paused. "Well, I know that'd be impossible, but let's keep the lowest profile possible. Have an explanation ready for putting a few tanks here and there. You know the sort of thing—part of regular army maneuvers in the area, et cetera. . . ."

"Les," the army chief told General Limet, "it's yours if you want it."

Limet thought long and hard. He'd just moved his wife and three teenage kids for what he'd told them was the last time in his career. And he'd promised that he wouldn't take any combat duty if given the option. His plan was a few years in Washington and then retirement to Florida. And a couple more years after that he could legally become a lobbyist—play golf, earn a bundle.

"There's something else I want you to consider, Les," added Shelbourne. "It's more than likely that whoever commands this force will become very unpopular with the American public. It's all very well now that everyone's blood's up, but there's bound to be a lot of squawking after. When the public really understands what this is—Americans spilling American blood— there's bound to be recriminations. In short, the history books may not be very kind to you. And you won't have an entirely free hand." He explained the president's hesitancy on the matter of artillery and tanks.

There was a long silence as Limet pondered the gamble, thought of the future of his kids and how he'd given his word to his wife. No one outside knew how much a military wife had to put up with. She, after all, deserved some consideration. And the kids.

Then there was his mom, eighty-seven, short-term memory shot to hell. Soon it'd have to be a private old folks' home. You know what they cost a *month*? On the other hand . . .

"General, give me an hour."

"Okay. But no later, Les."

"On the dot, sir."

Shelbourne's phone rang at 1600 hours. Les Limet would take command of the antimilitia force. He felt he couldn't let the president down, family consideration notwithstanding.

"You don't sound very happy about it."

"Well, I've had something of a skirmish with my family."

"Les, I don't want you to go into this halfhearted or half-assed. Lives'll be riding on it. For political reasons the president wants a relatively small force to go after these two murderers, or, I should say, suspects. In and out. If this madman Mant commits any more forces, you could suddenly find yourself outnumbered. We don't know exactly how many militia—"

"I understand, sir. Don't worry. I'll do the job."

"Very well."

CHAPTER FIFTEEN

THE PRESIDENT ADDRESSED the nation for the second time in as many days. On the advice of his aides he kept it short, to the point. ". . . The confrontation which the militias have chosen, between themselves and the government that represents the American people, cannot be allowed to stand. Operation Cleanhouse will be commanded by General Lester Limet of the United States Army. As reluctant as I am to bring force to bear on fellow Americans, the operation has to be carried out if law and order are to prevail." He paused and looked straight at the camera. "It is distasteful, regrettable to all Americans, but ultimately it is the rule of law that is being so flagrantly broken and it is the safety and security of your children which must be assured."

All the networks carried it. In Monterey, watching the president's address while visiting his sister-in-law—a duty he'd promised his late wife he'd perform on a regular basis—retired general Douglas Freeman's eyes were filled with tears of utter and inconsolable rage and frustration. America going to war and him not in it? It was unthinkable, monstrous. Goddammit, it was immoral! How many times had he telephoned the Pentagon and warned them about the militia? And now not a single call for advice—not even a whisper—from Les Limet. Compulsively busy, Marjorie, in the kitchen, started the blender, sending streaks of static across the TV picture.

Freeman felt like getting up, picking up the electric cord, and strangling her. This constant business of hers was nothing less than goddamn sabotage of his TV viewing, and sabotage was what Les Limet would have to watch out for with the militia. This would be a hit-and-run fight, and if Limet thought he was just going to walk in and face them down, he was in for a rude surprise. Operation Cleanhouse! Christ, what kind of namby-pamby name was that? Reminded him of Marjorie's endless vacuuming. Should've called it "Bulldog," something with some guts in it. He zapped off the snowy TV with the remote, got up, went to the toilet, blew his nose ferociously, and over the roar of the cistern looked in the mirror as if addressing his staff in 'Nam, telling them that what Les Limet needed to know was that this was a *civil* war, a fight within the family, and that civil wars, as history, including America's own Civil War, had shown, were twice as savage as any other. Different wars— different tactics.

Ah! He couldn't stand himself like this. He detested self-pity.

Les Limet, already en route to Washington State, was putting Shelbourne's advice into practice. While it wasn't his intent to use artillery against fellow Americans, Limet had ordered an M-1 tank platoon—four tanks—at Sedro Woolley on the western side of the Cascades and six M1A1 tanks to be airlifted to the now-extended airstrip near Lake Chelan on the eastern side of the mountains and fifteen miles south of the Pateros FBI, BATF field HQ, which Limet would use as his headquarters. Limet was soon being flown by helicopter to Pateros from Spokane.

Latrell and Hearn had been integrated into McBride's Bravo Company with surprising ease. And if the federal authorities thought that any militia in the country would believe them about the alleged crimes of the "two suspects," whose names and descriptions had been given out with all the same hoopla of the "two suspects" in the Oklahoma bombing, who by the federals' own admission turned out to have had nothing to do with the bombing, then they were being incredibly naive. In any event, Latrell and Hearn were both growing beards and Hearn had ditched his swastika and they were serving as riflemen in 2 Platoon ahead of Rymann's rearguard squad, whom Lucky McBride had now left as he and the remaining one hundred ninety of Bravo Company made their way into the Sawtooth Wilderness.

And if Mant had any concerns about the guilt or innocence of Latrell and Hearn, any doubts were quickly erased by the sudden violence of the federal Ninjas' attack on his men by the river. And with the president's announcement of an invading force, it was quite clear to General Mant and every member of McBride's Bravo Company moving deeper into the Sawtooth Wilderness that their very existence was now at stake. That it was a case of hitting the federals before the federals hit them. Yet Mant had ordered them to dig in, to bar the way above War Creek to Ames's cabin. It was a time for Bravo Company and its commander to remember Colonel Vance's entreaty in Spokane—to obey HQ no matter what their own fears and assessment of the situation might be.

Having the luxury of time in which to prepare for Limet's assault, Mant had set up a line of twenty-two-man OPs—observation points—along Highway 20 as it wove its way through the high Cascades. The road was now closed to all but federal military traffic, the latter consisting mostly of Humvees armed with a swivel-mounted heavy 50mm machine gun patrolling the winding hundred-and-eighty-mile highway all the way between Pateros on the eastern side of the Cascades to Sedro Woolley in the west.

While his force of about a thousand men, including Major William McBride of the 82nd Airborne at Fort Bragg, Lucky McBride's brother, were being contacted, giving him an overwhelming five-to-one advantage against the militia's contingent moving toward Ames's cabin, General Limet was en route to the FBI and BATF field HQ near Pateros. It began to rain. In the Cascades the precipitation turned to snow.

Far to the west, beyond the Cascades on the flat plains about Sedro Woolley, sixteen soldiers stood beneath canvas lean-tos by their platoon of four tanks, making a small fire of anything that would burn in a pierced four-gallon drum. For all their modern equipment and cold-weather uniforms, including new Kevlar helmets, the soldiers, like those of old, waited, stamping their feet to keep warm, coffee mugs in hand, their occasional laughter and small talk subdued but heard clearly enough by a nine-man squad of Washington militia.

Helmut Werner, the militiamen's leader, glanced around at his men waiting behind the cover of a barn no more than seventy yards from the M-1 tank crews, the tanks parked in staggered fashion about ten yards apart along the highway. Werner looked at the farm vehicle, a three-ton truck they had "borrowed," then at his watch, there being no radio instructions on order of Mant because of the federal army's superior electronic eavesdropping ability.

It would be dark within five minutes but Werner knew his squad couldn't move for another ten in order that both his squad and another hiding three miles outside Pateros on the eastern side of the mountains would move together.

Two army Humvees, having been on patrol through the Cascades, came west along the Sedro Woolley road. They stopped by the tanks, taking half of the tank crews back to a motel a quarter mile away from which they could be rushed back to the M-1s should they be required to move up into the Cascades twenty miles farther east.

"That's dumb," said Komura, one of Werner's militia

squad, as he watched the two Humvees driving off. "Only leaving two men to a tank."

"You complaining?" asked Werner.

"Nope. But I'll bet the Humvees are gonna come right back with relief crews."

Werner was biting his bottom lip. Sammy Komura was probably right. If the squad moved now it'd have to deal with only eight unarmed tank crewmen instead of sixteen if he waited. He checked his watch again—two minutes.

On the eastern side of the Cascades at the other end of Highway 20, the crews of six M1A1 tanks were not being relieved, and they, unlike their western M1 compatriots, were being snowed upon while waiting, motors running, for the imminent arrival of General Limet.

Back near Sedro Woolley on the western side, the two minutes were up, and with the other eight members of his squad in the back of the truck, Werner, in farmer's overalls, drove out to the main road and turned right toward Sedro Woolley. One or two of the tank drivers around the oil-drum fire saw the truck pulling out from the farm in the distance but paid it no mind.

On the eastern side of the mountains Rymann's rearguard squad of militiamen, less the two men killed in the firefight with the Ninjas, were advancing through heavy timber toward the platoon of six M1A1 tanks. The tanks' engines were running but their gas turbines were remarkably quiet for a motor that could drive the fifty-five-ton M1A1s at over forty miles per hour. As yet unheard by Rymann's squad, General Limet, in an armed Humvee with two MP outriders, was approaching, having just left the Pateros field HQ a mile back.

* * *

As Werner drove the farmer's truck along the Sedro Woolley road toward the four faster and smaller 105mm M1s, he was wishing they could have used fire-and-forget Arpac IIs, but Mant's orders were that no antitank missiles be used for the time being. It was, in Mant's words, only "early days," and he was advocating conservation of missiles whenever possible.

Near Sedro Woolley, Werner's truck was about twelve feet away from the oil-drum fire when he stopped it and waved to the eight tank drivers clustered around the drum fire. "How ya doin'?"

"Cold," replied one of the drivers, leaving the fire, walking toward the truck. "You hear 'bout this road bein' closed?"

"Closed?"

"Yep—'cept for military vehicles. Government orders. We're havin' some trouble with militia boys other side of the mountains."

" 'S'at a fact?"

"Yes, sir. You want to get—" The tank driver stopped, a Smith & Wesson .38 pointing right at his head. Werner got out of the truck. "Hands up where I can see them. Turn around. Quickly!"

Before the other drivers and crewmen knew what was happening, the tank driver had his hands up and the militiaman was telling them what to do. "All of you stand still or your buddy gets it," Werner warned. "All right, boys!" With that, the back of the three-tonner came alive, spewing out Komura and seven other militiamen, all with balaclavas covering their faces, weapons pointing at the tank men, who were too openmouthed to do anything. As far as the tank crews knew, the militia was supposed to be a hundred and fifty miles to the east around Twisp and—

None of the tank crew was armed.

"Off with your boots," ordered Werner. "Then your clothes. Hurry it up!"

Within three minutes the men were down to their underwear.

"I said all off! Do it!"

In the next minute the eight crewmen were naked. "Right, start walking west to the motel. You can warm up there." Most of the tank crewmen were shivering already. "C'mon," one of them shouted. "Run!"

A couple of the militiamen were laughing.

"Shut up!" said Werner. "Do your job. Pick up their uniforms on the way back to the truck." Six of the nine-man squad sprinted toward the four tanks. Each man dropped two HE grenades at once down the "hole" of each tank, keeping its hatch open—more air meant more fire—then ran back to the truck as the grenades exploded, the truck's engine running, all the tank crew's clothes now aboard. The truck was already moving as the last militiaman, Sammy Komura, jumped aboard, the first two tanks exploding, the other two roaring with fire. Now the tanks' 12.7mm machine-gun ammo started popping. A few rounds of 105mm exploded, then a gas tank ruptured, sending wild orange arcs of burning fuel shooting into the drizzly air, some of it falling on the other tanks nearby.

Now Werner's squad could hear sirens in the distance as police cars and military Humvees raced to give chase, only to be delayed by the infernos that had been tanks, the air filled with putrid dense black smoke curling upward as the interiors of the tanks continued to burn fiercely, belching toxic fumes. Soon the wailing of ambulances could be heard, confusion reigning supreme at the motel and at the site of the gutted tanks, Werner's truck heading fast into the darkness of the Cascades.

* * *

A hundred yards from the Pateros side's six tanks, Rymann's squad was at a loss about what to do. With the snow falling heavily, the tank crews, already in a much higher state of readiness because of the failure of the FBI's Ninja attack, were inside the tanks. The only ones Rymann's squad could see were the commanders of the first and fourth tank in the line of six doing an "Israeli," heads out of the hatch looking about, the only two tanks not "buttoned up." Ovitz, the easygoing klutz of two days before, was subdued. He was no longer a youth. Something had happened to him inside those woods beyond the tall green grass. He had not only defended his position well, he had taken out two of the Ninjas. His prestige was high. Even with the militia's radio communication all but silent, except in the most urgent cases, knowledge of what Rymann's squad had done had spread throughout the militia's mountainous redoubt. Here were the guys who had taken out a whole squad of the best tactical team the FBI had.

In the fast-fading light of the foothills, hand signals weren't feasible, and Rymann was forced to whisper to his squad. "Ovitz, you know where automatic is now?"

"Fuck you."

"All right, you and I hit the two bunnies sticking out of their holes. The rest of you'll have to move up to the edge of the road with your Molotovs. Now, don't light up before Ovitz and I fire. That'll be your sig—"

"Shit," said Ovitz. "What's this?"

Not twenty yards away through the snow-weighted foliage two outriders and a machine-gun-topped Humvee were pulling up behind the six tanks, the tank commander at the rear of the tank platoon throwing off a snappy salute to a man emerging from the Humvee.

"Who's he?" asked one of Rymann's squad.

"Maybe that general we heard about on the radio."

"Plan's changed," said Rymann. "We'll all open fire on my '*now*.' Ovitz, you and I still take the two—" All six tank hatches were opening, crews getting out to see the big cheese. Rymann waited till they were all out.

"Now!" and the squad opened up, the stuttering orange enfilade of fire kicking up snow all about the bunched-up men around the general. Immediately the tank crews began to scatter, some toward their tanks, some diving and rolling into the ditch on the far side of the road, the softly falling snow dusting the M1A1s, Rymann yelling at the squad to stop any of the remaining crews from getting into any of the tanks, to prevent the 12.7mm atop the Humvee from coming into play. One of the brutish-looking turrets began moving, its main 120mm and coaxial machine gun turning ominously about toward the militia.

"Holy shit!" someone yelled, at once terrified and surprised that at least one man of the four-men tank crews must have remained in the tank as the officer in the Humvee arrived, the officer now lying on the road, either faking it or badly wounded, several other bodies nearby.

"Let's go!" yelled Rymann. The tank turret's 120mm was now pointing right at them but didn't fire. A bluff by a lone driver aboard the tank? By now several other army men were scrambling up on their tanks, disappearing down the hatches. Only one of Rymann's militia squad managed to get close enough to hit one of the M1A1s with his Molotov. The bottle exploded against the side of the tank, creating an impressive-looking fire, but none of the flaming gasoline had spilled down the hatch, and the fire did little, if any, damage. Thirty seconds later it was doused with a CO_2 extinguisher, vomiting out its white foam while a tank commander on the road, one arm holding the other, which was bloody and hanging limply from his shoulder, yelled at his men to fire the tank's machine guns in the direction of the attack.

"But, sir," said one of the crewmen coming up from the ditch, "they're gone by now."

"Do as I say!" the officer screamed, and within thirty seconds all of the tanks' 12.70mm and 7.62mm machine guns, including the 12.70mm atop the Hummer, were chattering, firing into the forest, bullets zipping, thudding into the heavy timber, setting leaves a-tremble, shucking off snow, sending bark flying, the gunners unable to see anything but forest despite their infrared sights.

The attacking militiamen had vanished as quickly as they had appeared, the thin layer of snow near the tanks' outports melted by barrel heat, sending thin streams of water down the sides of the tanks, the cold air reeking of cordite.

"Couldn't see anything, sir, 'cept trees," one of the other tank commanders told him. "They were well gone by the time—"

"Be quiet!" snapped the wounded officer, a major. "And see to the general."

"The general's dead, Major."

"You sure?"

"Yes sir. We tried CPR but there's no pulse. Nothing."

"All right, put him in the Humvee. I'll take him back. Meanwhile I want you men to withdraw from this position back to Pateros until we get infantry protection— which should've been here in the first fucking place." He looked around at the dead. Eight bodies. "Put 'em all in the Humvee." The major paced, then went on, "The shit's gonna hit the fan over this, boys, but there's one thing we can all agree on, right?"

One tank man looked blankly at another, then at the major. "I don't understand, Major."

The major grimaced. He began to shiver, not only

from the cold but because shock was starting to get him. "If anyone asks," he began, shock making his voice sound strained, hesitant, "which they will, we were on the ball, right? We returned fire. Don't anyone clean those twelve-point-sevens till I give the—" He fell to his knees and one of the crewmen helped him to the passenger side of the Humvee. Now his teeth were chattering but he managed to order the remaining men to make sure none of the gasoline was left in the outriders' motorcycles. He didn't want the militia to get at any free Molotov fuel. The two MP outriders were dead.

"How many militiamen attacked you, Major?" Marte Price asked him as he was being evacuated by helo from Pateros for surgery in Yakima. Drowsy from the medic's morphine shot, he told her it was a "platoon-size militia attack. Least thirty—maybe forty—men."

The president was livid, shocked. In the first real army engagement with the militia he'd lost ten men, "one of them the *general* in command of 'Houseclean'!" He'd forgotten it was "Cleanhouse" but no one dared correct him. There were so many advisers in the Oval Office they'd had to bring in extra chairs. He turned his wrath on the army chief of staff. "Jesus Christ, the press is *crucifying* us! Marte Price on CNN has some military expert opining that it's elementary that armor should never be without infantry, that it's *elementary*. How do you explain that, General?"

"I can't, sir," Shelbourne replied. "Only thing I can think of is that there must have been a communications problem from General Limet's HQ."

"*Problem*? You mean screwup. 'Course, we won't know because General Limet's dead! We're in the process of sending in a thousand-man force and their commander is dead!" There was a palpable silence in the Oval Office before the president asked gruffly, "Who else can we send in?" No one was eager to risk his reputation with suggestions. "The truth is," the president continued, "that no one, including me, anticipated the . . . the sheer ferocity of this attack, the militia's ability to react in this way."

"Ah, Mr. President," said Delorme, the senior aide, "there is one man who did. Douglas Freeman."

There was a groan from someone in the white leather lounge chairs.

"You might recall," Shelbourne cut in, "I did mention him, sir. He's been bugging—I should say he *was* bugging—Les Limet about it. Said he had some—" The general almost said "plan" but watered it down for his own safety. "Freeman apparently had some idea of how we might deal with them. As I say, we did mention him, but he's retired."

"Well, then, unretire him. Get him on the phone."

The secretary of the interior stood up. Dammit, someone had to say it. "Mr. President, General Freeman is a *soldier*, not a diplomat." There were several murmurs of agreement.

The president was nonplussed. "I don't *need* a diplomat. I need a *soldier*."

"Yes, Mr. President," put in an aide. "But if you're concerned about political fallout here and overseas— well, I think what Mr. Secretary is saying is that Freeman isn't always circumspect in what he says to the press. To put it bluntly, he doesn't like them."

"Who does?" There was a smattering of laughter that eased the tension, but the secretary of the interior was going to have his say, and never mind the light relief.

"Mr. President, when I was in the state department he periodically referred to the department as the 'DOLS'—

the 'Department of Lies.' " One of the joint chiefs, an admiral, couldn't hide a smirk, and Interior saw it. All right, see how the joint chiefs liked this one. "And I might add," the secretary of the interior continued, "that it is well known that General Freeman refers to all those in the Pentagon as *fairies*. This is a term of abuse he uses not for gays but for anyone who disagrees with him. His staff used to try to prepare him—*muzzle* him, would be a more accurate description—for press conferences, but you can never rely on him, as I say, to be circumspect. He disdains all members of the government and it's said that like his hero, Patton, he believes in reincarnation. He's a loose cannon!"

"Can he fight?" asked the president.

"Yes," Shelbourne answered. "But he does ruffle feathers. He takes absolutely no notice of public opinion, and sometimes bends orders to his own will. Once in Vietnam when he was specifically told not to violate Laotian territory but only to probe with patrols, he launched a drive of at least battalion strength which, when questioned about, he claimed was 'a reconnaissance force'!" General Shelbourne paused but then felt compelled to add, "He has nothing but contempt for polls and the press, as has already been mentioned, but if there's a headline to hijack he'll do it."

The president was nodding sagely. "Get him on the phone. I want to talk to him personally."

"It's the president," said Marjorie, just like that. She might as well have said, "It's the milkman."

"Mr. President."

"General, we haven't met, but you've been mentioned as someone who might help us with this militia problem. How do you feel about that?"

"I'd have to have full control, Mr. President. Not have

my command with one hand tied behind my back by some damned civil servant."

At the other end of the line, his aides saw the president visibly taken aback. "Command! My God, General, I haven't said anything about you commanding anything."

"Pardon me, Mr. President, but I couldn't think what else you'd be calling me about?"

"Advice?" the president suggested.

"About how to do it? Mr. President, sir, Les Limet, God rest him, was a good man—logistically. You needed anything from condoms to corned beef he'd have it there and on time. But tactically speaking he was out of his depth. Genius for organization but no tactical or strategic ability to speak of."

"I'm glad you don't speak ill of the dead. How about *your* tactical and strategic ability?"

"I'm good at both."

"I see modesty doesn't stand in your way."

"Mr. President, I'm a son-of-a-bitch, but I'm *your* son-of-a-bitch. The militias have to be stopped. Freedom to bear arms doesn't extend to civil insurrection."

"Glad to hear it, General, because I've been told you're an admirer of the militias."

"An admirer? No, sir, though by God, from what I hear on the news those boys near Pateros had guts, taking on a tank column. 'Course, damned tanks should never have been there without—"

"You admire their politics?" the president interrupted. "It's been said that you do."

"No, sir, but I *understand* their frustration with the government. In my view, government's gotten too big, too intrusive, from the boardroom to the bedroom. In any event, I'm for more decentralization."

"*Are* you?"

"No offense intended, Mr. President."

"None taken, but I have to know where you stand. Intelligence sources are telling us that there are more people than we realized in our armed services who sympathize with the militias."

"I understand them, Mr. President. I don't support them."

"Good. Now there's one other problem. There's a consensus that you're a 'loose cannon' vis-à-vis the press, et cetera."

"I tell it as I see it."

"As *you* see it. I would hope you have tolerance for other points of view among your colleagues."

"Certainly, but if I'm in command, after everyone's put in their five cents' worth *I* make the final decision, as you have to."

Clever, thought the president. This general might be outspoken, but he was no fool.

"General, if I were to give you command of what was General Limet's force, how would you go about dealing with this militia at large in the Cascades?"

"Mr. President, I assume this conversation is on scrambler?"

"It is."

"First, I don't need a thousand men. Moving that many in that country up there—might as well ask a bulldozer to be quiet. But if I had them I'd employ the bull's-head strategy. Used against the British by the Zulus at Rorke's Drift. The bull's head is the frontal thrust, then the horns, outflanking movements, left and right. But unlike the Zulus, I'd close the gap at the back. Box them in. Surrender or annihilation."

The president started as if he'd been jabbed by a pin. "Annihilation!"

"Sir, the militia is the enemy. Those jokers understand

only one thing—force. They have to be given a clear choice."

"General, you've just about talked your way out of a job. The priority is to get these two murder suspects out for trial. Anyway, assuming you could box in this company . . ." The president consulted an aide, then spoke again to Freeman. ". . . this militia company of theirs with a smaller force than that assigned General Limet, how long do you think it might take you?"

"A week!"

For a moment the president was at a loss for words, his aides listening in on the speaker, shaking their heads disbelievingly.

"Well," the president told Freeman, "I'd give myself a little leeway if I were you, General. They're in their own backyard up there and this militia general, Mant, may have a few ideas of his own."

"Does this mean I get the job, sir? C-in-C, federal forces?"

"On one condition. That if you are successful—if you *do* box anyone in—there'll be no talk of annihilating anybody. There will only be talk of ending the fighting. I do not want to hear, read, or otherwise be advised that you intend to issue any such surrender or annihilation ultimatum to the militia. And you are not to use aircraft against them. No strafing or bombing."

"And if our recon aircraft are fired upon?"

"Then you may return fire, but only—and I want this fully understood, General—*only* to the point of suppressing the militia's fire. No further."

"Yes, sir."

"I'd like you to take command as soon as possible—from Pateros."

"I can leave immediately."

"How many men will you need for the strike force, General?"

"A hundred."

"A hundred? General, the smaller the force the better politically, but only a *hundred*?"

"Audacity, Mr. President. *L'audace, l'audace, toujours l'audace*! I have a few tricks up my sleeve."

The president held one hand over the mouthpiece, telling his aides, "Well, he sure as hell doesn't lack confidence." He removed his hand from the mouthpiece. "Where are these hundred to come from, General?"

"I've already made a list. Most of them are from Delta Force, Rangers, and SEALs. Men I've worked with before. Men in the army whom I trust."

"As opposed to men in the army you don't trust?"

"I didn't intend it to come out that way, Mr. President."

"But that's how it came out, General. As I've told you, I know some army types are supportive of the militia, but I hope you're more circumspect about that with the press."

"I have a press officer, sir."

"You need one," the president said.

Within the hour CNN announced the appointment of Freeman as C-in-C of Operation Bulldog, a name change, as Marte Price at Pateros HQ reported, the general had apparently insisted upon.

In Washington, D.C., the talk at State was that "Bull-at-a-Gate" had been put in charge of "Operation Bullshit" and was headed for a fall.

In Monterey that evening, Douglas Freeman, his gear packed, waited for a car from the recently reopened Fort Ord to come pick him up for the ride to the airport. For a moment the newly unretired general felt uncharacteristically apprehensive. Was it because he'd so confidently told his commander in chief that he needed only a hundred men for his strike force? Had "George C. Scott" bitten off more than he could chew? Or was it a realization by a veteran of many wars that this was a different mission than all those that came before, that this *was* a mission where patriots would clash, American against American? It hadn't happened since the Civil War. In that conflict, the bloody horror of American against American could to some degree be psychologically camouflaged by calling it a battle of the North against the South. That way you could almost believe there were two different peoples fighting, same way as Americans used to talk about the North Koreans and South Koreans, North Vietnamese against the South Vietnamese. Illusions—they were all brothers and cousins, fathers and sons, one against the other.

What would he feel the first time he had an American in his sights? Would blood prove stronger than cause? You'd have to be damn careful, too, with many of the militia wearing the same fatigues—army surplus—as the strike force. How many would fall to that oxymoron—"friendly fire"? And it was dangerous stuff psychologically for a soldier to be thinking about the enemy as men just like you. POPS, the army's psychological operations unit, would have its hands full. Yet these men in the militia had just killed nine FBI agents, eight tank crewmen, two outriders, and General Limet. By doing that they had placed themselves beyond the pale.

He heard the army staff car pull up outside, the embossed stars on its stiff metal flag catching the front porch light, and involuntarily Freeman found himself entering his general's mode. He straightened up as an officer and gentleman, decreed so by act of Congress, and said good-bye to his sister-in-law as warmly as good manners required. Marjorie merely nodded and closed the door.

"Back in the saddle, eh, General?" the driver of the staff car asked.

"By God—Brady. Is that you?"

"Sure is, General. I hear we're getting up a team. A hundred true and strong."

"Jesus. Where'd you hear that?"

"All around the base, sir."

"Huh—so much for White House security."

"Sorry, sir."

"Not your fault, Brady. Mine. Should never have told those bastards at the White House. Goddamn place is leakier'n a two-dollar toilet."

"Yes, sir."

"Well, Brady, if it's all over the base it's a good bet that some of the militia know."

The general was wrong—*all* of the militia knew. And General Mant's aide-de-camp, Colonel Somers, had already passed on the order for all militia units in the Northwest to be ready to move to ACON Four. Mant intended to overwhelm Freeman's troops at first contact and annihilate them—teach the federals a lesson they'd never forget. If you stood up against them now it would deter them in the future. And Mant had it on good authority from the Washington, D.C., militia that the White House had forbidden air strikes against the militia. A bonus that meant it would not be an air-land battle but strictly a land battle, the kind his militias, under veteran instructors like Lucky McBride, had been training for all over the country.

"D'you know, Brady," Freeman asked his chauffeur, "that we sent five hundred thousand men to the Gulf War?"

"Figure it must've been around that, General."

"You learned that from the news reports, right—CNN?"

"Yes, sir."

"I know one thing CNN didn't tell you. Best-kept secret of the war."

"What's that, sir?"

"That we also sent thirty-five thousand dogs."

"You serious, General?"

"Damn right I am." He snatched up the cellular phone and immediately put it down. Open line. Too insecure. "When in hell will we be at the airport?"

"Quarter hour at the most."

"Good."

By the time they arrived, Freeman had encoded a request to the U.S. Army's canine corps in Fort Gordon, Georgia. Though he doubted the militia was crazy enough to use gas warfare against his Cascades Strike Force, a dog or two would be invaluable as early detectors of any biological or chemical weapons—obviating the need for cumbersome NBC—nuclear, biological, and chemical warfare—suits that would greatly inhibit movement, the very noise of moving in them through mountainous terrain a severe handicap. This way each soldier need carry only an emergency CW—chemical warfare—syringe.

CHAPTER SIXTEEN

IT WAS ARMY Chief General Shelbourne on the other end of the Pentagon–White House scrambler line.

"What is it?" asked senior presidential aide Delorme. "The boss is asleep."

"Better wake him up."

"It's three A.M. Is it that urgent?"

"Mr. Delorme, the militias of Washington, Oregon, Idaho, and Montana have declared independence. Secession from the Union."

Delorme was stunned. *"What?"* he said. "They can't do that!"

"They have. And what's more, they've got thirty-six thousand men—two divisions—to back it up. You think they're bluffing after that Ninja debacle? Jesus Christ, they've just taken out six tanks and killed Les Limet! They're not fucking around, Delorme. You'd better wake the boss. We've got a goddamn insurrection on our hands."

"Does the press know?"

"They will in about ten minutes," the general answered. "We received an intelligence report from one of Treasury's boys."

"Secret Service?"

"Yes—deep cover in the militias. The information is that Mant is about to make a public statement." Delorme pressed the red button. "Where will they broadcast from?"

"We don't know. Apparently it's been prerecorded on video and radio. It'll be on all the networks and CNN no doubt and it's going to be relayed through WWCR—Worldwide Christian Radio—out of Michigan and by TECM—Texas Constitutional Militias—e-mail network. Those bastards code everything, including the goddamn weather, but you can bet this announcement'll be in plain language. And of course it'll be all over the Internet."

The president arrived, disheveled, in robe and slippers. His hair was combed but he was unshaven and looked about sleepily, shocking Delorme with a loud red, white, and blue nightshirt that the aide had never seen before. He thought the boss wore pajamas.

"Orange juice and coffee," the president told Delorme and took the phone. He listened to General Shelbourne.

"General, are you sure this isn't some militiaman half-full of booze giving your man a story?"

"I'm sure, sir."

"Well, what're we doing about it?"

"We've alerted I Corps at Fort Lewis, Washington, the Hundred and Sixty-third Armored Brigade at Bozeman, Montana, and the Hundred and Sixteenth Cavalry Brigade at Boise, Idaho. They're our major combat units in the Northwest."

"Are they regular army?" asked the president.

"I Corps is, as part of our Continental Sixth Army. The others are National Guard units. Sir, I know you want to keep the guard units out of it, but they're available in the area."

"Point taken, General. But let's hold off any deployment. This militia news release may be all piss and vinegar—just to get attention."

It wasn't. As Shelbourne and the president spoke, the Second Washington and First Idaho regiments, ten thousand militiamen in all, were deploying along an east-west line following Washington State Highway 14 running parallel to the Columbia River where the river's course formed the border between Washington and Oregon. The Third Washington Militia Regiment of five thousand men was meanwhile racing west through thick forests of maple, Sitka spruce, hemlock, and Douglas fir to cut Interstate 5, forty-five miles from the coast, and 101, on the coast, the main south-north supply arteries leading up from the big army bases on the coast in California.

Twenty minutes later the militia alliances of Michigan, Oklahoma, Illinois, Texas, and Florida vociferously joined what they termed "the Great Crusade." Another hundred thousand men.

The shape of the rebel Northwestern states took the form of what the press quickly called the "cleaver," its blade made up of Washington State, Oregon, northern California, and Idaho, its handle by Montana and North Dakota. Below the cleaver there were smaller areas of insurrection, as in Yosemite and Yellowstone National Parks, and of outright chaos such as in South-Central L.A. In the latter, white militia sympathizers taunted blacks, who answered violence with violence. Asians and Latinos tried to stay out of it while protecting their stores from rampaging mobs but found themselves drawn in when the looting began. This time, however, the latest L.A. riot wasn't filmed close up by any TV station. A local KTLA Channel 5 camera crew and reporter had been shot to death by rioters not wanting to be identified. All TV coverage was from the air, though one helo was hit by small-arms fire as it tried for a close-in zoom of a bloody confrontation between police and rioters near the Jordan Downs Housing Project.

Within two hours U.S. Army and Marine heavy-air-transport bases throughout the rebel states were under fire, and strategic rail lines all over the United States— the only other way, apart from highways, for the U.S. Army to rapidly move large numbers of men within the continental United States—were blown. Anyone who ventured forth on the highways of America was literally taking his life in his hands. Freeways became deserted, after the Teamsters Union refused to put their drivers at risk until the roads were made safe. The lifelines of the United States were seizing up. Chaos threatened. *The New York Times* said it all: CIVIL WAR.

Amid all these cataclysmic events it appeared that people had completely forgotten about Charlie Ames. It was as if the man had disappeared into thin air. Besides, the big "pix" news this hour was that militia general Mant, wherever he was, had just ordered, via the Net, all militia units to fly the militia standard, a Confederate flag with four rifles top and bottom forming two *M*s.

The heart of the collapse was northern California, from Sacramento up to the Oregon border. Here, for years, in a country of rugged individualism, people, including ranchers, farmers, artists, loggers, and fishermen who had often fought among themselves over how best to pre-serve what land and resources they had, had always agreed on one thing: they wanted to break free from the south. Southern California, starting from San Francisco down, especially Los Angeles, was viewed angrily by these northerners as a pig on the teat of the north, con-stantly draining the latter's water and other natural resources. Secession had been a common topic up here for over eighty years, and in June '93 almost half of California's fifty-eight counties voted to secede. This was the country of the spotted owl, country that stretched from the Redwoods of the coastal plain to the Sierra Nevadas, with the northern end of California's Central Valley between.

Rightly or wrongly, the northerners also believed that they held their land in deeper spiritual respect than did the "bright-lighters" of the big cities to the south. The commercial tentacles that extended from San Diego and L.A. and San Francisco were seen as a constant threat to the northerner's simpler, more natural way of life, a threat of increasing governmental regulation and taxation even though some of those regulations helped preserve the giant redwoods and other resources in what the northerners called "God's country." Among the angry, self-reliant northerners, though their values and outlook differed, were the marijuana growers whose plantations, in a climate ideal for growing the weed, had been hidden for so long but lately had received hard hits from the Drug Enforcement Agency. *More damned federal legislation.*

A bright-lighter from New York, visiting the quaint, Victorian-style village of Mendocino just a hundred miles north of San Francisco on California's north coast, once said to local logger Jim Nye, "I don't understand all this militia business out here in the West, this tension between you folks and Washington, D.C. What's the story?"

Silently Nye took out his commando knife. They were outside the Mendocino Bakery and Café. Kneeling, he traced out a rough shape of the continental United States, then he drew the knife down the middle. "East o' that line," he told the bright-lighter, "five percent of the land is owned by the federal government. West of it, over fifty percent is federal. Out here you can't even take a piss without the federals tellin' you when and how. The most endangered species out here, friend, isn't the spotted owl—it's us. Free men. Old Jean-Jacques was right: 'Man was born free but everywhere he is in chains.' Federal chains. We aim to break 'em." The opening sentence of Rousseau's *Social Contract* had become a kind of mantra among the country's militias.

When the news flash came to the village of Mendocino, Jim Nye was sitting in Roaster's Inn, his rough hands clasping a mug of strong black coffee, watching TV and rolling homemade cigarettes. Because of the BLM—the federal Bureau of Land Management—regulations about clear-cutting, he was out of work and couldn't afford tailor-made smokes. A couple of unemployed fishermen, also victims of federals—in this case, Washington, D.C.'s yearlong ban on coastal fishing—sat at the next table playing gin rummy.

"This just in from our Seattle affiliate," read the TV announcer. "Militias in Washington State, Oregon, Idaho, Oklahoma, Texas, Florida, Illinois, Michigan, and Montana have declared themselves independent countries—in what they say is an act of secession from the United States. They are requesting that all militias in the rest of the country do likewise."

A cheer went up from the crowd in Roaster's.

"The president has described the militias' declaration as not only unlawful but a 'clear and present danger' to the integrity of the United States. He has placed all federal troops in the nine affected states on DEFCON 3, the third highest of five peacetime alerts. The president has also given senior military commanders in the rebel states authority to issue 'weapons-free' status so that the federal troops might immediately combat any action by the militias which the government deems hostile to the good order and security of the United States."

"Fuck you!" shouted one of the fishermen. More cheering and table thumping in Roaster's. Logger Jim Nye didn't say a word, just sat there with his coffee, a smile of deep satisfaction spreading over his weathered face. See how the fucking enviros liked this—militias of nine states on the move. Might frighten a few spotted owls along the way.

With the coastal highway 101 and the I-5 inland already being intercepted by the Oregon militia, Jim Nye figured the best thing his northern Cal militia unit could do was make sure that none of the side or "loop" roads, between Mendocino on the coast and Piercy, about eighteen miles inland from the coast, could be used by the army trying to rush troops north of San Francisco into Oregon. Best place to stop the federals if they tried this would be the crossings over the Navarro, Elk, and Big rivers. If, on the other hand, the California federals went northeast on 40 through southeast Nevada in an effort to swing through southern Idaho and Wyoming to attack the militia's left flank, then the militia of Nevada would deal with them. The Nevada militia wasn't that big compared with those of other states, containing only one battalion of a thousand men, but numbers were deceptive. Activists in Nevada didn't mess around and wouldn't be intimidated. In the early 1990s, well before Oklahoma City, they'd blown up federal offices in Reno and Carson City.

Jim Nye had gone to the Mendocino Bakery to get one of their famed tamales just to celebrate, and as he drove to his home twelve miles east of Mendocino, he kept dropping his false teeth then clenching them again, a sign that he was as excited as he was anxious. He might be out of work because of spotted-owl freaks and the federal government, but now he could strike back—and he wouldn't have to hurt a soul. Nye reckoned he was one of the best loggers in the Northwest—hell, in the United States—and if there was one thing he'd learned from his old man, but never had a chance to use, it was how to lay an abatis, a tree blockade. The area had already been chosen by General Mant's HQ for just such an eventuality. Now he was going to do it, jam up the side roads. It wasn't something any fool could do. When the eco freaks saw it they'd have a goddamn heart attack. That alone made it worth doing.

All over Washington, Oregon, and northern California, militiamen like Jim Nye were responding to the call. And some, like Davy Smallwood in the Redwoods up near the California-Oregon border, would get the call not on the Net but by landline phone. Before he reached home, Smallwood's wife, Brenda, had answered, and when a sexy-sounding woman's voice said, "Tell Davy it's time to pick up Minimi," and hung up, Brenda got the shock of her life. The kids were fighting over whether to watch reruns of *Home Improvement* or *Extra*, she had bread about to come out of the wood-burning Fisher, the timer was sounding off, the smoke alarm was screaming, and in the confusion she'd thought the caller had said "Mimi." In the early days, a hundred and fifty years back, a lot of French-Canadian fur trappers had been in Oregon when the British Hudson's Bay Company was the big cheese in the territory, and the French-Canadian trappers had stayed on and so there were French names all around. Mimi? Some French tart Davy was seeing on the side?

"That's what she said, Davy. Go get Mimi. Who the hell's Mimi?"

Davy tossed his tractor cap onto the hat stand and

shook his head, laughing. "*Minimi,* Brenda, *Minimi.* In the federal army they call it a SAW—Squad Automatic Weapon."

"Well, heck, why didn't she say that?"

" 'Cause the federals might be listenin' in."

"Shoot. Don't you think the federals would know what she meant anyway?"

"Naw. Too stupid. Minimi's a limey word."

"Davy?"

"Uh-huh?"

"You tell me where you're goin'?"

He made a haven't-we-been-over-this-before? face. "You know I can't tell you, hon."

"You look after yourself," said Brenda, putting her hand on his shoulder.

"Always have."

"This is different, though. This isn't a drill, is it? This is for real."

"Gotta help the brothers up in Washington and Oregon, Bren. They're layin' it on the line. A man has to go."

"You least know how long?"

"Long as it takes."

She'd been over this many times in her mind, but now that it was here it was different. Felt a lump in her throat. She and Davy had their rough times—who didn't?—but they'd made it this far and they were as happy as any couple could be, given the federals had screwed Davy's livelihood. Too proud to go on welfare, they'd eked out a living collecting mushrooms for the Japanese market. In his dad's time in World War II, the Japs had sent over flame balloons that they had designed to descend over the West Coast to start massive forest fires. The United States had won the war and now, mused Davy, here he was scrabbling around like a goddamn sixties hippie

picking mushrooms for some Jap businessman in Tokyo.
Country had gone to hell in a handbasket. Screw Tokyo
and Washington, D.C.

"It'll be in the Redwoods," she said. "Won't it? Federal
land?"

All he told her was, "We're just gonna give the federals
a little fright. Hold 'em up long enough for the Washington and Oregon boys to consolidate their positions."

"Consolidate." Brenda knew that was a militia word.
"Thought they had over thirty thousand coming down
from Idaho and Montana to help 'em. Surely that's
enough."

Davy smiled at her naïveté. "Honey, that's the point.
They're *comin'*. Ain't on the Columbia-Snake line yet.
And the federals are sending up three divisions—that's
over fifty thousand. We gotta help slow 'em up—buy
time for our boys along the line."

The "line," 570 miles long, ran west to east along the
Columbia River, which formed both a wide natural moat
and the border between Oregon and Washington, and
then followed the course of the Snake River as it swung
southeast to form part of the border between Oregon and
Idaho. As such, the line effectively boxed in Oregon in
the shape of a "7," the corner of the 7 passing through the
Snake River's Hell's Canyon National Recreation Area,
the stem of the 7 forming the eastern border between
Idaho and Oregon.

Davy kissed Brenda and gave both kids an extra-long
hug. "You behave yourselves and take good care of
Mom. Okay?"

"Okay. You going to the A-and-C, Daddy?"

He mussed their hair and left.

The A-and-C wasn't a railroad nor a hardware chain. It
stood for the Anderson and Central Valley militia in the
northwestern corner of California. Even so it was some-

thing of a misnomer, for it really stood for Anderson and *North* Central Valley, but militia leaders, always sensitive to the misappropriation of acronyms, didn't want the particular confusion that might arise if they called it ANC—the Communist-driven African National Congress.

It was a small militia, barely a company of three platoons and fewer than a hundred men, but along with the larger Northern California militia, it would, because of one of those unexpected quirks, have a decisive effect on the course of the war and, coincidentally, on the price of marijuana all across the United States and Canada.

A-and-C's designated task from General Mant's HQ was to cause as substantial delays as possible to the federals on coastal Highway 101 running parallel to the coast, and on Interstate 5 about ninety miles in, so that the Washington and Idaho and Montana regiments could have more time to deploy along the Washington-Oregon border as well as along the Snake River running southeast, protecting Idaho's western flank. Jim Nye's platoon of thirty men was to act as mobile reinforcements for either highway ambush or for "side-road contingencies" should the U.S. Army convoys use the side roads along the coast.

The first ambuscade involving Jim Nye and Davy Smallwood, not in the Redwoods but on Interstate 5, was laid at night in a cutting approximately twelve miles north of Sacramento and twenty-five miles southwest of Folsom. The militia let the advance guard of a BFV—Bradley fighting vehicle—and a Hummer, with a swivel-mounted .50-caliber machine gun atop, pass through the high-sided cutting.

When the militia's platoon leader saw the enemy's vehicles, fifteen of them, fill the circle of his Owl fourth-generation low-light-sensitive pocket scope, he fired the flare. As soon as its loud pop was heard by the two fifteen-man squads, one on either side of the road, the thirty militiamen opened up with AK-47s, pouring a hail of 7.6mm into the Hummer, the first three and last two troop-laden trucks. There was a splintering of glass and the Hummer went into the S-shape defensive driving pattern but to no avail. The vehicle, its driver hit, slammed into the side of the cutting, its rear wheels still spinning on the road, burning rubber with nowhere to go. The trucks behind screeched to a stop, and several smashed into the vehicle in front of them. Soldiers jumped out over the tailboards onto the I-5 as the second truck in the convoy erupted in flame. The third truck's cooling fans exploded like so many airborne coins, reflecting the descending light of the parachute flare, and the stink of burning gas and oil filled the air.

The turret of the rearguard twenty-five-ton Bradley, an M2A1 with 30mm of appliqué armor added, swung to three o'clock, its 25mm chain gun and its coaxial 7.62mm machine gun elevated sharply to about forty-five degrees as were several of its port-firing M231 Colt 5.56mm automatic weapons. The 475-round-a-minute chain gun got off one burst before the Bradley was hit mid-right side with a Loral Aeroneutronic Predator HEAT—high-explosive antitank—round, its shaped charge striking the Bradley aft of the mission computer, penetrating the vehicle's half-inch-steel-plus-one-inch-aluminum armor, releasing a jet of molten metal, scalding and blinding the crew and setting off the seven TOW missiles in the BFV's left-side launcher. The resulting explosions caused the instant vaporization of the vehicle's nine-man infantry squad's blood before they could exit and deploy. Two militiamen, though high up on the culvert's lip, suffered superficial burns on shoulders and legs from the hot metal fallout.

The advance BFV, an M3 or Cavalry Scout Bradley, with its crew of three—and two more Bradley infantry vehicles now a mile farther down the I-5—swung about on the all-but-deserted highway, terrifying a family inside a stopped car, the Bradley's metal tracks spitting sparks in the tight U-turn as it quickly attained its maximum of forty miles an hour, its chain gun already filling the predawn sky with long white dashes of tracer despite it being out of effective range because of the obstructing contours of other culverts.

By the time the Bradley drove off the highway to charge up behind the militia, it, too, had been hit by a fire-and-forget Predator II antitank missile at a distance of 130 yards, the explosion lifting the rear of the twenty-five-ton vehicle off the ground, the wall of heat and concussion from the disintegrating Bradley knocking the Predator operator backward, one of the black foam-rubber end sleeves of the stubby launcher tube whacking another militiaman, causing his AK-47's burst to fire dangerously high, toward the militia squad on the other side, striking Davy Smallwood, killing him instantly. The *whoosh* of the heat wave was immediately followed by the taste of burning rubber.

With the first three trucks and rear two stopped dead, a Bradley knocked out, and four of the remaining trucks aflame, the A-and-C militia platoon leader didn't need his nightscope, the dancing light of the burning trucks providing all the illumination his thirty men required. The federals, on the other hand, could see only the odd tongue of flame from the militia's AK-47s and only a few of the militia's World War II army-surplus helmets.

The federals had no place to hide, fire coming down on them from either side, their only protection afforded by scrambling under the few trucks that weren't burning or by throwing themselves flat against the sides of the culvert, neither of which allowed them to return any effective fire. And now grenades began rolling down either side of the culvert, their explosions killing and wounding the federals who'd taken refuge there. Within fifty seconds of the militia opening fire, thirty-two federals were dead, forty-eight wounded, blood, burning trucks, bodies, body parts, and chaos spread all over the I-5.

Within five minutes of the start of the ambush, the militia were in their four-wheel Jeeps and were gone. An enterprising and very brave federal sergeant, with a squad from one of the rear trucks, who ran to the end of the western side of the cutting to come 'round back of it in the dying flare light, found only piles of expended 7.62mm casings and grenade pins scattered along the top of the cutting, and one helmet.

It was the first action of its kind since the American Civil War to have taken place on an American highway, not counting the Indian wars. Its ferocity and the fact that it had obviously been so well planned, down to nonconflicting fields of fire to maximize the damage, stunned the Pentagon, even as every available federal, civil, and military ambulance raced toward the scene. The ambushes of the M1 tanks, General Limet's death, and now the I-5 incident made it clear to Army Chief of Staff Shelbourne and the commander of the CONUS—Continental U.S.— Sixth Army that the roads were the militia's final line of defense, or rather attack, and this made every federal, from senior officers and NCOs to enlisted men, aware of the horrendous potential of the militia. If the vital road arteries throughout the United States were not "secured from militia hit-and-run guerrilla tactics" then, as Shelbourne put it to the president, "federal forces are at a decided disadvantage in terms of maintaining 'logistical efficiency,'" or as he put it to senior officers of the Sixth Army, "Without safe highways we are in deep shit. How in hell can we fight the bastards if we can't get to them to fight, for Christ's sake?"

"Advance units," suggested his aide, Major Baun.

"We *had* an advance unit in these Bradleys," Shelbourne retorted. "And according to the goddamn militia Internet reports, it was destroyed by an antitank missile."

"I mean advance units in force," said the aide.

"Major, we haven't got enough men in the entire United States Army to plant a man every ten yards along every highway in the country—even if we wanted to. And if we did, the goddamned militia could pick them off."

"Air transport," the major suggested.

"Not fast enough," Shelbourne responded. "Not in the army air arm."

"We could ask the air force." The major was gutsy, which is why Shelbourne had selected him, as Freeman had selected Colonel Norton, a fellow veteran, as his aide. Both aides would stand their ground despite the bad temper of their superiors.

"General," the major continued, "I don't think this is the time for interservice rivalry. If we need the air force, let's ask them."

"Oh, it's not that I'm worried about," Shelbourne answered. "The trouble is those militia pricks have threatened the airfields and airports. Bastards've brought the civil airlines to a dead stop. Everyone's thinking of that TWA 800 flight in 'ninety-six out of JFK."

"Use out-of-the-way fields."

"A possibility," Shelbourne acknowledged, "but there's still the problem of not being able to move overwhelming ground forces fast enough. Christ—took us months to build up our Gulf War force and we had nothing but cooperation from civil airports. Now they're all scared shitless. Besides, the moment we use out-of-the-way fields we immediately multiply our logistical problems—food, ammo, and gas. And then the pricks could hit and run, until we secured the base." The general looked straight at the major, Sam Baun. "Jesus, Sam, it's like Vietnam."

The major conceded the point. The phone rang and Baun answered it, listening grim-faced. "Thank you." He turned to Shelbourne. "We have to get something going. That was NSA. CNN and Murdoch's news channel are already covering the site of the ambush—world news."

Shelbourne bit his lip, pondering the problem. "Maybe," said Baun, "Freeman's mission will get us out from behind the eight ball."

Shelbourne nodded, aimed his cigarette-pack-sized "Automap" pocket computer toward the wall, and selected TPC F-16B, the map for northern California, now projected on the wall. His hand was shaking slightly, and before Baun could notice, he put the Automap on the desk, which unintentionally altered the focus. "You're right, Sam. We have to get out from under this—and fast. Let's hope Doug Freeman can get us on the board. Meanwhile I think I have a surprise for our militia friends. Put the Eighty-second Airborne at Fort Bragg on alert. We'll bypass the I-5 *and* the 101."

Baun didn't get it. "You mean, sir, we'll bring back all the convoys heading north from California?"

"No," said Shelbourne. "To suddenly recall two divisions would be to tell Mant's boys what we're up to. Besides, we can't just give away northern California— unfortunately. It'll be one of our major staging areas. No—have the convoys proceed, but slowly, at least for a while. Going slower won't eliminate the danger of hit-and-runs by the militia, but it'll keep their heads down, hopefully limit the damage. And"—he smiled—"it'll get the militia thinking we're *all* coming by convoy."

Now Baun could see it. "Slip the Airborne over the Oregon-Washington line. Get behind them."

"You got it," said Shelbourne. "And in front of them." He was looking at the map at the four-mile-long Astoria Bridge over the Columbia River from Astoria, Oregon, to Washington State, now designated as "AB," and the two bridges over Youngs Bay to the south of Astoria. "Secure AB across the Columbia. Because if we don't have *it* we have nothing. No point in bringing thousands of our troops up from California to fight Mant's people if we can't get across the friggin' river. Point is, sat pix show Mant's main defensive line is on the northern side. Makes sense. He sure as hell doesn't want to get caught with the river behind him. He's on the northern side because he wants to use the river as a moat against us." Shelbourne walked closer to the map, looking at the east-west course of the river that formed the border between the two states. Walking into the beam of the projected map, Cannon Beach, about twenty miles south of the border, was projected on his neck. "Trick is to get the Eighty-second Airborne *behind* them—secure the AB on *his* side before he realizes it."

Shelbourne lit up a Havana—smuggled in through the mail by a Canadian NORAD liaison officer—and sucked in so hard the cigar's tip turned from red to bright orange. *"Bridge at Remagen."* He beamed, blowing out an acrid cloud of thick bluish gray smoke whose shadows moved across the wall map like storm clouds. "If we get there in time," he added, smiling, stabbing at the wide mouth of the river, "we'll take the big bridge from him before he knows what's hit him."

"Good," said Baun, his tone hopeful but nervous because he was thinking of another bridge, in 1944, that Airborne troops had been sent to secure over the Rhine. And it wasn't the bridge at Remagen that Shelbourne had just referred to but the bridge at Arnhem—a bridge too far—an unmitigated disaster for the Allied paratroopers. And almost certainly the federal Airborne, like Freeman's militia force farther north, would be outnumbered by the enemy until the main-force reinforcements arrived from the much more populous south.

CHAPTER SEVENTEEN

CASCADES. DAWN. THERE were three choppers carrying Freeman's force of one hundred. The first was an SOA (special operations aircraft) long-range four-crew-member MH-60K Black Hawk helo carrying Freeman and twelve SOF (special operations forces) troops. The other two choppers were big CH-47 Chinooks, each with forty-four SOF troops aboard, all three choppers approaching the eastern foothills of the Cascades. In the Black Hawk, Freeman went up front, telling the pilot to lead the hundred-man force into an LZ that was west of Twisp and that would place him and his men on a gradual slope with the north-south-flowing Methow River behind them. TIS pix (thermal imaging satellite photos) had identified "leopard spots," a warm spot cluster, possible body heat, each cluster consisting of approximately ten micropoints of heat and located ten to fourteen miles west of Twisp in the direction of the Sawtooth Wilderness area and Ames's cabin.

"Shouldn't be a cluster in there," said the pilot, doing battle with a rush of static and the sustained roaring of the Black Hawk's engines, the rotors maintaining a cruising speed of around ninety to a hundred miles per hour. It was uncomfortable, the helo bucking because of the hodgepodge of cross air currents and drafts coming off and going down to the sharp saw-toothed snowcaps of the Cascades. "It's a national park in there," added the pilot, tapping her knee map.

No one answered her, too busy hanging on during the bumpy ride, each of the troops in mottled, khaki-green, hooded, second-generation ECWC, Extended Cold Weather Clothing System, loaded down with sixty pounds of equipment. In the main they carried 8.9-pound increased-accuracy M-16 A2 rifles and M249 SAWs, both weapons using the heavier NATO 5.56mm ammo. Two men in each squad of ten were equipped with ANIPAS-13, thermal imaging day/night-vision weapon sights, a half dozen of the troops also carrying new lightweight 5.65-pound M4 carbines, a collapsible-stock version of the 8.9-pound M-16 A2.

It was misty in the north-south Methow River valley around Twisp and the helo pilot's intense concentration was evident from the beads of perspiration on her forehead. Freeman was, ironically, an early convert to equal opportunity, his rationale, since his first use of women in Korea, simply being that if "skirts" could show they were, like men, entitled to be shot *at* then they could be involved in combat. Besides, she was a damn good pilot, and as they descended she showed why, as long, trailing wreaths of mist, seemingly perverse in their intent, congealed to block any clear sight of the landing zone Freeman had chosen. The general was now instructing the two big Chinooks a few hundred yards behind the Black Hawk to follow him in but not to touch down until his twelve men had secured the LZ and had assessed whether the ground, in long grass by the frozen river, was firm enough to take the 53,900-pound weight of each Chinook.

Freeman's aide, Colonel Norton, was perplexed. Having three choppers land in the same LZ was hardly the best way to initiate the general's Zulu or bull's-head tactic: one force keeping the enemy occupied by seeming to hit them head-on while sending the bulk of your troops out into two horns or flanks. Closing the trap from the rear. "Wouldn't it be better, General," Norton suggested, "to split your force now into the three components?"

"What in hell for?"

"Bull's-head strategy."

"Oh, that—that was bull*shit* strategy for White House consumption, in case there are militia moles in Washington, which I'm sure there must be, by the way. We're going to move a lot faster than any damn bull's head, Norton."

"How?"

"Hold on!" the pilot shouted as the Black Hawk began a gut-wrenching series of fast up-and-down motions, creating powerful pushes of air that blew into the mist, dispersing it beyond the landing zone. It was a trick the helo pilot had learned from one of the helo's machine gunners, a Vietnam vet.

True to his reputation, General Freeman was first out the door. Expecting a soggy landing, he was surprised to find the ground firm, from early-morning frost. Carrying a semiautomatic Remington eight-round shotgun loaded with number-four buckshot and fléchette cartridges, and a Colt laser-aiming .45-caliber with silencer as his holstered weapon, Freeman signaled the others to follow.

Within ten seconds the twelve Special Forces troops were out, and in another fifteen seconds nine of them had fanned out to form a fifty-yard-diameter semicircle facing away from the river. No enemy movement was seen, though Freeman took nothing for granted. He had good reason not to, as minutes before starting this mission, Intelligence had informed him that he was probably up against a Lucky McBride, apparently a 'Nam and Gulf vet who'd become something of a legend in the militias. Besides, Freeman knew that any noise the militia might have made would have been smothered by the roar of the Black Hawk as it took off and the noise of the first of the two big Chinooks coming in, the high-country air heavy with gas fumes, troops scuttling out to further fortify the perimeter.

Five of Rymann's rearguard militia squad hadn't been able to get near Freeman's LZ even though POP—Pateros Observation Post, one of the many OPs along the mountain road—had called in the approach of the three lizard-pattern camouflaged federal choppers, one Black Hawk and two Chinooks. Each OP had a tough-terrain vehicle, and the one requisitioned by Rymann's squad was an Isuzu Sidekick Jeep with room for only four of the nine-militiaman squad, the rule being that one militiaman, the driver, had to stay with the vehicle in the event it needed the camouflage net to be thrown over it. The Jeep had roared out of Twisp so fast that Rymann and his weapon were almost flung out of the rear seat. "For Christ's sake," yelled Rymann. "We want to get there in one piece!"

"Gotta beat those black helos."

"They're not black," said Rymann, shaking his head, his voice whipped away in the Jeep's slipstream. It was one of the militia's abiding obsessions, this conviction that the government was periodically sending out "black" helicopters on secret missions. Maybe the air force was trying out prototypes of the new Comanche helo. Whatever, as in so many parts of the country, there had been reports for years in the Northwest about black helos. Despite the advance warning from POP and other OPs along the route through the Cascades that Freeman's three helos were on their way, descending in the area outside Twisp, the "Sidekick" Jeep didn't make it in time to do anything about the landing of the Black Hawk or the first big Chinook, and barely arrived in time to see the second Chinook approaching. "Pull up in that culvert!" ordered Rymann, sure that if they went much farther they'd be in a clear line of fire from any ground force that had alighted from the first two helos. As they came to a hard stop, mud and snow slurried beneath the vehicle.

"Can you do it?" asked Ovitz, sitting next to Rymann, the latter gripping the Jeep's steering wheel so hard his hands had gone white as the snow above the tree line.

Rymann didn't answer, standing up in the Jeep. "Nobody move!" he commanded, closing his right eye, sighting the big Chinook above the frozen curve of river and white-green mountainside, the scope's crosshairs bisecting the big bird. He squeezed the trigger. The Stinger missile shot out of its tube, crimson-tailed, the hot backblast hitting the far side of the culvert behind the Jeep, sending up a cloud of stinging, gravelly dirt. Seconds later the ground-to-air missile's main engine ignited, propelling it at over eight hundred miles an hour, homing in on the Chinook.

The helo's fuselage imploded, bits of it flying through the air, followed by an enormous orange explosion whose sound wave hit the culvert seconds later as fiery bodies and debris tumbled earthward all over the LZ, some of the forty-four Special Forces still alive and aflame as they were falling, screaming, hitting the ice that was the frozen river like fiery comets, sliding uncontrollably, backs and necks broken, those still aflame giving off an unpleasant sweetish odor as body fat continued to sizzle till extinguished by fire-melted ice.

Though they were all combat veterans, Freeman's remaining fifty-five men out of what had been a hundred were clearly shaken by the sudden and violent loss of their comrades. In a matter of seconds the strike force had been cut in half.

"Into the trees!" Freeman shouted, immediately deciding against all instinct not to waste time or risk any of his men by sending them across the bend of river behind them on a seek-and-destroy mission to silence the Stinger. And in that moment of quick decision Freeman realized he had made a fatal mistake. Yes, the pilots of all three choppers should have released flares while descending, to "dummy off" the Stinger missile's passive infrared homing device, as they'd done in 'Nam and as the Russians had done in Afghanistan against the militia rebels there. But "Operation Bulldog" was *his* responsibility and Freeman knew he'd have to take the rap for it. He could only thank God that no media people were along, like CNN's Marte Price, no videos of the explosion, of dead bodies tumbling, to be transmitted worldwide.

He had screwed up and immediately felt that the pressure on him to get something to show for it had increased twofold. The death of so many of his men only reinforced his determination to apprehend both Latrell and Hearn—alive—so they could be punished. After causing the death of forty-four of his men, shooting would be too good for them—too quick. *If* he caught them.

But what concerned Freeman now as he hastened to consolidate his drastically reduced force of fifty-five was how much more high-tech weaponry the militia might possess. Or was Mant blowing a limited high-tech wad in this engagement, hoping to bluff his enemy in the Cascades into disengaging? Certainly no one, even among the intelligence agencies, had been able to provide much information on Mant or his tactics, other than stating the obvious, that he was a "shadowy" figure, at pains to keep his identity as little known as possible outside the militia. Beck and Albright reported that even in Spokane before hostilities had begun and before he had left town, Mant had spent nearly all his time in his hotel room.

"We could request an air strike," Norton suggested.

"No," said Freeman, refolding a map of the area into a manageable size, using his knee as a table. "I don't want to order in any air strike. White House is very antsy about that and the networks'll have spotters at every damn air base in Washington State. What I'm worried about . . ." He paused, looking at the map quadrants covering the area where the Twisp River began. By following War Creek, one of the Twisp's tributaries, back to its source, he would be taking his men farther into the Lake Chelan–Sawtooth Wilderness, closer to the Ames cabin, which was rapidly becoming a militia shrine. His men would be in high-snow country, which even hardier types avoided in winter and spring.

"Source of this creek," said Freeman, "is pretty close to the site of the Ames cabin, where the TIS pix showed the thermal emissions."

"Might have moved by now," Norton suggested.

"Possibly," Freeman conceded, quickly folding up the map. "We'll find out soon enough."

CHAPTER EIGHTEEN

North Carolina

IT DIDN'T TAKE a genius to figure out something was up at Fort Bragg. With all leave canceled and with blood-product supply companies up in Raleigh and down in Atlanta suddenly much busier than usual, it was obvious to anyone that a major exercise or mission was under way, though the destination and ETD were being kept secret till the last possible moment.

Since the big shake-up in '96 when army brass, in reaction to *Newsweek* and *Time* articles, rooted out members of the skinhead white-supremacist gangs in the 82nd Airborne and other units of the regular army, some skinheads had now simply let their hair grow to regulation length and took care they didn't have any new tattoos showing, and thereby escaped detection. In any case, First Amendment rights made it difficult even within the armed services to prevent verbal dissemination of racist views or the underground hate sheets like the *White Warrior*. Leroy Chess, whom his buddies called "Cheese," was the de facto leader of the Fort Bragg chapter of the White Dragons, and he put a call through to the Portland chapter. All he said was that "the boys from Fort Bragg are probably comin' up," then he hung up so as to beat any possible trace should the federals have infiltrated Portland's militia HQ and tapped the line.

Upon receiving the news, the Portland White Dragons relayed it by motorcycle courier, not trusting the phones, to the militia's northwestern command in Portland, who after consultation with Mant, in letter-for-number code, ordered "DESTROY FORT BRAGG IMMEDIATE STOP REPEAT IMMEDIATE," for as Mant told Colonel Vance, if the militias did not inflict as much damage as possible "early in the piece," then they would pay dearly for it later.

"Besides," said Mant, "we have to demonstrate to all our members across America, quite fearlessly, that the militias' course *is* set, that the die is cast, that we have committed ourselves irrevocably to winning the war."

It was then that things started to go wrong. When the A-and-C militia, flush with their victory over the convoy on I-5, got the message, there wasn't a doubt in their minds. Hadn't they been told by Colonel Vance, the N.W. liaison officer on his round of speeches, that local militias would get orders from HQ that at times might not seem to make sense but that were vital to carry out? And the A-and-C, including Jim Nye with his itch to make an abatis, had no doubt that the federals, as Nye had predicted, would quickly turn from the I-5 and try to make an end run up along northern California's scenic coast road through Mendocino, Caspar, and then Fort Bragg, where the road crosses the Noyo River.

Historians would later recall that on June 10, 1944, a similar "tactical error"—i.e., screwup—in France over two places with the same name, Oradour, had resulted in the massacre by the Das Reich Division of all the inhabitants in the *wrong village*. Similarly, the A-and-C in its haste, as in the case of the Das Reich Division, swiftly obeyed the order from Mant's HQ, knowing, as Vance had assured them months earlier, that no order would have been given had there not been a purpose. Besides, there were two obvious reasons why the Fort Bragg they knew on the northern California coast should be attacked: one, it was situated by the strategically vital river crossing that clearly had to be destroyed in order to stop the federal reinforcements that were coming up from the south; and two, the A-and-C militia were only too aware of the ever-constant fact of federal infiltration of the militia. Probably one or more of the buildings in this otherwise sleepy little coastal town must be being used as fronts for a federal electronic eavesdropping unit of the kind the federals had set up around the little town of Jordan in Montana, monitoring everything that went in and out of the Freemen's sophisticated computer center. Feds were likely carrying out the same kind of eavesdropping they'd done at Waco, Texas, putting tiny microphones in the milk cartons that were delivered to Koresh and his followers.

At 0700 hours, the A-and-C, including Jim Nye, in their rough fleet of twenty-eight four-wheel-drive vehicles, arrived at Fort Bragg. The leader of the A-and-C and the other twenty-nine members of the militia company were fast, methodical, and at first, as polite as their business permitted. The Fort Bragg police station was stormed quickly and the dispatcher ordered to call the town's half-dozen most prominent citizens to the station. Children were handled with particular care but were moved, forcibly if necessary, same as some adults who had to be taken out at the point of a gun. The last house, redolent of fresh coffee, was owned by the mayor's twenty-year-old son, Sean Makeery, a prominent environmentalist on northern California's coast, who protested vehemently, calling the section of four militiamen led by Jim Nye "thugs and goddamned fascists," and told them to get off his property, a clapboard bungalow with moisture-sodden cedar shingles, green here and there with moss. His young wife, Rachel, standing in the background in hair curlers and smelling of conditioner, was furiously dialing the police station until, after a few tries, she realized the lines had been cut. Two squad members started escorting Sean out through the living room, but he suddenly went limp, just sat down, one leg either side of the doorjamb. "Fuck you!" he shouted at them.

"Let him be!" said Nye. "Stupid son-of-a-bitch." He knelt down, the blue steel barrel of his Colt .45 nudging the environmentalist's ear.

"Don't hurt him! Don't, please—" began Rachel, her face pale, voice trembling. They could hear several pops—shots?—outside.

"Shut up!" Nye said, without looking at her. "We're not gonna kill 'im, though that's what the little fucker deserves. Him and his fuckin' spotted owls have done for this country. Ruinin' people's lives all up an' down this coast."

"I'm not trying to—" began Makeery.

"Shut the fuck up!" said Nye. "Now listen to me. You listenin'?"

Nye waited. No answer. Makeery's wife fainted, one of the squad catching her just in time, dragging her into one of the old-fashioned stuffed lounge chairs.

"C'mon, you guys," said the A-and-C leader, stomping into the small house. "This is the last—" Suddenly there was the boom of a tremendous explosion. The whole house shook, a pair of bone-china dolls on the mantel looking like they were doing a jig. Mrs. Makeery was conscious again and screaming.

There were more popping sounds outside, coming from the direction of the police station nearby. A militiaman burst through the doorway, red-faced, drunk, and said something to the A-and-C leader.

"Shit!" said the leader. "You sure?" he asked the drunk, whose brandy breath seemed to fill the room.

"Positive," said the drunk.

"Shit!" said the leader again, then he turned sharply to Nye. "C'mon! Get 'em out of here. Bridge is blown but we still got work to do."

Nye put the .45 away, telling Sean Makeery he had two choices. "Come with us or die in the fire." His wife made a dash for him, clung to him, and urged him to go. The leader was sprinkling a bottle of canola oil all over the kitchen, then tossed a match.

"Knock 'im out if you have to!" he said. "Now let's go!"

Once the fire started, Makeery moved, agape at what was going on. In Bosnia! In America. Outside, the environmentalist stood dumbfounded. Everything was burning, the whole town on fire, the sharp bang of a furnace bursting somewhere down the street. But there were no other people, no neighbors. His wife, her voice barely audible above the roar and crackling of flame—the only other sound the barking of dogs—asked the A-and-C leader where everybody else was. He didn't answer but was issuing orders beyond the shadows cast by the madly dancing firelight.

"Where is everybody?" Rachel repeated.

"Over the other side of the river," Nye eventually informed her roughly. "Where you'd be if you'd done what you were told." Now she saw her bungalow totally enveloped in flames, the heat on their faces pushing them farther back, Sean and Rachel in each other's arms, the firelight showing them in silhouette. Nye taunted Sean Makeery: "Now, when you get your insurance for the new house, what're you gonna build it out of, eh? Good ol' redwood or fuckin' spotted-owl feathers? I lost my house to the fuckin' mortgage company. Now we're quits, asshole."

"Let's go, Jimmy," said a militiaman.

Nye, using his left hand to protect his face from splatter, fired one shot and the environmentalist crumpled to the ground. Rachel, a madwoman silhouetted against the flames, clasped her head in her hands and screamed, her torso bending up and down like those "A-rab women" in mourning.

When the A-and-C roared north out of Fort Bragg, they were again flush with victory. No way, with the spring runoff strong as it was, would the federals be able to cross the swollen Noyo easily. The coast road had now been denied them. 'Course, there was still 101 running parallel to the coast, and sooner or later a major defeat would have to be inflicted on the federals to show them who owned all access northward from the heavily populated bright-lights of the south. But for now the militia was holding its own on the coast. The A-and-C leader said it was "too bad about the folks in Fort Bragg." All right, so things had gotten a bit out of hand, but hey, this was "hardball." Americans had to choose, same as they did in their first civil war. You were for the rebels or against them. Simple as that. It was, as Mant had told them, "a fight to the finish." There could be no middle ground. And listen, the "lesson" of Fort Bragg would spread soon enough: "Anyone who cozies up to the federals—gives 'em 'safe houses' from which to operate against the militias—pays the price." The federals should thank God the women and children hadn't been shot as well—like they would be in any other country.

As young Rachel Makeery was stumbling in shock through the huge, frenetic shadows of the fire, she tripped and fell. Getting up, she reached down for balance and felt her hand warm and sticky. It was the dead body of a local policeman, who, though off duty, had nevertheless come out with his handgun only to be shot dead by the militia. There and then, even before she'd heard of the massacre at the police station, where someone said a deputy had tried to draw his gun, Rachel Makeery knew she would fight the militias with everything she had, that she had become their implacable enemy.

Mant, though inwardly furious when he heard of the razing of the Fort Bragg in northern California and not the one in North Carolina, wasn't a man to lose his temper, and grimly, matter-of-factly, he assessed the political and military implications. Though initially tempted to distance the militias from the blunder unequivocally, he realized that to do so would signal all other units in his army a lack of confidence on his part in local commanders, which in turn would encourage second-guessing on their part or, as Colonel Vance advised much more bluntly, would induce them to think more about "covering their ass than about obeying orders from HQ."

"Look after it, Colonel," Mant told Vance.

Within twenty minutes the Internet and preselected reporters—CNN's Marte Price couldn't be reached—were told by Vance that Fort Bragg, northern California, a "highly classified clandestine federal arms depot and communications center," had been "neutralized by forces of the United States Militia Corps, Northwest Division." And furthermore, any others "offering aid and comfort to the enemy will be dealt with severely. There can be no half measures in the defense of freedom. Members of the militia have been fired on and regrettably have had to respond in kind. No women or children have been harmed."

CNN's *Headline News* boss, Jack Wilde, refused to carry the militia announcement because of the militia's demand that it be preceded by the playing of the "revolutionary" anthem, "The Star-Spangled Banner," accompanied by a background of Old Glory and the militia flag flying side by side.

"All right," Vance told him, the colonel's voice crisp and arrogant on the phone, "we'll give it to Murdoch." In the absence of any report yet from Marte Price, Jack Wilde agreed to run it. In the minds of many viewers throughout the country, the incident at Fort Bragg in California was a defining moment. Either you understood it from the point of view of the militia as being an initial and, however bloody, necessary action on the part of pro-freedom fighters against oppression and overwhelming odds or you saw the militia as simply an army of gun nuts and kooks fighting the tide of progress.

For General Shelbourne, who at the Pentagon had given up referring to "Fort Bragg"—no one knew which one he meant—the military implications of Mant's attack on the northern California town were far more serious than any divisions it had caused among America's civilian population. Quite simply it meant that Mant's forces were completely unpredictable, having demonstrated they could strike at will—a situation that the president had reminded Shelbourne of not five minutes before.

More worrisome was the question of how Mant's HQ learned about Sixth Army's intention of using the coast road. Militia informants in the army, of course. And if they knew this much then they probably knew about the 82nd's precise departure time—H hour—even if they weren't sure of exactly where in the Northwest they were headed, as Shelbourne had issued orders to General

Trevor, commanding 82nd Airborne, that no one below company commanders, like Major William McBride, should be told of the battle plan.

Whatever the case, the Fort Bragg incident in northern California caused Shelbourne grave concern over his impending attack against the Oregon-Washington border at the mouth of the Columbia, where the river thundered head-on into the giant swells of the Pacific Ocean. Accordingly, he ordered elements of the Fifth Continental U.S. Army from Enid, Oklahoma, to be prepared, to reinforce, to deploy westward as the 82nd Airborne readied to leave for the Columbia delta on its mission to secure the Astoria Bridge. Meanwhile the bulk of Shelbourne's forces from California, the most populous state in the union, would be sent up the coast and northeast through Nevada so that Mant's army, now manning the Columbia/Snake River front, could be trapped in a huge east-west pincer movement, as well as having to battle the 82nd Airborne, while I Corps up at Fort Lewis in Washington State remained on DEFCON 3 alert should a militia breakout in the Cascades materialize. For the moment, however, until he secured the roads leading up from southern California, all Shelbourne and anybody else in Washington could hope for in the way of victory was for Douglas Freeman's force of commandos to defeat the militia company in the Cascades.

Fort Bragg, North Carolina, is so large it can overwhelm a new soldier in the 82nd Airborne or any other of the nine units stationed there, and the White Dragons provided a steady point of reference, a like-minded club for any Nazi skinhead who felt homesick. But there was a price for membership. You had to provide five CDs of music from "Skrewdriver," the British band that had become the standard-bearer of the hundred-thousand-strong

International Skinhead Alliance whose SS motto, "Blood and Honor," signified hatred of all minorities, particularly drug addicts, homosexuals, Jews, liberals, and, in Europe, Gypsies. It was a hatred shared by such American antiblack, anti-immigrant hate groups as Chicago's RV—Romantic Violence; WAR—White Aryan Resistance; Nebraska's NSDAP-AO—the Nationalist Socialist German Workers Party—Overseas Organization; West Virginia's National Alliance; and southern California's Aryan Nation, which had nurtured Michael Hearn.

At Fort Bragg, the second part of initiation for membership in the White Dragons was to demonstrate a fearless resolve to flout army—i.e., federal—rules and regulations that encouraged integration in the armed forces. Accordingly, White Dragon leader Cheese reminded not only the newcomers to the group but all members that they had an obligation to sabotage any actions planned against their brothers in the militia. One way of doing this was to undermine morale, calling the families of all black personnel in Fort Bragg's married quarters and telling them their nigger husbands, brothers, sons, were going to be shot in the back. Just for variety, Cheese would call up the wives of black soldiers and tell them their husbands were having affairs with the wives of white soldiers, Cheese citing names and dates and saying he was calling because he hated to see white women polluted.

By the time the 82nd Airborne was approaching H hour, interracial tension among thousands of soldiers at Fort Bragg, but particularly in the 82nd Airborne, was the worst it had been for years. Among the eighteen thousand men of the 82nd, two men in particular were distressed: Major William McBride, commanding officer of Charlie Company, Second Battalion, Third Regiment, and Sergeant Randy Nye, first platoon, Alpha Company. Among so many men there were in fact dozens who had relatives serving in the thirty-six-thousand militia force now forming the Columbia/Snake River front, but Nye and McBride, while unaware of each other's existence, knew where their brothers in the militia were. Major William McBride knew his younger brother, Lucky McBride, was in the Cascades, and Sergeant Randy Nye had received a letter the previous week, before the start of the war, from his twin, Jimmy Nye, a logger-cum-militiaman, the letter bearing a postmark of Mendocino in northern California. In it Jimmy told Randy what a "fuckup" the federals had made of the logging industry and complained of the new "artsy-fartsy gun legislation" the feds were considering and how

remember in 'Nam the night they announced Bobby Kennedy was shot by Sirhan Sirhan, how the whole bar erupted in cheers and the guys saying how they ought to give Sirhan a fucking medal for shooting that pinko liberal bastard. What's the matter with you, Randy—you're in with the wrong crowd. Fucking assholes in Washington trying to get gays in the army. Joke up here is why did the queer want to go to Fort Meade? Because it's in Mary Land.

In with the letter Jimmy had put an out-of-focus photo of a bumper sticker: I LOVE SPOTTED OWL ... CASSEROLE and a poster of Adolf Hitler giving the Nazi salute with the caption EVERYONE IN FAVOR OF GUN CONTROL RAISE YOUR RIGHT HAND. *Come on over*, Jimmy told Randy. *The militia needs more good men like you.*

When Randy finished reading the letter he'd thrown it away, but not before he'd torn it up into little pieces. He had enough problems without worrying about his brother. Six years before, Randy's wife, Pamela, had given birth to a baby girl with Down's syndrome. They'd known before Nancy was born that she was going to be retarded, or what the politically correct called "mentally challenged." Hell, now, thanks to DNA, they could even tell what diseases you'd have from just a spec of embryonic liquid. Randy had wanted Pam to abort. Pam didn't want to. They'd tried to discuss it rationally, but pretty soon it had turned ugly. Randy had written Jimmy that whenever the TV news covered the latest pro-life or pro-choice punch-up you could cut the silence in their living room with a knife. Jimmy didn't say a thing about it when he wrote back—all he could talk about was the militia. But Randy interpreted his brother's silence as a clear commentary, knowing that, because of the influence of the Christian Right, the militias were by and large antiabortion, seeing pro-choice as a further erosion of morals in America. By now young Nancy was six and at school the teasing had begun, and the angrier Nancy got—she wasn't retarded enough not to know pain—the worse the teasing became, the other kids deliberately drooling and rolling their eyes. Pam was distraught and Randy, trying to comfort her, told her one of America's greatest columnists had a Down's child. "Well," Pam, her nerves frayed, retorted, "you're not. And on your army pay we can't afford the special care she needs."

"What d'ya want to me to do? Run for president?"

"You could be more understanding."

"I am."

"No, you're not. I can see 'I told you so' in your eyes."

"I never said a word."

"You don't have to."

"Look, honey—" She brushed him off.

Sex was out of the question. Randy was getting grumpy with his squad. And to make matters worse, two of the four black guys in his nine-man squad were acting strange, like they were suspicious of everyone, including him, taking jokes the wrong way, seeing racial stuff where there wasn't any—least none that Randy could detect. Maybe it was the usual excitement and anxiety before a mission? The weather? Or both—hotter this spring than usual. Randy felt guilty about wanting to get the hell away from the base, see some action. No more arguing with Pam and—God forgive him—time away from young Nancy. It was awful—he'd talked to the padre about it—not loving Nancy as much as he should. One day he was in a cold sweat, telling the padre—God help him—that he was embarrassed by her. The padre said he understood, that it was more common than generally known. This made Randy feel even worse about it. Dammit, he didn't want to be common in that way. Wanted to rise above that—distinguish himself as a man in the same way as he'd distinguished himself in 'Nam, be one of those fathers who loved his kid no matter what. "Unconditional love" was the buzz phrase these days.

The platoon's lieutenant, Gene Tyre, called him in and told him they'd all finally been given the green light. Tomorrow morning, 0800. In action within forty-eight hours. Randy was looking forward to it. This was his job, this was what he knew how to do. He'd have a clear objective now, a problem that could be solved. His squad was his family. After the target briefing he was going to give his men a pep talk. Usual stuff—no matter what your personal problems you had to leave them behind. *Concentrate* on the job at hand. If you didn't, you'd be dead. "Seize the objective"—the big bridge over the Columbia. "And hold it. No matter what."

CHAPTER NINETEEN

FOLLOWING THE LINE of the frozen War Creek tributary, pushing farther into the wilderness, Freeman's fifty-five-man force moved quickly but cautiously for fear of ambush. The creek, towering ridges and mountains either side of it, ran for another two miles into the Sawtooth Wilderness before it petered out in the high country that fed it. Four miles northeast of their position was a road that might have been used for artillery support to be brought in from Pateros—if he had more time. He didn't. The only other man-made feature was a section of the Pacific Crest Trail eight miles northwest, near Battalion Creek, deep in snow.

"You sure about not calling in air support?" Norton asked. "I'd say that Stinger attack negates the president's restriction."

"Maybe," Freeman replied. "Maybe not." He signaled the strike force to stop for a break and, talking softly, told Norton, "Even if the president gave us permission to bomb them—and we'd have to get it right from him, which I don't think we would—the only effective way of clearing this thermal patch we're heading for is to napalm them, especially as I suspect they're dug in."

"Jesus!" said Norton, his voice low but urgent. "You can't do that, General."

Freeman, whose eyes had been searching the two high ridges north and south of him, looked hard at Norton. "You think we can use iron bombs?"

"Well, it's an alternative to napalm," said Norton, wishing he'd never brought the subject up.

Freeman gave a noncommittal grunt, adding, "I already have to explain the loss of half my force in that downed Chinook. Anyhow, by the time I fart around getting permission for an air strike from the president—he'd have to take a poll—enemy could have moved. We're in a Vietnam situation here, Norton. They hit us, we pursue, and they withdraw into thin air." He looked around at the mountainous redoubt. "This country favors *de*fense, Norton, not *off*ense."

Of course, Freeman knew Norton knew the Sawtooth Wilderness favored the militias. The general was merely thinking aloud. He was well aware that unless he acted quickly, Mant's militias from Winthrop to the north and the Pateros area in the south could close in on him from both flanks. And he would still have the Twisp militia in front of him—a three-walled box—his only means of escape being behind him, a retreat to the east, back along War Creek to the Twisp River and the Twisp River road. And with only a fifty-five-man force at his disposal, he would be outmanned about sixteen to one. And there had been the intelligence report before he'd left that even more militia members from Spokane were slipping around the federal roadblocks to join Mant's forces in the Cascades.

Confronted by the overwhelming odds, Douglas Freeman made one of the most momentous decisions of his career, deciding that he, too, could unilaterally request help from Spokane. Freeman signaled his radioman over.

His name was Sager but everyone called him Andy because of his facial resemblance to Detective Andy Sipowicz on the old TV drama *NYPD Blue*.

"Andy," Freeman told him, "time to bounce a memo off that satellite to Fairchild AFB."

"Yes, sir."

"Request air support. Give 'em these coordinates, reference the TIS pictures, and tell them I want pinpoint bombing—right on the button."

"Yes, sir," Andy answered, happy to be sending a message that would damage the opposition before he and the rest of Freeman's strike force had to confront them.

"General," Norton warned him, "I know I was the one who first brought up the idea of air support, but, sir, that's dependent on—"

"The president," said Freeman sharply, his voice still low but with a distinctive edge to it. "By the time those fairies in the Pentagon come to a decision, we could be trapped, Norton. We can't afford the wait." Norton had always trusted Freeman's military decisions, but right now he could see a court-martial staring them in the face and he felt obliged to warn Freeman that his order to his radioman violated the mission's rules of engagement.

"I know that," Freeman answered brusquely, "but what would you rather be—alive and court-martialed? Or politically correct and dead?"

The question of court-martial aside, it would have made much more military sense to use low-flying Phantoms or F-111s, but in ordering a B-52 strike, Freeman knew what he was doing—in effect making the target an abstract thing, a target that Americans bombing Americans would not see—a mere map reference miles below.

Andy told Freeman the message had been received by Fairchild. Freeman signaled his force to move forward, telling Norton that they'd better hope some "asshole at

Fairchild" wouldn't check with Washington, D.C. No one did, bombing runs from Fairchild on air-force ranges being commonplace. Only difference here was that the designated area happened to be in mountainous wilderness instead of desert. And it was only a hundred and twenty miles away—a short mission, a cell, three B-52s, the best answer all around for iron bombs. They'd bomb from high up well out of Stinger range. Probably wouldn't even see the target, given the rainy gray cloud cover over the Cascades. It would all be done by computer. A hop, skip, and jump really, compared with the old long-range stuff from Okinawa to North Vietnam.

Rymann's four-man Stinger group back by the junction of the Twisp River and War Creek where they had downed the Chinook were now joined by the rest of his squad in another Jeep bristling with weapons.

"We can't carry all this stuff," Ovitz complained.

"Don't bitch," said Rymann. "We'll leave the Stinger rounds here with the two drivers in case the federals try to ferry in more troops. The other seven of us'll take the rest of the gear."

"Fucking heavy," said Ovitz.

"Quit your squawking. You've been trained for it."

"Doesn't mean I have to like it."

"C'mon," Rymann urged. "We don't get a move on, Freeman's outfit'll be off the riverbed back into the trees."

"Well, at least," said Ovitz, "we won't have any trouble tracking 'em in this wet." Rymann told the two drivers to get the two Jeeps under cover and to keep a sharp eye out for any more helos. "Those big Chinooks are no good at NOE," he said, meaning nap-of-the-earth flying, where choppers flew low, hugging the earth's contours to avoid radar detection. "But the small helos can slip in so you mightn't get any warning from our OPs along the road. Take it in shifts. Have the Stinger armed and ready."

"Right," said one of the drivers as Rymann, on point, signaled the patrol forward. Despite Ovitz's griping and monumental foul-up with the AK-47, Rymann knew the remainder of the men he'd chosen from I Platoon Bravo Company were well trained. They not only knew how to use a variety of weapons but they were physically conditioned to the rainy "liquid sunshine" of the Northwest. And they were used to this rugged, high terrain, where the reduced oxygen content of the thinner air demanded much more from a fully loaded man than did the lower country. In a firefight it could be an edge that could tip the odds in your favor.

Rymann had one more advantage, knowing that Freeman's Special Forces ahead of him would have to proceed with turtlelike caution once they left the frozen creek surface and went back into the woods, given the slaughter of the federal tank crews at the hands of Rymann's squad outside Pateros, and the earlier loss of eight members of the FBI's elite HRT. Rymann's squad, on the other hand, could move as fast as possible and, he hoped, get a chance to attack Freeman's force from the rear *before* it came to the end of the frozen ice and entered the trees that led to Rymann's fellow militiamen, en route to Ames's cabin.

CHAPTER TWENTY

JIM NYE WAS tired after the three-hour, 150-mile drive north of Fort Bragg to the Redwood National Park near the California-Oregon border, chosen by Mant as the best site in which to consolidate southern Oregon and northern California militias for a stand against federal troops driving north up the coast. A federal engineer battalion had already forded the Noyo River at Fort Bragg, and a second column of federal troops was coming up north of Sacramento, where a downed bridge across the Sacramento River on the I-5 had been, as in the Noyo case, crossed by a one-lane pontoon bridge. In short, the federals had been delayed for five hours but had not been stopped, the supply line now stretching like an enormous snake all the way up from San Francisco, splitting at Sacramento into three columns, the coastal (west or left of the central valley on 101), the column north through the central valley on the I-5, and the northeast column to the right of the Central Valley on U.S. 80, weaving its way through the Sierra Nevada northwest of Lake Tahoe.

On all three routes the federals were preceded by fully armed AH-1S Huey Cobra Scouts cruising at NOE altitude just above the treetops, the pilot locked onto his terrain-following radar, his tandem seated copilot/weapons operator ready with the forward-mounted 30mm gun and rocket launchers, the army being pressured by the Sierra Club and National Forest Service not to use rockets and/or incendiary material for fear of starting forest fires. Firefighting brigades all over central California and the Pacific Northwest were put on alert, although around Lake Tahoe the spring thaw had not yet rid the area of snow and those in the affluent lodges around the water were looking out on depressing vistas of slate-gray lake and snow reminiscent of the scene that lay before Al Pacino in *The Godfather* as he'd sat staring out at the same gray lake, pondering his brother's betrayal in another kind of civil war.

Two of the three columns, all three consisting of hundreds of camouflage-painted U.S. Army trucks, Bradley fighting vehicles, and forward motorcycle riders, reported that they were proceeding as ordered without incident, despite the delays caused by the downing of the Fort Bragg bridge and the delay caused to the right-hand column because of the ambush on I-5. The middle column, however, was still delayed by the sabotage of the bridge across Shasta Lake in the Shasta National Recreation Area 162 miles north of Sacramento and had to head northeast in a detour on the 299 and 89 to get back onto the I-5. For all three columns it was as if the militia had disappeared. Which it had, except for the buildup of militia troops, including Jim Nye's A-and-C in three areas: the Redwoods National Park on the 101, the Mount Shasta National Forest Area a hundred miles to the east, and near the town of Truckee ten miles north-northwest of Lake Tahoe.

In the wealthy, built-up areas around the high, world-renowned twenty-two-by-twelve-mile lake, where mansions, posing as houses, look out on the normally blue water that in places was over a quarter mile deep, tourists and residents alike thought the militia/federal clashes were far away, confined to the Pacific Northwest. That is, until the militia, via the Internet, informed the population of Lake Tahoe, those living on both the eastern shore in Nevada and the western shore in California, that Interstate 80, California State 50, and all side roads, such as the 89 from the Squaw Valley ski area, leading to Interstate 80, were closed by order of the militia.

It was one of the few times around the shores of Lake Tahoe that developers and environmentalists were as one in their outrage at being largely cut off from the outside world.

Ignoring Tahoe City's police call to stay off the 89 and claiming the militia announcement was all "hillbilly crap," a couple of local entrepreneurs and National Guardsmen in their mid-twenties, nicknamed the Blues Brothers, concerned about fear of the militias keeping the high-spending tourists away, strapped on their shoulder holsters. They hopped into their Suzuki four-wheel-drive and, radio blaring hard rock despite south Tahoe's noise bylaw, headed up around the western shore to Tahoe City, then west toward the 89 that ran north, parallel to the Truckee River, which in turn flowed toward the junction with Interstate 80. If there was a roadblock they'd parley with the hillbillies, throw some cash about.

It didn't occur to the Blues Brothers that the militiamen involved might be from Tahoe, that the militia might be some of their neighbors, NIMBYs—Not In My Back Yard types—who, having been born and raised in the Tahoe area when it was pristine, now wanted to stop the influx of others who wanted to enjoy the lake. Maybe they were NIMBYs who had known the area when it was free of the water pollution caused by the chemical-filled dust blown eastward out of California's overcultivated Central Valley and by ruptured sewer lines leading away from the lake. Maybe they were NIMBYs who had been there *before* there were 214 ski lifts, *before* TRPA (the Tahoe Regional Planning Agency) and CATO (California Tahoe Conservancy) had to fight to preserve the lake against any more neon and urban blight. Or were they NIMBYs trying to stop the development of adult peep shows, more casinos, high-rises, strip joints, and arcades as well as the heavy traffic fumes and traffic jams that clogged the seven-mile stretch between Pope and Nevada beaches? The Blues Brothers were doing well with their casino and were already in preplanning buy-offs to try to squeeze through the environmentalists' legal loopholes.

The sun was out on 89, the lake a vibrant blue, the road deserted, which wasn't usual, given this time of morning. The only things the brothers had seen moving in the evergreen forest that spilled down below the snowcapped Crystal Range mountains were a peregrine falcon hovering high above a Jeffrey pine and a rush of young paintbrush plants bending in the pine-scented breeze. The sudden and complete isolation of Highway 89, the absence of even an early-morning fisherman on the Truckee streaming by to their right, was the first sign that everyone else might be heeding the militia warning. Brian, the elder of the brothers, was the first to suggest, since all the braggadocio of their south Tahoe sendoff, that maybe they should've got a "posse" together. "Strength in numbers," he said.

"Too many cooks spoil the broth," answered the younger brother, who was driving. "I still think it's a bluff, but if it isn't, it's better just the two of us turn up. No threat, right?"

"Then we'd better take off our guns."

"Fine," said Troy, the younger one, driving with one hand slipping the 9mm between the seat and his thigh, barrel toward the dash. They had turned right at the junction, a signpost pointing east to Reno, Nevada.

"Shit," said Brian. "Maybe we should turn back, Troy. I mean, you know all that stuff up on the coast. Fort Bragg. Pretty nasty."

"Yeah, because that was the army versus the militia. We're no threat." He paused. "Oh hell, let's just see. First glimpse of a roadblock and we stop and turn around. Simple as that."

It was even simpler than Troy imagined. There was no roadblock, just the sudden *thwack* hitting their gas tank, then another round slamming into the radiator and a fine mist of blue antifreeze on the windshield.

"Holy shit!" It was Troy, hitting the brake, tires screeching, the Suzuki going out of control. "Jesus— Jesus—" and they flipped, the roll bar sending out a trail of sparks, a *whoof* as the trail of gasoline caught fire, like some long, burning snake slithering across the center line. Troy, upside down, still strapped in, his hair wet with what he thought was blood, smacked the seatbelt release, dropped to the road, and immediately tried to unbuckle his older brother, now dazed and disoriented.

"Brian!" Troy yelled. "You okay?" A stupidity he'd recall till the end of his life. He reached in the backseat, which was flaming, managing to free Brian, the latter's jeans on fire. Troy dragged him faceup to the shoulder of the road and started throwing dirt on the flames, putting them out, panicking, waiting for the next shot. It looked worse than it was, Brian's leg hair singed. He was walking away, the wrong way, Troy having to turn him around and push him off the road where their Suzuki was blazing. "C'mon, let's go," he said, nervously glancing at the woods. Had they aimed for the gas tank or had it been a fluke? Two shooters or one? Troy wasn't interested in finding out. In his haste to get away from the Suzuki he'd forgotten about their guns and the cellular. As the two men, dry-throated, walked back toward Tahoe, they kept nervously looking back along the road and at the forests on either side of them, the silence of the road now pregnant with danger, causing them to run in panicky fits and starts until they were out of breath, Troy wishing he'd saved the 9mm.

CHAPTER TWENTY-ONE

DYLAN RICE, A rancher's son near Fort Laramie, Wyoming, was seventeen and had eyes the color of coal. They were so black, he knew from the comments of others, that you couldn't see the pupils, and the joke in Wyoming's militia was that if you had a night job to do, send out Dylan—nobody'd see his eyes. Dylan hated the stupid joke but didn't protest because he knew that if something dangerous had to be done, the militia would likely give it to his pa, providing he wasn't out herding up mustangs with the helo, and Dylan'd get to tag along.

Dylan was a quiet boy with one great passion: he loved to drive. His aim in life, apart from fighting the federals, which came as naturally as hunting jackrabbits, was to

drive in one of those long car trails like that Safari in
Africa and the 'round Australia tour. Your car had to be
tough, you had to be tough. Every weekend Dylan, sometimes with his buddy Lorne, would just take off. His pa
said Wyoming was the most beautiful country on God's
earth, and that with little more than half a million in the
whole state, it was still one of the few remaining areas in
the U.S. you could travel in safely. But just in case there
was trouble, Dylan always traveled with a .30-caliber
rifle in the cabin of the pickup and his old man had a .357
Magnum in a big dust-proof Ziploc bag tucked away
under the seat. It wouldn't fit in the glove compartment.

Dylan and buddy Lorne, who was also seventeen, had
both grown up in that quiet, independent kind of way that
marked so many Western ranch kids, but now and then
they'd have a ding-dong argument about where to go on
their drives. Lorne had seen this movie, *Jurassic Park*,
and had a thing about driving southwest on the 34, then
up to Medicine Bow and the Como Bluff Dinosaur
Graveyard. But old bones didn't do a thing for Dylan,
unless the conversation was about his bone and the
chances of getting it into Elizabeth Wain, who always
smelled of roses and lived down in Cheyenne and was
the object of intense rivalry between the two boys.

No, what Dylan wanted to do was scoot on up north a
bit, avoid all the tourists heading into Yellowstone, drive
up between the thirteen-thousand-foot Bighorn Mountains to the east and the Absaroka Range to the west,
across the Wyoming/Montana line, and on over to Little
Big Horn, where Custer had made his last stand.

If Lorne had a thing about dinosaur bones, Dylan had a
thing about Custer. Sometimes, standing alone at Little
Big Horn, with only the wind and bowing grass for
company, he felt like he was the reincarnation of his
hero. The thought of Custer standing brave like that,

murderous Indians all around him, moved Dylan to tears. It was as if he was standing up to a last charge by the federals. He was imprudent enough this day to share his feelings with Lorne, who pointed out that Custer had *been* a "damned federal." They had one hell of a row, finally venting their anger at each other by standing back from one of the red, white, and blue shield signs that proclaimed FEDERAL LAND NO TRESPASSING and riddling it with .30 rounds. Then they flipped a coin to see whether they'd go north to Custer's last stand or southwest to the dinosaur bones at Como Bluff.

"The bones!" Lorne announced triumphantly, looking down at the coin.

"Piss on it!" said Dylan, neither of them knowing that the toss would be the turning point in their lives, because at that moment General Shelbourne, 1,500 miles away in Washington, D.C., was ordering Wyoming's National Guards' 115th Field Artillery Brigade in Cheyenne to proceed "with all possible haste" west northwest to meet up with the eastern column of California's three-pronged attack against Idaho's southern flank.

Leaving Fort Laramie, driving fast southwest toward Medicine Bow and the bones, Dylan Rice was in a sulky mood, the only thing worth seeing south of Fort Laramie in his view being Laramie itself, forty miles west of Cheyenne. Laramie appealed to him because it was once the roughest town in the West: whores, cattle, thieves, cardsharks, Butch Cassidy, and the first woman in the United States to be elected to public office. Dylan picked up the cellular and phoned the ranch. "Pa, me and Lorne's goin' down to Como Bluff—see Lorne's bones."

"No, you're not. Where the hell you been? What's wrong with the damn cellular? Battery shot?"

"I'm talking to you, aren't I?"

"Don't be a smart-ass. You must've just come into

range. Now, you skiattle down to Cheyenne—never mind going on to those damn bones. I want you to go to see Morton about those two gaskets I need for the helo."

Now Dylan came right out of his sulk, sat up straight behind the steering wheel like someone had jabbed him in the backside with a spur, because going to see Morton in Cheyenne meant only one thing: the Wyoming militia were going to hit the federals. About time. He looked across at Lorne. "You hear that?"

"What?"

Dylan waited for a few seconds, glancing out at the sage rushing by. He loved secrets, but secrets were no good unless you could share them—tease 'em out a little. "Means we're gonna hit the tracks."

Lorne didn't get it.

"Orchard Valley Junction," Dylan explained, bright-eyed and keen. "Just outside Cheyenne. We knock it out—we take out three lines. No trains north, south, or west of Cheyenne."

Lorne—just like Lorne, Dylan thought—shrugged as if it was no big deal. "So the federals won't move by rail. They'll use the highway."

Sometimes, thought Dylan, Lorne wasn't so bright for a militia guy.

"Not troops, you dork," Dylan told him. "*Tanks*. You think they got a HET for every fucking tank?" He meant the army's Oshkosh Heavy Equipment Transport truck. "The way they like to move their M1s is on flatbed rail-cars, a battalion of over sixty tanks and Bradleys in one pull. We're gonna cut the interstate highways, too—70, 80, and 25."

"Well, let me out," said Lorne. "I don't want to mess with explosives."

"Who said anything about explosives?"

"Thought that's what you were going to Cheyenne for."

Dylan was shaking his head in merriment. "Not out here, man. Feds got all explosives tagged since Oklahoma. They got chemical markers in 'em. Can tell what batch they're from. Doing the same with fertilizer. They can trace it real quick."

"So," Lorne challenged, "how 'bout all those explosions we been hearin' about in California and stuff?"

"They're full militia units. They don't give a shit whether the federals can trace it or not. Fed shows his frappin' head out there, he'll get it blown off, that's what." He slowed for a deer crossing the road. "In Wyoming we haven't got any big units of militia. Smaller groups, right? We got to stay undercover, man, till General Mant moves up the Northwest."

"Well," said Lorne, "good luck, but I want out."

"All right, I'll drop you off wherever you want."

"Long as it's before you see Morton." He paused. "You guys are nuts."

"Thought you were up for it?"

"Not in the middle of town, man. No way."

"You prick," Dylan joshed. "You're gonna look up 'Lizabeth, right?"

"No," said Lorne unconvincingly. "I just don't aim on gettin' my balls shot off doing your old man's dirty work."

Dylan didn't like that. "Ain't *his* dirty work. Militia wants it done. You know that we planned this a long time ago. Or have you forgotten? Have to say it, man—you look 'bout as scared as a jackrabbit."

"Well, maybe I got more fucking brains 'n a jackrabbit. You want to get yer balls blown off, you go right ahead."

"I told you already we ain't gonna use explosives."

"Then how you gonna do it?"

"C'mon and see."

"No thanks."

As they drove past the airstrip where America's youngest aviator, Jessica Dubroff's, plane crashed on takeoff in '96, Dylan tried to engage Lorne in conversation. But Lorne wouldn't respond, and when he got out he was still pissed at Dylan but knew he was doing what was right. He walked past the rodeo arena and the Frontier Days Old West Museum to the phone booth. A soldier was inside. There were soldiers everywhere. Lorne hadn't seen so many military vehicles since the heyday of the ICBM base here at Warren Air Force Base. Seemed like the town of fifty-seven thousand had swollen to twice its size and he heard talk in the shops, which were doing a roaring trade already, that more khaki was expected up from Fort Carson due south in Colorado. Apparently the regular army's Fourth Mechanized Infantry Division down there was moving north up the I-25 to join Shelbourne's other forces in what the federals hoped would be a concerted and decisive attack against the rogue states of the Northwest, namely Washington, Oregon, Idaho, Montana, and northern California. So much for army security, but with such vast distances of green plains, mountains, and sagebrush desert involved, and with the world's media crawling all over, it was impossible for the Pentagon to keep strategic planning secret; only tactical moves by individual divisional commanders in their AOR—area of responsibility—could hope to be kept confidential, and even then not for long.

When Lorne got through on the phone to his mom back in Fort Laramie, he told her what Dylan was up to and she told him he'd done the right thing, and to leave everything to her and catch the next Greyhound home.

He lied and told her the buses were "booked solid" and he wouldn't be able to get one out till eight the next morning. Maybe he could stay over at Mrs. Wain's house. No hotel rooms left—army had taken 'em all. His mom said she'd clear it first with Mrs. Wain, which she did, then she phoned the Cheyenne Sheriff's Department and told them just what that fool Dylan Rice was up to. She'd known his mother and knew she wouldn't approve of Dylan being involved in any kind of violence. Besides, she was doing him a favor. "If the boy starts monkeyin' around with the Union Pacific and Burlington Northern, he's likely to get his head blowed off."

"Appreciate the call, Mrs. Reeth. We'll pick 'im up. You say he's going to see a Mr. Morton?"

"Yes."

"You have an initial?"

"No."

"Well, can't be too many of 'em. We'll be in touch." When he got off the phone his deputy looked up. "Think she knows about the new reward?"

"Preventin' sabotage of federal property?" said the sheriff. "Now, Ray, a neighbor might do that in Noo York City, but out here? C'mon now."

Being a cautious man and anticipating some weather or mechanical-breakdown delays for his three columns heading north, General Shelbourne had ordered the National Guard's 116th Cavalry Brigade in Boise, Idaho, to attack north—though he had done so reluctantly because of the treasury secretary's uneasiness about overseas money markets reacting to the belief that too many regular-army units were involved. Shelbourne had also ordered the National Guards' 163rd Armored Brigade in Bozeman, Montana, to attack southeast in an effort to prevent the Idaho and Montana militias' Mountain Divisions heading west from reaching the north-south section of the Snake, which separated southeast Washington and northeastern Oregon from the heel of the Idaho boot.

Shelbourne watched Major Baun pointing at the war room's map in the White House bunker, not knowing exactly how to describe Mant's Idaho and Mountain Divisions to the president's press secretary. The Mountain Divisions were not classifiable as either infantry or armored but rather a combination of both, veterans like Washington militia's Lucky McBride, now in the Cascades, having had the liberty and six years to adopt the best, and to dump the worst, features of each. The ski battalions that made up the division owed a lot to some veterans of World War II whom the militia had invited, in years past and under false pretenses, to form YASC— Young Americans Ski Clubs, as Hitler had used weekend "Glider Clubs" to build up the Luftwaffe. Some kids had come from as far away as Chicago to be instructed by these veterans of the old WWII U.S. Mountain Divisions on all the techniques of skiing and shooting from that long-ago war. These acted as FORMS, or force multipliers. That is, one veteran instructed twenty skiers; each of those twenty then taught twenty more, and each of these, twenty more. In the space of a few weeks of training around Sun Valley, but away from what the militias called "the rich little piggies" of Sun Valley's fashionable slopes, twenty veterans would end up training sixteen thousand peacetime combatants. Furthermore, the extent of the Mountain Division's mobility, and indeed that of the militia in general, was not yet fully appreciated by Shelbourne or his staff, and only began to become evident when reports of widespread sabotage of roads and bridges in the high country from California to Wyoming started streaming into the Pentagon.

The militia's modus operandi was simple but effective: they used snipers and/or ambush—as in the case of the militia's ambush of the convoy on I-5 and on Lake Tahoe's 89. The snipers stopped the convoys by taking out lead and rear vehicles while the rest of the militia poured down fire on those men and vehicles caught in between and hightailed it across country before the feds could organize anything like a counterattack. As a result, convoys were now being preceded by Cobra scout helos. But soon there simply weren't enough helos and, as Shelbourne pointed out, just as important, not enough helo fuel depots to permit coverage of "every damn bridge in America." Plus, after the hit in the Cascades, there was now the added threat of Stinger missiles. And to make matters worse, militia who had blown the Interstate 5 inland were reportedly dressed in civilian clothes, driving nondescript cars and pickups, blowing up their assigned target often as not at night, then speeding off, either back to their militia units or, in some cases, to their homes. "The FBI and BATF," Major Baun told Shelbourne, "are going nuts. They don't know who the hell they're looking for. Anyone can be a saboteur. One guy they were lucky enough to get because a box of detonators blew before he could blow Amtrak's 'Pioneer' line outside Boise, Idaho, was sixteen years old."

"So what happened when they took him in?" asked Shelbourne.

"*Nada*. Zilch. He wouldn't say squat. Interrogators said he'd obviously been well trained. Wouldn't even give his name. Said he couldn't be tried in adult court because all federal courts were—get this—'repugnant to the laws of God.' *Repugnant!* And he's only sixteen."

By day's end Shelbourne's computer-projected "incident map" printout of the United States, particularly the West Coast, looked as if someone had taken a pepper shaker to it. "Jesus Christ!" said the general, clearly shocked. "Has the country gone stark raving mad?"

Baun gave him no comfort. "We didn't realize how much antigovernment feeling there is out there, particularly in the West."

"Ah," said the general, "if you ask me the damn militia's just a goddamn excuse for every no-good son-of-a-bitch to act up."

"To some extent," Baun agreed. "Looks that way in South Central L.A. Still, General, I think we'd be unwise to assume they're all like that. Some of them are doing more than just acting up. One report indicates that there's a lot more local support among citizens than any of our intelligence services predicted."

Another of Shelbourne's aides entered the room. "General, we're on radio link with the Airborne. They're about to go in."

Flying over the Columbia, Major William McBride felt his gut tightening. He had made hundreds of jumps, more than a dozen into combat, but always the solar plexus went into a knot as he readied to lead his men out of the great yawn of the Hercules' door, ready for the plunge into nothingness, hoping to hell that the weather Joes were right and that stratus cloud rolling in from the sea would hold off long enough for the Airborne to see landing zones clearly.

The thundering roar of the planes drowned out anything but a shout, the jumpmaster complementing his words with unambiguous hand signals, palming his hands abruptly toward the paratroopers as if pushing them back.

The jump light was red.

"Get ready!" called the jumpmaster.

"Get ready!" they bellowed in unison, still sitting but ready to rise as one.

"Stand up!" shouted the jumpmaster.

"Stand up!" came the shouted reply, the stick of jumpers heaving themselves and a hundred and nine pounds of weapons, ammunition supplies, wrist-sized GPS—Geo Positioning Systems—emergency rations, water, communications equipment, entrenching tool, night-vision goggles, cellulars for section commanders, and other assorted tools of battle, each man's face invisible in camouflage paint.

"Hook up!" yelled the jumpmaster.

"Hook up!" Each man affixed his yellow static line to the cable.

The jumpmaster brought his hands in on his chest, elbows straight out. "Check equipment!" Each man did so, starting from the back, and when the first man in the stick reported, "Okay!" the jumpmaster bellowed, "Stand in the door!"

Major William McBride shuffled forward under the weight. Other planeloads were already out. The red light turned to green.

"Go!"

McBride stepped into the void.

Icy cold.

It was a world of screaming slipstreams and icy swirling grayness, the early-morning stratus sweeping in from the sea, reportedly clear beneath a thousand feet.

Below a sky rapidly filling with an aerial armada of C-17s and Hercules transports that jettisoned flares to evade heat-seeking Stingers, a young woman, Zoë Nadet, was out picking wildflowers on the Washington side of the four-mile-wide river. She had told Ralph, her husband of two years, that she'd pick one flower for each year since his birth date—twenty in all—then she'd head back to their small, three-room cabin in the nearby woods. But now she stood in the tall riverine grass and gazed up in terror-fueled awe as the big planes thundered above her at no more than a thousand feet. Ralph, running back to the cabin, was already on the cellular alerting militia HQ in Astoria, on the Oregon side six miles across the river, that he figured a drop was imminent.

"Roger that," had come Astoria's reply. "We've got it covered. Everyone's on war alert. You report to Bravo Two-Fi—uh-oh, here they come. Best stay where you are, Bravo Three. Do what you can."

"Roger."

When Ralph flicked the Motorola cellular closed, he was scared. B-25, Bravo Two-Five, was the river sector several miles east of his cabin and was his company's rendezvous point by the river. He and Zoë liked living by their lonesome, but right now he would have appreciated having the remainder of his hundred-man militia company around him. But he'd known that by the time he got there, B-25 would most likely be in action. It was up to him to live up to the militiaman's credo: "To do whatever you can wherever you are," and within a minute he was out of the cabin, loaded AK-47 in hand, slamming home a thirty-round mag, running down toward a clear patch about the size of a baseball diamond that opened up from the edge of burned-out woods and spilled tall grass down to the river.

The first khaki chutes he saw opening just below the clouds at about eight hundred feet were coming down several miles east of him beyond Jim Crow Creek and toward the rocky bluff of the fort in Fort Columbia State Park. But in the cabin Zoë heard on the radio that enemy paratroopers were also landing on the seaward side of Fort Canby State Park, situated on a north-southeast crescent that jutted out into the river mouth. Now the sky above the cabin was becoming thick with parachutes, some of them now descending near the old fishing village of Chinook and the marshlands near the tiny community of Stringtown. East of the Nadets' cabin, beyond the strategically vital two-lane, four-mile-long Astoria Bridge that connected Washington State to Oregon, the river spread out, eight miles wide, and it was here in a spongy expanse of European beach grass that Washington State's western militia and the 82nd Airborne made first contact. The main bulk of the Airborne's "Force A," the five thousand allocated to drop just north of the river, were soon strung out between the hilly country around 401 in the east to the flat and narrow twenty-two-mile-long Long Beach Peninsula ten miles to the west. The peninsula constituted the north-south stem of a rough "b"-shaped area seven miles wide at its base and just under a mile wide at its narrowest part along the north.

Paratroopers were landing everywhere and that was the problem. On the Washington State side of the river they should have been concentrated in a pocket around the Long Beach–Seaview township, but some of the infamous fogs of the area—the river is so big, it creates its own weather system—had moved in rapidly from the sea. This, combined with low stratus and unexpectedly strong winds inland, at five hundred feet, had swept the Airborne off target, causing what surviving paratroopers would later call the Astoria FUOMP, or Fuckup of Monumental Proportions.

Had militia general Mant wished for a disaster to be visited upon his enemy, he could not have designed a more felicitous combination of factors. The local high-altitude winds coming up during the drop hadn't been predicted, and all the paratroopers filling the sky could do was try to steer themselves away from the narrow one-and-a-quarter-mile-wide, twenty-seven-mile-long Long Beach Peninsula that lay between the Pacific and the broad reaches of land east around Willapa Bay. Over 1,200 men touched down on the peninsula but were scattered about the Long Beach–Seaview township and up and down the length of the peninsula, miles away from the AB sector instead of around the northern base of the Astoria Bridge where they were meant to be concentrated. The remainder, over a thousand of the 5,000-man force, were continuing to come down on the base of the "b" in the Willapa Wildlife Refuge around Bear River and on sandbars in the river where low tide's retreat left expanses of mudflats, reed-filled estuaries, and seawater marshes. In short, every soldier's nightmare. And to boot, they were dropping into this sodden landscape, with some well over a hundred pounds of equipment on their backs and swarms of militiamen closing in from Seaview on the coast and from the 401 eleven miles inland. Many militiamen, taking whatever high ground they could, were shooting with impunity into the khaki-green sky, "picking off federals," as one local put it, "as if they were skeets."

Earlier, when Major William McBride saw the carnage beneath him—swirls of salty water where men had fought to jettison their loads and ended up drowning, automatic fire from the militiamen spraying the water of the estuaries so densely it had looked as if it was hailing—and smelled the pungent odor of marsh and mudflats rising up to assail him, mud exploding, militia 60mm mortar rounds pockmarking the flats, water rushing in to fill the craters with a deadly foaming quicksand, all he could do was curse his company's luck. He'd pulled the pin from a grenade, dropping it far below him, hoping its shrapnel would clear his own personal landing zone. From there he might be able to rally and collect enough men to launch a local counterattack.

Several hundred feet away to his right he spotted a militiaman distinguishable from the regular army only by a darker green smock and World War II GI helmet, swinging what looked like an AK-47 in his direction. McBride let fly with another fragmentation grenade and, yanking on his chute, prepared for a feet-perfect landing or flare. Instead he felt his feet sucked into a mud bath and saw the chocolate water rushing up to slap him in the face. He closed his eyes, heard the grenade explode, then a scream, and held his breath, hands instinctively going out to break the fall. He hit the quick release. Nothing happened. He was abruptly jerked back as the chute, catching a sudden gust of wind, took off over the flat, dragging him unceremoniously along in the mud, his body slithering and twisting, hands flailing for balance, so that now one second he was on his back, the next windsurfing on his stomach across the watery muddy surface. It saved his life. Militia bullets were kicking up mud-water spouts behind him, but the bursts of semiautomatic fire were too slow for the sudden gusts of wind. Cursing aloud, he hit the quick release again, felt himself slowing. The chute was gone. Quickly he unhitched the M-16, slipped off its barrel protector, flicked the safety to off, and let fly with a three-round burst in the direction of two oncoming militiamen fifty yards off. He saw one flung back, the other reaching down, pulling his wounded buddy toward tall grass that covered both banks of an estuary.

Not seeing any of his men nearby but bodies strewn all over in the distance, McBride now briskly snatched his pack with one hand, M-16 in the other, and made his way into grass, wiping the mud from his face with his sleeve and slowing his breathing as he helplessly watched the chutes of the last sticks open, inviting another fusillade of militia fire from the ground. Several of the descending paratroopers slumped like heavy bags, their bodies jerking spasmodically, blood spraying around them, before hanging limply, dead before they hit the ground, then dragged along the mud by their chutes, as Bill McBride had been, their bodies turning as if still alive.

"Smells like a fucking toilet!" McBride swung about at the words. It was a sergeant, his 82nd Airborne patch, unlike the major's, unobscured by mud, sweat trickling down his camouflage face paint. "Lost the whole fucking platoon." The major didn't recognize him as anyone from his company of a hundred and twenty, but then again he couldn't be expected, even as a company CO, to remember everyone in his command. Man's name was Nye. Randy Nye. "You one of my boys, Nye? Charlie Company, Second Battalion?"

"No, sir, sorry. I'm Alfa Company, Third Battalion."

"Jesus!" said McBride, pulling out his notepad-sized computer map. "We should be way apart." It told him just how scattered the Airborne was. "We're spread out to hell and gone."

"Air force," said Randy Nye disgustedly. "Couldn't drive a friggin' bus, let alone hit an LZ."

"Wasn't all their fault. What we need to do is get consolidated before these bastards pick us off one by one." There was a temporary break in the clouds, the sun came through, and fetid steam began rising from the mudflats. McBride felt his ears pop, the air around him vibrating with the rush of mortar rounds exploding and the crackle and stutter of small-arms fire. He and Nye both knew CAS—close air support—was no go, given the fact that militia and Airborne were engaged in close-quarter battle. Even helo gunners wouldn't be able to distinguish between friend and foe. McBride turned and looked beyond a sea of reed grass in the direction of Seaview–Long Beach and could hear the deeper tattoo of heavy machine-gun fire, then a sound that reminded him of a demolition derby in full throttle, and now he could smell gasoline fumes along with the putrid odor of marsh and mudflat gases, an army of soldier crabs moving rapidly en masse across the tide-sculptured mud bank nearby.

"This is gonna be fun when the tide comes in," said Randy Nye.

Bill McBride grimaced but nodded as if he'd already thought of that. In fact he hadn't, preoccupied as he had been by the problem of how to gather enough men into one place to launch a counterattack, before they were all chopped up piecemeal by the militia, whose strength he estimated was at least equal to that of the Airborne's on this north side of the river. He only hoped that at least the AB had been taken and that across the wide river on the southern, Oregon, side the situation was different.

It *was* different. It was much worse. And the Airborne hadn't taken the AB. The militia held both ends of it as well as the northern end of the smaller six-hundred-yard-long *Old* Youngs Bay Bridge, designated YB. A second bridge, the two-mile-long Youngs Bay Bridge, also spanning Youngs Bay south of the town, had been blown. By whom and on whose authority no one knew.

Twenty-two miles farther south, where the Pacific Highway met Oregon's State Highway 26 coming west from Portland forty-five miles away, the militia had thrown up a blockade three miles north of Cannon Beach and a few miles inland from Ecola State Park. The junction was eighty miles west of the Pacific Crest Trail over which you can walk the more than two and a half thousand miles from Mexico to Canada virtually without stepping out of lands under the control of either the Bureau of Land Management, the National Parks Service, or National Forest Service, a fact that further irritated the militias.

On the coast, several hikers were near the junction where the militia also blew up the 101, immediately in front of a National Guard company. Nineteen-year-old Sonia Loeson, a second-year student at Oregon U, was among them.

When a private from this company, furious over the discovery that other people were actually trying to kill him, came across the hikers in the nearby woods and saw that none of them had been wounded despite being so close to the detonation, something in him snapped. These hikers—he knew the type, young, antimilitary, environment nuts. "You!" he shouted, waving his M-16 at Sonia.

"Hey, man!" said one of the hikers, a bearded, scraggly-haired youth. "She didn't do—"

The guardsman fired and blew him away. "Rest of you 'cept her—scram!" he screamed, and they vanished into the woods. The guardsman was getting excited looking at her. He knew what these women were after, with no bras and tight-assed shorts—stuck-up bitches just like the ones who'd spurned him at school. "Take it off!" he commanded. "All of it!" and waved the M-16 at her. Terrified, she did as she was told.

"I'm gonna fuck you!" he told her. "Gonna fuck you till it comes out your chin. Come here!"

Trembling like an aspen, she walked falteringly toward him. "You got AIDS?" he demanded.

She tried to speak but couldn't. Instead she nodded, and managed a choked "Yes."

He grinned. "Lyin' bitch. You ain't had it before, have you?"

"Yes," she said, "I—"

"Turn around, bitch—wait a minute. Let me see your tits!"

She turned back toward him, eyes downcast, as if somehow her downward look might shame him, protect her. His left hand grabbed her breast and squeezed so hard she yelped like a puppy.

"Shuddup! Shut the fuck up! You hear?"

She nodded.

"Turn around."

She did so and he pushed her up against a tree in dense bush several yards in from the trail. "You put your arms round the tree. Go on!" Cradling the rifle, he took out a condom, slipped it on, and after he'd wiped some grease off the barrel with his finger, he used it to—

"Hey!"

He spun around, his fly open, his tumescence clearly visible, and fired a wild shot at the intruder, another guardsman, who fired back but hit Sonia Loeson, who fell, mortally wounded, and died a few minutes later as her would-be rescuer cried, holding her hand, her assailant having disappeared into the woods.

The unit to which both guardsmen belonged had been rushing along the sixty-nine road miles to the coast en route to the south side of the Columbia, where they were to support the beleaguered elements of the 82nd Airborne. Unexpected winds had carried over three hundred of the unlucky paratroopers beyond the sandy beaches of Clatsop Spit and Fort Stevens into the area of sea where the Columbia's mouth and the Pacific Ocean rage in an eternal argument over what General Mant called "the most dangerous bar in the world," black, rusted hulls of sunken ships still visible from the shore. Other paratroopers on the river's south side, who were supposed to land near the AB's southern end in and around Astoria, had been swept beyond the town, over Old Youngs Bay Bridge, onto Clatsop Spit around Fort Stevens and beyond, into perilous marshes and sloughs. A few miles north of them fierce house-to-house fighting erupted in downtown Astoria and along the town's cliffs and steep roads where many old, stately homes stood and where two hundred forty men of Bravo and Charlie companies of the Fifth Airborne Battalion had landed.

The militia, which had secured both the northern *and* southern ends of AB, the longest continuous truss bridge in the world, now lost the southern end of the bridge, where they were overrun by a hundred and ninety-four men from FEDFOR's Airborne. The paratroopers, unlike most of their comrades, had actually landed where they were supposed to and made a running, firing-at-the-hip charge against the dug-in militia. General Mant, though hundreds of miles north of the battle, knew that this was the Achilles' heel of the war on the Astoria front.

As well, the militia had to retake the southern end of Old Youngs Bay Bridge if they were to stop FEDFOR. But as every soldier knows, nothing is simple in war, and in these initial hours the inevitable confusion and fog of combat were shrouding the battle. Nevertheless, General Shelbourne could discern three major areas of urgent concern, namely that the capture of the Astoria Bridge, crucial to his outflanking the militias, depended on the outright capture of the Old Youngs Bay Bridge, which in turn depended on FEDFOR's California forces and its National Guard's 41st Infantry Brigade reinforcements from Portland getting past the militia in the Cannon Beach area.

Shelbourne's nerves were strung taut. He had awoken suddenly at three o'clock that morning from an apocalyptic dream of Portland under siege, all but unprotected except for a brave, ill-equipped police force, the city's 41st Brigade, now gone from the city—en route to Astoria—on *his* orders.

Fourteen miles north of Astoria, beyond the river's

mouth, the more than two thousand Airborne troops blown too far west of the base of the "b" were now fighting for their lives all down the twenty-seven-mile strand of Long Beach, the "b"'s stem. Over a hundred and seventeen paratroopers—twenty from Major Bill McBride's command—had dropped into the wind-chopped waters of Willapa Bay, east of Long Beach sand spit, and drowned. Only a few squads of these troopers, including a 60mm mortar team and communications section, made it to terra firma, coming down on Long Island in the bay, where they frightened thousands of seabirds into flight and from which they could hear fighting south and west of them but could not as yet see anything but elk and more birds, flocks of black cormorants and gulls among the more than seventy species that nested on the rocky island.

Under the initiative of a very wet and cold corporal, the mortar squad set up shop on the southern tip of the eight-mile-long, two-mile-wide island seven hundred yards across a channel from a dock that stuck out from the Willapa Wildlife Refuge office. There were several canoes and yellow-painted kayaks on the sand beneath the dock but no militiaman in sight. Sooner or later, though, the corporal figured they'd come looking for the owners of the chutes they'd seen descending over the island and at which they had probably taken potshots. Another thing the mortar-squad corporal was sure of was that any militia, given the wide-open approach to the island, would wait until dark before they pushed off from the dock. He'd let 'em get halfway across the channel, then, he promised his six-man squad, "We'll blow the fuckers clean outta the fucking water!"

Five miles west of the mortar squad and Long Island, on Long Beach Peninsula, the Airborne was strung out all along twenty-seven miles of beach, from Seaview to Leadbetter Point State Park. Some men had expended all their strength, wading ashore under fire from cars, trucks, and hastily commandeered tour buses, which, bristling with heavily armed militia, were speeding up and down Highway 103, pulling off at the touristy townships' beachfront accesses and in some cases driving on the beach itself. Here they jumped out of the vehicles, unleashing a rain of deadly fire upon the hapless Airborne, many of the latter cut down before they cleared the pounding surf, others within feet of the boardwalk, the scene made even more chaotic by the thousands of terror-stricken residents and tourists frantically running away from both the Airborne and militia invasion, racing south along the 103 from Long Beach–Seaview township toward the exit onto 101.

The civilians' intended escape was thwarted, however, by an auto wreck outside the bed-and-breakfast house by the visitors' information center at the junction of 101 and Pacific Highway, where a militia pickup collided with a Beach Cab, the taxi so badly smashed that the first four digits of the phone number on its side disappeared into a V of metal, "905" visible but scorched by the fire now consuming the cab, its driver miraculously unharmed, two militiamen dead on the road from massive head injuries, others limping about in shock through broken glass, the driver's face streaming blood and the radio thumping out Roy Orbison's "Dream Baby."

From Long Beach to the hill-surrounded fishing port of Ilwaco at the base of the "b," where the airport, like other local landing strips, had been blocked by militia-strewn four-gallon drums of sand on the runways, the slaughter of the Airborne continued. Many of the paratroopers were pinned down on the beaches, trying to use their packs as cover, sand flicking up all around them as they were hit, in many cases at virtually point-blank range, in what the militia were already calling the "Long

Beach Turkey Shoot." The bloodied water's edge was littered with dead, surf crashing against their bodies, rolling them over as indifferently as it had washed dead-head logs ashore on the beach, the bleached white logs affording the besieged Airborne the only real shelter from the deadly fire of the enemy's highly mobile force.

At first, when the ad hoc assortment of militia vehicles had come to a screeching halt from Seaview's Bolstand Avenue to Oysterville and Leadbetter State Park and militiamen began jumping out, some Airborne had thought they were up against a ragtag enemy. It appeared so, especially from the dress of the militiamen, many without the telltale militia uniform and WWII helmet, as if truckloads of armed boardwalk hooligans had arrived willy-nilly to raise hell. But the apparent disorder of the militia was only that—*apparent*. The militia's interlocking and deadly fields of fire soon told the clusters of Airborne, some of whose weapons were jamming from sand and overheating, that they weren't up against amateurs but against men who were good shots—men who didn't waste ammunition.

In the first sixty minutes of combat along the peninsula, forty-two militia were killed, excluding those at the site of the car crash; sixty-three wounded. The Airborne's dead was in excess of 497, nearly 1,116 wounded or missing in action. In all, over 1,500 Airborne casualties—a near 10 percent rate of loss if applied to the whole division.

Shelbourne pulled out the stub of a half-smoked Havana from the pocket of his old gray West Point robe, now tight around the gut, and tried to wet it with his tongue, but there was no saliva, his tongue dried by anxiety, the cigar, instead of rolling about comfortably in his mouth, sticking to his tongue like a finger in a freezer.

And he felt just as cold. A 10 percent rate of loss might not mean that much to civilians; to a general it was a nightmare.

The situation was made worse by the fact that Mant's militiamen had been ordered to ignore badly wounded comrades in the field except to take their weapon and ammunition, leaving them to the federals, who were then obliged to Medevac them out, thus tying up more federals both at the front and back in the military hospitals and hastily erected POW holding areas, creating a serious drain on manpower the FEDFOR vitally needed at the front. In any event, Shelbourne knew that at this present *rate* of casualties, the highest for the 82nd since Arnhem, such losses were unsustainable—that unless immediate help was forthcoming, in a few more hours the 82nd Airborne would cease to exist as a fighting unit.

At the Columbia River's mouth, on the Oregon side, at the site of the first U.S. settlement in the American Northwest, fighting, like that at Long Beach, on the Washington side, was at close quarters, an Airborne company managing with interlocking fields of fire to force militia infantry back toward the big river, cutting them off from the remainder of the militia forces on what was now the Astoria front.

As well as the continued fighting in the town itself, there was house-to-house mayhem on the heights above the river, many of the old, carefully preserved homes there gutted or ablaze. The trapped Airborne used flame-throwers, sending long arcs of orange fire streaking brilliantly against the green of the town's flora, creating the illusion that the houses under attack were actually sucking in the flame. The resulting fires were creating fierce back-drafts, sending flames roaring skyward. It was the area's most violent display of man-made power since Fort

Stevens—established by order of Abraham Lincoln at the mouth of the river in the first American Civil War—was shelled by a Japanese sub in June of 1942 as it trailed fishing boats through the river's mined channel. At Fort Stevens itself, retreating militia sought protection behind the fort's moat, amid the old concrete batteries.

It being a Tuesday, the fort, much of it now reconstructed, had been closed by museum officials, but militiamen, desperate to hold out until reinforcements came across Youngs Bay from Astoria, had quickly blown down the doors. Unluckily for them, the Airborne, in one of its few successes so far in the battle, continued to hold the southern end of Old Youngs Bay Bridge and were managing, albeit barely, to prevent militia troops from crossing over it to assist their comrades. And the situation of the militia at Fort Stevens worsened as Airborne troops pressed home the attack, the cavernous old gun batteries now sprouting with M-16s, hunting rifles with scopes, and shotguns, reverberating with the sound of gunfire. The aged battlements of the first American Civil War was being chipped away by FEDFOR fire, puffs of mortar and stone flying into the air, temporarily blinding several militiamen wearing contact lenses. In their frantic efforts to get the grit out of their eyes, the men momentarily left gaps in the defense, and the Airborne, their blood up, angered by reports of the slaughter of Airborne on Long Beach, quickly exploited the situation. Firing into the gaps, covering their designated attackers, the paratroopers raced forward, M-16s on burst fire, SAWs on full automatic. Breaching the gaps, they cleared out an old gun-battery emplacement, killing the fourteen militiamen inside, the noise like strings of firecrackers set off in a Dumpster, the engagement at close quarters so fierce that the Airborne attackers had been sprayed by the blood of the now dead and dying defenders. One of the latter, a militia sergeant, his stomach blown open and entrails sliding down his thigh, looked up with the eyes of a wounded animal pleading to be put out of its misery. An Airborne soldier, face streaked by grime, camouflage paint, and blood, and drenched in perspiration despite the cold dampness of the place, quickly looked around for his squad leader, a sergeant with a Gulf War scar across his chin. The veteran signaled the Airborne soldier to step aside, put his M-16's barrel against the militiaman's temple, and fired.

At Fort Clatsop—another historic site on the river's Oregon side, designed by the great explorers Lewis and Clark, whose extraordinary journey of discovery had opened up much of the West—another battle was raging, only here the situation was reversed. Over fifty Airborne and nineteen terrified tourists were taking refuge in and around the old log building and its adjoining visitors' center. The Airborne's radio operator was still alive, but his set had been shot up and was effectively destroyed. Children were screaming, their mothers, some of them hysterical, trying to protect them as glass and wood chips flew, several of the children urinating in fright, others strangely silent in their terror. One of the tourists, a young man in jeans and matching denim jacket, lay dead, spread-eagled on the floor, a neat hole in his forehead, his nut-brown toupee, which had come askew at the back of his head, shiny wet, lying in a plum-colored pool of blood and brains. An Airborne lieutenant told everyone to shut up, took one of the women's sweaters, white, shoved its sleeves between his black grenade-launcher barrel and rifle barrel, and thrust it out a window. In a matter of seconds the firing died down, then ceased.

"You surrendering?" came a militiaman's voice.

"Hell, no!" yelled out the Airborne's lieutenant. "We've

got civilians here. Want to let them go." He paused. "All right?"

There was silence around the log building, though the firecracker popping of distant fighting could be heard.

"All right," came a militiaman's voice. "But not in a bunch. One by one. Two yards apart."

"Give us a minute," said the lieutenant.

"What for?"

"Lot of kids in here. Pretty scared. Have to settle 'em down."

"Hurry it up!"

The lieutenant, his voice subdued, turned to a private. "Myers, that dead civilian. Was he with anybody?"

"Doesn't look like it, sir. One of them just covered his face—tryin' to get the kids not to look at him."

"Quickly," said the lieutenant. "Get into his clothes. I want you to take out a sitrep—tell somebody what the hell's going down here and bring back help."

"Yes, sir."

"And Myers?"

"Sir?"

"Take off your dog tags. Give 'em to me."

"Yes, sir."

"And don't get blood on his shirt or jacket."

Myers made no attempt at privacy. There wasn't time. He stripped down to his khaki underwear, took off the dead man's clothes, quickly pulling them on, several children still sobbing, one of them passing wind in fright, no one saying a word.

"Hey!" came a shouted voice. "You use those civilians as a shield, you got no chance. We'll kill everyone, man! Now send—"

The door swung open and the nineteen civilians, including Myers at the rear, walked out slowly, one by one, as agreed on, hands up, except for some of the children, who, though still scared, couldn't resist glancing about, trying to see who had been shooting at them. But only one militiaman was visible, his left hand out, pointing in the direction of the parking lot. In his right hand he held a .30-caliber Sporter rifle with scope, two handguns in holsters at his side, two bandoliers of ammunition crisscrossing his dark green battle smock. A World War II steel helmet covered his head, a thick elasticized canvas band around it holding a small plastic bottle of clear fluid, and a dirtied square first-aid pack stuck into the band, his helmet's strap resting against a dark, bearded chin. The children were already bunching up nearer the person in front of them. Suddenly the rear half of the column stopped. One of them, a scruffy, acne-faced teenage boy, said something to the militiaman. The militiaman listened, scowled, then brusquely waved the boy on.

Inside the log building, the Airborne lieutenant withdrew his M-16 from the window and took out the white sweater. He knew that as soon as the column got past them, the militia would resume firing. He had three fragmentation grenades ready, lined up on an old macramé-covered table in front of him. The lieutenant was under no illusions; if someone didn't get here soon, he and his men would be wiped out.

As Myers at the back of the column drew close to the bearded militiaman, the latter drew him aside. "You come with me," he told Myers, jabbing him with the .30 Sporter toward a clump of trees well away from the fort and the column of evacuees en route to their vehicles. In the distance, firing grew more intense, but whether it was Airborne or militia reinforcements Myers couldn't tell. Up ahead he could see some kind of vehicle, a truck, barely discernible beneath a khaki-green camouflage net, green-painted steel plates welded to its side, front, and back, a slit for where the driver sat, six more slits along the side serving as firing bays. A door slammed shut and a militia captain emerged from behind the armored pickup. "Who's this?" he asked the bearded militiaman.

"A kid told me he's a federal. Took off his uniform and switched it for a dead guy's clothes. Tryin' to sneak through to find more federals—bring 'em back against us."

The militia captain, his face showing the strain of the fighting, stared at Myers. "Well, is it true?"

"Hell, no. I'm no soldier. I was here visiting the fort when suddenly I look up. Parachutes everywhere and next minute—"

"Go get the kid!" the captain ordered his militiaman. "Hurry. I haven't time for this bullshit."

A few minutes later the militiaman returned with the boy.

"You sure about this?" the captain asked him.

"Yeah," said the teenager, frightened by the increasing sound of gunfire punctuated by explosions, mostly grenades, but also the *crump* of mortar rounds. "I saw him changing clothes."

"Strip!" the captain ordered Myers. When he got down to his khaki army-issue underpants and singlet Myers knew he was a POW. The militia captain looked at the acne-faced teenager. "You better get back to the convoy. We'll be white-flagging it."

The teenager hesitated, looking first at the captain then at the militiaman, who had his rifle pointed straight at Myers's heart.

"Don't I get no reward?" said the teenager.

"You'll get a kick in the ass if you don't get out of my sight, you little prick," said the captain. "Go on, piss off!"

The kid was running back toward the ad hoc convoy of

cars and a couple of motorbikes that were getting ready to go out under a white flag. Suddenly the militia captain drew his Sig Sauer .45, pointing it at Myers, and told the militiaman, "Go tell 'em to hold that convoy—till I say they can go."

The militiaman did as he was told.

Myers was sweating.

"Nothing personal," said the captain.

" 'Course not," Myers replied, finding it difficult to get enough spittle to talk. "Just doin' your fuckin' job, right?"

"That's right," said the captain, unabashed. "You're on the wrong team."

Myers tried to swallow but couldn't. "Yeah, well— you don't have to kill me, do you?" His knees were trembling.

The militiaman with the .30 Sporter came running back, and Myers, though preoccupied with his fate, noticed the man wasn't even slightly out of breath. Contrary to what the Pentagon had told the Airborne, the militia weren't a bunch of out-of-shape wannabes. They were fit, well armed, and from what he'd seen at the fort and here, well disciplined.

"What's your name?" the captain demanded. "And rank?"

"Myers. Private first class."

"Well, Myers—"

"Incoming!" yelled the militiaman, and all three of them instinctively hit the dirt as an artillery shell passed over in that peculiarly air-shuffling sound, crashing into a copse of trees about seventy yards off to their left, shrapnel whistling through fir, lacerating trunks and shredding branches, a tall column of damp earth and moss erupting. "Jesus," said the militiaman, a Vietnam vet. "One-fifty-fives."

Myers started to run and the captain fired, the .45 hitting the federal in the right rear thigh, bringing him down. Myers had just given the captain an idea. He turned to his fellow militiaman. "Truss him up and put him in the pickup."

"Get him a medic."

"No. Fuck him. Just truss him up. Then get two and three platoon here—or what's left of 'em."

"Break off the attack on the fort—"

"Burn the fuckin' fort now the civilians are out. Save grenades. Use gas from the pickup. We're pulling out—for the time being. We've got nothing in this area that can do anything about one-fifty-fives. Go on. Move!"

"Yes, sir."

Chain-smoking and dressed in farmer's overalls, Louis Keel, forty, looking fiftyish, pulled off California's 99 near Fresno, two hundred miles north of Los Angeles in the San Joaquin Valley, part of the Central Valley between the Pacific coast and the Sierra Nevadas. He was watching elements of Fort Irwin's 177th Armored Brigade pass by, heading northward in all their magisterial might, FEDFOR M1A1 MBTs—Main Battle Tanks—having replaced the brigade's old lighter M551 Sheridans, which had once played the opposing force, or OPFOR, as a "Soviet"-designed Red force against Blue units at the National Training Center in the Mojave Desert. A battalion of fifty-eight M1A1s on truck transporters was preceded by six scout five-crew-member M-3 Bradley Cavalry Fighting Vehicles, each sprouting a 25mm chain gun and TOW missile launcher. Behind the tanks came six M106A2 heavy 107mm mortars followed by mechanized infantry being transported in nine-man-squad Bradley IFVs—Infantry Fighting Vehicles—the hatches of both M3 scout and M2 infantry Bradleys open, drivers and commanders doing an "Israeli," heads out for better visibility.

In all, it was an impressive array of American power moving along the highway. And this was only one battalion of five. But as he watched them go by, Louis Keel wondered how many of them would do an Israeli in combat. He figured they'd button up quick enough. Keel tapped out an unfiltered Camel, lit it, and took a long drag until he felt the smoke spreading deep in his lungs, calming him. He would have taken a swig of his home-made hooch, but lookit, he told himself, what you don' need, Louis, is some federal pulling you over for a Breathalyzer. Reminded him of the story about this guy being pulled over by a cop for speeding.

"I wasn't speeding," says the guy, but his wife says, "Yes, you were, dear." He gives his wife a dirty look. Then the cop says, "You also went through a red light." "No way," says the guy, but his wife says, "It *was* yellow, dear." The guy gives her another dirty look. "And," says the cop, "your plates have expired."

"Oh," says the driver, "I paid for 'em but they haven't come yet." His wife says, "Yes they have, dear—they've been sitting on your desk." The guy's had enough of his wife, so he reams her out, calling her all kinds of names. The cop looks across at her and says, "Does he always speak to you like this?" and she says, "Only when he's drunk."

Louis chuckled, took off his sweat-stained felt hat—it was getting too hot—reached over to the passenger side, and from under a mess of old newspapers and magazines that, like him, smelled of stale smoke, extracted an old, worn copy of *Time* magazine and propped it up on the steering wheel with Theodore Kaczynski looking knowingly out at him. Using his cigarette as a pointer, Keel

began another of his daily conversations with the
Unabomber and lit another cigarette without realizing it.

Let the federals call Ted Kaczynski the Unabomber,
but to Louis Keen he was Theo. "Theo," Louis explained, "you made one big mistake, boyo. You pig-
frigged around—one little piggy at a time, see? What you
shoulda done if you were gonna go a piggy at a time was
hit a big piggy like we done that attorney-general bitch.
And don't mess with goddamn letter bombs. Just hittin'
the symptom, Theo. Just hittin' the symptom. What you
gotta eliminate is the cause. Like you lance a pimple here
an' there, man, doesn't do no good. Pimples come from
the diet, right? Too much sugar, Theo. Gotta get everyone off the sugar. But hey—" A long piece of ash fell on
the Unabomber's face. Louis blew it off. "But I'm not
criticizin' . . . well, maybe I am, just a tad. But hell, don't
take no mind. I'll carry on, you don't have to worry 'bout
that. But I'm goin' for the cause, Theo, not a little piggy
here an' a little piggy there, but a whole bunch o' piggies.
Goin' to eliminate the appetite for sugar, Theo. Gonna go
south. Bunch o' piggies at one time. Nighty night,
Babe!" Louis shook his head in amusement at his own
joke and lit another Camel. Now he had three going at
once—two in the ashtray, another between his lips. "Like
a goddamn Vietnamese," he told himself. "Ol' Jesse
Helms had it right when he saw the little brown monkeys
smoking two cigs at a time, in 'Nam." Jesse had told the
tobacco conference, "Now, *they're* the kind of people we
need." Louis grinned approvingly. As far as he was concerned, the antismoking crowd were a bunch of goddamn
fascists.

He looked back at Theo, who he could see was still
looking at him. They understood each other. It was
like looking at that painting by that wop painter, the picture of Jesus carrying the cross, all beat-up but looking

out at you and you knew he knew. Nothing had to be said. You knew what you had to do. "Theo," Louis said very softly. "Jesus' name be praised. You're the Unabomber. I'm the Multibomber." He paused and let the smoke come out any way it could. It was as if he was on fire. " 'For I have seen the darkness,' saith the Lord, 'and I will bring ye the light. I will always—' " Louis choked up. He knew himself to be a hard man, but Jesus' promise that "I will always be with you" never failed to move him to tears. He blew out another dense cloud of bluish-gray smoke. Then, with all the reverence for Jesus he could muster, he looked at Theo one more time. And like a father saying good-bye forever to his son, he breathed in deeply, in order to say his piece without breaking down, and told Theo Jesus' promise: "I will always be with you."

Tears were streaming down his sun-creased face as he put the *Time* away and pulled back out onto 99, the sweet smell of vineyards, the cloying dust from the valley, and the stink of exhaust from the army convoy stuffing his nose, causing more tears. But these weren't tears of sadness or joy, as when he thought of the Lord, but more a kind of allergic reaction that he, like Theo, had to modern America. For Louis it was a symptom of the greed that kept polluting the air and poisoning the rivers, a symptom of the "me" generation—of all the little piggies. He'd thought of the contradiction in what he was doing, his pickup spewing out more polluting fumes, as he drove toward his target, but as Theo knew, sometimes the ends justify the means. Besides, the target had come to him in a dream, as dreams had come to the angels of the Lord, and it was well known that to get at the devil you sometimes had to use the tools of the devil. Didn't Jesus throw out the money changers from the temple? He didn't *ask* them to leave, He *threw* the fuckers out—had to knock over a few tables in the process. Louis chuckled and shook his head, side to side. Geez, the California Highway Department was gonna go absolutely ape when they saw what that goddamned armored convoy had done to their roads. Oh well, Governor, if the militia had its way, the convoy wouldn't be making a return trip.

It was so hot now, it was hard to breathe. Even the crows seemed drag-assed, just sittin' on the poles. Crazy, wasn't it? Louis thought. So hot down here when up in the Sierras, little piggies were skiing.

CHAPTER TWENTY-TWO

OFF CAPE DISAPPOINTMENT, the wall of foam-streaked sea rolling inexorably toward the Columbia bar was over three stories high, and it was coming straight at the Day-Glo orange coxswain aboard Cape D's white-hulled coast-guard rescue boat, its blue-and-red stripe all but obliterated by spray.

"Pitch swell!" he yelled, the engineer repeating the call, the massive wave striking the boat a few points off the starboard bow, the boat leaning precariously to port, shuddering as it climbed up and up, then strangely stilled for a second at the apogee of its precipitous climb before the sudden plunge into the bowel-chilling void above the next trough. After months of training, this was the man's first real rescue attempt as coxswain. And if a beginner's sheer terror of battling the monster waves had abated for him, he was still fearful of the swells' tremendous power. One of the two crewmen was yelling at the other aboard the four-man vessel. He was shouting not in anger but in order to make his advice heard over the sustained crashing of the huge Pacific rollers over the bar, where hundreds of ships had met their end. "If we'd been a few points further over we'd be under by now! Got to keep 'er bow and—"

"Pitch swell," yelled the coxswain. *"Breaking!"* A wall of boiling white water hit them, rivers rushing down the gunwales, surging about the scuppers and wheelhouse, the coxswain fighting the wheel, one of the crewmen grasping the vertical safety rail with both hands, the force of the tons of water threatening to tear him loose and suck him straight back over the stern. "There's one of—" The rest of his alert was drowned in the thunder of the next wave, his right hand indicating a heaving green blanketlike patch of dye and what looked like a pink cork—a man's face in the gray valley between troughs. It was one of the paratroopers who'd been whisked out over the narrow spit of Long Beach by the wind shears and dumped unceremoniously into the raging seas.

"Throw 'im a line!" yelled the coxswain, but the crewman had already tossed a lifesaver to the man, who was now gesturing frantically, if a little woodenly, his body seizing up in the frigid ocean. Cape D had already called the coast-guard choppers from the Oregon as well as the Washington State side, and it would be a helo that would have to pull most of them out. Over eleven had been spotted in the immediate area, the rescue boat doing

what it could in the mountainous seas to keep the downed
paratroopers afloat.

"Don't understand it!" the coxswain shouted to the deckhand. "Droppin' 'em anywhere around the Columbia—
should have life vests."

"They do!" the deckhand shouted back.

"Then what the hell's goin' on? Flappin' their arms
about like they don't have any."

"Probably their packs pullin' 'em under."

"Life vests should support—*pitch swell!*"

The Airborne's orange B-7 inflatable flotation devices
were supposed to keep a paratrooper and full pack afloat,
but the CO_2 cartridges weren't inflating the vests, and by
the time many of the Airborne had switched to the "by-
mouth" inflating tube, their packs had dragged them
under. Most had managed to jettison their loads and
bobbed up to the churning surface, where they tried to
inflate the vests by mouth, an all but impossible task in
the heavy seas.

Though all were much younger and fitter than the
average fifty-year-old man, they were exhausted and cold
and were quickly succumbing to the coast guard's fifty-
fifty rule—the fact that an average fifty-year-old man
swimming in fifty-degree water, like that off Cape D,
will have a fifty-fifty chance of swimming fifty yards.
Any farther is a matter of sheer luck, genetics, and
fat. Going into the fetal position to reduce the loss of core
heat would help, but sooner or later—sooner in the
huge seas off Cape D—the lungs, brain, and other
organs would surrender their warmth. The heart, at first
racing, would slow, hypothermia setting in. Hands and
feet would go numb, followed by uncontrollable shivering and shaking, then blacking out. Some, if picked up,
would be so disoriented they might dive back into the

water, mistaking it for the surface, hallucinating. Then death. Most would be dead within the hour. Only that rare individual would survive, and cold statistics showed that he would most likely be bigger and fatter than any of the combat-fit Airborne.

A "Dolphin" coast-guard chopper appeared below the cloud cover like a friendly white bug, its red stripe barely visible then disappearing in the bank of fog rolling in along the river where the two bodies of water mixed—a glimpse of flashing navigational lights visible now and then—the Dolphin now heard but not seen. There was a flash of orange light, then a tremendous boom above the crackle and thumps of the battle and a rain of fiery debris, two of the chopper's rescue crew tumbling down into the river, the militia's Stinger having exploded right below the engine's cowling.

High above Astoria, in the 125-foot commemorative tower atop Coxcomb Hill, overlooking a vista that included the Columbia River, Youngs Bay, and through long layers of fog, the town itself, a militia machine gunner waited. When an obscuring layer of mist cleared, he let fly with the first long burst of fire from a marine-corps M2406, a converted M240 medium machine gun. Its synthetic stock reflected a beam of sunlight as the gunner shifted the weapon, on its bipod, to the other side of the tower's lookout, directing his fire down on Lego-sized Airborne as they dashed from one burning house to another along Jerome Avenue. Long white sheets with roughly drawn red crosses on them hung forlornly out of Columbia Memorial Hospital, less than half a mile to the north of the tower. Now, as they darted from house to house in close-order battle with the militiamen, the Airborne, as well as worrying about being fired at from all around, had to seek shelter from the machine gunner in the tower.

Northwest of the tower, across the river, Major Bill McBride, crawling through the estuary grass, Sergeant Randy Nye behind him, heard a rustle up ahead and stopped. He flicked off the safety and waited. Nye did the same. All they could hear was running water. The tide was coming in. Despite all his training, McBride wanted to shout, "Airborne!"—concerned about a possible blue-on-blue—friendly fire—but he suppressed the urge. There was another rustle of grass, this time behind them, McBride guessed about fifteen feet away. Randy Nye on his right side turned as quietly as he could to face the front so they would both have a hundred-and-eighty-degree field of fire. They heard the grass moving again at three o'clock to McBride, who told himself it was probably nothing but a few nesting birds—hell, they had landed slam bang in the middle of a wildlife refuge. Besides birds there were larger animals—elk and bear in these parts. There was more movement off to his left, and in a burst of sunlight that sliced through the gray over-cast, a rotten-egg, hydrogen-sulfide-gas smell rising from all around the estuary, shot through with the sickening stink of rotting fish. Maybe that was it—the noise—some scavenger bird cleaning up a carcass. Now there was the sound of distant firing north of them from the direction of Long Island in Willapa Bay and the increasing noise of water gurgling into the estuary nearby. Bill McBride fig-ured they had a half hour at most before he and the sergeant had to move, whether they liked it or not. Either that or drown.

The coast-guard crewmen were overwhelmed. The Airborne were dying faster than they could haul them aboard the sea-pounded rescue boat. Other boats, including one from Astoria, were on their way, but only five men were picked up out of the dozens in distress as a stiff northwester whipped waves, cresting in front of the boat, to new frenzies.

A larger Oregon Coast Guard vessel, a cutter, was steaming at flank speed to assist, and each time it hit a wave, a dull, sickening thud reverberated through the ship, followed by a shiver of metal, the spray over the bow descending like a tropical rain, the well deck awash in waist-deep water as a rescue crew, their safety lines affixed to the rail, struggled to ready their smaller boat. But by the time they had launched, they had managed to save only two men from the ferocious surf. A coast-guard H-60 Jay Hawk rescue helo fared better, having avoided flying over the "b" to avoid Stingers by first heading out to sea farther up the coast before coming into the coast, and popping infrared "sucker" flares as an extra precaution.

One of the two Airborne the helo rescued was going into hypothermia, hallucinating, not really knowing what was going on. The other man, however, still had most of his faculties intact and would never forget the sudden fall of the Day-Glo-red-clad rescuer who came down in the freezing sea, was lost to sight for a moment, and reappeared not more than twenty feet away in a towering gray wall of water that was streaked with angry veins of foam and boiling sand. Again the swimmer reappeared, doing the Australian crawl, and lifted high by a wave, stopped momentarily, putting up an arm as if signaling for help but actually doing so as a way of retaining buoyancy as the wave crested, beginning its downhill rush. It was only after being manhandled into the coast guard's harness, his body collapsed like a bag of potatoes and winched up, that the rescued Airborne man realized his rescuer was a woman.

As the man who was hallucinating was hauled up, the coast guard only now realizing he was the worse off of the two, he began jabbering something about seeing dragons and cartridges. Shortly after, he died. At first no one had paid any attention to his hallucinatory raving, too busy getting him warm. And it would be several hours before eleven men still alive, out of the dozens who'd been swept out to sea, would come to the same conclusion—that, like the ill-fated Airborne at Arnhem who'd been issued bum radios, they'd been issued bum CO_2 cartridges that had failed to inflate the vests before the men could ditch their heavy loads and use their "by-mouth" inflating tubes.

There was, to put it mildly, "heavy shit" flying at Fort Bragg, North Carolina. That night a call for a congressional inquiry was under way. Ashen-faced, on CNN, the prime contractor in Atlanta for the DOD's water-safety vests swore by everything he held sacred that every batch had been tested.

"How?" the interviewer asked.

"Ah, well, like you do anything else. Chocolates, for example. You know—you, uh, pick one out of a batch and test it. If it works, the batch is fine."

"But you don't test every cartridge—"

"Ah, no—hell." And here the contractor made a serious, if understandable, gaffe. He smiled as he said "hell." He didn't think there was anything funny about the death by drowning of over fifty members of the 82nd Airborne, but was simply expressing incredulity at the newsman's stupidity. How in hell did he think you ran a business? Say you're making chocolates—what do you do, eat every one to make sure it's okay? But whatever he meant, that smile did him in. The station's switchboard lit up, jammed with outraged callers demanding that their tax dollars not be used for any DOD acquisitions from this contractor. Forty minutes later the contractor died of a heart attack.

Thirteen miles northeast of Columbia bar, at the southern end of the eight-mile-long Long Island, the Airborne 60mm mortar crew had begun bracketing a small flotilla of militia kayaks and canoes when the latter were halfway across the channel between the mainland and the island.

Suddenly the militia found themselves in an exploding river, columns of roiling water shooting skyward all about them, the gray-colored water turning white and sizzling. But instead of panicking, as the six men of the Airborne expected, the militia spread out in a V, which necessitated the mortar crew recalculating its aim even as the distance between Long Island's shore and the militiamen narrowed to less than two hundred yards. Spumes of foaming salt water erupted with every *thoomph* of a mortar round. Soon the angle of mortar fire would be so acute as to be almost vertical, as the two arms of the militia flotilla neared the marshy shore of the island.

"Let's go!" ordered the mortar chief. "Back into the woods. Too many of 'em." The Airborne squad leader covered the mortar crew as they collapsed the weapon, snatching base plate and barrel, quickly retreating into the brush, four squad members hauling away the unfired 60mm round cases. The point man was alert, knowing there was a distinct possibility that other militia and/or Airborne were on the island.

By the estuary, McBride again thought he heard something, his elbow moving to nudge the sergeant's boot, when the grass by them exploded in action and McBride fired. There was a strangled cry, feathers filling the air, the huge albatross crashing to earth, writhing in the greenish-brown estuary grass, splattering it red, the bird with one wing all but shot off and hanging uselessly, the other flapping furiously.

"Shit!"

The comment was made by Randy Nye, the major's outburst now having betrayed their position to all and sundry. McBride knew they'd now have to move. Bending over, he led off in a crouched run to higher ground above the estuary, expecting to come under fire at any second. But they reached high ground and more grass behind a scatter of weather-whitened driftwood, and it occurred to McBride that if they'd been in 'Nam he might now be dead, the sergeant's monosyllabic commentary having ID'd them to the enemy as Americans. But here in their own country, their identity remained unknown, so long as they'd only been heard and not seen. For this reason, though, the danger of a blue-on-blue remained high and McBride, chagrined by his mistake, embarrassed in front of the sergeant, was bothered by something else, the killing of the albatross. He remembered himself and his brother "Lucky" as youngsters, their father, a West Coast fisherman, recounting the story of Coleridge's *Ancient Mariner:* "Water, water everywhere and not a drop to drink," of how the Mariner was doomed because he'd killed the albatross, a seaman's age-old harbinger of good luck—of land ahead. They could still hear the big bird, whose normal wingspan was in excess of six feet, thrashing about downwind, unable to lift off. Exhausted, the bird collapsed and lay dying.

The sea breeze grew stronger, sending a shiver through the incoming tide, pushing a brown scum of detritus into the estuary grass that now bent with the wind, revealing for McBride and Nye a squad of WWII–helmeted militia infantry hurrying to cross a salt marsh several hundred yards east of them—nine militiamen strung out, a few yards apart. It was too good a target to ignore. McBride drew a bead on the point man, aimed slightly ahead of him, and squeezed off a three-round burst. The man fell and for a fraction of a second McBride could see a glint of sunlight—perhaps the militiaman had a scope.

McBride and Nye were now firing together, one militiaman, the rear-end Charlie in the squad, returning fire, as bullets splattered the water of the marsh about him, his seven comrades increasing their speed, making for a clump of grass-entangled driftwood on a hump of marsh that resembled a beaver dam several hundred yards off. The first two of the now eight-man militia squad were kneeling, firing as their comrades continued to run, then two of these would kneel and fire in a leapfrog race across the marsh, the shooters now having spotted a tongue of flame from Randy Nye's M-16. The militiaman's fire was kicking up sand about the two Airborne men's positions, forcing McBride and Nye to back off their high ground, McBride left, the sergeant right. The militiamen were nearing the weed-sprouting driftwood, their rear-end Charlie shooting southward at a right angle to McBride and Nye, who now saw the reason for the militiamen's dash across the salt marsh. A platoon-size force, about thirty to forty Airborne, had broken out of cover, coming from the general direction of Fort Canby State Park at Cape Disappointment, five miles to the west. McBride had reloaded and was making life difficult for the rearguard shooter while Nye continued firing at the front of the fleeing squad.

On the rugged shoreline of Fort Canby State Park and Cape Disappointment, what would become known as the "running rock" fight was under way, its combatants, like most men at war, too preoccupied with their immediate local problem—to scale a cliff up to the park proper—to pay much attention to any other sector of the vast, militia-Airborne battle that was now raging all over the far southwestern corner of Washington and northwestern Oregon.

The Airborne lieutenant and his troops in Fort Clatsop, near where the Airborne's Myers lay wounded and trussed up in the back of the homemade, armor-protected pickup, were still surrounded by militia. The militia captain, Nestar, who'd shot Myers, worried about the Airborne 155mm shelling. Wanting to extract his men, he ordered the militia to Molotov the Fort Clatsop log building. Two attempts had failed, both militiamen shot dead by the beleaguered Airborne before they'd even cleared the woods, the gasoline firebombs exploding in their hands.

On the rocky shoreline of Fort Canby and Cape Disappointment, Airborne were firing up at the cliffs from behind the huge, house-size rocks at the surf's edge, but as the tide came in, the Airborne's position became untenable, some of the 270 paratroopers who had touched down there already up to their waist in the frigid water, the bodies of dozens of dead Airborne floating all around them, corpses swept in against the rocks by fierce eddies of foaming water as the tide kept coming in, covering the flats, the sound of the crashing ocean muting the din of gunfire and seagulls screeching on the seaward side.

"Get that guy out of that fucking tower!" ordered the Airborne division's General John Trevor.

"Roger that," replied the Second Battalion's CO, whose Third Company was pinned down by the machine gunner high above them and by two militia companies moving in from Highway 30, which entered the town from the east. "Problem is, General, every time we get a bead on 'im he ducks down in the tower, then turns up on the other side to give our guys grief south of the town."

"I don't want excuses, Colonel. You have a Stinger?"

"Ah—we lost a lot of equipment in the marshes and—"

"Find one! Take him out, Colonel. Now!"

"Yes, sir."

The colonel heard the staccato of the machine gunner and saw his men pinned down as the militia were regaining ground, including the smoking, charred skeletons of what an hour before had been grand old Oregonian homes built a hundred years before, when, after Portland, the town had been the biggest, rowdiest, and most affluent in the state. The colonel's second in command had doubts. Even if they could rustle up a Stinger, would the heat-seeker antiaircraft missile home in on the machine gunner? "Only one way to find out," the colonel replied. "First, we have to get one."

The call went out over the radio. There weren't many around, as the last thing the Airborne had anticipated was a militia air attack. An Airborne section commander near the reservoir on the north end of Shively Park, a half mile south of the town, said he had one and the colonel told him to take out the machine gunner on high.

The militia could hear the Airborne's radio traffic, but as it was scrambled in transmission it sounded like gobbledygook. Nestar, the militia captain eight miles away on the Oregon side, who'd ordered the Molotov attack on Fort Clatsop's log building, urgently wanted to know what was going on—to grab a few prisoners. But as soon as the choking Airborne exited the log building amid billows of dense black smoke, they were shot down at point-blank range in a hail of militia fire. Only two Airborne, one a radioman sans radio and the other a soot-covered rifleman, survived.

Meanwhile a few hundred yards away in the copse that hid Myers, the militia's only prisoner so far in that area, a black Airborne corporal named Duncan, from Chicago's south side, who like so many others had overshot the drop zone, came across the hybrid armored pickup that contained Myers, weak from blood loss. Duncan had already seen at least ten dead Airborne—including an officer whose binoculars he now had and two with their throats cut. He untied Myers, speeded on by the sound of the triumphant militia returning from the slaughter at Fort Clatsop. Using his body as a crutch, the corporal helped the wounded man away from the truck into a denser growth of trees, but not before slicing the armored pickup's tires. At that moment Duncan saw two things simultaneously. The first was the long, huddling groups of civilians, which included the acne-faced boy who had ratted on Myers, waiting nervously by their cars, the lead vehicle a battered 1994 Chevy Blazer bearing a long pole with a white T-shirt hanging lethargically on its tip. The second was a militiaman with a scoped .30 Sporter approaching with two captured Airborne soldiers, hands clasped in surrender atop their heads, coughing from the smoke they'd inhaled. One of them was the radioman sans radio, who'd been captured escaping the burning log building; the other, a short, slight-looking individual, his hair and eyebrows singed, face and Airborne shoulder patch covered in soot, which made him look like a bedraggled performer in a minstrel show. But no one was laughing, not even the triumphant, bearded militiaman with the .30 Sporter, a man who, unbeknownst to Duncan, had lost over six of his comrades and seen over a dozen wounded in the final assault on Fort Clatsop.

* * *

Farther north, on Clatsop Spit at Fort Stevens, the Airborne had rallied behind the moat of the old Civil War earthworks and turned its concrete batteries, half-buried in the sand dunes, into a formidable defense position for *this* civil war. Thick, white-flowered growths of evergreen salal bushes, many already ripped asunder by erratic FEDFOR 155mm artillery fire, quivered in the sea breeze, a baby twister that threatened zero visibility and was thus a perfect cover for an enemy assault. The blown sand hissed on the moat like rain.

North of the river mouth the debacle on Fort Canby Beach, a result of the the parachute drop gone awry—in itself a tragedy for the Airborne—would cost its commanding general, Trevor, any further career promotion unless he could redeem himself by some quick and decisive action. His sin wasn't the overshoot—the pilots of the transports would have to answer for that—rather it was his failure to provide enough cliff-storming equipment for his troops. His not unreasonable assumption had been that as the drop would occur over the gently undulating and flat land of the delta, no such tools as collapsible ladders, grappling lines, etc., would be needed. Instead he had opted, sensibly on the face of it, for extra arms and ammunition. But failure, Trevor knew, took no note of common sense, or good intent; the dead floating off Fort Canby Beach were his responsibility and his alone.

The only thing that prevented the annihilation of his men, strung out in the beautiful sparkling mist that wrapped itself about massive dark rocks in gossamers of sea spray, was the fact that some seventy paratroopers had come down on the lee side of Fort Canby State Park, on Waikiki Beach behind Cape D—"D" for Disappointment—in front of the cape's coast-guard station. Amid all the confusion, with the militia's attention primarily on the big overshoot of hundreds of paratroopers, these seventy troopers were able to obtain the heights above the eastern side, where they began to harass the militia, who were thick along the clifftops on the westward, sea, side.

By now these militiamen were running low on ammunition and some of their weapons were so hot that rounds were cooking off. The seventy-man Airborne attack succeeded. Despite the chaos of the overshoot, most of these seventy were dry, having landed on Waikiki Beach unencumbered—unlike their comrades on the eastern side—by wet clothes, boots, and load-bearing vests. They also succeeded because of the cool leadership of one lieutenant, Gene Tyre, who, in a textbook case of fine radio linkup, managed to coordinate not the kind of every-man-for-himself situation that was dictated by conditions on the seaward side of the cape, but rather a *concentrated* and superbly orchestrated attack against the militia's rear, which cost the lives of six of his men. This attack caused momentary panic in a militia platoon of thirty men a mile south of the North Head lighthouse who, up till now, had been firing down, unopposed, on the half-drowned Airborne.

Believing, because of the deadly and simultaneous concentration of fire behind them, that a force of well over company strength must be pressing home an attack, the thirty militiamen began a hurried withdrawal north toward Seaview, four miles away. Here they planned to join the militia's main body of over four thousand, who by now had joined battle with the Airborne north and south of the Columbia River, knowing from their highway observers, like Louis Keen in California, that more FEDFOR reinforcements were en route from California.

The withdrawal of the militia platoon along the Fort

Canby State Park allowed Lieutenant Tyre and his remaining sixty-four men to reach the top of the bluff and form a semicircular defense. It was no more than fifty yards wide, but their fan-shaped field of intense fire allowed the beleaguered Airborne below the cliffs a way out. Within minutes a steady stream of Airborne were coming off the beach, their sodden clothing making their camouflage battle dress darker and more difficult to see in the photographs taken by a recon plane lucky enough to have found a hole in the fibrous cloud that now covered the entire six-hundred-square-mile battle zone.

When General Shelbourne at the Pentagon saw the fax pix of the northwest front's battle area, overlaid by a clear plastic sheet with salient landmarks and legend, he shook his head. "Look at this, Baun," he instructed his aide.

"Anything in particular, General?" Baun asked, unable, except in a few locations, to differentiate friend from foe.

"Place names," said Shelbourne irritably. "Everything out there's a goddamn *fort*. That's the mind-set we're fighting against. They see everything as a state of siege by the federal government."

"Perhaps," Baun suggested, "unless Washington— D.C., that is—is mistaking a symptom for the cause."

The general looked up quickly from the map, glowering. "What in hell are you talking about, Baun?"

"Well, sir, they had to fight hard to make it out there— out west. It's really quite recent in our history."

The room had fallen silent—everyone looking at Baun. "Ah, well, you know," the major continued, "the Oregon Trail and all that. It was tough—not that long ago—and then the federal government goes and claims all the land. If you see—"

"What's the matter with you, Baun?" Shelbourne challenged. "You got a screw loose? Goddammit, man, you sound like that screwball Mant or that propaganda minister of his, Vance."

The hostile reaction had blown Baun off course for a moment, but, dammit, he was supposed to be an aide, a devil's advocate sometimes, not a suck-up—not what he knew General Freeman would call a Pentagon fairy. "General, I'm not saying I agree with them, only that I think we should understand them—if we're to defeat them."

"Of course we're going to defeat them," snapped Shelbourne. "And . . ." He hesitated. He was losing it. "Well—what do you think we should do?"

"Exactly what you're doing, General. What Colin Powell said he'd do to the Iraqis. Cut them off—no way out—then kill them."

Shelbourne nodded sagely, but inside he was a troubled man. Already he had American blood on his hands. Even if he won he knew he'd never rest easy with it, that it would haunt him for the rest of his life. Right now "they" were the "enemy," but he knew deep down that some of those so far faceless men must have fought beside him in 'Nam and it sickened him to his stomach, his outburst at Baun a measure of his growing dis-ease. Yesterday a kid at school had told his grandson that the general was a murderer.

As Airborne Corporal Duncan, near Fort Clatsop, was helping the wounded Myers to his feet, he had seen the militia captain, the bearded one with the .30 Sporter, and the two bedraggled-looking Airborne who'd been taken prisoner coming from the direction of the burned-out log building. One of the two Airborne POWs, the radioman with the singed eyebrows and comical minstrel look, was told by the militia captain, Nestar, a man of above-average height, mid-forties, with hard blue eyes and a faint white scar on his chin, to stand abreast of the other three. Militiamen were now gathering in the parking area less than a hundred yards away. The 155mm howitzer shelling had ceased, but whether this was due to the Airborne gunners suddenly realizing that civilians were in the area of the state park or whether the howitzer crew of eleven had been taken out by militia, Nestar had no way of knowing. In any event he had no intention of having his men trapped, ordering them to mingle with the civilians in the parking lot.

"I don't like this," opined the militiaman with the .30 Sporter. "Using civilians as—"

"You don't have to like it!" Nestar snapped. "Just do it."

Sporter hesitated. "How 'bout these two guys?" he asked, motioning to the two federals with his rifle.

"Go join the civilians. I'll be there in a jiff."

Corporal Duncan, concealed by trees and scrub brush beside Myers, who was groaning with pain, was so close he could hear the militia captain clearly despite increasing arms fire, and dared not move, praying that Myers, now slumped against him, wouldn't give them away. Through a curtain of thick green leaves he saw the militia captain waving one of the Airborne POWs over with his .45. When the man, the one resembling a minstrel showman, his hands still on his head, was no more than four feet away, Captain Nestar told him to sit without lowering his hands. Next Nestar, the barrel of his Sig Sauer catching a glint of sunlight through passing cloud, told the minstrel to kneel, which he did, awkwardly, hands still clasped atop his head. Hidden in the bush, Duncan was so close he could see the whites of the man's startled eyes.

"What's your EC?" Nestar asked.

Minstrel said nothing.

Nestar pulled back the hammer with his left thumb. A southpaw, noted Duncan, as if this detail meant something. It didn't—it was merely his mind refusing to believe what was happening and Duncan knowing that if he fired at Nestar, he and Myers were dead men. And what would that profit the Airborne, with militiamen all around, not a hundred yards away, forming a motor convoy in the parking lot with at least one civilian in each vehicle, and each truck sprouting machine guns and other small arms?

"What d'you mean, EC?" Minstrel said bravely, unconsciously heightening his comic look as he sat up like a startled bird, with his soot-black hair sticking up and his white-eyed, black-streaked face, his aggressive response a blind for his fear. "EC? You mean the European Common Market?"

Nestar pulled the trigger—a bang, Minstrel's black head flung back in a shower of blood.

"Jesus! Jesus!" It was the other POW. "Jesus! Jesus!"

Nestar turned the .45 on him. "You know, too," he told the prisoner. "It's not just the radioman. Everyone in the unit knows, right, in case the radio guy gets dumped? Well . . ." Nestar glanced down at the dead man's face— or rather the portion that was left—now plum red, the dead man's blood made dark by his blackened face. From the terrible aspect of the corpse's head wound, Duncan knew the militia wasn't using regular field ammo but probably some kind of dumdum that spread out to fist size on impact, particularly on bone, a round that smashed everything in its path. Now Nestar could hear the deeper-toned staccato of a heavy machine gun—a 50mm—and another sound. Somebody was coming in a Hummer, probably with the gun mounted atop the cabin for 360-degree traverse. Nestar pulled back the hammer.

"Rosebud!" said the POW. "It's Rosebud."

"Thanks," said Nestar, and shot him. What was the point, the militia captain told Sporter as he joined the "civilian convoy" exiting Fort Clatsop State Park, of letting the federal go after he'd given the fucking password?

"Christ," Sporter told him. "You didn't have to kill him, Captain."

"Oh, and what would you do? Take him out in this convoy?"

"We could've."

"Listen!" Nestar snapped, hopping aboard the lead white-flagged Blazer and thumping its cabin as a signal for the convoy to get under way. "We can't afford the time to fart-ass around making special arrangements for one goddamn federal. My job is to get you guys out so we can hit 'em again, not lose my whole fucking company. Can't you hear that point-fifty coming toward us?"

Sporter didn't respond.

"Besides," said Nestar, "you've got no fucking business questioning my orders. We're gonna win this war. We've got to win it or we're toast." He paused. "You want to do this again?" The sweep of his left hand, holding the .45, took in all the land north of Clatsop, across the river where the sound of fighting was no longer coming in surges but was a continuous wave of noise punctuated by the deep thump of what Sporter took to be air-dropped FEDFOR howitzers, two of which he saw coming down now over the Willapa Wildlife Refuge. What he was hearing, however, was the boom of an Abrams M1A1 120mm cannon belching fire and fury. In a morale-stunning move, a FEDFOR of several Hercules had landed on a long strip of highway south on 101 and disgorged three main battle tanks.

"Well," Nestar pressed angrily, "*do* you want to do all this again?"

"What'ya mean?" replied Sporter, not looking at the captain but at a roadblock up ahead. The barrel of an M60 poking out of it, it was a hastily thrown together barrier of driftwood manned by a squad of Airborne, some with marsh reeds in their helmets' camouflage net. Nestar told the driver—a civilian, scared out of his mind—to slow but not stop.

At the blockade an Airborne sergeant and his squad of eight had all weapons off safety as they saw the lead pickup approaching, its white flag held prominently aloft by a very nervous, pimple-faced kid.

"Stop!" the sergeant ordered. "Or we'll shoot."

Every Airborne weapon was sticking out atop the logs now like the quills of a porcupine.

"No, you won't," said Nestar defiantly. "We've got a bunch of civilians here. We're giving them safe conduct out of the area."

"Like hell you are!" the sergeant shot back. "You're using them as a shield."

"We're giving them safe conduct. So you'd better—"

"Turn 'em over to us. We'll give them safe conduct."

"They don't trust federals," Nestar said contemptuously, and tapped the driver's shoulder. "Put 'er into low and go forward. Don't try to go around 'em. We'll bog down. Got it?"

The driver, shaking, started to speak, but nothing came out. All he knew was that there were lots of guns and itchy fingers all around him. He nodded vigorously.

"Fine," said Nestar. "Now just stay cool."

"Turn 'em over to us!" the sergeant repeated.

Nestar's .45 rested on the driver's shoulder, its chromium-plated steel barrel nudging the civilian's neck.

"Yellow basta—" the Airborne sergeant shouted, not

finishing because of women and children. Angrily he waved his men to drag the whitened logs of driftwood off the road. "Hiding behind women's skirts."

Most of Nestar's militiamen, crowded into the civilians' cars, couldn't bring themselves to look out at the federals. Sporter was red-faced with shame, and as they slid past the Airborne, seeing thirty or so federals that had been positioned and staggered along either side of the road only as a blur, he was unable to meet any of the enemy eye to eye.

The Airborne sergeant had only a minute at the most to glimpse the militia captain during their brief exchange, but he wouldn't forget him—around five-nine, beefy but not overweight, his face with a hard set to it, "like Rod Steiger," one of the Airborne said, with hard, blue eyes. His passing glance at the federals was full of undisguised contempt, his fixed gaze telling you that the only rules in this war were that there weren't any, not if you wanted to win. It was a stare that would earn him the name "Laser" among the Airborne. The latter would also learn that Nestar was a graduate of the CIA's clandestine Phoenix Program in Vietnam in which over nineteen thousand suspected Communists were "eliminated."

"Nestar," a humiliated Sporter asked him, "what did you mean back there? About did I want to repeat this. You mean hiding behind women's—"

"You hold your tongue. And you call me *captain* or else you can get back to rolling bandages." Nestar saw the white flag begin to dip and shouted up at the acne-faced boy. "Hey! You keep that upright, you little turd, or I'll whup your ass! Got it?"

"Yes, sir."

Nestar, still looking ahead for any sign of the tanks whose cannon he could hear shooting from beyond the southern end of Old Youngs Bay Bridge, continued to harangue Sporter. "I mean that if you don't want to have to fight these federals again you're going to have to beat them and I mean *bury* them. Now! Washington's got a hell of a lot more men'n us. More troops, more supplies—you name it. But like everything else in the federal government, it takes 'em a week to decide whether or not they should take a crap. We've got a window of opportunity . . . here. We've got them off balance. We have to finish them, beat them so badly that even if they get their second wind they'll figure—the rest of America'll figure—it isn't worth it. Then we'll *really* have our own country. But if we're going to win we have to make it clear that the cost of trying to stop us is too high. We have to win. Anything less and we'll have to start all over again." With that, Nestar instructed the driver to continue on toward the Astoria end of the big bridge by first crossing the Old Youngs Bay Bridge—map reference YB—still held by the Airborne on the southern side and by the militia at the northern end, the Airborne now getting artillery support from a FEDFOR 155mm howitzer over half a mile east from marshy Daggett Point.

Despite swamp conditions the eleven-man crew of the howitzer had improvised with two-by-four pallets, used in the drop, to stabilize the 155's split-trail legs and were now making the area around the southern approach pylons to the Old Youngs Bay Bridge uninhabitable while trying, successfully so far, not to do any damage to the bridge itself. A militia company of a hundred and twenty men tried to rush the bridge but were met by resolute and well-aimed M-16, SAW, and 81mm mortar fire from the Astoria side of the bridge, three quarters of a mile to the north, and the continuing howitzer bombardment from Daggett Point, three miles to their east.

Then, quite unexpectedly, something happened that changed the Airborne's fortunes with respect to both ends of AB and the northern end of YB. Below the stratus cloud hundreds more chutes were coming down in and about Astoria onto an orange, streamer-marked Airborne-secured LZ west of Shively Park, where the Airborne had secured a perimeter. From here the Airborne would attempt to regroup, bringing all their stragglers together, and dash "hell-bent for leather," as the Airborne's General Trevor so unoriginally put it, down Seventh Street, across Olney Avenue to the northern side of YB, a distance of about five hundred yards. Before they could launch this attack, however, the major in charge impatiently awaited the landing of another two platoons of thirty-five men each. These were now coming under intense fire both from the ground and from the Astoria tower, where the machine gunner, though he was firing beyond his weapon's most effective range, was still able to create havoc, shooting up into the descending forest of parachutes with an abandon that threatened to overheat the barrel.

It was later claimed that the reaction of an Airborne captain on the ground about a thousand yards north of the tower on Irving Avenue, who had come across a Stinger and operator, was part of a brilliantly thought-out plan, but it was in fact sheer luck. Shortly after the militia machine gunner had commenced firing on the descending Airborne, who couldn't fire back for fear of hitting fellow paratroopers, the Airborne captain ordered the Stinger operator to fire. The soldier, his right cheek against the launcher's sight housing, his eye on the iron sight, activating the infrared sensor, waited for the tone. There was none, but he had the tower in the open sight and pulled the trigger. The five-and-a-half-foot-long, 2.76-inch-diameter missile was launched, its solid fuel rocket giving off a backblast so powerful it momentarily scooped out a trough in the water puddle behind the soldier, the missile now deploying its eight control vanes, the soldier listening intently amid the unending cacophony of the battle. He heard the high-pitched tone, signaling that the 6.6-pound high-explosive-head missile was in lock-on, streaking at over 1,400 miles an hour to the target's heat source, in this case a very overheated M60. A brilliant flash was momentarily reflected in the low stratus by smashed glass, the tower's top wreathed in swirling dense white smoke. At that moment there was a rush of Airborne troops eastward along Irving Avenue across Sixteenth and east from the burned-out remains of the bed-and-breakfasts as troops, bottled up for so long by the militia gunner in the tower, hoped to make up for lost time.

A recovering heart patient, watching from a window at Columbia Memorial Hospital, cheered wildly as the smoke cleared and it could be seen that the machine gunner, along with his weapon, had vanished. The militiamen at the base of the column who'd been guarding the tower entrance against attack were still scattering from the falling debris, one militiaman who for whatever reason didn't have a helmet felled by the machine gun's red-hot breech, which killed him instantly. A surge of radio traffic, like a huge sea swell racing at the Columbia, rolled through Astoria with the news that the tower gunner had been taken out.

The removal of the gunner was the impetus for an assault against the Astoria end of YB. In fact, one was already under way when the machine gunner had been killed. Nevertheless, the news had galvanized all the paratroopers in and around Astoria, lifting them out of the defensive mind-set they'd assumed after the overshoot mess, which had struck at the heart of their tactical integrity as a fighting unit and temporarily, fatally for some, slowed them down. The success of the Gulf War notwithstanding, this mess wasn't unusual in the first hours of any offensive, especially when, like Arnhem in '44, it involved so much swampy, low-lying terrain.

If the three thousand Airborne north of the Columbia were infused with renewed purpose, their fellow paras five to ten miles away on the Columbia's south side, in and around Clatsop County, were still involved in what historians would later call a "consolidation of forces." This meant they were trying, in one paratrooper's words, to find out exactly "where the fuck we are."

In fact, small, handheld GPS—Global Positioning Systems—did tell the Airborne exactly where they were, in terms of map-grid reference, to the nearest three feet. But the Airborne was still desperately trying to match up targets with ad hoc groups of forces that had been blown way off course, groups the regiment sergeant major described as "wanderin' around the battlefield—like freakin' zombies!" Compounding the problem was the fact that the militias had proved more mobile than even the most optimistic Pentagon prediction. It wasn't simply that the militia was better trained than most regular-army troops expected or that they had a veritable fleet of hard "knock-'em-sock-'em" well-equipped four-wheel-drive vehicles. Their real "ace in the hole," as Shelbourne had so mundanely put it, was that each militiaman knew the battleground intimately, including those involved in the dirty, no-quarter-given, house-to-house fighting going on in town even as militiamen at the northern end of Old Youngs Bay Bridge were trying to beat off the rush of five hundred Airborne. The Airborne assault on the northern end of YB had split into two prongs 250 yards apart. The western prong crossed Olney Avenue at West Marine, the eastern prong forcing the issue, charging through ethereal wisps of waist-high fog that had rolled in from Youngs Bay.

By this time, several miles east, on the northern side of the Columbia, Zoë Nadet had finally managed to reach her husband, who lay dead, his eyes staring skyward in an expression of complete surprise. Zoë heard movement in the river and grabbed her husband's weapon only to have it fly from her hands, her body punched back by an M-16 burst from an Airborne soldier who was wading frantically to shore against the current while another soldier behind him disappeared, his pack dragging him down after his chute collapsed in on him, lines tangling about his head, part of the chute still inflated like a small khaki-green balloon.

When the trooper who'd fired at the figure he'd seen on the riverbank staggered ashore and discovered he'd killed a woman, her left breast a bloody pulp, he fell to his knees. Her eyes were still open. His weapon fell from his hands into the blood-speckled weeds and he took off his helmet, water dripping from its canvas cover. He heard a rustle of grass, grabbed his M-16, and rolled, to no avail, the roar of shotgun blasts the last sound he'd ever hear, his body broken, sliding back down the bank, coming apart in the mud.

For both victor and vanquished in this short, deadly engagement, it had been the first human being they had killed, and except for those who had seen action in the Gulf War, it was like this for most of the militia and federals on both sides of the Columbia. And while most of them would never forget the bloody scenes, the bullet-ripped bodies strewn along the enormous reach of water running down to the sea, its grayness reflecting the gray of a leaden sky, the thing that would always stay with them was the smell. It was a mix of the spicy heaviness of early-summer plants, the salty tang of the Pacific on the strong sea breeze that swept in across the bar and up over the cliffs and dunes, and the putrid, nose-stuffing odors of urine, feces, and dead flesh. The smell and the impatient screech of gulls and other birds waiting to feast on the bloated dead.

But for now, such images had to be shunted aside in the sheer necessity of staying alive as the enemy pressed home its attack. Most of the fighting was no longer taking place mano a mano but by groups of combatants as the Airborne, only a few hundred stragglers left, collected together in units, albeit not their own, and engaged in specific tactical objectives such as that against the Astoria side of the YB. Aiding the Airborne was the fact that the militia was now feeling the shock of the Airborne's howitzers, which, though few in number because of the disastrous overshoot, began tearing apart any attempt by the militia to congregate in anything above section size. And there were situations around the approaches to both ends of AB where sections of even less than the normal ten-militiaman squad were literally blown apart by the 155mms that shuffled through the air over the river to land by pylons with devastating effect.

At the southern end of YB, however, where no explosions of artillery shells were sending spumes of earth and water into the air, some militia were now approaching battalion size. As Nestar's column approached the bridge from this end, the white flag was still held aloft by the now-weeping acne-faced teenager who had given away Myers to the very man who was forcing him to do this.

"Bastards!" the Airborne's General Trevor growled on the south side of Youngs Bay along the 26, looking north through his binoculars. "Scumbags!"

His aide, a colonel, concurred. "They're trying to blackmail us!"

"They're not *trying* anything," the general retorted. "Sons-of-bitches are *doing* it. How in hell can we fire on civilians? Damn!" He pulled down the binoculars. "You realize what this means? If we lose this end of the bridge we'll lose the whole goddamn bridge and they'll have our boys in Astoria cut off."

The general had known for some time that he was on the short list for promotion to the new chairman of the joint chiefs. A successful operation here might clinch it. A failure would definitely knock him out of contention. Well then, let Douglas Freeman as overall C-in-C, NWTO—Northwest Theater of Operations—make the call. Freeman had been so hot to trot, to grab the glory. Let "George C. Scott" take the responsibility.

Trevor turned quickly, striding toward his Hummer. "Let's kick it upstairs, Colonel."

"Yes, sir."

The general sensed the other's hesitation. "Out with it, Charlie. You think I'm abrogating my command." Off to the east they could hear the deep, gut-felt thump of another howitzer battery opening up.

"No, sir. Not at all," the colonel assured him. "Can I speak off the record?"

"Shoot!"

"It's political dynamite, General. I think you're absolutely right to give Freeman a chance to earn his pay." He paused. " 'Course, George C. Scott might kick it upstairs to Shelbourne!"

"No, he won't."

Geysers of salt water from an Airborne battery's fire shot skyward around the northern end of YB, the final volley as the attacking Airborne from Shively Park were getting too close to the militia. If the battery fired again they could very well hit their own men. On the southern side of the bridge the militia-cum-civilian column under Nestar moved onto the south end. It'd have to be a quick decision from Freeman. "My concern," continued the colonel, "is that we won't be able to reach him up in the Cascades."

"We'll reach him," Trevor replied confidently. "If he's got a cellular we'll get him. Dispatch a radio plane out of Spokane."

Despite his confident tone, however, Trevor was more worried than he'd ever been. He could lose the bridge while he was waiting.

Within seconds the colonel had contacted Fairchild Air Force Base in Spokane, sending the query about what to do vis-à-vis the civilians from Trevor, C-in-C FEDFOR Astoria NWTO, to General Freeman, C-in-C FEDFOR NTO. And then, still using that day's encryption code, "salmon," Trevor called his commander of the force at the southern end of YB. "Lieutenant, stall that fucker coming toward you with civilians in tow. I don't care how you do it, just do it. Stall 'im!"

"Yes, sir," came a hesitant reply.

Next, General Trevor called the Airborne's CO in Astoria, and could hear the rattle of small-arms fire and yelling in the background. "Pull troops from the town," he ordered. "From anywhere you can, to reinforce your rush at your end. Take it before this damned maniac puts civilians on your end."

There was a garbled reply.

"Say again," demanded the general, his eyes on the bridge.

The rush-force commander was confused. What civilians? Did the general mean the militia?

"I mean hostages!" Trevor bellowed, startling the Hummer driver who was concentrating hard on Highway 26 as more fog rolled in from the sea. "I mean," the general hurried on, "the mad-ass militiaman who's using a bunch of damned civilians as a shield—women and kids among them." It was obvious to him that his Astoria commander knew nothing about Nestar and his column.

"Not sure if we can do that in time, General."

"I don't want to hear what you can't do!" shouted the general. "Show me what you *can* do."

Trevor snapped shut his cellular, slipping it into his left-side holster, a standard-issue .45 in the other. "Goddammit, Colonel!"

"General?" asked his aide.

"Keep calling him back. Tell him we have to take that bridge. Us having the big bridge'll be no use to us or to the reinforcements from Portland and California if we can't get over Youngs Bay, for Christ's sake."

"Yes, sir."

Nestar was furious, his beet-red face contrasting sharply with the scar on his chin. Hearing the increased Airborne radio traffic, he'd tried to cut in with "Rosebud" as the entry word of the day, only to be met by frying-pan static. "Those two Airborne bastards," he told Sporter, "lied to me! Fucking bastards!" He glowered ahead at the south end of the Old Youngs Bay Bridge through the incoming fog. "All right, you bastards. I'm taking this fucking bridge! I'll 'Rosebud' you, you pricks!"

CHAPTER TWENTY-THREE

IN THE CASCADES, Marte Price was waiting impatiently for something to happen. Like all the other reporters she had been stopped at Pateros by the FBI, which, with General Freeman's agreement—indeed, with his encouragement—wasn't allowing anyone past the roadblock on Highway 153 just south of where the tank platoon had been routed, and General Limet killed, by McBride's militia at the beginning of the war.

Freeman and anyone else who was sent to the Gulf War had learned the great lesson of Vietnam: *control the press.* Allow them a reporter pool with access to daily briefings, but don't let them anywhere near the front, where they could transmit images of body bags and dead Americans. Do what Stormin' Norman did—corral them. Let them compete with one another in the heat of the press conference and turn all their energy and thirst for news in on themselves.

Marte Price had been in the Gulf as a reporter and knew the drill. She remembered how Bob Simon and his CBS team had gone into territory where they were told not to go and how they had been captured by the Iraqis. Schwarzkopf couldn't have asked for a better justification of his policy. In any event, never again would the

U.S. Army let reporters and photographers loose as they had in 'Nam.

Marte Price, however, had an ego as big as Douglas Freeman's. She hadn't become one of CNN's darlings by being content to stand around among the other reporters, and she refused to participate in the reporter's final act of frustration—interviewing other reporters. Along with the other correspondents, she had heard a rumor that apparently, when talk of sending a federal force to the Cascades was rife, some militiamen, about to head home after the aborted Spokane conference, had received an urgent call from General Mant to reinforce the militia in the mountains. Nearly all the reporters, who, incidentally, were making a motor-home renter in Yakima rich by camping out at the Pateros roadblock, had duly reported the rumor but did no more. Marte Price was the exception. She had gone to the most senior FBI agent at the roadblock, Tracy Albright, and asked her if the rumor was true.

Yes, Tracy told her, apparently Mant had made such a request, but as to how many had answered or would answer the call the FBI had no idea. It took Marte an hour in the "bizarre bazaar," as she called the collection of FBI, army, international and national press, and onlookers swarming about Pateros, to locate one of the charter pilots who was doing a brisk business bringing in reporters, to take her *out* twenty-seven miles north to the airstrip at Omak.

It was a small town nestled in the valley formed by the Okanagan River as it cut its way south through the mountains to join the Columbia a few miles east of Pateros. Omak, she saw, was the obvious point of entry into Mant's mountainous redoubt for anyone who, traveling west from Spokane, wanted to enter by the back door, avoiding the roadblock at the more immediate entry point at Pateros.

On the Omak airstrip she told the charter pilot to wait an hour. Then she took a cab—it looked like the only one—into town and asked to go to the busiest bar. The cabbie drove to the Triple C—Clark's Cider Cellar— pickup trucks aplenty outside, battered and mud-caked.

Though it was noon, the bar was dark, and crowded, smelling of stale beer and stale smoke, an old paper toilet-seat cover pinned up on the wall with BILL CLINTON'S CAMPAIGN POSTER written on it. True-blue, redneck country and no apology.

The room went quiet and heads turned. The barman took one look at Marte's to-die-for looks, her easy confident walk, poured another Bud for one of the men at the bar, and said, "A liberal"—like it was cancer.

"What can I do for you?" he then asked, big smile, happy to watch her breathe in the cream-colored sweater. In return, Marte treated him to her best sexy, redneck-winning smile. "I'll have a Bud."

"You betcha!"

She slapped a hundred on the counter and said she wanted to talk to any militiaman. She gave her cellular number to the barman—aloud—not expecting anyone to approach her in the bar.

"You a reporter?" he asked.

"You betcha."

There were a few grunty laughs.

She took a sip of beer and dabbed her lips with a Kleenex, telling him, "I'll be in town for the next half hour. Whatever I hear will be from an anonymous source. But I'm not paying for bullshit!" She downed her Bud and walked toward the "Bitches' " room, as opposed to the door marked "Sons-of-Bitches," to give them time, and on the way, her eyes now accustomed to the smoky darkness, she glimpsed a few militia uniforms. She thought she'd made a sufficiently no-nonsense appeal that her cellular should start ringing.

Nothing. After five minutes she exited the male dominion, rattling their chains with "Bye, boys!" Catcalls and whistles accompanied her exit.

Surely someone had recognized her. It was cold and she got back into the cab, telling the driver to wait. She received a call ten minutes later. She leaned forward, closer to the back of the driver's seat, and turned the volume way up. The caller said his name was Dan. Yeah, he was militia. No, he wouldn't tell her which militia, but if she wanted to talk, for the right price he'd meet her six miles out of town. "Green pickup," he told her. "Get out of the cab and wait."

"Alone?" she said. "You've got to be kidding. I'm staying in the cab. You come and see me."

"Cabbie knows me."

"That's your problem. I'll give you fifty for showing up. A hundred if it's good information."

"That's a hundred and fifty?"

"If it's good. I'll decide."

"I'll think about it."

"Fine. I'll give you five minutes, then I'm outta here."

"I'll think about it." He hung up.

"You hear that voice?" she asked the cabbie, turning down the volume.

"No," he lied.

She slumped back into her seat.

The charter pilot waiting for her at the airstrip had slipped another Flight Simulator game into his laptop and was losing when he saw a four-seater Cessna emerging from the gray canopy of rain clouds, coming in to land. He recognized the woman who alighted as one of the FBI agents from the Pateros blockade, but was not so sure about the man who was wearing a blue jacket with the letters ATF on the back.

When they came over to him they flashed their agency ID, introduced themselves as Tracy Albright and Alan Gordon, and asked him if he knew where Marte Price was.

He affected surprise. "How would I know?"

"Hey," cautioned Gordon, a twin for "Mr. Glad" only in a blue shirt and trousers, in his late forties, blond hair thinning. "We found out you put yourself up for hire. That's against ROE."

"ROE?" said the pilot. "That *Roe versus Wade?*"

"Hey," said Mr. Glad. "Don't try to be a smart-ass. You're in enough trouble already."

Tracy gave the pilot a smile. "ROE—rules of engagement."

The pilot shrugged. "They're your rules, not mine."

"They're everybody's," Tracy explained, "as laid down by General Freeman. Under the Antiterrorist Bill we're all, strictly speaking, under martial law." Tracy paused. She was relaxed, as much as she could be after Tony Beck's death. She touched the pilot's arm. "Is she in town?"

"Haven't a clue."

Al Gordon's blood pressure was rising. "You know she's a reporter—TV?" he said.

"Yeah, I recognized her." He didn't take his eyes off the laptop's screen.

Al Gordon kept pushing. "She didn't say what she was doing up here?"

"Nope."

"Okay," said Tracy. "We'll stick around for a while."

The pilot shrugged again, still not looking up. "Free country."

Tracy didn't like him, didn't like his cavalier, snooty attitude. He obviously thought playing with his laptop more important than answering their questions.

"Well," she told him, "it was a free country two days ago. Now we're under emergency powers."

"Uh-huh."

"Yeah," put in Al Gordon. "Means we could lock you up if we think you're holding out on us."

"Uh-huh."

"Yeah," said Al. "We could take away your laptop. I'm serious." He paused to let it sink in. "So did any militia come out to meet her?"

"No one came."

Gordon waited for a few seconds, then turned to Tracy. "Maybe we should take away his laptop."

"She took a cab," said the pilot.

"She tell you when she'd be back?"

He shook his head. *Screw the federals. No wonder they pissed off the militia.* He wanted to tell Al Gordon to fuck off.

"We'll wait for her," said Tracy.

"Free country."

CHAPTER TWENTY-FOUR

FREEMAN WAS FUMING. Here he was as far as he could go along War Creek, where the winding course of ice they'd been following ran out. And he couldn't push forward into the bush because he was waiting for the canine corps, which was set to deliver, preferably by helo but by parachute drop if necessary, the two "sniffer" dogs and handlers he'd requested.

He'd understood that it would take some hours to get the plastic-bagged clothes of the suspects in the attorney general's assassination from the room in the Spokane hotel. Meanwhile Freeman had given orders to his men deployed on either side of the creek to check their fields of fire so that if by chance McBride's troops were coming down from the "thermal patch" on the ridge near the Ames cabin to attack Freeman's force, the latter would be ready.

Andy, Freeman's radio operator, hastily tore a two-by-four-inch printout from his radio/fax printer and thrust it at Freeman. "C-in-C Astoria, sir." It was Trevor's question about what to do with civilians on Old Youngs Bay Bridge. Freeman thought about it, scribbled a reply on the back of the printout, signed it with a flourish, and handed it back to his radio operator. "Immediate, Andy. Top priority. C-in-C Astoria."

"Yes, sir."

Frowning, Freeman surveyed his own situation.

"Only thing worse than fixed fortifications, Norton, is sitting still. God, how I hate sitting still."

"Oh, I don't know," said Norton. "You've been on a few ambushes yourself, General."

"I have, but then we were setting a trap. We pretty well knew what was coming. But this . . . I'm not master of my fate here, Norton. I'm waiting for a couple of god-damn dogs."

"It's worth the wait, General. I think it was in character—original, brilliant." Norton paused. "Hope I don't sound like a suck-up?"

"Well, I couldn't think of any other way to find these

two bastards. Can't hold up a goddamn FBI sketch to the militias and ask, 'Would the suspects in Sheila Courtland's assassination kindly give themselves up?' " Freeman glanced out from their blind beneath an old moss-covered fir that had fallen by the creek's edge. "Dammit, I wanted to be in position before those bombers—"

"General!" It was Andy. "Sir, dog chopper's on its way. ETA 0120."

Freeman, visibly relieved, turned over his watch. Its luminescent dial was always kept facedown on his wrist so as to not give away position at night. It was 0112.

"Eight minutes," said Norton, "he'll be—" There was a terrifying Stuka-like scream—militia mortar squads had attached "freak-out" Nazi whistles to their rounds.

"Incoming!" someone shouted. The next second there was a loud *whoomp* and a shattering sound like broken glass, as the mortar round slammed into the frozen creek. Shards of ice spun in the air with the sound of gnats, and shrapnel whizzed into the underbrush either side of the creek. No one was hurt until the second mortar bomb exploded on the creek's northern side. The shrapnel hit a Ranger, and sliced off his left ear and nose. Bleeding profusely, another man went down with a gaping chest wound, his buddy yelling for a medic.

There was another scream followed by a fierce rattling sound of shredding undergrowth, the sharp odor of cordite in the air.

Already Freeman had designated a fire team of four to locate the mortar. It would have to be in an open space in the woods somewhere, otherwise the 60mm rounds wouldn't be clearing the trees. Two of Freeman's men carried 5.56mm M249 SAWs and two M203 M-16s with 40mm grenade launchers, and they split up into two pairs, going either side of the creek. Both teams moved quickly over the treacherously narrow strip of frozen ground between the icy creek and the trees, these under-growth-free strips along the embankment marking the high-water level of the creek during the melt that up here wouldn't come for another month.

The two teams heard another high whistle, and a round exploded fifty yards behind them as they approached a bend in the river. There was a stutter and both teams went to ground, AK-47 bullets kicking up splinters of ice, Freeman's four now returning fire at what they esti-mated was a patrol of about nine men. If each enemy sol-dier was carrying a normal load of two 60mm ten-pound rounds, in addition to their normal pack, they would have a total of sixteen, maybe eighteen, mortar rounds. They'd already fired four, leaving a max of twelve remaining. Meanwhile Freeman's two teams kept directing their fire in the general direction of the enemy patrol.

Abruptly the mortar ceased, its crew probably moving away from the Special Forces' machine-gun fire as ten more men from Freeman's position now caught up with the original four he'd sent out, adding their firepower. A half dozen of them slipped into the woods on the left-hand side of War Creek, forming a line, going quickly to ground amid fern and second-growth timber, waiting, the remainder of Freeman's force, forty-one in all, now coming to assist, a helo's *wokka-wokka* sound, a Huey, filling the rugged valley. Freeman realized that it was probably the sight of the helo that had caused the enemy mortar position to fold house and move into the woods, the militia assuming, correctly, that the Huey was sporting two M60 machine guns.

"Christ," said Freeman, glancing up at the chopper, "what a time to arrive. Andy, tell that Huey pilot to set down at the head of the creek. Behind us."

"Bit narrow," put in Norton.

"Or," said Freeman, his voice louder above the hard, chaotic noise of helo and gunfire, "lower the dogs and handlers in harness if necessary. And tell him we've got two injured for evac."

A few seconds later Andy reported that the pilot requested purple smoke.

"No!" Freeman replied. "It'd make a perfect target marker for that goddamn mortar—and tell those two machine gunners with him not to shoot *us*!"

"Yes, sir."

The firefight grew in intensity as the helo, taking advantage of the cover provided by the bend in the creek, began to descend toward the fifty-foot-wide slab of ice that lay just beyond, blowing up a storm of snow and brambles. Now the militia's mortar opened up again, the first round overshooting into the trees beyond the ice, the next two rounds exploding closer, both of Freeman's two-man teams estimating another eight rounds maximum, the helo pulling up over the trees out of range of the exploding mortar bombs. The next few mortar rounds landed on the western side of the creek, wounding another two of Freeman's men, bits of fir branch and frozen soil raining down with the ice, another four mortar bombs landing on the ice itself, cracking it so badly that what moments before had been a possible LZ for the helo was now a liquid mass of ice chunks and dirty water churned up by the explosions.

"Tell the chopper," Freeman yelled to Andy, "he'll have to deliver by harness."

"Can he make a pass with his machine guns?" Norton inquired, ducking as another rain of debris clattered all about him.

"No," answered Freeman, "I can't risk him getting close enough to get hit. Bastards may have a Stinger."

As Andy spoke into the radio Norton saw the Huey

returning toward them, hovering anxiously well beyond the broken-up ice. "Tell him to hurry up," Freeman told Andy.

Andy was in the process of transmitting when another mortar bomb came whistling through the air like a Stuka, and intuitively Freeman knew it was coming right at the HQ group. They all went to ground, heard an explosion, felt the earth tremble, a rush of heat over them, and a crash as if someone had hit Andy's radio pack with a sledgehammer. It might as well have been a hammer, the chunk of mortar casing embedded in the set having totaled it. Though the radio backpack had saved Andy's life, he was none too happy, uttering a string of expletives to vent his feelings about the militia, whom he repeatedly referred to as "dickheads!"

"All right, Andy," Freeman told him, indicating the mess that had been a radio. "Dump it and grab your rifle. Stay close. Might have to use you as a runner."

"Must nearly be out of mortar ammo," Norton opined, "if they were carrying two apiece."

He was wrong. Rymann's squad, carrying only emergency dried-food rations and water canteens, had loaded four ten-pound rounds a man instead of the normal two. Twice as many bombs as Freeman's force had thought. Freeman was in a dilemma. Should he forge on up toward the ridge where the thermal-patch pix had indicated the bulk of the militia force was, to carry out his mission of apprehending, killing if necessary, the two suspects in Sheila Courtland's murder, and risk the enemy squad harassing them from the rear? Or should he fight here and silence the militia squad but by doing so risk the withdrawal of his main company-size target indicated by the thermal emission? Above all he wanted to avoid splitting his drastically reduced force of fifty-five, some of whom were wounded badly enough for immediate evac.

Freeman decided to go over on the offensive right here against the enemy squad—at least wipe out the damned mortar that would otherwise dog his progress toward the thermal-emission area. While he and his line of Special Forces men on the western side of the creek moved slowly toward the enemy, a detached assault element of ten men, led by Medal of Honor veteran of Special Forces David Brentwood, went wide on Freeman's left flank to close in on the mortar squad's right, pushing it toward the frozen creekbed or as near as the danger of "friendly fire" would permit.

Among the most aggressive of Brentwood's assault team was an Australian-born 'Nam vet, Aussie Lewis, who had served with Brentwood on several of Freeman's Special Force insertions and was known to be an especially good close-in fighter. As much as David Brentwood was reserved, until it came time to fight, Aussie was free and easy with his opinions, which were liberally salted with four-letter words. He had once given English lessons to Vietnamese serving women, who, after offering hors d'oeuvres to high-ranking allied officers and being thanked, bowed and, as per the Australian's instructions, smiled sweetly, telling the officers to "Piss off!" The army's criminal-investigation department had never solved the case.

"'Bout fucking time we aced these assholes!" said Aussie as Brentwood passed on the order and the ten-man squad moved out. Meanwhile Freeman, knowing the chopper was getting low on fuel, had no choice but to let the Huey come in low above the trees, to try to deliver the two dogs and handlers by harness. As he spotted the chopper, which had been temporarily hidden by a dip in the trees, Freeman ordered covering fire. His men on either side of the creek opened up, the air soured now with the stink of the helo's exhaust fumes and filled again with the sound of battle.

Freeman heard another *whoomph*—the militia bracketing the already broken-up LZ, the chopper hovering just above the trees, beginning to lower a man in harness and a bamboo cage with black rubberized impact strips all about it. The man and his dog were suspended twenty feet above the roiling, ice-cold soup of shattered ice and dirty creek water, the pilot edging the Huey, its fuselage taking hits, closer to the margin of clear ground between the creek's edge and the trees.

Two mortar rounds, only seconds apart, smashed into the LZ, the Huey pilot feeling a push of hot air from the concussion, fist-size lumps of ice flying up and out in a V pattern. The dog handler slumped inert in the harness, the bamboo cage beneath him rocking dangerously. The pilot lowered them both to the ground, and Andy ran back from Freeman's position around the edge of the creek to disengage the slide hook on the harness. The handler was dead, not from the mortar explosions but from three bullet holes in his neck and head, a pinkish-gray ooze dripping down from inside his helmet. The dog was a medium-size, sixty-pound black-brown Belgian Malinois, unhurt as far as Andy could tell, and when released he sat by his dead handler's side as Andy extracted the man's body and immediately signaled the pilot to retract the harness cable.

The chopper veered away to the right, away from War Creek, even as the second handler and his dog were being hooked up, ready for their descent.

Moving wide against the mortar position, Brentwood's assault team was fired upon by the enemy squad's right flank. There were only four militia but they were in good defensive positions, using the heavy timber to maximum effect. Grenades were useless in the thick undergrowth, and Brentwood knew the only way to take them out was by getting in close. "Cover!" he shouted as he, Aussie, and two others moved from tree to tree, each man knowing from long experience that their buddies in the squad, three left, three right of them, would pour as much fire as possible at the militia defense while they advanced.

One of Rymann's militiamen, Sammy Komura, heard the dead man's click—out of ammo. He quickly reloaded and popped his head above a big log to get a line of sight. Brentwood fired a burst from the hip and Komura's head disintegrated. Aussie was less than twelve feet away as the blood-bubbling torso, all that remained of Komura, was flung back against a tree, and his buddy, a ranch hand from Montana, swung his M-16 toward Brentwood. Aussie fired his rotary-mag shotgun, twenty-seven pellets of hardened number-four buckshot shredding fern and blowing the cowboy militiaman back over a log, his face and chest ripped open, right hand still moving on his M-16. Aussie gave him another shot and his face peeled off. To the left, Aussie glimpsed one of his buddies going down, hit by a hail of AK-47 bullets a split second before the man who'd fired them was also killed. A militiaman raised his arms, and Aussie, covered by Brentwood, put his knife against the man's throat. "Two seconds, boyo!" he told him. "Where's the fuckin' mortar?"

The militiaman, who was in his mid-thirties, about as old as Aussie, moved his head back and to the right. "A hundred yards—" he told Aussie, his voice high with the threat of the knife. "'Bout a hundred yards."

With that, Brentwood's assault team quickly tied up the militiaman like a steer in a rodeo. They cut his shoelaces with one stroke of a knife and took away his boots, tossing them into the underbrush where he couldn't see them. Then they moved quickly through the second growth in the direction he'd indicated, nerves taut, looking, listening. There was a flash of light, a tremendous bang, a wide arc of red-hot ball bearings cutting down two of Brentwood's men, one slicing Aussie's thigh, his cold-weather camouflaged overlay sodden with blood. "Shit!" Now two men behind what Brentwood guessed must be a claymore-defended perimeter opened up with AK-74s—a faster rate of fire than the AK-47s. But Brentwood had their position pinpointed and called over to Aussie, "Willy Pete two o'clock."

"Got it!" Aussie answered. "Keep the fuckers occupied!" With that, ignoring his bloodied flesh wound, he swiftly moved from tree to tree, but only after checking for trip wires and/or claymores that might be set for remote firing, the sheer noise of battle about him deafening as Freeman's main body of forty—fewer by now—kept firing in the general direction of the mortar site, though they still couldn't see it.

Then Aussie spotted the small clearing, only twenty yards across, mossy trees all about it, and a pile of spent mortar-round carrying cases strewn about. He could see only the helmet top of the man feeding the mortar, the other man out of sight, no doubt kneeling near the base plate. Getting to within thirty feet of them, where he had a clear line of sight, Aussie pulled the pin, tossed a Willy Pete grenade, then another, their startling white light almost blinding in its intensity, especially given the overcast conditions, the explosions—long, spirally fingers of white-hot phosphorus—looking momentarily like some fantastic white spider whose multiple legs supported a beautifully incandescent blob above. The two-man mortar squad began screaming. The more they tried to smack out the pieces of fire all over them the more they screamed, the suffocation of the remarkably adhesive phosphorus tendrils achieved more by the wet underbrush than the two wounded men slapping at the chemical.

Both men, one with bad facial burns, were hustled back by one of Brentwood's assault team, Aussie and Brentwood staying behind to spike the 60mm mortar and collect the AK-47s from what had been Rymann's squad. Piling the now dysfunctional weapons under a big fir log, Brentwood, Aussie, and Andy grabbed some of the enemy's ammo for themselves. On their way back, adrenaline now subsiding, Aussie's injured left leg suddenly gave out and he fell to the forest floor. "I'll send a medic," said David Brentwood. "Hold tight."

"Would you like a beer?" Andy asked.

"Yeah."

"Who wouldn't?" said Andy, his *NYPD Blue* eyebrows moving up, shooting a glance at Brentwood, who grinned.

"Fuck you, Andy!" said Aussie.

"Promise?"

When the medic-cum-rifleman Lawson arrived, he brought a hangdog, apologetic look to every move. "Aussie?"

"Yeah."

"Used your morphine injector?"

"Nope."

"You'll have to. My main pack was shot to rat shit. The other medic's got some, but, well—old man says we gotta save it for the attack on the thermal-pix area."

"Huh, old man's right," said Aussie, "but I seriously doubt there's gonna be any thermal-body-heat area after this punch-up. Mant'll probably move 'em somewhere else."

"Well, anyway," said Lawson, licking his dry lips,

"we'll use your injector now for the pain, but listen, I lost all my suture stuff in that hit." Aussie was grimacing as the medic pulled the morphine Syrette from Aussie's helmet's elastic band and wiped his left arm with the patch of alcohol that left an ice-cold spot. Lawson plunged the Syrette into Aussie's arm, then threw it away and began to tape the wound.

The medic offered to help him walk back to Freeman's HQ position nearer the creek. "I'm not paralyzed, for Christ's sake."

"All right," said Lawson. "Be a fucking martyr."

"It's just a flesh wound, right?"

"Yeah."

"Then I can walk."

"Unless you lose too much—" Lawson looked down at the militiaman they'd left bootless and trussed up. He was dead, a neat hole in his forehead, the back of his head gone, its detritus already swarming with ants. Aussie had no sympathy for him. Life is hard; besides, the prick had sent 'em right into the claymores and they'd lost two more, Freeman's force now down to thirty-nine, their bodies under what had been their ponchos but what were now their death sheets. Then Aussie and Lawson saw the wreck that had been the Huey, in and around which several men were huddled, there now being no danger of fire since its gas tank ruptured. Ironically it had been brought down by Rymann's squad's small fire and not mortar shrapnel, the second and now only dog handler having successfully rappelled down with his canine before the Huey's tail rotor had been all but shot off.

"Do we have the squad leader?" asked Freeman. A lone militia prisoner, boots gone, said nothing, shivering with cold and fright though he'd fought well.

"What's your name, soldier?" Freeman asked.

"Ovitz, sir. Henry Ovitz."

"Unit?"

Ovitz said nothing.

"You're a problem, Ovitz—you realize that? We can't take you with us, so I guess I'll have to leave a man with you. We'll cuff you and I want you to sit nice and quiet. Understand?"

Ovitz nodded, obviously in awe of the general.

"You start trouble and my man here'll shoot you."

"Yes, sir."

"Good." The general left behind a Special Forces man, who had a foot wound so bad he couldn't walk, with two Mark-13 day/night flares and a purple smoke grenade for whenever a chopper could come in with litters to carry out the most serious cases from the battle zone.

Freeman and his thirty-nine, plus the dogs and lone handler, began their trek up the mountainside in the direction of the Ames cabin but focusing first on an adjoining ridgeline. The latter connected the bases of two mountain peaks and hid, at least to the naked eye, the TEA—the thermal-emission area—which any second now should be softened up by bombing.

Freeman's force was traversing the base of the mountain, heading for the TEA, when the B-52's string of bombs hit the ridge between the two mountains. Freeman was far enough off not to be part of any "collateral damage" but close enough to attack the militia's dug-in position before the militia had time to recover and re-organize after the earth-trembling trauma of a "stick" of B-52 ground-gouging HE bombs, some of which would not explode until they'd penetrated several meters below the ground. But without Andy's radio, Freeman had no way of asking the B-52 three-plane cell to delay their bombing run. By now the cell, so high as to be invisible even if there hadn't been thick cloud cover, would have already turned and be heading back to Fairchild.

Aussie was pushing himself to stay on Freeman's left in what was now a triangular arrowhead-formation assault, one three-man A-team to Freeman's left, assault team B, under Brentwood, to his right, a demolition team forming the rear echelon—the two dogs and the one surviving handler up front with Freeman's HQ section.

Each Malinois dog had a "bringsel," a four-inch stick hanging from its collar by a four-inch strand of fishing line, the dog ignoring the stick until it found the source of the smell it was tracking. Trained not to bark in such circumstances as required stealth, the dog, if it found its quarry, would take the stick in its mouth, returning immediately to its handler without any verbal command by the handler and with a minimum of noise. The two Ziploc bags containing clothing taken by police from Room 301 of Spokane's Imperial Hotel, where Latrell and Hearn had stayed, were clipped to either side of the handler's vest pack. The Malinois were legendary, having been known to track a quarry's smell from items of clothing that had been immersed in formaldehyde for years.

At the moment all Freeman and his men could smell was the deep, bone-chilling dampness of forest and undergrowth and an occasional whiff of skunk and dry dust and cordite thrown up by the explosions of the HE bombs that had turned quivering forests into moon craters. By now Freeman was sure that Lucky McBride's militia company, though having outnumbered his thirty-nine by at least five to one, must be all but annihilated.

CHAPTER TWENTY-FIVE

WHEN TRACY ALBRIGHT saw the taxi from Omak, she asked Al Gordon, BATF's replacement for Tony Beck, if he wanted to talk to Marte Price first.

"Not particularly," said Gordon.

"Ah," Tracy replied good-naturedly. "You want me to take the wrath of CNN?"

"Why not?" Gordon smiled. "ATF gets enough flak."

"We'll all get General Freeman's flak if we let anybody into the combat area. You know how touchy he is about the press."

"Marte Price *should* get flak. Way I hear it she's covered Freeman before. She should know the ropes by now."

"*Should* is the operative word."

As the taxi neared the plane a shower of rain passed overhead, nimbostratus clouds sweeping down from the mountains over the eastern foothills, where mist curled like tendrils of smoke.

As the taxi slowed on the airstrip Marte Price in the backseat turned to the militiaman who, as per her instructions, had joined her from the green pickup. "You sure you'll get the message through?" she asked him.

"No sweat."

"You screw around with me and—"

"I'd love to," he said.

"You screw this up and I'll do a number on you."

"Why would I? You've got more money to pay."

"That's right. Another thousand when I get there."

"Right."

By now the cab had stopped, and as Marte got out she smiled at the two agents. "I know. You're here to tell me to be a good girl."

"Yes," said Tracy. "You shouldn't have left the roadblock."

"Yes," added Al Gordon. "You could get hurt."

"I know," said Marte, turning to her pilot. "Back to Pateros, James."

As Tracy and Alan in turn walked back to their Cessna, Tracy noted that Marte Price had looked pretty pleased with herself. "Must have gotten a good interview with Max the Militiaman."

"Is that his name?"

Tracy laughed, touching his arm. "No—just made it up." It was the first time Al Gordon had heard her laugh since Tony Beck's death. He thought about having her on top, how he'd squeeze her breasts, gently rocking her back and forth.

When her plane took off, Marte Price looked down on the airstrip and saw the taxi, like a micro-toy. Then it disappeared, everything about her a swirling gray.

"In about five minutes," she told the pilot, "I want you to turn around and go back to Omak."

The pilot thought for a moment before he asked, "What'll I tell them after—when I get back to Pateros? I mean they'll want to know where in hell you are." He paused. "You're going into the mountains, right? The back way from Omak to Twisp. You know that road'll probably be sealed off by militia."

"I know," she said, her tone unconcerned. "Tell them—the FBI, whoever asks—that you took me to Grand Coulee Dam. It's about thirty miles southeast of us, right?"

"Yeah." He didn't sound too sure. She unzipped her belt pouch and gave him a hundred. "Look, tell them that after dropping me at Grand Coulee, you don't know where the hell I went. You couldn't be expected to. Okay?"

He took the hundred. He'd turn about in three minutes. "You be careful. Those militia boys are hair triggers these days."

"You know any of them?" she asked. "I mean any of those who are dug in up there?"

He was silent.

"The ones Freeman's up against?" she pressed. "Off the record."

"That mean you won't quote me?"

"That's right. Strictly between you and me."

"Yeah," he said, "I reckon I know a few. Used to do some crop dusting for some of 'em—like old Latrell. He's one the feds are looking for, right? Assassination of the attorney general."

"Yes."

The pilot turned the plane around, flying strictly on instruments. "Can't see a damn thing."

"Tell me about Latrell," Marte asked him.

"Real shit stirrer. Agin the government, 'gin every fuck—sorry."

"No, go on."

"Off the record?"

"Of course."

"Latrell goes looking for trouble."

"How 'bout the skinhead—Hearn?"

The pilot's right forefinger was tapping the control column. He knew the country well, but flying in pea soup was something he had never gotten used to. "If you like I can give you something for the record, but I'd need some encouragement."

"How much?"

"Five hundred."

"You think I'm Rockefeller?"

The pilot laughed. "That's very funny, you know. That's really funny."

"Why?"

"How 'bout four hundred?" he asked.

She gave an exasperated sigh. "Two hundred and you tell me. If I think it's good I'll give you another two."

"Two hundred?"

"Yes."

"Well, you said Rockefeller."

"So?"

"Apparently this skinhead Hearn calls himself Rock now."

"Wow," said Marte. "What a story. I bet the world's just dying to know that." She paused. "That's worth about ten cents—Canadian!"

"I'm not finished," he said defensively, easing the column forward as he began a gentle descent. "Rumor also has it that old Mant—well, he's not really that old, in his fifties I—"

"Fifty-four," she said impatiently. "He's fifty-four. At least we know that much."

"Yeah, well, the story is he put Latrell and the skinhead into the militia company Freeman's up against because he knows there's no way Latrell or the skinhead'll give 'emselves up. That way he puts some stiffener into those militia boys up there in Sawtooth. Smart move."

"What's Mant worried about?" Marte pressed. "Freeman's supposed to be outnumbered four, five to one."

"Well, Freeman's a pro, right? So're his boys."

"Uh-huh, like the tanks he left standing on the highway. Ones the militia blew the shit out of."

The pilot was surprised at her profanity. "That was before Freeman took over," he said.

She handed him another two hundred.

"You won't use my name?"

"I won't," she promised.

The micro-size taxi was still there waiting. As she got out of the plane and into the taxi, the pilot, who'd kept the engine running, waved, turned the plane around, and began his takeoff run.

Back in the cab Marte asked the militiaman if he'd gotten the message through to the militia who were patrolling the back road into Twisp.

"No problem. We're cleared all the way from Omak to Twisp. Thirty miles through the mountains. We've got to fly a white flag from the radio aerial. We'll probably be stopped once or twice, so don't mind if you see someone with an AK-47 coming out of the bush and—oh, shit!"

"What?" she asked. "What's wrong?"

He pointed at the rearview mirror. She could see nothing but the empty airstrip and rain. "Above!" he said, and she caught a glimpse of another micro-toy, a Cessna coming in to land.

"Step on it," the militiaman told the cabdriver. "Fuckin' feds."

"Jesus!" said Marte, slumping disbelievingly. "You didn't use a cellular to contact your buddies?"

"Yeah—why?"

CHAPTER TWENTY-SIX

WITH HIS RADIO gone, Andy was being used, to his intense displeasure, as a runner between Freeman's HQ squad and the assault-and-support teams that made up the thirty-nine-man force. Out on the left flank he told Brentwood's squad, then Aussie's, that despite the thunderous three-plane bombing, infrared scopes were still picking up thermal emission or hot spots from the top of the ridge, now only two hundred yards away.

The HQ squad of nine men would advance cautiously while the other two squads forming the arrowhead, thirty men in all including Brentwood and Aussie, peeled off in flanking movements. Aussie's squad would move right, Brentwood's to higher ground on the left, toward a scrub-covered outcrop three to five feet higher than the line of the ridge from which the federals' infrared sights were picking up the emissions. Snow covered the ground and dusted the trees. It began to rain heavily, as loud as a monsoon.

Someone whispered to Freeman that as most of the militia would be dead or still in shock from the bombing, the strike force should rush the enemy position. "No," Freeman replied, his voice all but lost in the noise of the downpour. "Place could be ringed with claymores."

"Bombing would have rid the area of that, sir."

Goddammit, Freeman told himself. What in Christ's name was wrong with his brain? Of course the bombs' overpressure and shrapnel would have detonated every Elsie mine and claymore within at least a hundred yards of the TEA.

"Would've thought they'd run off down the other side of the ridge," said Norton, "then on up to where the Ames cabin is."

Struck by a sudden sense of unease, Freeman shook his head. "No way. Those bombs start to fall—coming out of nowhere—you don't move, period. Don't you remember?"

Norton didn't answer immediately, then quietly said, "Something's wrong. You know what the Duke used to say. 'It's too quiet out there.' "

"It's raining, for Christ's sake," said Andy, the difference in rank not fazing the men in the Special Operations force. "Can't hear yourself think."

"Don't mean that," said Norton. "It doesn't *feel* right."

"I know," Freeman concurred, estimating that Brentwood on his left would almost be atop the high ground and Aussie's squad in position out to the right. "Somebody ought to be moving," he opined. "Moaning, whatever. Can't all be dead."

"Maybe we got lucky," said Andy. "Bombs got 'em."

Rain streaming from his helmet, Freeman checked both his flanks; he could see the M60 machine guns ready for action, one of the gunners having attached an empty soup can to the side of his weapon for a better belt feed in case his buddy got shot. That was when Freeman knew that Special Forces, as opposed to regular infantry, could make all the difference, since they were trained for extraordinarily swift action, attacking with a ferocity and determination not expected of regular enlisted men. But

Special Forces troopers, especially the SEALs among them, were also trained to wait and wait and then wait some more, if necessary, not to move, to convince the enemy they were not there. Two of Freeman's HQ squad looked again through their infrared and saw whitish patches of heat still rising from the direction of the foxholes along the ridge top. "Dead bodies," said one of the scope men softly. "They'd still give off heat for a while."

Freeman gave the forward signal and on either side of him his two machine gunners and the other heavily armed Special Forces in his squad moved up toward the ridge, crossing an old twenty-yard-wide firebreak; the dog handler was told to stay put with his two charges.

Soon the HQ squad, its flank squads in position, was so close to the TEA that they could see mounds of dirt— foxholes. Freeman gave the rush signal and within seconds the cratered area, trees split and smoldering from the bombing, some of the craters quickly filling with water, was overrun by Freeman's HQ squad. All around they could see what looked like kapok strewn about, giving the Thermal Emission Area the appearance of a town dump, the kapok coming from shrapnel-gutted ski mitts. "Dozens of 'em," said Freeman, perplexed. "What in hell—" He stopped, saw that the mitts were the kind warmed by small double-A batteries and smelling of mothballs.

At that moment two things happened. He thought of all the dumb ads—the little battery-run rabbit with the drum that just keeps on going and going—then he heard the first mortar whistling in. "Perimeter!" he yelled. "It's a trap!" The HQ squad broke from the moonscape of bomb craters toward the flanks, three of them caught in a mortar round's explosion, two killed outright, their body parts blown across the ground, the third man, his leg blown off, crawling toward the shattered trees at the perimeter of the mangy-looking, bombed-out landscape that marked the top of the ridge. David Brentwood and one of his Special Forces troopers ran back and quickly dragged him across the slippery earth into the trees as mortar shrapnel whistled overhead.

Firing was breaking out all over the place beyond the left and right flanks and from the summit of the ridge. Freeman, who in Southeast Asia had been called "Le Général Extraordinaire" and who had distinguished himself in the Gulf and many other incursions around the world, had been caught in a three-sided ambush because he and his men had been suckered into assuming the hot gloves' thermal emissions were those of troops dug in, confirmed by sat pix; meanwhile the militia had come back up the other side of the ridge from cold cover they'd been hiding in during the bombing.

But now Freeman's quick thinking, his ability for a split-second analysis of a situation and an equally fast response, came to the fore. Despite the cacophony of grenades exploding and small-arms fire all around him, the general was cool enough to discern that the only means of an escape, albeit a fighting one, was at five o'clock, away from the top of the ridge. Then he went high-tech, a little trick he'd learned not from all his years in the U.S. Army but from participating in some of the United States' joint maneuvers with his old enemies the Russians. He pulled out his ninety-nine-cent plastic whistle and blew two longs, his signal for a rough, wedge-shaped withdrawal; both his flanks pulled back to form the two sides of an inverted V, Freeman's squad remaining more or less in position to form the tip, and every man firing as they quickly retreated from the TEA back down into the bush. Freeman's inverted-V formation, with only thirty-six men remaining—three having been killed outright in the militia trap, two so badly

wounded they'd had to be left if the rest were to escape—
withdrew as fast as possible. Then ran.

"Holy shit!" yelled one of the militiamen next to
Hearn as the forward elements of the militia, their blood
up with an impending kill, Latrell not far behind them,
watched in amazement. "Look at 'em, Rock. Hot shots."
Hearn, alias "Rock," fired a long burst from his AK-74.
"They broke and ran, Rocky."

Rock ignored the militiaman, the skinhead's eyes on
one of the two Special Forces troopers left behind. The
man's legs had caught shrapnel from a mortar round earlier in the firefight and he'd been given a shot of morphine by a medic who'd had to retreat with Freeman's
force. Now he sat trembling in shock but looking up defiantly at Hearn. The skinhead shot him in the face before
rejoining the militia's charge after Freeman's routed
force.

"Ya-*hoo*!" shouted another militiaman, adrenaline up,
elated at having trapped and now scattering the opposition. "Special Forces, my ass! Runnin' for their lives,
boys. Runnin' for their lives," and he fired another burst
into the second-growth foliage, not seeing any of the
retreating soldiers but hoping to hit one of them anyway.
Freeman's boys were no longer firing, running so hard all
the militia boys could see now was trembling underbrush. The other wounded man from what was now
Freeman's platoon-size force was black, and when one of
the militiamen in the same platoon as Latrell saw him, he
stopped, pointed at the man's testicles, and fired a shot at
point-blank range before moving on. The black man's
ungodly screams echoed into the woods.

A hundred and fifty yards or so ahead, just beyond
the firebreak, there was the sound of a long whistle
quickly followed by two shorts, and now, even as
Freeman's ragged inverted-V-shaped formation kept

going downhill, its metamorphosis took place, the rough-shaped V changing into a straight line, left to right, that suddenly stopped, turned, and went to ground, the unseen militia still charging, a half minute or so behind them. It was here that the legendary physical and mental toughness of the Special Forces showed itself, its SEAL members having come from a training regimen that included daily runs of over six miles on loose sand beaches and seven-man boat crews having to carry a 425-pound inflatable boat up and down dunes and through swamps at night and having to pass through the infamous Hell Week. Some called it torture, striving for a level of fitness that most civilians believe unattainable by human beings, a level of fitness so difficult to achieve that the dropout rate during SEALs training is at times over 80 percent.

Training such as this, so much harder than anything the militias had endured, had washed out Special Forces hopefuls such as Timothy McVeigh, later arrested for the Oklahoma bombing. But now, as Freeman's inverted V became a straight line, it paid off. The Special Forces troopers were ready to charge back *up* the hill in a counterattack against the now winded and overly excited militia, who were crashing through the underbrush toward the firebreak in what they were convinced was a complete and utter rout of Freeman's force.

Rushing downhill pell-mell, the more than a hundred and sixty militiamen, Lucky McBride among them, ran into a sustained roar of automatic fire at the firebreak, each of the suddenly stopped Special Forces conscious of the drain on ammunition, not firing wildly in suppressive fire but picking his target, the roar of the guns so loud that even one of the dogs, trained to withstand such an uproar, was shivering in fright. Militiamen were dropping so fast that Aussie, in a burst of antipodean originality, opined that they were "falling like fuckin' flies" all along the treeless, snow-covered firebreak that allowed the Special Forces a clear field of fire.

Suffering a loss of only four of his men, Freeman's force had killed and otherwise inflicted over seventy casualties on the militia force that now, amid a sea of bullet-flicked snow, began a panicky retreat, turning around, recrossing the firebreak, or as Aussie told it, "dragging their asses" uphill. There was another long whistle and Freeman's strike force was up and not merely running but sprinting across the firebreak, the memory of over forty of their buddies killed in the shootdown of the Chinook above War Creek an added spur to their charge.

Another two Special Forces and eleven of the fleeing militia were killed within a hundred feet of the firebreak, its snow turning red, the Special Forces never hesitating, gaining on the militia whose panic, despite McBride's order to stand their ground, was now complete, the discipline of their squads broken.

It was every man for himself. Even those militia who stopped momentarily to catch their breath, turn around, and fire couldn't aim straight, their chests heaving, out of breath, most of their bursts spraying wildly and ineffectually into the trees. Freeman's force gained on them further, the Special Forces relentlessly maintaining their pursuit.

Aussie, cursing profusely at his injured leg because he couldn't keep up with his buddies, nevertheless found himself a useful job as fullback. He shot and disarmed any militia straggler who'd had the good fortune to have been bypassed by Freeman's terrible line but who resisted capture. Along with the canine-corps handler and his two dogs, Aussie was taking up the rear.

For some of the militia stragglers who were out of

ammunition or badly wounded, the mere sight of the two dogs was enough to encourage surrender, slowing down the Australian even more as he and the handler found themselves, albeit unwillingly, with the job of herding the captured militiamen and wounded Special Forces back to the firebreak. Here Aussie pulled out a signal flare, leaving its high, spiraling column of purple smoke to let "dust-offs"—Medevac choppers—know where to land to pick up casualties and POWs, thirty-seven in all, twenty-eight of them militia.

By now in full retreat, the first elements of the militia, Lucky McBride still among them, broke free of the trees, reaching the bombed-out summit of the ridge. Here they quickly sought the protection of the massive, lunarlike craters that beckoned to them like ready-made foxholes, albeit wet ones, many militiamen, including Latrell and Hearn, simply having the decision to seek shelter in the craters made for them, since the ground was so pockmarked it would have been difficult to cross the ridgeline without encountering one.

The steady rain made for knee-deep wading pools in the bottoms of craters, some of them strewn with split timber and other debris that had fallen after the initial explosions. But if they thought hiding would stop Freeman's force, they were catastrophically mistaken. The thirty Special Forces troopers, at first lobbing hand grenades, followed this by jumping into the craters, where they engaged already demoralized and exhausted militia in an unforgiving hand-to-hand combat. There was nothing heroic about this rain-curtained drama, men being slaughtered, bludgeoned by weapons, shot at point-blank range, slashed and stabbed by Special Forces double-edged blades and militia knives, the Special Forces' ferocity and skill so overwhelming in close fighting that this place above War Creek would come to be named Butcher's Ridge.

The bodies of eight Special Forces and thirty-two militia had fallen in the mud and dirty water of the craters, limbs and other body parts of another eleven militia and two Special Forces scattered, some floating in the bombed-out moonscape, the unceasing rain hampering the dust-offs' evacuation to Pateros. The dead militia included Helmut Werner and Rymann, who had undertaken the militia's first attacks on FEDFOR armor outside Sedro Woolley and the attack on General Limet and the tanks on the eastern side of the Cascades. What was left of Lucky McBride's militia was either surrendering or, led by McBride himself, beating a hasty retreat down the other side of the ridge into the Sawtooth Wilderness toward Lake Chelan.

But if there was evidence of a much-needed FEDFOR victory, even a partial one, here in the Cascades, miles away on the Astoria front there was the malodorous atmosphere of defeat.

When General Trevor, CO FEDFOR Astoria, received General Freeman's decoded response, he was taking a hurried dump by the edge of what unbeknownst to him was a cranberry bog. Watching Trevor use an entrenching tool to quickly bury his deposit and then walk several feet along the bog's edge to wash his hands, his aide was nervous. It wasn't the aide's first time in combat, but it was the first time he had deliberately delayed passing on a battle communiqué, and he realized that any delay before reinforcements could arrive would mean more Airborne casualties. Now he was arguing with himself— maybe it was just his good manners—history must be replete with incidences of messages withheld by subalterns until their superiors were off the can.

The general's ablutions done, the aide walked toward Trevor and handed him Freeman's response to Trevor's question about how to handle the civilians on YB, where Trevor's deputy commander, a mile away on the bridge, surrounded by a surreal scene of war, was nevertheless trying to hold a civil negotiation with Nestar while the boy with the white flag still struggled to keep it upright in the drizzle that had soaked the cloth. Trevor was reading Freeman's instructions:

FIRE ON THEM IF NECESSARY STOP TAKE THE BRIDGE STOP REPEAT TAKE THE BRIDGE STOP FREEMAN C IN C FEDFOR NTO.

CHAPTER TWENTY-SEVEN

RACHEL MAKEERY, THE wife of the environmentalist shot in the militia attack on Fort Bragg, had moved for shelter farther down the coast to Mendocino, where, had it not been for her sister Angeline, who worked in Ocean Effects, a store that sold upscale souvenirs of the northern California coast to the tourists and honeymooners, Rachel wouldn't have had a place to stay. The small, picturesque town was teeming with visitors, many, up from Frisco and L.A., feeling they were virtual prisoners in the town because of the state of siege imposed by what the media were referring to as the militia's "near-absolute control of the highways."

In fact, militia control was more apparent than real, but the media did have a point. Any local militia in the United States, especially those in the ten Western states, that had declared independence only had to say a road or highway was closed and it quickly became so. For anyone tempted to test its resolve there was the memory, reported ad nauseam by CNN, of what had happened to General Limet at Fort Bragg and the near-death experience of the "Blues Brothers"—now called the "Shoes Brothers" because of their hasty retreat in Nevada down by the Truckee River.

Constructing a perfect abatis at any time was difficult enough, making sure that all the trees you felled to block the road were more or less at a forty-five-degree angle to the road, branches interlocking to make their removal that much harder, but to do it in darkness, with nothing more than moonlight, took not only extraordinary skill with the chain saw but courage. No one to watch your back for secondary growth that might get caught up in the main tree fall or that might be shucked off in the primary crash, dead branches flying out like scythes. But Jim Nye had done it before, to block the coastal highway. But here, near the Oregon-California border, in the Redwoods, the remainder of his militia would position themselves in the giant Redwoods a mile back from Nye's abatis, creating one of their own *after* the FEDFOR coming up the coast had passed them. Thus they would trap the FEDFOR between the two Redwood blockades.

Down Mendocino way, militiamen "coast watchers" were alerted. "Coast watchers" was an old Pacific rather than Atlantic term, borrowed by the militia from the days of World War II when lone Americans and Australians, at very high risk, kept a sharp eye out for Japanese ships, reporting them by radio to the U.S. fleet. And it was an Australian coast watcher that helped JFK after his PT boat had been rammed by a Japanese destroyer. Unfortunately the coast-watcher radio transmits, however brief, also gave away what the Aussies called their "pozie"— position—to the Japanese. One of the militia coast watchers, Ray Marsden, a twenty-two-year-old in Mendocino, thinking he was cutting as heroic a figure as Rossano Brazzi, the handsome coast watcher of the movie version of *South Pacific,* was keeping tabs on the progress of the FEDFOR armored column making its way up the coast, which had been momentarily delayed by the downed bridge at Fort Bragg.

The problem with Marsden, however, was that his pride, specifically his desire to let everyone know he was a militia coast watcher, vied with the militia's need for secrecy. Marsden didn't tell anyone straight out, but with the infuriating posturing of a youth who had a secret but wasn't going to tell you, he managed to let you know, sort of, that he was a big-time operator.

By 3:00 P.M. at the Mendocino Bar, coast watcher Ray Marsden, in fatigues and "in-country" floppy hat, had seen more beers than armored vehicles, but was confident—and here he was correct—that the FEDFOR Armored Brigade, even after crossing more quickly erected pontoon bridges over blown bridges, would be behind schedule and wouldn't be passing through Mendocino for hours. At this time, in an act of will he thought worthy of commendation by General Mant himself, Ray switched from beer to pop.

Rachel Makeery felt awkward. Except for a few forays during her time at Oregon State U, she was unused to bars and wasn't quite sure of the procedure—how to look "cool." And her parents' disdain for saloons and the like made her feel guilty as well as naive. But she had worn a tight pink top and short white skirt. If she'd done this thinking she had to attract attention, she was wrong. Her figure wasn't Hollywood skinny but was full without being overweight, and Ray Marsden saw her the moment she entered and sat down at the bar near the old sixties Coca-Cola—dime a bottle—vending machine, the bar girl having witnessed no end of conversations started by that old red machine. It was an icebreaker, not that Marsden needed it. He sauntered up to the seat by the Coke machine. "This seat taken, ma'am?"

"No."

"Giddyap!" he said, exaggeratedly poking his finger at her. "Kramer," he said by way of explanation. "The old *Seinfeld* show."

"Oh yes," Rachel replied, not having a clue about what he was referring to. She and Sean hadn't watched TV much, being too busy with the NORCEW—Northern California Environment Watch. She smiled shyly at him, he lifting his Canada Dry to his lips, making it foamy and watching the small, lustrous triangle of white panties under her skirt. Despite the turmoil of her conflicting emotions, Rachel had decided to go through with the seduction; after all, the militia had murdered her husband in cold blood. But then Marsden, despite his fatigues, hadn't actually said he was a member of the militia. Maybe he was just a wannabe? He suggested they go for a drive—to a lookout point.

"Sure," said Rachel, not caring that he might be too drunk to drive and remembering how in college, those girls who'd risked premarital sex had talked about how too much alcohol would make "it" limp anyway. And though he was now drinking Canada Dry, she could smell his beery breath.

                            * * *

Sitting in the white, gazebo-like lookout, a copy of the
one down at Elk Cove, overlooking the vast blue Pacific,
Ray Marsden was oblivious to the grandeur of nature,
overcome by the smell of Rachel's hair, the sensuality of
her neck and breasts, his right hand sliding up her skirt,
pulling her hard against him. She was rigid with resistance, he with lust, interpreting her resistance as a thinly
veiled attempt at propriety. She really wants it, he
thought, his hand moving from her crotch, pulling down
her panties, his lips still pressing against hers. He knew
the type, big act of no, no, and when she came it'd be
screaming and bucking like it was the Fourth of July.
Ray liked doing it here, outside—no traffic anywhere in
sight, the terrified tourists indoors, scared shitless of the
militia. "Go down on me!" he said.

   "No."

   "C'mon."

   "Have you . . . got a condom?"

   "Fuck the condom. Let's do it. Right here."

   "No. Someone'll see us."

   "Who? Goddamn federals are on the run! C'mon."

   "What about the militia?" she protested, pushing
him off.

   "Don't worry about them!" he said, growing more
impatient by the second. "They're up in the Redwoods."

   She allowed his finger to enter her, asking, "What
for?"

   "What?" he asked distractedly, feeling her moistness.
"Oh—they're gonna take care of the federals. Don't
worry about it. Nothin'll happen for a few hours yet. No
one'll see us, for Christ's sake." Frantic, he let go of her
panties, pulled out his wallet, took out a condom, and had
trouble ripping the foil. It slipped from his hands. He
bent down, heard her skirt or purse rustle, and felt some-

thing against his neck. She'd drawn the knife cleanly, deeply, across his throat. Wide-eyed in terror, his head went back, her left hand still grasping his hair, then he slumped forward, blood flooding from the gaping wound, his eyes still agog as he died.

"Now we're even, you piece of shit!" She got up, walked to the cliff's edge, and threw the knife over. It made a chopping noise like a helo for a second, then vanished from sight.

She returned to the truck, wiped down anything she might have touched, and began walking back to Mendocino.

Twenty minutes later she saw headlights coming toward her—three motorcycles about a hundred yards apart. Federal-army outriders. They slowed and stopped but maintained the distance between themselves, the second and third riders getting off their bikes, handguns drawn, not looking at her but at the bushes at the sides of the road.

"Ma'am," said the first rider, "you shouldn't be out here. Militia's everywhere hereabouts." He saw a splotch of blood on her white skirt, and his tone changed abruptly. "Could I see some identification, please?"

She showed him her Social Security card.

"You have a driver's license?" he asked.

"No. I don't drive."

"Where'd that blood come from?"

It was the first time she noticed it. The army rider saw her face was blank, expressionless. "A militiaman tried to rape me. I killed him."

The army rider was in a quandary. He should take her into custody. On the other hand, he had express orders to scout ahead and was on radio silence, unless he saw something that might inhibit the armored column coming up from the south a few miles behind him.

"Militia are hiding in the Redwoods," she said. "To ambush you."

She told him in more detail about Marsden and what he had said.

The outrider turned his bike around and told her to hop on, that he'd drop her off in Mendocino on his way to report to the armored-column commander.

As they neared Mendocino, slowing at a crossroads, she saw a poster advertising a thousand-dollar reward for any information leading to the arrest and conviction of a militiaman. Someone had crossed out "man" in "militia-man" and written "person."

The last thing Rachel Makeery was interested in was a reward, but the thought of such remuneration in return for the anonymous identification of known militia had piqued the interest of Mrs. Reeth—mother of Dylan Rice's friend Lorne—as well as interest throughout the country. People were infuriated by the likes of the Freemen in Montana in '96, who'd raked in federal-government subsidies for years even as they were avoiding all state and federal taxes. Overnight, once rewards were offered, the switchboards at FBI offices throughout the country were jammed. Many of the calls were simply cases of getting even, of settling old scores. A climate of suspicion had invaded the country and neighbor distrusted neighbor as Internal Revenue agents, acting on information passed on by the FBI from the calls they'd received, scoured neighborhoods looking for tax evaders who had been fingered by anonymous callers. One such accused was Stanley Merk, orchard owner.

As agents Tracy Albright and Al Gordon drove up to the orchard, their rented Acura passed over a drainage grille and shuddered. Normally it would be an occasion for comment, but neither agent spoke. Neither of them relished the assignment, but like manning the federal roadblock at Pateros, it was part of their job.

A man in dirty blue coveralls appeared from the rows of apple trees, an old double-barreled shotgun, open at the breech, in the crook of his right arm. Behind him they could see the front wheels of a red tractor that looked as worn as the man, a tall, weather-beaten type, whom Tracy guessed was in his sixties. Alan Gordon turned to Tracy. "You want to lead?"

"After you, Al."

"Thanks a lot, pal."

She smiled. "You're welcome." By now the man was nearing the agents' car, his face, Tracy noticed, looking softer in the late-afternoon sun than it probably was. But there was nothing soft in his expression—one of undisguised hostility. Al Gordon pushed the driver's window button, and as it purred open he was careful to make sure the man coming toward him could see his hands on the steering wheel, holding no weapons. "Hi."

Shotgun didn't answer, so Gordon spoke again. "You Mr. Merk—Stanley Merk?"

"What d'ya want?"

Normally the drill was to announce yourself as FBI straight off. Then nobody got confused, claiming later that they didn't know who you were before they shot you. But Al Gordon was going on gut feeling, he being a federal in militia country, and the small matter of a civil war in progress. "Are you Stanley Merk?"

"What d'ya want?"

"I want to speak with Mr. Merk."

"Well, you can't."

"How's that?"

"He ain't here."

"Know when he'll be back?"

"I'm asking the questions. You a federal?"

Tracy glanced across at Gordon. "Maybe I should give it a try?"

"Go right ahead," Gordon responded.

Tracy called out to "Shotgun," who was standing five yards in front of the driver's-side fender but off to the side. She figured if he fired, it'd go through Gordon's open window instead of the windshield and she'd have to slip down behind the dash to clear her .38. She waved a hand. "Hi, Mr. Merk. My name's Tracy Albright."

"So?"

The apple trees shivered in a breeze, there was a loud, mechanical coughing noise nearby as a farmhand started the tractor, and a wooden flatbed trailer emerged from the polished green rows of trees, the smell of dust and vinegary cider in the air. Tracy kept her silence while Gordon mumbled under his breath, "Guy in the tractor has a sidearm." Tracy nodded but kept watching Mr. Shotgun. The tractor stopped now right behind him, its engine idling, and she saw a blowup of a cartoon mounted on its right rear fender: a farmer with a machine gun asking, "YOU'RE GONNA REPOSSESS *WHOSE* FARM?" She wouldn't have taken much notice of the cartoon had it not been placed immediately below two two-foot-square boxes atop the fender itself. She thought she saw the end of a gun barrel sticking out of one and guessed it might be an M60. If it was, it was totally illegal, especially under the Antiterrorist Bill passed during Bill Clinton's first term, a bill under which habeas corpus was suspended.

"You better git, then!" said the one with the shotgun. The helper, whoever he was in the tractor, was now sitting sidesaddle, hands folded, waiting, but obviously in no hurry to see what would happen.

"Well?" Gordon asked Tracy. "Do we git?" Watching

the shotgun, Gordon drew his right hand slowly from the wheel and slipped the transmission into "R."

"Mr. Merk," said Tracy, holding her badge with her left hand, her right low, on the no-slip grip of her .38. "I'm from the Federal Bureau of—"

"Got nuthin' ta say ta federals. You're on private property and I want you off. Right now. Git!"

"All right," Tracy called out. "But we've every right to—"

"You ain't got no rights here, lady, or anyplace else. Don't you hear? We're independent."

"You agree, then," said Tracy, "with the militia?" She didn't give him a chance to answer before she tossed another question at him. "Are you a militia supporter, Mr. Merk?" She noticed the farmhand was out of his seat, standing now behind one of the boxes. She saw Merk's left hand slide almost imperceptibly down the gun's stock. Everything felt wrong.

"What've you got in those boxes?" she asked.

"Flamethrower," said Merk. "Some other stuff."

"A flamethrower? What do you use that for?"

"Flamethrowin'." The tractor hand grinned.

"Isn't that illegal?"

"Nope."

"It's legal," Gordon cut in softly. "The orchard owners use them to light smudge pots during a frost. Have to light 'em fast when the frost—"

Tracy saw Merk, unsmiling, raise the shotgun.

"We're going," she said.

"An' don't come back!"

They shuddered over the drainage grille again. Neither of them spoke for a while. Then Al told Tracy they shouldn't have backed off like that.

"Oh, don't go all macho on me, Al. You see that joker on the tractor? He had something else in those boxes."

"Another weapon?"

"What do you think? A caffe latte?"

Al shrugged, jerking the wheels to the road's shoulder, barely missing a pothole. There was a cinnamon smell in the car. He knew it was her—pleasant, sexy, not a perfume, but her. Maybe the adrenaline did that. Al breathed in deeply, staring at the black ribbon of road ahead, huge shadows spreading like undulating blankets across the sun-drenched green of the foothills, the snowcapped Cascades rising off to their left. He knew that inside the world of the mountains it would soon be night and that there, as within what was being dubbed by the press as the "Astoria Pocket," over two hundred miles to the south, the high-tech federal forces with infrared goggles and other night-vision equipment would turn night into day, and that for the first time on American soil, a battle would be carried on at night with the same intensity as it was during the day. Had Al Gordon also known that this meant that for the first time in history the FEDFOR night-vision equipment would mean a major drop of Airborne—reinforcements for Trevor—he would have been even more optimistic. At no time in the history of warfare had there been a major airdrop of thousands of men at night. It was ironic that the first such drop would involve Americans fighting Americans.

Adding to all this, a mile-long train of M1A1 tanks was at present en route to the Northwest from Nevada. Al Gordon didn't envy the militiamen once the FEDFOR's armored might came into play.

The war was unfolding as the experts had predicted, the early hours belonging to the militia because they started it—the element of surprise had belonged to them. But now that the federal leviathan was aroused, its weight alone must crush the militias who dared block its way.

"We'll get reinforcements," Tracy said suddenly. "We'll go back and get that son-of-a-bitch."

"Right," said Al, pulling over now to let an army convoy pass.

The only traffic, apart from Tracy and Al's car, moving in the west was military, FEDFOR convoys of men and equipment en route to the northwest theater around Astoria and Long Beach, to the northern theater of operations up around the Cascades, and through Nevada from California to what was being called NCTO— Northern Central Theater of Operations. The latter, not nearly as specific a location as the other two, was a label Shelbourne was holding in reserve for any clash that might take place between the FEDFOR's armored spearhead now moving up from California and the militia divisions moving south from eastern Washington State, Montana, Idaho, and North Dakota to reinforce the militia already in action along the Columbia–Snake River line. Just where they might meet, if they met, Army Chief of Staff General Shelbourne didn't know—only that it wouldn't be at night, because as his aide, Major Baun, pointed out, the U.S. Army was so superbly equipped with night-fighting equipment, as they proved in the Gulf—with laser range finders and infrared scopes aboard their M1A1 main battle tanks, Bradleys, and even on some Hummers—that the militia wouldn't dare mix it up with any FEDFOR after the sun went down.

Unfortunately for FEDFOR, however, no one had told the militia this. And under tough, all-weather training in the Cascades and the wide-open spaces of arid semidesert in eastern Washington, instructors such as Lucky McBride had acted as "force multipliers" and, like the instructors of the militia's all-weather Mountain Division, had trained thousands of militia in night tactics.

It was true, as the media never tired of pointing out,

that the U.S. Army had obtained for its soldiers the most expensive "black light" night-vision scopes, etc. It was also true, however, that the militia had purchased relatively cheap 2.9-pound Russian surplus night-vision 4.3X monocular nightscopes with auto-gain exposure protection, two AA batteries included, and head-mounted, hands-free 35,000X light amplification, again with built-in protection should the wearer suddenly be exposed to bright light, such as a flare.

CHAPTER TWENTY-EIGHT

COLONEL RICHARD LEIGH, born and raised in Boise, Idaho, had always had dreams of stardom in his head. A lean, tall youth with passionate ambition in his eyes, he'd been to Hollywood, hated it, and after two years of pumping gas had returned to Idaho dispirited but with his dream intact. In Hollywood he'd been an extra, a little fish in a huge pond. In the Boise Theater Players he could be a big fish in a little pond, and soon after his return he was receiving accolades from the *Idaho Statesman* and audiences alike. He had joined the National Guard at twenty-two, turned out to be a good soldier, and promotion had followed until he was now colonel commanding the Boise National Guard Cavalry

Regiment. But like so many in Idaho, he harbored a deep resentment of the federal government and in a tortured logic of his own held "them" responsible for his failure to achieve national recognition as an actor. He knew, as so many do, that he was as good a man as the president. He was also convinced that "they" had conspired to thwart him in his attempts to become a household name. It was no good pointing out to him, as his wife, Doreen, so often did, that he had achieved much in his forty years. So he didn't feel complete—who did? she asked. The point was, he was respected and admired in Boise. Oh, let the "bright-lighters" of the East be condescending about Idaho, contemptuous of "cowboys," "country hicks," and all that, but how many men had risen to the rank of colonel in the National Guard, had served in the Gulf War *and* been mentioned in *Newsweek*? So, was he satisfied? No. Hell, he told her, there were colonels everywhere. And that three-line mention in *Newsweek* had only been in the context of a piece on how Gulf War vets had contributed to the upgrading of the National Guard armored units. He confided in Doreen, and in her only, that as much as he knew Hitler had been disastrous for Germany, he, Richard, understood how the young Hitler must have felt being rejected three times by the Viennese Academy of Art. How it had made Hitler intent on revenge—determined to show the world.

Shortly after this confession, and quite abruptly, his behavior took a decided turn. Doreen remembered the exact moment. It had been when Clinton was taking the oath outside the Capitol at the beginning of his second term as president of the United States—as Richard's commander in chief. Doreen had been fondling Richard, he responding in kind. When he heard Clinton taking the oath he'd entered her roughly.

"Honey!" she'd said, half joking. "Don't get mad at

me. I never voted for him." He didn't laugh—not even a smile. Dead serious. The spell, if there'd been one, was broken and for the next five minutes she had to listen to a tirade as Richard lay, arms behind his head, glowering at the ceiling. "That's it!" he said finally. "That is *it*!"

Next thing she knew he returned home that evening telling her he was giving up acting altogether. It was true but it was also a lie. The streak of petulance that had always lurked in the shadows of his personality was now in the ascendant. He also told Doreen flatly that there was "no way" as a National Guardsman he could serve Clinton. It was a "matter of honor."

Doreen was confused. "All right, hon, but what's that got to do with quitting the theater?"

"Everything," he'd said.

What Colonel Richard Leigh hadn't told Doreen or anyone else that day was that from now on he was fully committed to the militia—he would make the federals pay—and that two days before he had met privately with General Mant. Mant praised Leigh's decision but impressed upon him the importance of remaining in the federals' National Guard and *not* resigning his commission. "You can be far more effective for us where you are," Mant told him. "Be patient. The call will come."

With that, Richard Leigh had undertaken his greatest role as an actor, that of a full colonel in the National Guard, loyal to the federal government of the United States.

Now, years later, Leigh was about to be involved in a terrible battle in a rattlesnake desert where no one expected a battle to take place. Again, for good reason. Hidden away in the dry, southeastern corner of Oregon, seventy miles west of Idaho and thirty-five miles north of Nevada, the fifty-square-mile playa—dry lake bed—of the Alvord Desert lay forsaken and, to most, unknown.

For good reason. Its loamy soil, powdery as talc, in some places pinkish white, was good for nothing but sage, lizards, and withstanding brutal heat. Real estate that no one cared for. Not even the wild beauty of the massive ten-thousand-foot-high, pine-studded Steens Mountain Range immediately west of it, or the Owyhee Upland to the east, could entice any but the hardiest of ranchers to settle there. Here, bobcats, golden eagles, and mountain lions outnumbered the ranchers whose herds of sheep and cattle grazed in the green spills of grass at the base of the Steens Mountain Range west of the desert even as the winter snows remained at higher elevations of this enormous fault block.

East of the mountain, heat shimmered above the salt-white Alvord, the edges of the desert marked by the sun-bleached bones of cattle and sheep. The FEDFOR armored cavalry National Guard unit from Boise, under the command of General Richard Leigh, had been on its way west with orders from Washington, D.C., to attack enemy positions along the Snake River when, shortly after noon, Leigh received fresh intelligence in a CTC—commander-to-commander—encrypted fax that another FEDFOR armored column, this one from California, thwarted by the militia's sabotage of roads and bridges, had turned east through northwestern Nevada into southeastern Oregon, obviously in the hope of making an end run up I-95 between Steens Mountain and the Owyhee Upland to the Snake River front.

In the fax Leigh received aboard his TOW-mounted Bradley M3 Scout, Shelbourne ordered him to join this second FEDFOR column at Rome, forty-five miles east of the Alvord Desert, and then together launch a concerted attack against the militia-held and strategically important railway depot at Burns, seventy-five miles northwest of the Alvord.

The electronics revolution that allowed Leigh to receive the unscrambled order from Shelbourne without going through a radio operator was of key importance, for it meant that no one but Leigh had seen the message directing the armored regiment of over four thousand men Leigh now designated NORFOR—northern force—to move seventy-five miles south and join the other FEDFOR regiment now designated SOUFOR. Leigh immediately gave orders for his regiment to stop. Exiting from the Bradley's turret basket, he hastily convened a conference with his five squadron, or battalion, commanders while his aide spread out a large-scale 1:500,000 map of southeastern Oregon. The "call" had finally come, as Mant had told Leigh it would, and Leigh, knowing precisely what he must do, gave the performance of his life. He was not known as a smiler, but now his normally stern expression took on an even grimmer aspect. "Gentlemen, I've just received word from General Shelbourne that we're going to be attacked by a turncoat regiment heading north on the Fields—Highway 78—route. We—"

"Burns?" said the second squadron leader, pointing to the strategically placed rail junction. "Militia reinforcements?"

Leigh could have kissed him. It was a comment that only enhanced his performance.

"Possibly," he conceded. "But whatever their intent, Shelbourne wants them stopped. Now. It might mean a night attack. Computer tells me that allowing for the fact that it's a gravel road, it'll take us three and a half hours at twenty-two miles an hour to reach them."

"We can go faster than that, Colonel," commented the CO of the fourth squadron.

"Our spearhead can," Leigh agreed. "But I don't want to leave our HETS behind, Ray, until I absolutely have to. Less wear and tear we put on our tanks the better. I prefer to let the HETS take us as far as possible before we unload." He was talking about the Oshkosh Heavy-Equipment Transporter System, M101 trucks and their M1000 trailers, which, tough as they were to haul the seventy-ton M1A1 tanks, could not exceed twenty-eight miles per hour in "off-road mode." And though it was officially a road between Fields and Highway 78, it was a gravel-dirt road and Leigh knew delays had to be factored in.

"Any indication they know we're heading for them, Colonel?" asked the first squadron commander.

"We don't know, George, but I don't plan to let them know we know. So, gentlemen, it's radio silence until we engage. One thing's for sure—I don't plan to waste time introducing ourselves." A little laughter there, fitting in nicely, it being obvious to Leigh that all five of his squadron commanders had accepted his lie without the slightest suspicion. Why wouldn't they? He'd never lied before. The only thing these five lieutenant colonels were concerned about was the best tactic to use against what they believed was a renegade regiment, one of them asking, "Colonel, how're we going to identify friend or foe? I take it they've got lizard-pattern camouflage, same as we do."

"Not a problem," Leigh responded. "We'll use an inverted V. Same as we did in the Gulf. Use your electrical tape. If anyone hasn't got theirs, put them on a charge—they should have it—and cut some V's out of air-rescue panels. And *everybody* wears protective goggles. It's going to be a mite dusty." Leigh now turned his attention to the map. "First squadron'll be the first to engage." He glanced up at first battalion commander, George Holt. "That's what you get for being number one, George."

"Yeah, dammit!" A smattering of laughter from the others, but it was more polite than heartfelt, the tension already setting in, except, it seemed, for Leigh, who, despite the grimness of his initial announcement, was now displaying anything but businesslike confidence. "George, you're going to get help from your mechanized infantry because before you engage, I want you to have Hummers and some of your five-tonners coat-trailing. Use runners and hand signals now to convey all your orders. That goes for all of you. Any radio traffic on our part before we make contact and we'll be in deep shit. Understood?"

"Roger."

"Another thing. I want our Hermits well protected." Leigh was referring now to the Oshkosh heavy expanded-mobility trucks. "There aren't any gas stations where we're going, and last thing I want is for any of our boys to be sitting ducks because they're on empty."

The only ones happy about the prospect of doing battle against a renegade regiment were those few, in every outfit, who, like George Patton and Douglas Freeman, enjoyed war, and those in the mechanized infantry of Leigh's regiment who were being designated as coat-trailers. The latter, in Hummers and/or Bradleys, were assigned the task of "going like hell," as Leigh put it, east to west across the desert terrain. Pulling sagebrush, tumbleweed, or anything else that would stir up enor-mous trails of dust, they would create the impression of massive forces on the move to the north so that the enemy, trying to avoid them, would turn away from the direction of their dust cloud into Leigh's trap, a massive ambuscade of armor behind which, ready to exploit the situation and to help defend their dug-in armor and long supply line, was a tightly wound spring of mechanized infantry complete with antitank missiles.

Leigh, like Patton, knew his history well and could expound at length on the importance of such technical innovations as the stirrup and how it allowed the rider to stay on his charging mount after the first hit, enabling him to strike again and again, and more powerfully than ever before, without being knocked off his mount. He could recite chapter and verse of Rommel's race to the sea in 1940, an almost unbelievable hundred-mile dash in less than a day, through the French, who before 1940 were thought to be the best army in Europe. Leigh had once astonished a colleague in the officers' mess with his ability to draw all Israeli and Arab troop and armor dispositions in the Six-Day War and those of the Gulf War right down to the British armored personnel carrier that was accidentally shot up by "friendly" American fire because its crew had forgotten to show the inverted V.

Today, however, Leigh was concentrating on the disposition of forces in Patton's victory over Rommel's armor at Al-Guettar. It too had taken place on a clear, hot day in the desert. He would spring a trap à la Patton, with a dash of Leigh originality: "shaken not stirred." He smiled at his private James Bond joke but soon pushed it aside. There would be no humor in what he had to do and he was no superman. He was, he knew, a very capable armored cavalry officer, commanding troops who would be decimated if he did not plan well. He carefully perused his battle plan, using a laptop to check the order of battle of his regiment of five squadrons: 220 M1A1 tanks, 215 Bradley M3s, 46 M109A6 self-propelled 155mm howitzers, 36 M106 heavy 4.2-inch mortars, and scores of maintenance trucks, Hummers, five-tonners, water-purification trucks, trucks carrying four days' supply of 60,000 MREs—meals ready to eat—heavy lift trucks, along with six heavy M88 TRV (tank recovery vehicles) and scores of mechanized infantry vehicles carrying into battle the four-thousand-plus men who had to be equipped with everything from condoms to sunscreen. They were men who would be involved in a battle against fellow Americans whose armored cavalry, like Leigh's, would be augmented by several air-cavalry squadrons consisting in all of thirty-four AH-64 Apache attack helos and twenty-one OH-58D Kiowa scout-cum-attack helos. The Kiowas, despite their mast-mounted laser/designator range finders, were a bit long in the tooth for Leigh's otherwise state-of-the-art air support but capable nevertheless of carrying both antitank Hellfire and the newly developed air-to-air variant of the ground-to-air Stinger missiles.

Shelbourne hadn't told Leigh what air support SOUFOR possessed. He didn't need to, for as well as having his tactics already thought out—even if it was to be a night fight—Leigh knew the United States Army's Order of Battle, which told him his helos would be out-gunned three to one in Apaches and two to one in Kiowas. But Leigh was confident that he was as good as anyone the FEDFORS could put against him—as good as Freeman, whom General Mant had brilliantly suckered into the Cascades, away from the kind of strategic battle Leigh was now facing.

Leigh knew his men were coiled, nervous. That was all right. A good performer, he told himself, should always be nervous—it keeps him sharp. By Leigh's estimate his regiment should be dug in east of the Alvord by late afternoon. So what if any of SOUFOR's helos spotted his force? They wouldn't suspect anything. What they'd see is the FEDFOR armored cavalry regiment from Boise stopped for the night, resting men and machines, waiting to make rendezvous with SOUFOR the next morning for what it would think was the joint attack on the militia railhead at Burns.

Leigh didn't expect any scout helos, given their voracious thirst for fuel and the fact that fuel was at an absolute premium out here in what many considered to be the loneliest place in America. Which is why Leigh got a fright around 4:00 P.M. A helo was spotted, but it had its navigation lights on. It was too far away to identify precisely but looked like one of those small jobs, a plastic bubble with a rotor on top, possibly someone using a helo, as they did in the Australian outback, to track down stray sheep or cattle. But damned if Leigh could see any sheep or cows.

Standing up in the Bradley, head and shoulders above the commander's hatch, Leigh looked around at his war machine, the combined rumble of its advance like the heartbeat of some great beast moving out beyond the towering wind-and-rain-sculpted citadels of volcanic stone known as the "Pillars of Rome." Silent and pink in the dying light, the pillars were momentarily obscured by the massive dust trail of the passing cavalry regiment. But all about him, unlike the desert he would soon be in, there was a field of green grass and it made the scene so ethereally beautiful that it was difficult to believe he would soon be at war.

CHAPTER TWENTY-NINE

WHAT THE MILITIA thought would be the battle for the Redwoods south of the Oregon-California line ended up being a rout. The commander of the FEDFOR armored column coming up the coast, tipped off by Rachel Makeery's intelligence, dispatched helos ahead of the column to digitally photograph the Redwoods along the 101, forty-five miles from Patrick's Point to Smith River on the California-Oregon border. The prime areas photographed were the Prairie Creek, Del Norte, and Jedediah Redwoods state parks, and despite bad weather the IDCs—infrared digital cameras—picked up the abatis, the trees felled by militiaman James Nye showing up like the tips of huge arrowheads across the roads.

But if the FEDFOR commander knew the location of the militia's abatis, and hence of their ambuscade, he was unsure of what tactics to employ, for in an age of acute environmental concern, his hands were tied. He could not call in CAS—close air support—or bombardment of any kind that, through fire, might destroy the grand old three-hundred-foot-high giants, earth's tallest living things, that were among the last of the once-mighty redwood forests, some of them over nineteen centuries old, the woods having attained nothing less than religious significance even among the most ardent loggers. General Mant knew this, and it was because the trees were so holy to the American psyche and to environmentalists all around the world that he had encouraged the 117th Oregonian militia to use the Redwoods as a base upon which any FEDFOR would be reluctant to fire.

Indeed, once news of the militia abatis had reached their commander, the men in the FEDFOR armored column, now coming up the northern California coast, were explicitly ordered not to use tracer. This caused the column several hours' delay as all belt, one-in-four tracer ammunition had to be checked so that the tracer rounds could be extracted. This also meant that the main 120mm tank guns, should they encounter targets outside the Red-woods, could not use their coaxial 7.62mm machine guns as any kind of range finder should their laser go out.

Unable to use tracer, artillery, or anything potentially flammable, including grenades, the column leader was an officer specifically recommended by General Freeman. He was therefore a man of exceptional initiative, calling an emergency meeting of all helo pilots and infantry officers, major and above. Tank commanders were summoned by company, that is, sixteen at a time, to be especially briefed, those trained in NBC—nuclear, biological, and chemical warfare—and those who had served in the Gulf. He also asked for any ex-loggers in the column. If there weren't enough of the latter he would, under the powers invested in him by the Antiterrorist and Defense of the Republic bills, conscript civilian loggers from anywhere en route up the coast.

When Tracy Albright, driving, and Al Gordon set out again from Pateros for Merk's orchard, they had company—another vehicle, a light gold '95 Lexus carrying four men: two agents from ATF, the other two FBI, armed with bulletproof vests, helmets, and an assortment of weapons. They would turn off the main road at twilight, around the time Merk would probably be having dinner, relaxing, if the old grump ever relaxed, and they wouldn't use headlights. They wouldn't be able to avoid the noise of the grille, but speed would be everything—catch him off guard. And if he was out in the yard he wouldn't be able to handle two cars at once. The minute they were over the grille they'd split, one car left, one right, thirty feet apart.

"What if his farmhand's with him?" Al Gordon asked Tracy.

"There'll still be six of us," said Tracy.

"I don't like it," said Al.

"Neither do I, but if we're going to make any kind of impression around here, we've got to bring Merk in for questioning. If he bluffs us the whole valley'll know about it and—"

"Yeah, yeah," Gordon cut in. "I still don't like it."

She smiled over at him. "Al, you're starting to sound like an old movie. Next you'll be telling me it's 'too quiet out there.' "

"It is."

Tracy took one hand from the wheel and playfully punched him on the shoulder. "Don't worry, Al, I'll look after you."

"Thanks."

When Louis Keel saw the oil pumps around Bakersfield hypnotically nodding up and down, he had the same impression he'd had twenty years ago: hundreds of black, redheaded grasshoppers frozen in place, driving you nuts with their up-and-down, up-and-down motion. A blight on the landscape. And the *noise*, a kind of shooshing and creaking sound that grated on his nerves. It was like so much of the modern world of machines. They were just plonked down there and, damn, all you could do about it, unless you were like Ted Kaczynski or Louis Keel, was accept it.

"Time, Ted," Louis said, pulling his battered Chevy pickup over to the roadside. He tapped out another Camel, lit it, and plugged the Mr. Coffee connector into the cigarette-lighter socket, poured a good cupful into the reservoir, plopped in a ground-coffee envelope, and switched her on. "Her," because everything in Louis's world had a gender. Ships were "she," trees were "he," and Bakersfield was a black bitch. God had always been "Him." And now the assholes were at work again and

"Our Father who art in heaven" was "Father/Mother who art in Heaven . . . may Your dominion come," and "Son of Man" had become "the Human One." Louis knew there could be only one answer. There had been only one answer down through the ages, only one remedy for the pollution of God's language, for the pollution of God's world. *His* world. Oh yes, you could ask them to stop it, to get back to basics, like Ted did in his manifesto, but what happened? In one ear, out the other.

And so it was that Louis Keel, seeing no contradiction in his thought, no hypocrisy in the lighting of the cigarette and what he was about to do, sipped the coffee and smoked his Camel, waiting for darkness, thanking God for the clarity of his vision, for the militia's decision to "stand up and be counted," for their stand against all the rottenness of "modern society," of "progress." Children in Africa were dying while movie-star piggies pouted and stamped their little piggy feet for another million in their little piggy movies, and flashed their boobs around Sun Valley and Ketchum, where Papa Hemingway had ended it all with a shotgun.

Louis finished the coffee, thinking how there must be a little piece of heaven reserved for a quiet smoke and coffee. He set the timer for an hour so when the nitrate fertilizer went off he would be well out of the area. The thought of nitrate, fertilizer, distracted him from the task at hand and he turned again to Ted, complaining that "there's another thing the piggies do—they find an island covered in bird shit—'guano' they call it—and next minute it's all gone, fucked the island, fucked the people, and all they care about are *their* little-piggy bank accounts."

Louis reset the timer now for a half hour. Problem with an hour was that the pickup, standing alone, might catch the interest of some nosy passerby. 'Course, he told Ted, he'd have to walk away real casual like, and half an hour might not get him clear in time.

He was walking away from the truck when he stopped and thought about it some more. Maybe he should've left it set for an hour? Maybe he was being a worrywart. A half hour should be fine. He didn't move. Only time he'd ever felt like this was years ago when his wife was still alive and they'd be about to go off in their motor home for some camping and fishing up around the Rogue River—where Clark Gable used to go. Now there were goddamn federal fisheries offices all over the place. Anyway, he'd find himself going back to the house checking, double-checking sometimes, that all his hand-guns were properly locked up and the alarm systems set. Then his wife would think she'd left the stove on. It was like a goddamn ritual. Now Louis, as though riveted to the ground, was thinking again of the pros and cons of reducing the setting from an hour to a half.

Jim Nye was proud of his abatis and stood amid enormous redwoods in Prairie Creek State Park, watching the road from the deep, primeval shade of the enormous trees. Beyond the road in a small meadow he could see Roosevelt elk grazing by a patch of vibrant ferns and red-wood sorrel. But Nye wasn't here to appreciate the surrounding flora and fauna, he was waiting for the first elements of the armored column to reach the abatis around the curve, and when this happened he would radio the militia monitoring the tail end of the column and they would close the trap by blowing two or three big trees across the 101. Then the militia, well hidden in the dark shade of the forest, would attack with LAW antitank rounds and Molotov cocktails. It wouldn't be necessary to kill the M1 tanks—a difficult job against sloped armor even for the LAW 80 with its 600mm penetration at six hundred yards—only to disable one of them, blow off one of its tracks, the twelve-foot-wide tank blocking the road and needing a heavy-vehicle retrieval vehicle. And how the hell were they going to move that up past all the armor stopped on the road and the hidden militia firing at it?

It was then that Nye heard the helos again. They'd been flying up and down the 101 since noon like a stream of frustrated gnats, and after an initial scare, Nye and the rest of the ambuscade militia paid them no mind. What could they do—start firing into all the woods along the 101, set them on fire? That'd look good on CNN, the federals burning the Redwoods. What was it that guy in Vietnam had said about the city of Hue reduced to ashes by the fighting? "We had to destroy it in order to save it." Thinking about this and just how smart General Mant had been, Nye was feeling pretty good, and that's when a swarm of twenty-plus FEDFOR helos in five waves of four abreast swooped low, almost at treetop level, not dropping flares because the militia in the thick woods could not see them nor, even if they did, get a clear shot.

But as the helos passed overhead, hundreds of black canisters descended, and within a minute the Redwoods were bathed in a heavy fog of tear gas. By the time the last wave of helos had passed, the gas was so thick it obscured the abatis, and the militiamen were fleeing the site, coughing uncontrollably, gasping for fresh air. More helos, Hueys, quickly followed with triple insertion—that is, with two ropes, one dangling from each side, three men with gas masks to each slipknotted, stirruped rope, six men to each helo. The choppers, some still above the clouds of tear gas that seemed to hug the Redwoods like the ground mist of an early morning, hovered as the soldiers slid down the ropes either side of the 101 right in among the fallen redwoods, a perfect defensive barrier. As these ten helos left, their place, in strict accordance with the armored column's commander's plan, was taken by ten more helos, whose soldiers and "inducted personnel" alighted not with weapons but with chain saws, whose timber-splitting noise soon filled the tear-gassed woods as they went to work at slicing up the fallen trees while the extraordinary Hummers, which never ceased to amaze all who saw them, bounced their way forward of the armored columns to go to work with their front-mounted winches, hauling away the segmented trees.

Helo-borne, gas-masked infantry kept pouring in. There were two midair collisions, the resulting fire contained, sixteen men killed; and one man, a logger who'd refused to shave his beard for a tight gas-mask fit, became violently ill, went into cardiac arrest, and died. But the militia had been routed and the armored column went on.

Stanley Merk had seen the dust trail from the two cars as soon as they'd turned off the highway and, using his cellular, called his farmhand, who was working rows not far from the house.

The Acura with Tracy Albright and Al Gordon was the first over the drainage grille and right away Tracy could smell the vinegary odor of cider, which was illegal to make without a license. Or maybe it was just the smell of rotting apples. The second vehicle, the Lexus, passed over the grille and swung left as planned.

Seeking to avoid any confrontation, Tracy decided to give the orchard owner, now coming out of the house unarmed, another chance. "Mr. Merk?"

"That's me."

Al made a how-'bout-this? face at Tracy. They could

see the tractor emerging from the trees about twenty feet left of the Lexus, hauling a load of fertilizer.

"We'd like to ask you a few questions."

"Like what?" said Merk, a mite testy but more conciliatory than before. The agents in the Lexus, as well as Tracy and Al in the Acura, had their windows rolled down, ready.

"We were—" Tracy stopped, the rattling of the tractor, which had now turned, passing between the two cars and heading for the gate, too noisy for her to continue. She glanced impatiently at the farmhand driving it and he said, "Howdy!"

She nodded hello and when the tractor had passed began talking again to Merk, who stood about twenty feet away, hands in the pockets of his dirty overalls. Al Gordon was on his cellular, telling the four agents in the Lexus to sit tight for now. "Looks like the old fart will cooperate after—"

He never finished the sentence. A voluminous belch of orange flame engulfed the Lexus, then the Acura, its feral roar like the flaming tongue of some ancient dragon, enveloping the six agents, three of them, aflame, fleeing the Lexus but brought down by another belch of flame, the farmhand laughing as they fell, Merk just standing there smiling, the farmhand yelling out that that's what federals "git when they mess with the militia." Merk heard popping sounds, rounds cooking off in the two cars, and only then did he move, the tractor already out of the gate before the cars' gas tanks blew.

CHAPTER THIRTY

AS HER MILITIAMAN driver, from Omak, had warned her, Marte Price's hired taxi, a black Chevy sedan, was stopped several times, despite its white flag, along the thirty-four-mile back road from Omak to Twisp as groups of heavily armed militia suddenly appeared around a curve in the road and emerged from the heavy bush. Each time Marte was pleasant, cash and notepad at the ready, asking the men if they'd heard anything about an expected clash between General Freeman's strike force and the militia. They hadn't, but said that the federal hotshot was in for a big surprise.

"You mean General Freeman?" she asked during one such delay.

"Yes, ma'am."

They were right, but not because of Freeman's bloody victory in the battle on the ridge, which they hadn't yet heard about.

She asked them if they could tell her where the combat was likely to happen.

"Huh, no secret about that," chimed in the driver. "To get anywhere near anybody you'd be best to follow the road along the Twisp River to the west." She gave the man a fifty and held up another fifty. "Anything else?"

One of the militiamen shrugged. "Word out of Twisp is someone heard a big explosion along the road. Sure as hell there's no public works going on there—road is back of beyond."

She gave him the fifty. The man lifted his slung AK-47 to pocket the bill. "I got a question for you," he told Marte. "You're a bigshot reporter—CNN, right?"

"Right."

"Then what the hell you doin' scribblin' in a notepad? Thought you'd be usin' a laptop, one of them little Dictaphones or somethin'?"

"Airports," she said. "They're supposed to be safe, but you never know when the X-ray machine'll wipe off your disk or tape."

The militiamen let Marte's car drive on.

CHAPTER THIRTY-ONE

"HELL!" MUTTERED LOUIS Keel. He knew why he had the feeling that he hadn't checked something; he'd forgotten Ted, left him sitting on the seat. Finally, released from his indecision, he walked back to the pickup, retrieved Ted, and bent to reset the timer to exactly half an hour again. What he didn't know was that the cheap alarm clock was defective.

The nitrate blew, a shock wave of orange fire rushing out so fast it appeared to those twenty or so miles away as a flash of lightning, but the explosion following sent up hundreds of fire plumes from the oil field, an inferno that reminded the Gulf vets of Saddam Insane blowing up the wells. The sky above Keen County became crimson, then turned darker, the scattered broken ground pipes glinting in the macabre scene.

CHAPTER THIRTY-TWO

THE PURPLE SMOKE from Freeman's position had been almost totally hidden, doused by the rain, but a thin curlicue had been spotted miles away by a national-parks helo flying adjacent to the Sawtooth Wilderness down along Lake Chelan, and he'd radioed it in to Pateros.

With radio contact with Freeman's force broken, the fleet of Medevac choppers, hitherto held back out of fear of more ground-to-air missile attacks, took off, ten of the twenty Hueys headed for the junction of War Creek and the Twisp River. The other ten, right behind them, would proceed to the firebreak clearing below Butcher's Ridge, both Medevac flights accompanied by flare-popping gunships ready to lay down suppressive fire, if need be.

*   *   *

Even above the pouring rain, Rymann's two-man Stinger team—the pickup's driver and another militiaman—in the culvert where Rymann had left them, could hear the chopping of the helos approaching and the noise of a vehicle coming from the direction of Twisp but couldn't yet see either.

In the lead Comanche of each group, the pilot, equipped with FLIR—forward-looking infrared goggles—watched a green-hued screen crossed by waves of thermal emission from the heater of the stationary vehicle in the culvert. Flares were immediately jettisoned and the lead helo's copilot wanted to fire a Hellfire air-to-ground missile at the pickup. But the pilot wouldn't give the order to fire, even though he had weapons-free status from the air commander. "We don't know who it is," the pilot pointed out. "Could be a civilian," by which he meant "nonmilitia."

"It's probably the vehicle that brought down our Chinook."

"Probably," said the pilot, "isn't good enough. We have to be—"

He saw a white line shoot out from the vehicle, racing skyward! "Flares!" he shouted, and as more flares were jettisoned from the choppers the Comanche immediately responded with two Hellfires streaking down toward the vehicle, its explosion turning the FLIR's image from green to shimmering white blossoms of light.

"Scratch one pickup!" yelled the copilot, shouting to be heard over the feral roar of his remote-controlled rotary machine gun, spewing tracer in and about the culvert, other choppers, Huey gunships escorting the dust-offs, letting loose with their side-mounted .50s, the gunners laying down a rain of fire in a counterclockwise attack about the site of the downed Chinook and the bodies of the forty-four dead Special Forces. The firing was so intense that even the partially frozen War Creek was peppered with bullets. Now the lead Comanche was low enough to see a second vehicle, a black sedan, heading toward the creek and flying a white rag from its aerial. Suddenly the vehicle, hit by ill-aimed—or was it intentionally aimed?—suppressive fire, skidded out of control and rolled onto its right side, crashing into the road's drainage ditch, nose down in water, its left front wheel still spinning.

As the second flight of Medevacs continued upstream toward the firebreak below Butcher's Ridge, the armed escorts kept on releasing flares and firing along the banks of War Creek, which was frozen solid higher up near the combat zone but cracking now and then from the enfilade of fire. Again flares were popped, suppressive fire stopping short of the zone for fear of hitting any Special Forces still moving in the woods, bringing down prisoners and/or wounded from the ferocious hand-to-hand battle that had taken place atop the ridge.

Back on the road, near the junction of War Creek and the Twisp River, Marte Price, stunned, covered in broken glass, blood all over her blouse, was trying to extricate herself from the front passenger seat of the black Chevy sedan. Over a foot deep, the lumpy, melting snow was being washed down by the rain, the frigid water leaking into the wagon through the broken front passenger window and rising threateningly as Marte managed to drag herself free of the seat belt, trying to stand up and, she hoped, get out of the wreck through the driver's door. The driver was slumped toward her, eyes open, his coat a mess of bloodied torn cloth and bullet holes, his mouth agape. She couldn't squeeze past him and she could smell strong fumes of gasoline but couldn't tell if the motor was still running beneath the shaking din of the first flight of Medevac choppers and escorts now landing to remove the bodies from the downed Chinook.

With water rising ever higher in the car, she scrambled over the front seat and reached to open the back door, its window now looking like a skylight, the rain dancing on it.

The door wouldn't budge.

She pushed the driver's window button for "down," but nothing happened. The freezing water had now reached her thighs.

Three hundred yards away, across the chopped-up ice that was the Twisp River, a perimeter had already been secured by the helo-borne troops, and medics were swarming over the area, but there was no one alive, some of the corpses' eyes missing, the chicken hawks having fled at the arrival of the choppers. Soon, their rotors still going, the dust-offs had been loaded with body bags. One of the medics, taking off his boots and shivering so badly his teeth were chattering, waded out a few yards from shore to grab a bloated body caught in a floating tree branch.

Marte spotted the keys in the ignition, reached over the slumped driver, and turned them. She felt a slight shudder, but the engine died. She tried the window button again. It still didn't work. The water was now up to her waist. "Don't panic!" she told herself, panicking. She reached over the dead driver again, who now looked decapitated, his torso completely underwater, pressed the horn, and reeled back in fright as it blared loudly. She pressed it again and this time kept her hands on it.

The officer in charge of the Medevacs, a major, barely able to hear the horn though it was only three hundred yards away, dispatched a squad of four men in one of the choppers to cross the river and investigate.

* * *

Six miles farther up War Creek the second Medevac force, also flanked with fire-suppressing gunships, was coming down in bad whiteout conditions, the rain at this higher altitude having turned to snow in what was now a blizzard, the militia POWs herded into bedraggled groups of six, the wounded—Freeman assigning priority to his men—being loaded into the choppers. Some, with possible spinal injuries, were placed on boards in litters affixed to the sides of the helos; others were blanketed and strapped securely inside. Snow kept falling.

Freeman knew that the helo pilots flying back to the Pateros MASH unit would be operating solely on instruments, dangerous enough in any weather but doubly so in a blizzard. But he also knew that to await any break in the weather would be to risk extending the "golden" hour—those sixty precious minutes immediately after a battle during which most wounded can be saved if they are gotten to a field hospital.

There were still isolated shots in the woods between the firebreak-cum-LZ and the top of the ridge as a few militia stragglers were caught trying to get past the cratered top to the far side of the ridge beyond which lay Ames's cabin. With the perimeter for the LZ now secured, a padre who had come in with the Medevacs was moving among the most seriously wounded, his well-intentioned ministrations, Freeman noticed, much better received by the more fundamentalist-inclined militia than by the Special Forces.

A dispirited Norton, squinting in the blizzard, emerged from a gust of wind-driven snow to tell Freeman that neither of the two suspected murderers, Latrell and Hearn, had been found among the wounded. " 'Course," Norton explained, "some of the dead—I mean their faces—are shot up pretty bad. Some don't have any at all."

This was one of those military realities that, by an

implicit understanding between the press and the military, was seldom reported, almost never photographed, and never ever shown on TV. The sight of American dead with bloody mush for faces had long been deemed too horrible for loved ones and the general public to bear.

"All right," said Freeman, helping to load another critically injured soldier, the IV bottle swinging wildly from its hook. "Tell the handler to let the two dogs go out. But only two men go with him—we need every hand here." Previously there had been the danger of the two Belgian Malinois being shot before they could be of any use, and so both dogs had been kept at the rear with the wounded Australian—who was making himself scarce so that he could stay until the last chopper of the mission took off. He got another morphine injection and had the two edges of his leg wound taped, determined to stay till the end of the mission.

"You're nuts," David Brentwood told him. "Get out of here while you can."

"No way, José. I want to see these two bastards who caused us all this grief. B'sides, I love to see dogs work. A good tracker is somethin' else. When I was a kid in Aussie I used to go out on my uncle's station and—"

"Station?"

"Ranch. Anyway, I used to go out and watch them for hours, herding the sheep. Beautiful thing to see—like a fucking ballet. You ever seen 'em work?"

"No. But I guess I'm going to." Brentwood and Aussie Lewis were buddies from way back, and if Aussie was staying to the bitter end, Brentwood was, too. "I suppose," Brentwood continued, "you're trying to show how tough you are."

"Yep."

"You're crazy. Could get hit by some sniper. We beat them but there must still be stragglers."

"Yeah," said Aussie. "But in this weather they can only see for about five yards in front of 'em. Anyhow I've got my—"

"Aussie?" It was the dog handler.

"Yo?"

The handler was opening one of the Ziploc bags containing clothing samples from the Spokane hotel room where the two wanted men had changed into their militia uniforms, one of the dogs already getting a good sniff of sebum, the oil an individual secretes from his skin. Each dog, though still on leash, had its bringsel, or wooden stick, hanging from its collar as the dog handler strode behind them across the firebreak. Aussie, with the M203 grenade launcher, the rush of morphine making walking easier, followed with Brentwood, armed with an M249 squad automatic weapon. They stayed a few yards back, on the dog handler's right, allowing the dogs to heel easily on the handler's left in the swirling snow that was being made worse by a departing helo's rotor slap.

Six miles back at the confluence of the Twisp River and War Creek, the regular-army sergeant in charge of the four-man squad aboard the Huey sent across the river to check out the horn-blowing sedan was first out of the chopper, which blew up an eye-stinging cloud of grit near the road's shoulder as it landed, the gravel raining down on the overturned car like hail. As the sergeant neared the Chevy he glimpsed a torrent of water and melting snow in the ditch but wasn't tall enough to see into the rear passenger window. He waved over the tallest of the squad, who quickly spotted a white, bloodless-looking hand banging on the glass and water rapidly filling the car.

"Get back!" he yelled at Marte Price. "I'll break the window."

Marte could see a blurred image of the soldier's face but couldn't hear him over the noise of the waiting chopper. The water was up to her shoulders now, the soldier turning, signaling the helo pilot to cut the engine. The motor died and the soldier shouted for her to get down. All she could do as he raised the butt of the M-16 was to take a deep breath and submerge, unless she wanted flying glass in her face.

The soldier hit the window once, producing hairline fractures. He hit it again and it went milky, a big white spiderweb of fissures with the consistency of taffy punched out fairly quickly. As Marte surfaced, the soldier told her to wait a second as he used his knife to bash and scrape out the edges of the broken glass, then hauled her out. She was barely conscious, her face and arms blue. The soldier lifted her over his shoulder and ran for the helo. "She's in hypothermia, Sarge!"

When they slid her into the Huey, she was confused, one of the first symptoms of her condition, and thought she was still in the car, her hands stretching out, pushing frantically at what she imagined was the imprisoning window of the car.

The two dogs were let loose, working a breaststroke pattern ahead and to the sides, coming back to the handler and sweeping out again, neither Aussie, Brentwood, nor the handler, several yards apart, saying anything. Any changes in direction were signaled by hand, requiring them to keep within sight of one another amid the second-growth timber where snow lay shallow on the ground, most of it being caught by the umbrella of pine and fir. The dog on the left flank returned as they neared the cratered open area, atop the ridge, the right-flank dog not yet in sight. The handler signaled Aussie and Brentwood to stop. Two minutes went by, every nerve taut, the sound of the choppers on the margin's LZ well behind them now, muffled by the woods. Somewhere nearby a skunk, no doubt frightened by the noise of the choppers and/or the proximity of three men and two dogs, must have sprayed, its acrid stench bringing tears to Aussie's eyes.

Before the chopper carrying Marte took off from the junction of War Creek and the Twisp en route to Pateros, the major in charge asked for two volunteers to lie down with her to give her as much body heat as possible. Thirty-eight men—including pilots—immediately volunteered. On the way back Marte gradually became conscious of a delicious warmth enveloping her, bad breath and the voices of the soldiers lying close in, either side of her. It was difficult to hear exactly what was said, but even in her semifrozen condition, the cold slowly, painfully, leaving her feet, her reporter's instinct made her struggle to listen. She had seen the bodies from the shot-down Chinook littered about and the last of them being zipped up in the awfully utilitarian black bags and, like her, carried into the choppers. The soldiers near her were saying that Freeman was in "deep shit," and she could only assume that after all the fighting the two suspects hadn't been caught.

The Malinois who'd been covering the left flank in what the handler called "butterfly wing"–shaped search patterns returned, his bringsel in his mouth. The dog handler immediately signaled Aussie and Brentwood that one of the two wanted men had been found. He put the dog on leash and let him lead—both Aussie's and Brentwood's weapons at the ready. The orders to Freeman, from Washington, where all the VIPs were "nice and warm and comfy," as Aussie put it, had been clear: the suspects should be "taken alive if at all possible." Neither Aussie nor Brentwood knew which of the two the dog had sniffed out, but they were prepared to kill if either of the wanted men shot at them, and to hell with Washington—a sentiment that Aussie knew any militiaman would understand.

The other dog came back, his bringsel still hanging from his collar. The handler leashed him, giving him to Brentwood. They could see broken fern and spots where the light covering of snow had been disturbed. But this could have been done by any of the more than two hundred men who'd been involved in the back-and-forth combat between the treeless margin of the firebreak and the cratered top of Butcher's Ridge. Aussie, with the pain in his leg now winning its battle with morphine, realized that he should have stayed back with the choppers, but he still thought of himself as the injured quarterback at the two-minute warning with the guts to see it through.

There was a sharp, whiplike crack and Aussie dove into the fern, the dog handler dead where he lay, another crack and the handler's dog leaped into the air, dead before he hit the ground with a thump. David Brentwood was down behind a mossy log and couldn't see Aussie, who was hidden by the fern, grateful that he had known the dog signal for down, the remaining Malinois beside him panting anxiously.

"Two o'clock!" It was Brentwood calling out. "A hundred feet."

Aussie silently commanded his dog to stay and crawled fast to the nearest tree that covered him, got his line of sight, and fired. Brentwood fired a burst a split second later, up and running through the fern, looking for the slightest move up ahead. He saw a navy-style watch cap forty feet away, and fired from the hip. There was a grunt like a stuck pig and he saw fern moving, gave it another three-round burst, and was on top of the enemy in seconds, the man covered in broken fern. Brentwood immediately tried to identify him, but blood covered his face, his eyes darting side to side like a cornered and terrified animal, his breathing shallow but fast.

Aussie arrived a few seconds later, calling the remaining Malinois to his side and feeling as if his leg was on fire.

"You recognize him?" David Brentwood asked.

" 'Bout the same build as that Latrell description," answered Aussie. "About the same age, too—in his early fifties, maybe late forties. But he doesn't match the police sketch. This guy looks . . . I dunno."

Brentwood, careful to use his arctic gloves, opened the militiaman's bullet-torn and bloodstained parka, then his top pocket. The dying man seemed to want to say something. Brentwood put his head closer and the man spat at him, bloody spittle running down his chin.

"You old prick," said Aussie, releasing his dog with one hand, gripping his M203 with the other. Brentwood found the man's wallet in the inside pocket of the parka. "No credit cards," he told Aussie.

"Figures," said Aussie, his eyes still searching about him as he let his dog off the leash to resume his search. "Lot of these militia guys don't carry any ID—especially credit cards. Think they're an international Jewish conspiracy against consumers."

The man coughed up more blood, then his head dropped to one side. Brentwood felt for the carotid pulse—nothing. Only now did he look for dog tags, not expecting them on a militiaman, but there they were: *Robert Brisco 1st Wash Militia*, one of those who had heard Colonel Vance preach to the militia—about the necessity of following orders, even if they didn't seem to make sense at the local level.

"Huh—silly old bastard," said Aussie. "What in hell's he doing up here at his age? Well, I'm not carryin' him out."

"What gets me," said Brentwood, looking up ahead through the trees toward the edge of the cratered ground, "is how come the dog he shot screwed up, leading us to him instead of one of the suspects? These mutts are supposed to be the best."

Aussie shrugged, clipping in a fresh mag. "Maybe whoever picked up the clothes took this old guy's clothes from the hotel instead of one of the guys we're after? Or maybe he was close to the two suspects, picked up their scent? I dunno."

The surviving dog was back at Aussie's side, staring up at him, tail wagging. The bringsel was in his mouth. Instinctively Aussie knelt down to pat the dog—and fell. "Shit!" he hissed. Brentwood had no sympathy for him. If Aussie Lewis wanted to show how tough he was, he should be able to carry on or he should have stayed behind—gone out on one of the helos.

"Give his leash to me," said Brentwood. "You wait here." Before Aussie could reply, he grabbed the dog's leash and, swapping his SAW for Aussie's lighter M203, moved off through the fern, which was now waist-high, praying that the dog knew what the hell he was doing.

CHAPTER THIRTY-THREE

COLONEL LEIGH SHOWED his four squadron leaders his plan for a "close overwatch" engagement, in which Bradley Fighting Vehicles and the regiment's mechanized infantry would be used on the flanks to stop interference with his main thrust of tanks as they rolled down the middle of the one-and-a-half-mile corridor between Steens Mountain to the west and the Alvord Desert to the east.

His commanders were appalled. Given the sandy terrain, this was surely a case where you should have *long* overwatch positions, your tanks at least a mile away so you could first pound the hell out of the opposition with Apache antitank helos, your howitzer, and heavy mortars before your tanks closed in. But Leigh had been spooked by the lone chopper he'd seen. It could have been an enemy Kiowa scout, and if the SOUFOR was alerted to the exact position of his NORFOR, even though SOUFOR would assume NORFOR was a friendly, it would rob Leigh's armor of complete surprise.

Leigh didn't want his tanks a mile away; he wanted them as near to point-blank range as they could get. And a long overwatch engagement, starting with NORFOR guns opening up, would blow any chance of surprise.

The ticket to victory was to hit them hard in those first critical moments. Furthermore, if SOUFOR had any sense of a trap, then in an "overwatch attack" they could send in their Apaches and Kiowas against Leigh, and Leigh knew that in aerial support SOUFOR had superiority in numbers. No, Leigh had decided he wasn't going to replicate Patton's attack on Rommel's armored column at Al-Guettar after all. He'd use part of it—have a squadron, in this case fifty, of his M1s dug in in defilade positions on a rise at the northern end of the Alvord, their guns pointed westward at a right angle to the gravel road eight hundred yards away and a mile from the towering cliffs of Steens Mountain. And when the remainder of his tanks, 170 coming south, got close enough to open fire, his dug-in tanks would also open up. Leigh's armor would then have SOUFOR boxed in on three sides, his NORFOR tanks straight ahead of them and on their right flank, and Steens Mountain on their left flank. The only way out for the federals would be to retreat, Leigh's highly mobile Bradleys "Delivering Pizza"—tank jargon for harassing the enemy at potential trouble spots on either flank—to blunt any breakout of SOUFOR's mechanized infantry. Leigh estimated that his NORFOR would have a maximum of only four minutes of surprise before SOUFOR could respond, getting over the initial shock, recognizing the inverted Vs that identified Leigh's tanks. But as Leigh's time in the Gulf War had taught him, a few minutes was plenty of time to lock on target with the laser and kill the opposing tanks.

"What about the helos?" asked the commander of Leigh's first squadron. "Ours and theirs?"

"There'll be one hell of a fight," Leigh responded.

"How about their Hellfires?" asked the third squadron's CO.

"We've got Hellfires, too," Leigh snapped impatiently.

"Yes, I know we're outnumbered in the air, but lookit. First we'll have the element of surprise—they're going to be utterly confused about what tanks to shoot at. They'll catch on to our inverted Vs soon enough, but by then our Hellfires'll have decimated them. That should more than even up the aerial battle."

"I'm not so sure," put in the first squadron's CO.

Leigh turned on him, the dying light reflecting gold on his desert goggles. "If you can't handle it, Colonel, I'll have you replaced. Now!"

"I can handle it . . . sir."

"Good. Now another thing. Our infantry is going to have to be ID'd. I want inverted black Vs on back and front and on shoulder patches." He paused. "And I'll want three Bradleys from each of you. Have the twelve of them go over to the west along the base of Steens Mountain." He paused again, then asked, "Problems?"

"Could be blue-on-blue," warned the first squadron's commander. "If our dug-in tanks fire and miss, the round could hit one of our Brads over at the base of the mountain."

"Granted," Leigh admitted. "But I'd sooner take that risk, George, than have the opposition use the base of the mountain as cover. I don't want any creeping Jesus to come 'round back of us by sidling along that flank. Besides, our boys shouldn't miss their targets. Way I set it up it should be a shooting gallery—for us."

"How about our howitzers and heavy mortars?"

"We'll give 'em a salvo—and I mean *one* salvo—before our tanks open up. After that our howitzers and mortar'll go 'long overwatch' and pound their tail—their backup supplies, their infantry, et cetera. But the range change on our big guns better be fast. Work it out with your officers and NCOs now. We'll meet in three hours—twenty-three hundred. Go over it again."

As they saluted and walked to their respective Bradley squadron HQs, the CO of first squadron—a thousand men—asked his three colleagues, "You think it'll work?"

"Don't know." The third-squadron CO shrugged. "I think he's trying to outdo Freeman and Trevor. Big egos—birds of a feather."

"Well," said the fourth-squadron CO, "I sure as hell don't want to outdo anyone. I'll just be happy to get through alive."

"Then, Bill," the first-squadron CO intoned, "you're gonna have to outdo someone on the other side."

Bill Cousins was thinking who it would be.

Leigh didn't smoke but liked to chew on a cigar, knowing as an actor that it gave one a certain éclat. Made him think of George Patton. He began chewing one now, he was that sure he was going to win. In three hours he'd meet with his four squadron commanders to fine-tune his battle plan, which would be subject to the reconnaissance patrol—two men in civilian clothing in a battered-looking pickup—he'd sent out at dusk.

In the early night he could hear a low-throated growl as an M1A1, a surprisingly quiet beast for its size, with dozer blade attached, dug yet another defilade position so that when the time came, the tank, like the other forty-nine tanks hidden behind and below the ridgeline, would simply have to move a few feet forward, up the protective incline, the M1's barrel and turret affording as little silhouette as possible as it fired one second and moved back down out of sight during the reload.

CHAPTER THIRTY-FOUR

IN THE MEDEVAC helo nearing Pateros, Marte Price was over the worst of her hypothermia, more conscious than ever of the bodies, one on either side of her, pressing hard against her, and the deafening sound of the helo's engine. Had she heard someone saying Freeman was in "deep shit" or had she merely imagined it in her earlier confusion? "Did you say something about General Freeman?" she asked, her throat parched, giving her voice a strained tone.

"Yeah," said the soldier, "but don't say I told you."

"I won't," she replied in what was undoubtedly the strangest interview of her life—lying on the floor of a Huey, naked except for bra and panties, wedged in by a man, stripped to his underwear, on either side of her, blankets piled atop them.

CHAPTER THIRTY-FIVE

THE DOG WAS rigid. Fifty yards ahead, through the falling snow, Brentwood could see some of the craters left by the bombing, the snow around them thicker than it was on the protected forest floor. Crouching low, he moved off half right so as to approach the group of three or four suspect craters from the southeast; that way, if whoever was there took to the woods closest to them, they would be heading southwest into Aussie's cone of fire. Of course, the dog might be leading him to a corpse, a number of which lay about; they wouldn't be picked up until the wounded of both sides had been ferried back to Pateros. The craters should have been "swept" clean, but since they hadn't been, Brentwood figured that after Freeman's counterattack back up the hill, some of the badly wounded militia stragglers, or even Special Forces not yet accounted for, had been unable to get farther than the craters, and were now holed up in them.

Brentwood, left hand in front of the dog so the animal would stay, and finger on the M203 trigger, advanced slowly. There was movement at a crater's lip. Brentwood dropped down, bullets whistling at chest height through the trees behind him, the staccato sound of an AK-47 splitting the air. After he'd rolled toward a fungus-covered log for cover and rose to return fire, he saw two men, Special Forces from their garb, dashing into the woods far left, heading toward Aussie's fire sector. The moment he glimpsed the Special Forces uniforms Brentwood called out to Aussie, "Don't shoot!" But he was too late, the Australian letting the SAW rip. One man took a full burst that knocked him off his feet, his face disintegrating, the second man going to ground screaming, "No! Don't shoot! Don't shoot!"

"Get up!" Aussie yelled. "Hands up and stand still!"

Hands trembling, the man rose from snow-dusted ferns. Neither Aussie nor Brentwood recognized him at first, especially as he was dressed in a Special Forces uniform, stolen from one of Freeman's dead, and had grown a stubby beard. Brentwood went over to have a closer look, flipping off the man's Special Forces helmet.

"Hearn!" said Brentwood. "Right?"

The skinhead shook his head. "Rock!"

"The fuck you are!" said Aussie, limping toward him, pointing to the dead man a few yards away. "Your mate?" he asked Hearn. "Latrell?"

Hearn nodded. It irritated Aussie. "Can't you talk?"

"Yes," said Hearn, fear now giving way to sullenness. But he said nothing more, staring ahead as if watching something or someone deep in the snow-curtained woods. Brentwood handcuffed him with a white plastic strip and told him to start walking.

As they neared the firebreak Aussie and Brentwood expected everyone who hadn't yet been Medevac'd to stare at one of America's most wanted militiamen, but only a few paid him any attention, most too exhausted to care. They'd be hearing it all on CNN anyway. Hell, it was going to be as big as the Oklahoma bombing trial.

Aussie and Brentwood would be heroes, the lucky objects of Freeman's reflected glory—but it was not yet clear whether Freeman would be celebrated at all, for at the very moment Hearn and what they thought was Latrell's body were loaded aboard a dust-off with Aussie and Brentwood riding shotgun, General Douglas Freeman's fate was very much in the hands of Marte Price, who, in Pateros, was recovering in an army hospital tent, sipping hot black coffee laced with Jack Daniel's. She was pursuing the question of Freeman being in "deep shit."

"Well," one of her warming buddies had explained to her, "there's a rule in the army that says you never—I mean *never*—leave an area without having someone pick up all the CEOIs." Marte took another sip of coffee. It teed her off when people used acronyms without explaining them. Sometimes it was merely from habit, but other times it was just to make themselves look important and the listener stupid. Marte still said nothing.

"Ah, CEOIs," the other soldier explained, "are communication electronic operating instructions. Codebooks. You take 'em from the dead, whatever, but you never leave an area without collecting them. At the junction of those two rivers back there, where the Chinook was shot down, the CEOIs had been left behind." He paused. "It's a court-martial offense."

"He's right," said the other soldier. "It's a career stopper. No doubt about it. Major, major screwup."

Marte was entering this information on her laptop, her notebook having been lost in the water-filled car. "And Freeman's responsible," she asked, "for not having done it?"

"Yes, ma'am. He's the man in charge."

"I mean," said the other, "it mightn't seem that big a deal to a civilian like yourself—no offense, ma'am—but in the army it's very serious. See, the enemy could get hold of it and read whatever you shackle—that means whatever you encode. Once they've got your code, well, they can do all sorts of stuff."

"Yeah," said her second warmer. "They could call your own arty—artillery—down on you."

"Uh-huh," said Marte, without looking up. "But the militia didn't have artillery?"

"No, but they were the enemy. Could've done other stuff if they'd got those CEOIs."

Marte Price sipped her coffee. All along she had wanted to be the first reporter to get the story out to CNN's millions of viewers around the world. Instead she'd ended up in a ditch, damn near drowned, lost her notes, gone into hypothermia, and meanwhile every damn TV reporter in the country was on-screen, "Live from Pateros," giving the army's official, White House–sanitized version of events and adding humorous asides about CNN correspondent Marte Price being "warmed up" by two "very, very lucky guys!" Meanwhile no one was allowed anywhere near Hearn, one of the two suspects who, along with Ames, as everyone in America knew by now, had sparked the entire Northwestern rebellion.

Marte closed her laptop smartly, put on her face, fixed her hair, pulled on her tight white spandex top, popped a couple of mints to kill any hint of the Jack Daniel's in her coffee, and went to see the general who had just finished his press-pool conference outside his trailer. She'd heard that Freeman was in a buoyant mood—that he'd been ordered by Shelbourne (that is, by the president) to take over command of the Astoria front. Not surprisingly, Marte's boss, Jack Wilde, at CNN, had asked her to continue covering Freeman.

Major Norton politely but firmly told her that if she had any questions she'd have to wait for the next conference, scheduled "live" for tomorrow morning at 0600—for the 9:00 A.M. news in New York.

"Oh," she said, her tone one of surprised disappointment. "I was hoping to see him about leaving the CEOIs."

Norton paled. "CEOIs?"

"Yes," she said, smiling ever so sweetly. "The codebooks."

Norton glanced about nervously. "Ah, well, you'd better come in. The general and the two men who apprehended the suspects are on the phone at the moment with the White House, but I'm—ah—I'm sure they won't be long. Would you like some coffee? Cookies?"

"No thanks. I'll wait."

"Ah . . . yes. I'll go tell him."

"Thank you." She was still smiling.

When Norton entered the general's room at the end of the trailer, Freeman was still on the phone.

"Thank you, Mr. President, I appreciate that." Aussie Lewis and David Brentwood were standing awkwardly, albeit at attention, next to the general.

Freeman put down the phone with happy anticipation in his eyes. "Kudos from the president, Norton. Medals for these two men. Going to give the team a presidential citation." He paused. " 'Course those men"—Norton knew he meant all the Special Forces men who had been killed, especially those shot down in the Chinook—"maybe it'll be something for their families. Might help ease the pain." He paused again. "You believe in the hereafter, Norton?"

Norton shrugged. Right now he believed in courts-martial, and the moment Aussie and Brentwood were excused he recounted his conversation with Marte Price.

"Jesus Christ!" Freeman exploded. "We aren't in Vietnam. The enemy isn't—" He stopped. He knew there was no excuse. The enemy *was* the enemy, wherever you were. He'd screwed up. "Norton, go get Lewis and Brentwood and send 'em back here. Meantime you get to that temporary morgue we've erected and get every CEOI. That clear?"

"Yes, sir."

Marte Price was pressed for time and she knew Freeman admired people who got straight to the point.

"Miz Price," Freeman said pleasantly, stepping forward to meet her as Norton left. She took the general's outstretched hand, held it for a second, then told him that the "CEOI story" interested her, adding quickly, "Of course, I'd be much more interested in getting an exclusive interview with this Hearn."

"Would you?"

"Yes."

Aussie and Brentwood entered the trailer. Freeman ushered them toward her. "Gentlemen, this is Miz Price of CNN. She claims that I forgot to collect CEOIs from the dead of the Chinook shoot-down. Naturally I wanted to correct this mistaken notion of hers and have her meet the two soldiers whom I instructed to collect all the CEOIs and deliver them to Major Norton."

David Brentwood was a little slow on the uptake, but Aussie didn't even blink. "I wish you hadn't, General." He looked down at the bandage around his left thigh. "My leg'd sure be in better shape."

"You were wounded at the river?" asked a surprised Marte Price.

"Yes, ma'am. Damn militia—sorry, ma'am, I mean *some* militia—sniper nicked me just as I was collecting the last of the CEOIs. 'Course"—he nodded with mock derision at Brentwood—"my mate here . . . not a scratch, as usual." That was Aussie's second lie. David Brentwood had almost died once from a wound received during a Special Forces' intervention overseas. Brentwood grinned. Hell, everybody else was lying their ass off—he might as well join in the fun. "Beginner's luck," he told her.

"And you delivered the CEOIs to Major Norton?" she pressed.

"Yes, ma'am."

"I think," Freeman cut in, a touch of displeasure in his voice at the notion that his word had been doubted, "you'll find Major Norton will substantiate that."

She paused, but she wasn't finished. "Of course," she said, smiling. "I'm sure the major will. Still, I'd like to dig up a little background on it—you know the sort of thing, interviewing everyone at the scene." A heavy silence descended on the room, which lasted only seconds but seemed like an eternity to Brentwood. Aussie didn't mind—he was happy just watching Marte Price breathing in her spandex.

"Tell you what," Freeman suggested. "I know how pressed you are for time—news deadlines and all that. It'd take some time to dig up that background you want." He paused. "Of course, I'm sure you know there's no way I could violate the prisoner's constitutional rights to a fair trial. FBI's been very insistent on that point. Quite frankly, Miz Price, there's no way I could let you talk to the surviving prisoner." Marte began to say something, but Freeman continued: "But I could offer you an exclusive interview with these two men. They were the ones who captured him."

Marte Price turned to Aussie and Brentwood. "You two brought Hearn in?"

"Yes, ma'am," said Aussie.

She had her laptop out. "General, I get an exclusive

here, right? I mean no one else has talked to these two men."

"No one. It's your story." He paused. "Now, how about that *background* for the CEOI story?"

She couldn't have looked more beautiful. "Oh, I wouldn't worry about that, General. An interview with these two gentlemen would be just fine."

"Done!" he said, trying, unsuccessfully, not to sound too eager. "There is one stipulation, however. We don't like Special Forces to be shown on camera. I'd like you to do it in silhouette. There are some real nuts out there in the militias who'd love to retaliate."

"Oh." Marte sounded genuinely surprised. "I thought this defeat would be a body blow to them."

Freeman shook his head. "We only fought *one* company of them. There are hundreds of companies on the Astoria front and hundreds more all over the country."

It was an ominous piece of information and one that Marte Price would use in her exclusive report. "I wouldn't be at all surprised," Freeman added, "if there wasn't an attempt by the militia to snatch Hearn from custody. That'd be one way for them to show they were still a force to be reckoned with."

Before Marte faxed the story she told her boss, Jack Wilde, in Atlanta that "Freeman thinks we're going to have a lot more trouble with the militia now. What d'you think?"

"Well, for what it's worth, I think he's right. They've got more martyrs—Waco, Ruby Ridge, and now Butcher's Ridge. There'll be a surge in membership all over the country. And they're sure as hell going to dig in on the Astoria front."

"God help us," said Marte, but it wasn't God she was thinking of, it was Freeman. No matter how big his ego or his white lies, the man didn't flinch. No other commander she could think of would have admitted as candidly that "Butcher's Ridge" was named after him. He was willing to allow the appellation to go into the history books, unadorned and brutal as it was. She only felt it fair that he be acknowledged in her report, not as a payback for the exclusive interview but for his undeniable attributes as a soldier. He had gotten the job done, and she told this to America. The other networks, however, did not celebrate Freeman, pointing out that the suspected assassin, Latrell, was unaccounted for. Dental records had now shown that the man that David Brentwood and Aussie Lewis had thought was Latrell was not, in fact, the suspect, and speculation was that Latrell, one of the two most wanted men in America, had craftily planted items of his clothing on the other, dead, militiaman in order to mislead the dogs. In any event, neither Lucky McBride nor Latrell had been accounted for, and rumors that they, along with some other survivors of Butcher's Ridge, were already on the Astoria front were flying fast.

CHAPTER THIRTY-SIX

TRUE TO HIS word, young Dylan Rice of the Laramie chapter of the Wyoming militia didn't have any explosives. All he was given by Morton, his contact in

Cheyenne, was a sledgehammer and a long-T-handled wrench, which he and Morton took to a particularly lonely stretch of track south of Cheyenne. In an age of high-tech their method was old but effective. Morton unscrewed the bolts that held the sleepers and rail line in place. Once he had loosened them, Dylan unscrewed them by hand, then, as Mort moved on to the next sleeper, he took the sledgehammer and knocked out the wedges from between the bolt seat and rail. Most aspiring saboteurs would then have pulled off the segment of rail line and let it fall down into the grass or, using their tow-truck rig, hauled the length of track away. But not Morton. He told young Dylan to leave the rail length alone. It didn't make sense to Dylan, but he was too junior in the militia to question his superiors. All that Morton said by way of explanation was that a rail track was an odd thing to haul up into your pickup, and if the federals saw you—and Cheyenne was crawling with federals—they'd arrest you. And given the suspension of habeas corpus in the Antiterrorist Bill, they could hold you as long as they wanted. "Understand, Dylan?"

"Yeah, but—well, I mean can't we haul the rail away? Hide it somewhere? Without a rail the gap in the line'd hold 'em up much longer."

Despite the danger of what they were doing, Morton, keeping an eye out for any signs of federals, army or police, smiled at the youngster's naïveté. "Dylan, the engineer on a locomotive, if he's doing his job, is constantly keeping watch up ahead for any problems—dead stock, or live stock for that matter, on the rails, a tree fall. Anything. And now they've got what they call a FOLS— Forward Line Sensor. But it doesn't matter whether the engineer uses his eyes or the FOLS. If he can't see a break, he'll just keep going and the whole shebang goes off the rails. Then the federals are really in the shit 'cause

then they need a train crane to come out to get the locomotive, and whatever other car or flatbed has come off,
back on the tracks. We're talking a lot of hours here—
maybe days. Whatever it is, it means the federals are
stalled! Then we come in with our mobile stuff and really
do some damage. They've got all these tanks and APCs
sitting on the flatbeds with nowhere to go—sitting ducks,
my friend!"

Dylan was in awe. He could listen to guys like Morton
for hours. Morton was so smart when it came to all this
stuff—had to be seven days older'n God.

By now they were sweating and had three lengths of
rail loose but were leaving them in place so to all appear-
ances the line looked A-OK. "This," said Morton, "is
going to be the mother of all derailments."

As they walked back to the truck they saw a spiral of
dust, a vehicle about a mile north of them coming from
the direction of Cheyenne. Fast. Morton pulled a pair of
binoculars from his truck. "Son-of-a-bitch. It's a
Bradley. Federals! Let's scoot, Dylan," and they headed
south. Within a minute the pickup was doing sixty mph,
leaving the Bradley far behind.

"Mr. Morton . . . ," said Dylan, voice tight with alarm.
South of them was another Bradley. Morton was tempted
to pull off the road, go cross-country, but just as quickly
he decided not to. Cross-country was a Bradley's home
turf. Now, in the fading light, the air was filled with
white streaks. Tracer.

"Goddammit!" Morton shouted. "They're getting the
range. God—" The inside of the windshield was suddenly obscured by blood and bits of hair and scalp. Dylan
reached for the wheel, Morton's deadweight on the
accelerator, his torso slumped toward the dash, but it was
too late. The pickup lurched hard left, Dylan's attempt to
bring it back straight futile, going at such speed it rolled

three times then spun, the teenager dead, felled by the binoculars that had acted like a missile inside the cab, another half-second burst, four rounds, from one of the Bradley's 25mm chain guns ripping him apart.

Federals about to move west out of Wyoming toward the militia's Snake River line released an incident report to the media, noting that the Mark II, not the Mark I Forward Line Sensor, had been used. The calibration of the Mark II, the report stated, was so sensitive that it detected not only track "rumble"—that is, the distant sounds of vehicular traffic on the rails—but also the "smaller" sounds, the most frequent being the rail-transmitted noise of a lone steer or elk crossing the tracks.

In reality, the FOLS had had nothing to do with detecting the sabotage. The Bradleys had been dispatched from Cheyenne because of Mrs. Reeth, who reported what her son, Lorne, had told her about his buddy Dylan Rice going to see Morton. The Cheyenne Incident, as it was being referred to, made the midnight news in Washington, D.C., and New York, and the nine o'clock news on the West Coast, where General Trevor had, in desperation at the failure of negotiations and at the repeated urging of General Freeman, given the order to an Airborne infantry major to order his men to open fire on YB, the Old Youngs Bay Bridge.

"Civilians, too, General Trevor?" asked the major, his face creased with disbelief.

"Yes, dammit, Major. Clear the bridge!"

"But, sir—"

"Clear the bridge!"

Two seconds after the shooting began—not all of the major's men fired—it abruptly ceased, one of the Airborne yelling, "Fucking murderer!"

On the bridge, pandemonium had broken out, those civilians not yet hit bolting in panic back to the southern end of the span, several dead militiamen as well as civilians scattered about, one child sitting immobile in shock next to its mother, General Trevor's men no more than two hundred yards away. Two things immediately caught Trevor's attention: the figure of the militia captain, Nestar, crouching behind and holding what Trevor, through his binoculars, could see was a girl, maybe five or six years old, and a boy of about fourteen or fifteen standing in front of Nestar, the white flag the boy had been holding on the bridge speckled red.

"Who told you to stop?" Trevor yelled at his men, only a few feet away. No one answered, but Trevor could hear one of the major's men sobbing.

"Shut up!" Trevor shouted. "Goddammit, we have to take this bridge. Remember Fort Bragg!"

The men, including the major, were nonplussed. Fort Bragg to them was North Carolina. What in hell was the old man talking about? It sounded as if he was cracking up. He was still shouting, "Clear that bridge! Or you'll have a lot more Fort Braggs! That's an order!"

Trevor's aide, a visibly shaken man, spoke quietly to the general. "Sir, I think it best . . . maybe you should back down." He had meant to say "back off," but that isn't how it came out.

"Back down! By Christ—"

"Sir, I meant—"

"Not me, Colonel," said the general, so incensed he didn't hear his aide anymore. "I get an order, I carry it out. And I expect my men to do the same." He turned his rage on the Airborne major. "I want the name of every man who disobeyed my order and I want it in five minutes, Major. Do you read me?"

"Yes, sir."

With that, Trevor stormed back to his command Hummer.

On the bridge, Nestar was threatening to shoot the girl and the teenage boy unless the Airborne's attack on the northern end of YB also ceased immediately.

Caught in a twister of conflicting emotions—despair at having given the order to fire, humiliation at his men not following through, self-loathing for having given the order in the first place—Trevor was now pacing back and forth beneath the camouflaged canvas lean-to that unrolled like a trailer-home annex from the Hummer. Now and then he'd stop by the real-time computer-generated map on his ruggedized laptop. But although the results of this or that engagement were being fed it, the basic quandary hadn't changed: the militia now held both ends of YB as well as the big Astoria Bridge. This battle was very close to being lost. Without the bridges, his FEDFOR was like a boxer trying to fight with one hand behind his back. And now the final humiliation came through the laptop: he was to be replaced in the field by Freeman.

Soon he had to deal with the rumor, traveling by inter-squad radio even as he spoke, that he, General Trevor, C-in-C 82nd Airborne, had lost control and that the impending loss of YB would enable a flood of militia to cross over into Oregon if he couldn't get a handle, and quickly, on the Nestar situation. Increasing the pressure to near breaking point was Trevor's certainty that his slippage of command would create confusion and defeat, and cause more lives to be lost. Already rumor was rife across the din of the battlefield that Trevor had blown it, that Washington would probably bring in Freeman to sort it out.

The general demanded coffee—as if he needed pumping up—and for the umpteenth time stopped at the computer map. There were no longer as many blue— Airborne—units clustered about YB's northern end.

Either some of the Airborne there had surrendered . . . or been killed? In any event there weren't as many as five minutes ago. He tried to call the northern sector of the bridge. No response. Now blinking amber dots informed him an encryption was on the way. By the time he was handed his coffee, the decoded message from Chief of Staff Shelbourne was coming on-screen in plain language. GENERAL FREEMAN ON WAY TO ASSIST NWTO STOP.

More humiliation. The final "to assist" sounded even more insulting than outright replacement would have been. Trevor threw his coffee away in disgust. "To assist" meant to take charge. Trevor told his aide, "Well, by God, I won't be—roll up!" he ordered his driver. "Back to that squad!"

He was there in under three minutes despite the thickening fog. He grabbed an M-16 from the man who he guessed had been sobbing and brought it up hard into his shoulder. Fog rolled on and off the bridge like passing ghosts. Nestar, Laser, whoever the hell he was, was still edging toward the northern end, circling with his young hostages, then abruptly changing pattern so as to confuse any hopeful sharpshooter. The motion of Nestar with the two kids as shields looked bizarrely like a six-legged spider sidling along the bridge. Trevor, his brain racing as if Freeman was literally about to drop in and stymie his career, leaned against the Hummer, stopped, went back for the squad's M60 instead, rested it on the Hummer's hood, set the range . . . and couldn't fire at the children. In the next second they were swallowed by mist.

He had failed to carry out the most fundamental rule of the officer corps. He had asked—*ordered*—his men to do something he wasn't prepared to do himself: kill children. And he had lost the bridge.

"C'mon, General!" came a sarcastic cry. "You can do it!"

His hand moving as if it were made of lead, his eyes dulled by knowledge of what he had done, Trevor forced himself to pick up his binoculars. In the circle he saw the bodies of two children who had been cut down by his order. Killing the children like that—it was as bad as My Lai. *American* children. It was murder any way you cut it. And he hadn't even the guts to do it himself.

Nestar had won. He was now in control of the bridge, his shield the two children.

As darkness closed in, the fog grew still thicker, and on CNN, via military feed line from the Astoria front, it was announced that the victory of General Freeman over the Cascades militia had been overshadowed by the loss of YB—Old Youngs Bay Bridge.

In Washington, D.C., Shelbourne was pleased by the Pentagon's speed and smooth handling of the Trevor situation. The fact that the press had not yet caught on to it only proved once again the effectiveness of the armed forces' "post-'Nam" determination to keep the media out of the combat zone.

In the zone itself, however, morale had plummeted. What Trevor had tried to do, his order to shoot the children, was repugnant to his soldiers, Americans who were already killing Americans. There was a crisis of command right through the 82nd Airborne.

CHAPTER THIRTY-SEVEN

GENERAL SHELBOURNE GUESSED correctly that the only thing holding the 82nd together right now was its superior discipline, its collective memory of what it had proudly done in the past, and, perhaps the strongest bond of all, the fact that they were all in the same boat, under fire, kill or be killed. Nevertheless, Shelbourne was a deeply worried man. What was troubling him most was the possibility of mass desertion in the 82nd, an unthinkable possibility only hours ago.

Freeman had won the Battle of Butcher's Ridge, but if he had expected a public outpouring of praise for his achievement, he had, uncharacteristically, miscalculated—and badly. *The New York Times* and a score of Democratic-party congressmen who had never liked what they saw as the George Patton–like side of Freeman pointed out that in June 1996 the FBI had ended the "seventeen-person standoff" in Jordan, Montana, without firing a shot. So what was so brilliant about Freeman killing nearly two hundred Americans to get at two?

Freeman was asked for his reaction on the tarmac of Fairchild Base in Washington State en route to assuming personal command of the Astoria front, a command that incidentally he and aide Norton believed the White House had shrewdly fobbed off on him in order to have him handle another unsavory and politically explosive situation. If it went bad it'd be his fault, not theirs.

Freeman began his response to the press as professionally as he could, not taking offense at the *Times'* back-handed congratulations for his capture of Hearn but withholding "final judgment" until the general's forces had captured Latrell—*if* they caught him, and if they ever managed to arrest Ames, the militiaman who, as the *Times* pointed out, had "quite obviously evaded the best General Freeman could throw at him."

"Goddammit," said Freeman, ignoring Norton's attempt at damage control. "I wasn't fighting against two killers. Doesn't anyone understand that I was fighting a company of highly trained militiamen? Our intelligence sources report that they were led by none other than one 'Lucky McBride,' a man known to be a Vietnam and Gulf War veteran, twice decorated with the Silver Star and a man highly knowledgeable about the terrain. The press drawing a comparison between the siege of the Montana Freemen in 'ninety-six and this situation is nonsense. You can't talk to you people. Lead's only damn thing you understand."

There was a cluster of reporters, flashlights popping, and the constant *whirr-click-whirr* of photographers.

"Your strategy going to be any different from General Trevor's, General?"

"We'll see."

The reporter from *The Washington Post* momentarily broke free, ahead of the scrum. "That mean you disagree with Trevor's tactics?"

"It means nothing of the sort," said Freeman, without breaking his stride. "General Trevor is a damn fine soldier. Some generals never get near the front. Too comfortable back in headquarters. Not Johnny Trevor! He was up forward—where a leader leads. Need more men like him."

"You mean, General," shouted the *L.A. Times*, "that the army brass isn't aggressive enough?"

Freeman paused, causing a pileup behind him. "What I say, ladies and gentlemen, is what I mean." He strode off again, the pack following like a gaggle of geese.

"General, Rodman here—*Chicago Tribune*. There's been talk of civilians being fired upon as—"

"Yes," Freeman cut in. God, he loved all this attention. "Civilians *were* shot—*murdered* is the correct term—at Fort Bragg by the militia. That's the kind of people we're dealing with."

"No, General, I mean civilians shot by the 82nd Airborne in Astoria."

"Perhaps," said Freeman. "Friendly fire can't be helped sometimes, particularly when the enemy is hiding behind the skirts of civilians, using them as hostages."

"General Freeman," asked a tall, lanky woman. "*Seattle Post-Intelligencer*. Rumor is that the Airborne received a direct order from you to shoot civilians if necessary."

"I gave an order to clear a bridge."

"Even if it meant killing civilians."

Freeman stopped, the crowd flowing around him. "What'd you say your name was?"

"Patricia Arless—*Seattle Post-Intelligencer*. The word is, General—"

"What would you rather have, Ms. Arless? A quick ending to this war or a long-dragged-out conflict during which *both* sides take twice as many casualties?"

"But, General," riposted Arless, "the talk is that the bridge has been taken by the militia."

"Ms. Arless, you're telling me there's 'rumor'—

'talk'—'word.' I won't know what the situation really *is* until I've had a chance to see for myself." He was boarding the aircraft.

"But," yelled a tabloid reporter, "have you stopped ordering civilians killed?"

"Yes!" Freeman shouted, and disappeared into the army-air 747 transport. Norton was yelling at the reporter, trying to qualify Freeman's yes, but couldn't be heard over the high scream of the engines.

Through the wizardry of electronics, some papers already featured front-page stories about Freeman before his plane had landed in Portland. The tabloid headline of one of them, the *New Hampshire Clarion*, blared, FREEMAN STOPS KILLING CIVILIANS.

The general was so furious at the sight of this that despite the pride he took in not being a pill popper, by the time he'd been driven—airstrips in and around Astoria having been wrecked—to the Astoria front, he'd chewed six butterscotch-flavored tablets for acid indigestion.

Norton had no sympathy for his boss. What Freeman should have done was to "no comment" everything. Like Norm Schwarzkopf, Freeman wanted media people kept at a distance, as they had been in the Gulf War, but he also wanted the glory, and like it or not, the media were the vehicle of fame.

"Should've kept my damn mouth shut!" he told Norton. "Look at that headline, Norton. That's like the old one, 'Have You Stopped Beating Your Wife?' Either way, yes or no, you're dead. Bastards! Goddammit, Norton, I'm back to square one. And all because I didn't get that son-of-a-bitch Latrell."

"And McBride," Norton added dryly. "Lot of media are making him out to be some kind of Robin Hood."

Freeman pulled his leather gloves on tightly. It was

cold in the plane, the way he liked it—he could think better. "Norton, I'm *personally* gonna shoot that McBride son-of-a-bitch. Prick's become a symbol." He paused, fingers pressed together like a spire. He sat back against the seat. "By God, I admire him, whoever he is. Like to shake his hand. But I'll shoot him instead."

"Ames?"

"I'll shoot him, too."

With that, Freeman turned his attention to the large computer screen that was showing him a real-time digital sitrep of the Astoria front. "Look at this, Norton. Biggest goddamn mess since Arnhem. Our people scattered to hell and gone—sand dunes, tidal flats, swamps, and house-to-house in the town."

"You have a plan, General?"

Jaw clenched as he studied the map, Freeman nodded slowly. "Believe I do, Norton. If you were Mant, what's the last thing you'd expect here? I mean both sides of the river?"

"I know what I *would* expect. More reinforcements for Trevor—I mean for our side."

"Uh-huh, but where?"

Norton was getting tired of this. Knew a kid at school like Freeman. Wouldn't tell you anything—first you had to guess. It was like they were on *Jeopardy!* But Norton also knew that it was Freeman's way, testing his ideas out on his aide, who he knew was a good thinker and devil's advocate. A sounding board.

"I would think," said Norton, "that our FEDFOR troops would come in here." He was pointing east of the Astoria Pocket.

"Yes," Freeman agreed. "And how?"

"Armored column," Norton suggested.

"Paratroops?"

"Not after what happened. Dropping meat into a grinder."

"Exactly!" said Freeman.

"So that's what you're going to do?"

"I'm going to order another major drop from 82nd Airborne. Going in to help their buddies. Tremendous morale booster after this Trevor screwup."

"But, General, if Mant's troops are ready and waiting . . ."

Freeman was shaking his head. "No. Listen, Norton, we go at it full bore with our boys now on the ground. That'll keep Mant's boys busy. We only drop into Airborne-held territory this time. And we make history, Norton. We drop in total darkness—everyone with NVGs." He meant night-vision goggles, specifically the lightweight Gen-III third-generation model 2777. The replacement Airborne, Freeman told Norton, wouldn't be seen by the militia, who, despite their equality in firearms and tactical training, would probably have only a night sight here and there.

"What if it backfires, General?"

"You're a negative bastard, Norton. Always see the gloomy side. *L'audace, l'audace*, Norton. *Toujours l'audace*."

"I know, General. But I'm paid to caution you."

"Like the small boy in the victory parade, eh, Norton?"

"What parade's that, General?"

"When Rome welcomed home a victorious general and his soldiers, the general would ride in a chariot, and amid all the pomp and circumstance a boy would keep whispering into the victor's ear, 'All glory is fleeting!' "

Norton nodded approvingly, but knew that Freeman believed you could take glory with you—that glory in this life would be with you in the next life, for, like Patton, Freeman believed in reincarnation, the soul immortal, with only its container, the body, changing. Once, during the Gulf War, on one of those star-studded Arabian nights that seemed to explain why astronomy had first been the province of the Arab, Freeman, in a confessional mood, had told his aide that he had fought on American soil at the battle of Vicksburg in the first American Civil War and told him how, felled by grapeshot, his body had emptied its blood and freed him to reenter the never-ending spiral of history.

Now he recalled how at one point along War Creek, though he'd never been in the area before, he knew exactly what he'd find around the next bend—a circular jumble of rocks with a split waterfall. He was right, and once again he had experienced the feeling that, because they know no other word for it, modern men call "déjà vu."

He became aware of Norton's voice. "How many, General?"

"What?"

"How many reinforcements are you going to ask for?"

"A battalion," said Freeman. "With artillery. That'll shake Mant from his sleep."

"You think he's here? At the front?"

"I know he's here. I *feel* the son-of-a-bitch."

CHAPTER THIRTY-EIGHT

THE TACITURN COLONEL Leigh was a great believer in the KISS rule—Keep It Simple, Stupid—when it came to tactics. Five companies, seventy of his tanks from first and second squadrons, waited in the Alvord Desert in their defilade positions, only desert and the lone gravel road lying between them and the towering cliffs of Steens Mountain two miles away to the west. The remaining 150 tanks two miles east of them were deployed in two-line-abreast formation.

Eschewing single-column, wedge, or echelon formations, Leigh had decided on the rail-line maneuver, as this way the left column had to worry only about the enemy on its left side, the right column about the 180-degree arc on its right, the lead tank of each line concentrating on the 180-degree arc in front. If the lead tank was hit, the line would simply move around it, the next tank in the line becoming the lead. In this way, Leigh hoped to deny SOUFOR's tanks a flank attack on his armor.

He would know in about thirty minutes whether it was a good plan or a disaster. His seventy defilade tanks were so well dug in that each was behind a "triple"—that is, hunkered down with three levels, or mounds of earth of differing height, from which to fire. The top level allowed the tank to come up from its ditch and have an unobstructed field of fire, as well as permitting it to depress its 120mm gun should it need to engage the enemy infantry at close range. The second, lower step permitted a "pop-up, duck-down" firing mode, with the M1's turret and gun barely visible. The third step was your basic deep ditch wherein the tank was completely hidden, neither hull nor main gun visible to the enemy, the range given to the tank gunner by observers outside the tank.

But now Leigh was having second thoughts. What commander didn't before H hour? He reminded himself how General MacArthur, beset by doubt, was ill the night before the landing at Inchon. The Good Book told you to take no counsel of your fears. But Leigh knew if he didn't achieve surprise, that if SOUFOR's commander suspected anything was amiss, all he'd have to do was send a squadron or two of *his* Abrams M1A1s in a "Hail Mary" around Alvord's dry lake and hit Leigh from the rear.

In that case, even if Leigh's seventy had time to climb out of their defilade positions, they would find themselves unwittingly exposing their underbelly, which, next to the top of the turret and rear, was the tank's most vulnerable area. Leigh had sent out Bradley M3 Scouts to run INTWAR—interference/warning—but they were limited in their mobility since their presence could give away Leigh's ambuscade. And then there was that lone helo he'd seen. Had it been a rancher or a Kiowa army scout? But there again, he told himself, where would you be if you didn't take risks? Victory belonged to the brave.

Standing alone outside his Bradley M3 HQ, Leigh poured himself a coffee from his thermos and noticed his hand was shaking. He felt, rather than saw, his way into the Bradley—no lights, no radio, no smoking, and no coughing, and all the ranges having been "lasered" out for the defilade tanks, the 150 sitting quietly to the east, the 155mm howitzers and heavy mortars and the Bradley infantry vehicles behind both the defilade and open-area tanks. All had been computerized and were ready, waiting. If he won, if he defeated SOUFOR, Leigh knew it would be a tremendous victory for the militias and a humiliating defeat for Freeman's forces, and Leigh would be as famous as Lee, who had brought the federals to their knees in the first Civil War. If he lost . . .

Within each of Leigh's 220 tanks, the silent computers were performing their magic, their sensors sniffing and feeling the desert night, digitizing the atmospheric conditions: heat, wind strength, humidity—anything that, along with barrel droop, the type of ammunition used, and the temperature of the turret, might affect the shoot. Inside the turret's bustle, aft of the commander, an assortment of forty shaped-charge HEAT (high-explosive antitank) and APFDS (armor-piercing, fin-stabilized, discarding sabot) rounds were neatly stacked, an additional six rounds stowed in the hull behind the commander's seat, the loader sitting to the commander's left, the gunner in front, and forward, outside the turret, away from commander, gunner, and loader, the lonely driver.

Little was said as the minutes ticked away, each of the tank's four-man crew alert to his responsibility, the commander specifically responsible for the security of the tank's right side, the loader for the left, and the driver for the front left-side, right-side 180-degree arc, each man watching the computers' monitoring panels as well as thermal sights. The commander, a sergeant or other NCO, busy like the captain of a ship, oversaw everything, all four men acutely aware that with tank rounds coming at you at better than a mile a second, a split-second delay could mean annihilation. Inside, the tanks reeked of sweat, not the usual smell of perspiration but more bitter smelling, infused with the adrenaline of fear and, for some, high excitement. And once you were in battle there were no toilet facilities. If you had to go, you went, and would hose it out later—depending on water rationing.

Incredible though it seemed, the driver of one of the defilade tanks, six feet forward of the other crew, had fallen asleep behind his motorcyclelike hand controls, his ribbed and semi-inclined cushioned seat too comfortable by half, and his body already tired from the strain of waiting. It was a common problem in the M1.

Outside the tanks, below the lip of the defilade positions, anxious infantrymen also waited, fingers nervously tapping weapons, Leigh's plan to allow half of SOUFOR's armor to pass his defilade's midpoint before opening fire. No CAS—close air support—would be possible for SOUFOR because once NORFOR's artillery, tanks and heavy mortars, and infantry-fired antitank weapons opened up, there'd be so much dust in the air that identification of friend or foe would be virtually impossible from the air as one mighty fusillade crashed in on what Leigh hoped would be a surprised enemy. This was a commander's dream, having time to place your forces precisely where you wanted them. What could possibly go wrong? Leigh asked himself. He had ordered three Bradley M3 scouts to videotape the victory, to be shown later on CNN. Two things would immediately follow a win here. It would deliver a crippling psychological blow to the morale of Freeman's forces and a corresponding rise in the militia's morale. This would force Washington to talk about an accommodation in the seceded states' favor. And second, it would result in a surge of new militia recruits. Everybody loves a winner.

It was still dark and the desert's immense silence seemed ready to explode.

"They're in the corridor." The defilade tank commander's voice was calm, controlled, yet even his tone conveyed the tension he felt as the first of SOUFOR, three M3 Bradley scouts, edged into view, then a long line of Oshkosh M1017/M1000 heavy transporters, M1s on their backs.

"Jesus," said one of Leigh's NORFOR gunners in defilade, seeing the first tank through his sight and getting its reticle, or yellow dot, in the crosshairs. "The fuckers are being hauled!"

"Wake up, Texas," the tank commander commented wryly. "This isn't the fuckin' movies." He meant that given the fact that SOUFOR was coming from hundreds of miles away, his gunner's expectation that SOUFOR's armor would be moving on its own steam was naive.

For Leigh, however, the spread-out nature of SOUFOR's column posed an immediate tactical problem. Though he half expected their M1s to be on transporters, the distance between them meant that if Leigh had his tanks in defilade fire too soon, he would take out only a handful of the enemy's tanks at the cost of alerting the entire column, which was yet to hove into sight. On the other hand, if he let SOUFOR's squadron of transported tanks pass his defilade tanks, he was risking imminent discovery.

He gave the order to engage.

"Gunner! Sabot! Tank!" came the order in the fifty tanks. TIS—thermal imaging system—allowed each gunner to see his target, white on black or black on white, his choice. "Identified!"

Each gunner's laser range finder had the distance to target, 700 meters, 875 yards, displayed on the green screen.

The loader, hearing "Sabot!", already had an APFDS—armor-piercing, fin-stabilized, discarding sabot, or penetrator rod—round in the 120mm gun's breech. The breech slammed closed, the loader, punching in the hollow "ready to go" white square that appeared adjacent to the range readout, yelled, "Up!"

"Fire!" yelled the commander.

"On the way!" shouted the gunner, simultaneously squeezing the trigger—total time from command to execution five-point-two seconds, each of the seventy defilade tanks sending a long, thirteen-pound, aluminum six-finned tungsten dart at over 3,000 miles an hour slamming into ten of SOUFOR's Oshkosh-pulled tanks. Each struck in a one-square-inch area with the force of a ten-ton cement truck traveling at seventy mph.

The M1 has the best rolled-steel armor the world has ever seen, but it couldn't take this unless the dart hit the sloped armor on such an oblique angle as to glance off, and two did. The other eight tanks, however, exploded as buzzing superheated fragments began spalling, flaking off from the interior of the tank because of the tremendous impact, the white-hot fragments setting men and machine afire, the turret hatches blown off, belching enormous Roman candles of fire shooting so high and with such intensity that they brilliantly illuminated the edge of several salt-lake beds, or playas, a quarter mile away as if the latter were white china. Leigh could hear SOUFOR's panic on the radio net.

"Red Three. Red Three. We're hit!"

"Clear the net."

"Say aga—"

"Clear the fucking *net*!"

"Johnny's bleeding badly—it's on my sights. I can't read. Get 'im off me. Shit!"

"Shut up. Calm down. Keep fuckin' *calm*!"

"I'm goin' higher," said one commander. "Green Channel. Get off the fucking net!"

Leigh's gunners had already smacked the ammunition door switch with their right knees, the bustle's main magazine door opening, another round quickly extracted by the loader, and in one movement, through a hundred and eighty degrees, slid into the breech. The scream of artillery shells could be heard as Leigh's 155mm's opened up in a deadly creeping barrage whose rounds, because of Leigh's quick information, did not pound the already-disabled tanks but rather began falling on the tail of the SOUFOR column that snaked back for miles beyond the Alvord and through the ghost town of Andrews.

It was a brilliant move on Leigh's part, for by having his artillery pound the enemy column's tail, he was not wasting ammunition on the M1s on transporters up front, letting his defilade tanks on the southern edge of the corridor and his tanks at the northern end of the corridor deal with any armor that might attempt to break out.

The rising sun bathed the desert in a golden light and the gunners quickly moved to optical sighting rather than remaining in thermal-image mode.

SOUFOR, as its radio traffic showed Leigh, was in utter confusion and shock. Radios still sounded like the Tower of Babel. Their reaction was slower than anticipated, and in two minutes they lost nine more tanks, on transporters, even as other tanks, their transporter ramps clanging down, rolled off the semis' flatbeds into battle. Two tanks, while still on their transporters, fired at the flashes of Leigh's defilade tanks, an action not appreciated by the two transporter drivers, who, without earplugs, were deafened by the boom of the 120mm main gun, the flaming belch of hot gases from the barrel's fume extractor momentarily blinding them as well, the combined shock of noise and color rendering them incapable of responding intelligently to the screaming voices on the radio.

Most of SOUFOR's gunners couldn't see the inverted Vs on the sides of Leigh's tanks, the latter being dug in in defilade positions and only appearing briefly in the great clouds of dust created by SOUFOR's own panic. Now Leigh's fifty M1s at the northern end of the corridor started sending rod-penetrator and HEAT rounds screaming southward into SOUFOR's already-confused squadrons, only one of Leigh's tanks taken out by a HEAT round that caused spalling inside, the hot fragments of steel and ceramic tile liner flying about the interior, blinding the gunner and short-circuiting the digital systems, rendering the MIL Standard 1553 data bus inoperable, wiping out the DID—driver's integrated display—the stunned loader staggering forward into the recoil of the tube, or main gun, as it fired, its 118-ton punch driving one of his helmet's earphones into his head, killing him instantly. The driver, isolated up front, was frozen in fear, the gunner in the turret basket hearing the sergeant commander's voice screaming, "Unman! Unman!" Everybody was getting out as fast as they could, the gunner, using his forward hatch directly under the cannon, literally cut to pieces by superheated steel debris as a rod penetrator sheared off and broke against the four-inch-thick, seventy-five-degree-sloped-steel armor of the next tank in defilade.

"Smoke!" Leigh ordered. "Cover in smoke."

It was a quick but calculated decision, Leigh knowing it would create problems for his infantry but afford his tanks in defilade extended protection, for even though the TIS—thermal imaging system—could slice through it, the smoke would make identification harder. There was another reason Leigh was gambling with smoke. At any moment he expected his Apache gunships, and then SOUFOR's, to enter the fray. His helos would know that any tank in the corridor south of Leigh's northern echelons was the enemy, but SOUFOR's pilots would enter a smoke- and dust-filled two-mile-wide corridor, having to identify before firing. The alternative would be what had happened in the Gulf War—behind all the PR about the video war—losing more men from blue-on-blue than were lost from enemy fire.

"Gunner! Heat! Twelve o'clock!" It was a SOUFOR commander who was about to send off a high-explosive round toward Leigh's tanks, coming at him just over a mile dead ahead, the gunner's target a shimmering white on black, 1,500 meters, the amount of dust particles in the air degrading the laser ranging system by the second.

His right knee on the blast-door open switch, the loader hauled out a fifty-five-pound HEAT round, the blast door closed, and he swung the round into the tube's breech. "Up!"

"Fire!"

"On the way!" The tube—or gun—jerked back and the HEAT round was off, a fume-extractor fan purring, reducing the acrid smell of cordite in the turret, the barrel now in counterrecoil forward, the breech opening, shucking the hot shell base into a bucket on the floor, the rest of the shell's casing having combusted during firing. The bullet-shaped round, having traveled at over a mile per second, slammed into the target NORFOR tank, the downward-pointing charge inside the round exploding, sending a long tongue of molten metal through the armor at twenty thousand miles an hour, causing heavy spalling of steel-ceramic tile that penetrated the magazine door, causing a sabot round to explode. The bulk of the explo-

sion vented through the magazine's top blast panels, the
fire extinguisher nozzle automatically activated, drench-
ing the badly wounded loader. The gunner, seeing the
FCEU—firing control electronics unit—was out and the
loader down, took over loading duties. The commander,
a lieutenant in his override position, pressed the red
"slew/slave" button, swinging the turret through a thirty-
degree arc in less than a second, centering a target.

A second HEAT round struck two of the tank's three
vision blocks on the right side of the commander's
cupola, and following the tremendous explosion and ball
of flame that engulfed the tank, the driver, strapped in,
couldn't get any response. Inside the turret, six feet aft of
him, the IVS's—intervehicular information system's—
electronic page was smashed, only the three "mode"
switches remaining intact. And the two SINGARS—
single-channel ground and airborne radio systems—were
dead.

In a matter of seconds the driver could hear the roar of
a fire above his hatch, like the sound of a waterfall. But
the hatch was hot to the touch, so he opted for the other
exit behind him into the turret, but it was jammed shut.
The temperature was rising. It was the forward hatch or
nothing. He could hear the coaxial machine-gun rounds
cooking off, but it was still the hatch or nothing as he
gingerly opened the hatch. The fire, hungry for oxygen,
licked in, and despite his Nomex fire-retardant suit, his
hair caught on fire. By the time he suffocated it with
his helmet, he had third-degree burns to his scalp.
Screaming, not knowing what to do, peeing himself to
dampen his legs, he flung open the hatch. As he exited,
the fire enveloped him, and aflame, he jumped off the
tank, hit the desert sand, and immediately started to roll
to snuff out the flames. The driver in the next tank,
wanting to get away from the burning tank loaded with

ammo, its fuel tanks carrying over 450 gallons of diesel, shoved his M1 into first reverse and, turning the handlebar wrist throttle, gunned the vacuum-cleaner-sounding 1,500-horsepower gas turbine from zero to thirty miles per hour in nine seconds, backing over the other driver, whom he never saw.

Three seconds later the tank of the dead driver exploded into a roaring column of fire over a hundred feet high, transforming the soft morning light into dust-filled glare.

By now, SOUFOR's tanks, their commanders over the initial shock of being fired upon by what they now believed must be a renegade militia regiment, began peeling off, east of the sagebrush-speckled corridor onto the edge of the white playa of the Alvord, away from the smoke and dust and into sand dunes. But almost instantly they attracted the first attacks of Leigh's thirty-four air-cavalry "Uglies" or AH-64A Apaches. Things were coming apart, and though in theory the Apaches' missiles were supposed to lock onto a laser from an independent source—either an infantryman or Kiowa or other helo scout—thereby "painting" the target, the reality was different. Gulf War and 'Nam veterans alike were having as much difficulty as those who had never been in action before. Again it was the problem of differentiating friend from foe, and Leigh's NORFOR, though also thrown into some confusion by tanks that looked exactly like their own, still had the advantage of the attacker in knowing, by means of the IVS's electronic pages that went from tank to tank without any voice intervention, where most of his tanks were.

The SOUFOR Apaches also arrived to do battle, but not until seven to eight minutes after the twenty-four NORFOR Apaches. Though the NORFOR helos, like those of SOUFOR, would soon have to be recalled because of the high risk of blue-on-blue incidents in clouds of sand and in smoke thrown up from Leigh's tanks, Bradleys, etc., those eight minutes during which Leigh's helos had been unopposed took a terrible toll on the federals.

As each of the Apache pilots and gunners brought their craft above the high sand dunes and looked at their assigned targets—pilots at the less-armored Bradleys and now Hummers; gunners at tanks "painted" by their own laser beam—PNVs, or pilot night-vision sensors, projected data displays onto the MIDDs (miniature data displays), the pilot's helmet-mounted display recording the changing data in his line of sight wherever she or he moved their helmet. Meanwhile one of the Apaches' computers continued calculating fire-control vectors over the undulating sand dunes and the whiteness of Lake Alvord's playa, the relatively thin tops of SOUFOR's tanks easily perforated by laser-sliding hundred-pound Hellfire missiles.

During this battle of the Alvord, Leigh's twenty-four Apaches went "alone" against the tanks—that is, conditions being inimical to using other helos as "painters," each Apache, mostly using the dunes as pop-up, duck-down cover, rose and fired two to three of its sixteen missiles, using the helo's own onboard laser designator. As soon as the first tank was hit, the Apache swung its laser onto the second target, this second missile already in flight, its laser nose seeker causing it to veer sharply to the new on-target beam and so on until all sixteen Hellfires were expended.

During all this time at least half of Leigh's Apaches were simultaneously engaging mechanized infantry personnel carriers, Bradleys, and Hummers with the Apaches' underbelly-slung, 1,200-round, 30mm armor-piercing chain guns, their barrels spewing down fire at ten rounds a second. SOUFOR's Bradleys were by no means silent and took out three of Leigh's Apaches, with their deadly antitank TOW missiles, which almost rivaled the Hellfire in their penetration capability. But the Bradley had a major flaw—or, as Leigh had pointed out in one of his more jocular moods, it was a "motion-challenged vehicle" insofar as it had to come to a complete stop in order to fire its TOW missiles. This proved to be a deadly delay, time enough for Leigh's air-to-ground Hellfires to kill most of SOUFOR's Bradleys as well as over seventy-eight of SOUFOR's M1s in those early minutes of confusion. It wasn't as impressive a score as had been racked up in Kuwait, where at one juncture over five hundred Iraqi tanks had been taken out at the cost of one Apache, but here in the Alvord it was spectacular enough. After all, Leigh's helos had been up against the best main battle tank in the world and had devastated SOUFOR, who, by comparison, had only managed to take out or disable thirteen of Leigh's tanks. By the time SOUFOR's twenty Apaches had withdrawn, the Alvord corridor resembled the road to Basra in the Gulf War, a sea of scrap metal that only minutes before the Americans had hit it was a traffic jam of fleeing vehicles.

The sagebrush country was littered with the split road wheels of tanks, unraveled tracks, the hulks of burned-out Abrams and hydraulic fluid that had bled black on the dry salt pans or been soaked up by the sage-dotted sand. Here and there men, or rather what was left of them, were draped and smeared over exit hatches. Some of them, charred corpses, were on the sand, twisted into grotesque shapes by the infernos, others missing limbs and heads, the Alvord sky filled with spreading plumes of dense black smoke.

*　*　*

"What the fuck happened?" asked a battle-shocked boy of eighteen. It had lasted less than thirty minutes, not much more than some of the murderous Iraqi engagements of Desert Storm, Colonel Leigh killed in the final moments, incinerated in his command tank. Over 1,283 tank crewmen and mechanized infantry were marked "X," over 2,000 "W" in SOUFOR's regimental log, the remainder, "M" for missing in action, the whole debacle sending an earthquake through the Pentagon about the increasing dangers of blue-on-blue in the civil war. It also paralyzed FEDFOR commanders and their officer corps. *Jesus, look what happened in the Alvord.* The mystery of the inverted Vs was never solved because the Pentagon assumed that Leigh had, through no fault of his own, been informed incorrectly, tragically, that SOUFOR was renegade and, as any good officer would do, tried to stop it. And did so.

It was an enormous victory for General Mant, for now every FEDFOR, from private to general, was gun-shy out of fear of killing one of their own. Mant immediately ordered "maximum effort," intending to capitalize on the mood of hesitation, which, as *The New York Times* conceded in its editorial, had spread like a malaise through the U.S. Army. As he gave the order Mant remembered the advice a famous racing driver had given him. The instant a terrible crash occurred, the man said, every driver momentarily eased up ... except for him: he put his foot down on the accelerator—as hard as he could.

CHAPTER THIRTY-NINE

LATRELL WAS OUT of control. And so were a lot of militiamen, buoyed, almost delirious, by the news of the great FEDFOR defeat in the Alvord, in which billions of dollars of federal equipment, meant to be thrown against the militia, was now so much junk, a somber lesson to Washington of just how much damage could be done by those units, all of them in the northwest cleaver, who had officially declared, or were now declaring, themselves on the side of the rebels.

Overseas, the value of the U.S. dollar fell dramatically while shares in General Electric, General Motors, Martin Marietta, Hughes Systems, and other defense companies soared. International coverage of Russia's problems in the Republics paled in comparison with the Battle of the Alvord, and in the frantic ensuing media search for "accountability," the cry was out for Shelbourne's resignation. Freeman was still being celebrated for his victory at Butcher's Ridge, but his detractors were demanding louder than ever to know where in hell was Ames, who had started all this bloodshed, and where in hell was Latrell, the prime suspect in the assassination of the attorney general of the most powerful nation on earth?

The foreign press in particular was having a field day

at America's expense. Washington could put a man on the moon but they couldn't apprehend a known militiaman and suspected killer of one of their highest officials. In the English-speaking world, only the more serious British and Canadian papers empathized with the United States' position, with the difficulty in a democracy of combating the militia. Italy and Germany were sympathetic, the Russians were saying "*See*, you have your own problems." The French were gloating, seeing every point lost by America as a gain for them. By the third day after the Alvord, Freeman, having taken over command from Trevor, was, as an unoriginal CNN announcer said, "Behind the eight ball." The federalist supporters were demanding that he end the war with a crushing blow against the militia's Astoria front, where morale—particularly that of Latrell and Ames, who fought there, though they had never met—was at an unprecedented high.

There was another reason for the militia's elation: whereas they had held the Astoria or "Big Bridge" from the beginning, they'd had a "close-run thing" with YB, Old Youngs Bay Bridge, until Nestar, aided by continuing bad weather, recently claimed it. This meant that the militia now had consolidated its hold on the bridge and therefore on the southern—Oregonian—side of the Columbia. And while officially the militia told the press that they were "dismayed" by Nestar's use of hostages, which "wouldn't be condoned or repeated"—unofficially they were, as Mant told Colonel Vance, "damn glad" they had both YB and AB, for this meant they could reinforce and resupply the Oregon militia's spearhead on the southern bank.

In Washington, the air-force chief advocated bombing the militia, "as we did in the Sawtooth Wilderness."

"The problem with that, General," the president told him, "is that they aren't *in* the Sawtooth Wilderness."

"Yes, sir, but I'm sure that with a smart bomb we could—"

"General," the president cut in, "you can't be sure of anything. We bombed hell out of that ridge in the Sawtooth and we still haven't got this Latrell, Ames, *or* this media legend-of-the-moment, Lucky McBride. All I need is for another civilian to be killed near either of those bridges and this goddamn thing could blow up in our face. *Again!*" He paused, realizing anger was overcoming his usual statesmanlike demeanor.

"But, sir," Shelbourne persisted, gamely for a man on the brink of being reassigned. "The bridges are a different matter than the Sawtooth Wilderness. YB is a quarter mile long. AB is four miles long. Once the weather clears—"

"*If* it clears," the president interrupted again. "Sorry, go on, General."

"Well, sir, if we get a clear shot at it, even for a few moments, we can aim at the middle of the bridges. That gives us a safety zone—if we miss."

"Correct me if I'm wrong, General Shelbourne, but isn't it true that contrary to public opinion and neat, highly selective Gulf War videos, hitting a bridge, even with smart weapons, is a very tricky thing?"

Before he could answer, the air-force chief cut in. "We'd need weapons-free status for that."

"You have it!" said the president.

Amid the pervasive gloom of the White House, the president and his assembled cabinet finally received some good news later that afternoon. Air-force fighter-bombers had taken advantage of a momentary break in the cloud and fog over the Columbia and had successfully bombed a thirty-foot section of the Old Youngs Bay Bridge. That was the good news. The bad came fifteen minutes later when it was learned that one of General Trevor's forward observers on the southern side of the Astoria Bridge had seen black-clad figures, the militia in fatigues, hurrying out through the fog from both ends of the Astoria Bridge, herding hostages before them and placing them at two-hundred-yard intervals across the bridge.

"Dammit!" said the president, letting the report fall from his hands. "We still need to cut that Astoria Bridge if we're to cut off the militia's supply line. That's the key." He shook his head. "Cunning bastards"—he apologized to Patricia Wyeth, then continued—"they know after the outcry about Trevor ordering those civilians shot that we won't bomb the bridge so long as hostages are on it. How low can you get?"

"They're desperate," said Shelbourne. "Despite their high morale, Mant knows that no matter what gains they've made, Freeman'll wipe them out if they can't hold that bridge. At first Mant was ready to blow it up if he couldn't hold it, but now he's gotten cocky. He's got so many men on the south side of the river, he has to have the bridge to win."

The president's forehead was creased with worry lines. "Ask Freeman for his take on the situation."

"I already have," Shelbourne answered. "He warns that if the militia have this bridge, they can enlarge the war. If we deny it to them, we win."

The president shook his head. "But what in hell can we do with all those hostages there? As soon as we move toward the bridge, they shoot the hostages."

CHAPTER FORTY

LUCKY McBRIDE AND Latrell had fought together in the Sawtooth, but that's as far as it went. McBride took an instant dislike to the other militiaman, who had been forced onto him by Mant and whose eyes had the gleam of the zealot. McBride didn't know whether Latrell had been involved in the killing of the attorney general, but with a zealot he knew anything was possible. McBride was in the militia because he was fed up with what he saw as government by federal bureaucrats whose only allegiance was to themselves and not to the country, bureaucrats who didn't even begin to understand the West—same as they didn't understand 'Nam. But as far as he could tell, Latrell was a straight-out hater, hated everything and anyone who stood in his way, like all this Nazi shit he and Hearn had indulged in, Hearn with a swastika tattooed on his shoulder. Hearn hated authority, period. McBride hadn't liked the skinhead either, but the trouble was that Hearn and Latrell were both damn good fighters and had given as much as they took on Butcher's Ridge. And McBride knew that, in some respects at least, the militia was no different from the army. You had all kinds of misfits in the army, too. Witness 'Nam—he'd seen as many psychos in uniform as he'd seen outside.

The trick was to organize them, harness their mad energy into a fighting force for your cause, and Mant, though it had taken many years, had achieved this with the help of men like McBride, who felt that in 'Nam their government had forsaken them, men who had come home to a country that didn't want them, men who wanted a country of their own out west.

After McBride and Latrell reached the Astoria front, Latrell was quickly assigned to the general defense of the Astoria Bridge, to what the militias called "posse" defense—mobile squads of men, usually nine or ten, whose job it was to be on call for any emergency, to plug any hole that the federals might open in the militia's defense.

The presence of McBride, now in charge of a battalion, lifted morale on the Astoria front even higher. Already a legend for his gutsy defense of Butcher's Ridge, no matter that he was eventually forced to withdraw, the 'Nam-veteran-turned-militia-force-multiplier was also feted by the underground press across the country. For many Americans the fighting on the Astoria front was reducible—perhaps because it was easier to grasp than a bunch of situational maps—to a showdown between Freeman and Mant, the latter represented by Lucky McBride. The fact, dug up by CNN's Marte Price, that Lucky McBride's brother, Major William McBride, was a federal occasioned no particular surprise, as so many men had brothers, fathers, and other relatives fighting on opposite sides, each believing in their cause as passionately as those opposing them believed in theirs.

Ames, on the other hand, didn't believe in any cause, not now that his wife and children were gone. How could God permit that? What possible lesson, what possible good, could come from their murder? Nothing. For

Ames, what had to be done was as clear as the nose on his face.

Keeping his head down in the fog as small-arms fire crackled all around, Norton reached Douglas Freeman as the general was leaning over the front of his Hummer, consulting the topographic map of the Astoria front, and clearly he didn't like what he saw. "This Astoria front," he told Norton, "what the media is calling the Astoria front is starting to look more like a goddamn bucket." His gesture swept across the map from Mount St. Helen's to the coast. "And a leaky bucket at that. Norton, we've got to stop this militia buildup before they break out. Only way we can do that is separate the head from the tail. Sever that goddamn Astoria Bridge."

Norton didn't bother answering; his boss was thinking aloud. Still studying the map, Freeman continued: "The militia's strong suit is their intimate knowledge of the Northwest and their mobility. By the time our guys figure out where they are, Mant's boys have moved again. Only way we can defeat them, Norton, is to cut off the supply tail, slow their momentum long enough for us to launch a major concerted armored attack. That's what *we're* best suited for. But"—Freeman sighed, only now looking up at his aide—"we have a slight problem."

"How to cut the bridge?" Norton suggested.

"Yes," Freeman acknowledged. "But more than that. I know these sons-of-bitches, Norton. We're going to have to make a double play before we win the series."

Norton was taken aback. Surely *the* priority was the Big Bridge, the main artery pumping the lifeblood of supplies across the river. "What's the double play, General?"

"Norton, if you wanted to knock out federal forces' morale here, what would you do?"

"Bump you off, General."

"Damn right. You get rid of my tactical genius, Norton, and FEDFOR is in deep shit!"

Norton didn't crack a smile. The general meant every word and Norton figured his boss had earned the right, from his famous tank "retreat" feint as part of the U.N. force in Siberia to his Southeast Asian battles with Chinese regulars. He wasn't slow to accept either responsibility or praise, didn't mind being right up at the front as he was now rather than in some safe HQ well back from the fighting. Which was why, he told Norton, he had to try to get Mant. "Mant's cut from the same cloth, Norton. Stays close to where the action is."

"He wasn't at Butcher's Ridge, General. Least I didn't see him there."

"Don't be so goddamn literal, Norton. Besides which—and it bothers me to say this—but Butcher's Ridge, *my* Butcher's Ridge, wasn't the main battle. For political reasons, yes—to get Hearn and this other joker—"

"Latrell."

"Yes. It still is politically important with the world watching for us to get Latrell, but militarily, Norton, here"—he stabbed at Astoria with his gloved fingers—"here is where we have to break their balls militarily. And intelligence reports place Mant in the area."

"Can they be more specific than that?" Norton asked.

"Not at the moment. They're trying to triangulate militia radio traffic—on the assumption that the center of all the buzz must be the HQ."

"May not be a very sound assumption, General."

"No, but it's the best we've got so far. In any event, I want you to stay on it. Make it your priority, Norton. Find out precisely where he is."

"Yes, sir. Meantime, General, what about the bridge?"

"SEALs," said Freeman. "I've already made the request. Navy's been pissed off about being left out of the proceedings anyhow." He looked up at Norton. "Well, now's their chance to send in a team. Blow it up."

"The whole four miles?" Norton joked.

"Told them I'd settle for a span, Norton. Enough to stop the militia's goddamn trucks getting across with those hostages aboard." The general stood up, dropping his pen disgustedly on the map. "It's a wonder the militia doesn't tie the poor bastards to the hoods of their pickups. I tell you, Norton, this business with the hostages—this Nestar prick—is the most despicable aspect of this war. This grew out of Waco and the Freemen." The general sighed heavily. " 'Course, it's as old a tactic as war itself. Despicable, though. We should've known the kind of people we'd be up against after the Oklahoma bombing."

"When are the SEALs going in?"

Freeman glanced at his watch. It was one o'clock in the morning. "They'll be coming downriver now."

The SEALs—Sea, Land, Air warriors—seven of them, in wet suits, faces blackened, crouched low and all but invisible in the darkness, were aboard an IBS—Inflatable Boat, Small—complete with weapons, sea anchor, carbon-dioxide cylinder, ropes, and enough C4 plastique to take out six pylons. Now all the training at Coronado, from the use of the new PRC-624 waterproofed handheld VHF/FM radio to the BUD/S—Basic Underwater Demolition/SEALs—course, would pay off, including the long hours of running in sand carrying a 250-pound log, of two-mile ocean swims, of having to run fourteen miles in less than two hours, of having to dive with legs and arms tied behind their backs, of having to perform a blind breakdown and reassembly of all weapons in the dark against the clock. Each of the seven men was also highly trained in marksmanship. All their training had been designed for just this kind of mission.

On the northern side of the river, over sixteen miles east of the Columbia's mouth and eight miles east of the Astoria Bridge, the seven SEALs were navigating their way carefully downriver in the deep channel through fog and the maze of sandbars and marshes that, for the most part, lay on their left-hand side, south of the Tongue Point Channel. Soon the channel would swing southeast, cutting diagonally across the river toward its southern shore and passing beneath the highest part of the bridge, whose superstructure at this point roughly resembled a smaller Golden Gate, over two hundred feet high. From its high Astoria side, the bridge sloped down to run for two miles, much of it on steel matting, twenty-five feet above sea level and across the sometimes visible Desdemona Sands. Then it rose again to a height of forty-nine feet above the north ship channel before descending once more as it neared the Washington State shore.

The SEAL team, under the leadership of Lieutenant Gus Morgan, after following the Tongue Point Channel for several miles, both shorelines of which were under militia occupation, planned to cut away midway across the river, at this point five miles wide, avoiding the higher Golden Gate–like span in favor of the long, twenty-five-foot-high, seventeen-foot-wide, two-lane steel matting section of the bridge above Desdemona Sands. Here, they hoped, they could anchor the IBS in the thick fog and, swimming a short distance to the bridge, plant "earmuff"-shaped charges on several of the four-foot-diameter concrete pylons that held up one of the 140 eighty-foot-long concrete spans.

Even with night-vision goggles the navigation required would have been impossible without the team's handheld

GPS—Global Positioning System—units by means of which the orbiting satellites, through their complex array of onboard computers and atomic clocks, could give the SEALs their position on the river to within fifty feet. Land forms, even close-by islands and sandbars, were notoriously unreliable to use for navigating, for even if they could be seen through the chilly fog, reference points were difficult to find because of changing shapes brought on by the ebb and flow of the tide. A sandbar now visible might shortly disappear, or vice versa.

One of the seven men, Petty Officer Bryan Seth, checked the "earmuff" high-explosive charges, so called because, although they looked like large champagne bottles, the SEALs intended to put one on either side of selected pylons, giving each pylon an "earmuff" look. Another man, hunkered down in the boat, using a blue-lensed pencil light, checked their position against his knee map that was encased in a clear plastic water-proofed pocket and told Gus Morgan that they'd soon require a surge of power from the Mercury outboard. The outboard was relatively quick, and given the five-mile width of the river, the almost continuous crackle of small-arms fire along both shores, and the occasional boom of bigger guns, Morgan knew the whir of the motor would probably be lost. Still, when it started up, Gus Morgan intuitively felt apprehensive as he wondered whether his was the only vessel on the river. If he were Nestar, in charge of the bridge defense, he would have boats out looking despite the fog and wide reach of the river. As if the mere thought of it had brought it on, Morgan heard a soft slapping noise off to his right and signaled to the others, most of whom had heard it also.

Muscles taut, the seven men strained to see through the foggy darkness, several of them, including Petty Officer Seth, already suffering headaches from the night-vision goggles. Seth saw a long shape in the darkness. The next instant they felt a thump followed by a long, scraping noise, and the boat was abruptly smacked off course. A string of obscenities would have followed had they not been trained to maintain silence on such ops. The big log continued on its way. Lieutenant Gus Morgan flipped up the safety of his stubby Heckler & Koch MP5A5 submachine gun and exhaled in a sigh of relief.

PO Seth felt a sudden chill on his cheek and wondered if a breeze was starting up. He hoped not, because it would mean an end to the fog that along with the cover of darkness afforded them protection from discovery by the militia. Did Nestar have sentries along the entire length of the bridge—four miles? Would he even guess that Freeman had ordered the bridge blown? Seth was aware of the man next to him hunkering down again to check their position relative to the bridge, still several miles downriver, and he thought about how his ten-year-old son would like one of the pencil-beam lights. The thought caused Seth to force his mind back to the mission, knowing that even a momentary lapse like that could jeopardize the whole op. The blue pencil light went off.

In anticipation of the bridge's destruction, Freeman was ordering a company of fourteen M1 tanks forward three miles to the south of the river on the Lewis and Clark Road. This north-south road led up to YB, the Old Youngs Bay Bridge, and for the most part had been retaken by Freeman's FEDFOR, reinforced now by the Portland National Guard unit that had broken out north from the battle at Cannon Beach. Other armored units were also moving toward the Astoria Pocket, and Freeman was confident, as he told Norton, that if and when the Astoria Bridge was cut, the militia's morale would plummet, at least among all those on the southern bank who would suddenly find themselves cut off from Mant's milk cow. At least that was the plan. It all depended on the bridge.

Though the tanks began to move up, they did so at a snail's pace, the drivers barely able to see the road and fearful, with good reason, of booby traps, for while the M1, "the Beast," was an awesome monster, it was a blind monster in the fog and in the smoke from fires deliberately started by the militia to mix with the fog. And along with their forty APDS and HEAT rounds, Freeman's tank crews were also carrying the knowledge of what had happened in the Alvord, where other M1s exactly like their own had suddenly opened fire on SOUFOR and wreaked havoc on the federal forces. Many of Freeman's tank crews were Gulf War veterans and they knew that even at ten mph, a good clip in combat despite all the PR pictures of tanks galloping at forty mph across the countryside, the danger of a blue-on-blue was as real as any potential attack by the enemy.

Militia troops could not see the tanks at first but heard them as a low-level growl, remarkably quiet given their sixty-plus-ton weight. Militia TAKS, or tank killer squads, were also moving *toward* the sound of the M1s coming cautiously along the road, other tanks, encouraged by those already advancing, moving in the direction of the river, some on the coastal 101 missing the right-hand turn that would have had them link up with the Lewis and Clark Road and instead following the train tracks to the small town of Warrenton before they turned right, coming close to the militia-sabotaged Port of Astoria Airport. Here militia troops defending the airport were equipped with LAW antitank missiles. Moving down the drainage ditches, the militia were out for engine kills, where the missile would not be aimed at the sloped front armor or thick sides of the tank but at the engine grille at the back, which along with the tank's belly and turret top was its most vulnerable spot. Anticipating this, Freeman had ordered his own infantry down the ditches to run interference for the BUFs, or "Big Ugly Fuckers," as they were affectionately known to the foot soldiers. The fighting here was chaotic and hand-to-hand, men coming upon each other in the fog unsure of whether it was friend or foe, recognition possible by helmet shape alone, and if you didn't have a helmet you were shot, stabbed, or both—those out of ammo using their entrenching tool to chop and fell the enemy. Now and then the M1 tanks were able to fire: directed by a FEDFOR infantryman, some tank commanders, doing an Israeli, head out of the hatch, hosed the drainage trench with the turret-mounted .50-caliber machine gun and the loader used the 7.62mm machine gun above his hatch, sending long red-and-white dashes of tracer streaking out into the night.

There was the bang and pop of parachute flares fired and opening up, turning the fog into huge canopies of incandescent whiteness, revealing lumps of tanks and stalks of any infantry gutsy or panicked enough to move rather than freezing as the flares descended. Despite the FEDFOR infantry, four engine kills were made within twenty minutes of the start of Freeman's armor movement, two crews saved by the sprinkler dousing the fire, the engine a write-off, three of the eight men killed and two badly burned as they exited the flaming tanks. One M1's HEAT rounds started to explode as a crewman, aflame, exited his tank, running into a rain-sodden field immediately beyond the drainage ditch that was now the site of more brutal and unforgiving close-quarter combat. The stutter of AK-47s and M-16 bursts punctuated the screams and oaths of dying men, fallen helmets thudding on the roadway—in the militia's case, clattering, because they lacked canvas covers—fiercely contested firefights breaking out all around the airport perimeter, particularly near the long northwest-southeast runway.

As difficult as it was for Mant's men to maintain possession of the vital airport and the shorter landing strip thirteen miles east near Svensen, south of Russian Island, the foggy conditions favored the militia's defense, since they rendered any attempt by Freeman's FEDFOR to ferry in Airborne troops extremely difficult. Even the red warning lights atop the Astoria and Old Youngs Bay bridges were thought to have been obscured by the fog, but in reality, the militia, under Mant's express order, had shot out the lights, further ensuring nothing less than a suicidal descent for any gung-ho helo pilot. Though it was lifting in spots, the fog had also stymied Freeman's attempt to move in his 82nd paratroop reinforcements, who were now impatiently and, for many, anxiously, awaiting a firm order to either stand down or go for it. Freeman understood their frustration but had no intention of repeating the disaster that followed General Trevor's ordering of the initial jump.

"Jesus Christ!" said Freeman. "Where are those goddamn SEALs?"

Norton ventured into the back of a lead Bradley scout, closed the door, and turned on the red light. He felt as if he were in a submarine as he checked his watch against the roll-map overlay of the Astoria Pocket, seeing the hodgepodge disposition of the FEDFOR's units. Only two areas, one around the airport, the other around the marshes of Daggett Point less than a mile east of Old Youngs Bay Bridge, were shown as being civilian-free, most of the pocket still peppered by clusters of noncombatants who, unable to move because of the fighting, were a further impediment to any airborne drop. Norton switched off the light and banged his shin on the edge of the ramp door as he exited the Bradley. After rubbing the abrasion vigorously, cussing, and reminding himself that a lot of men in the pocket had a damn sight more to worry about than a bruised leg, he told Freeman that by his estimation the SEALs should now be approaching the bridge and—

Suddenly a rush of static invaded all cellular phones.

"Goddammit!" said Freeman. "They must have taken out the microwave tower near Westport. Get FEDFOR's engineers on the radio link. I want a dish up and I want it fast."

"Yes, sir," Norton answered. He wasn't normally a superstitious man, but he couldn't help recalling the old belief that bad things happened in threes: first the engine kills, second the microwave tower gone, and next . . . what? The SEALs swept away from the Astoria Bridge by the outgoing tide? Or had the Alvord been the first, the second the engine kills, the third the MW station? In which case . . .

"Knock it off!" he muttered to himself.

"What's that?" asked Freeman, looking through his NV binoculars and still not seeing much.

"Nothing, General," Norton replied. "I'm contacting the engineers by landline."

"Good." It gave Freeman an idea. "And Norton?"

"Yes, General?"

"Call CNN. Give it to Big Tits—Marte Price—that General Mant is dead. Killed in action."

"May I ask why, General?"

"Because then Mant's HQ—wherever the hell he's moved to—will have to reassure the troops that their leader is alive and well. That surge in radio traffic should tell us precisely where he is. Then I can go and shoot the bastard myself."

"Yes, sir."

While Norton went about contacting the engineers, Freeman said a prayer, a weather prayer to get rid of the goddamn fog. If God had stepped in at Bastogne in '44 to allow Patton close air support in Third Army's relief of the city, why in hell couldn't he clear the skies over Astoria?

In his southern Washington HQ hideaway, General Mant was equally sure that God in his beneficence would maintain the foul weather along the Columbia-Snake line, giving him more time to reinforce the front. There was already ample evidence of the Almighty's intervention on the side of the rebels. Look at General George Washington, leader of the revolutionaries against the oppressive federalism of the British. Washington's uniform was riddled with bullet holes, his hat had been shot off, and three chargers had been shot out from under him, yet he persisted in leading *his* revolutionaries at the front, unafraid of the enemy's fire, knowing God was on his side. Mant was certain it would be the same with him. He had asked for God's guidance at the very beginning of the war, and the stunning reverses suffered by the FEDFOR cavalry regiment in the Alvord were but one example of divine intervention.

Confident they must be nearing the bridge, Lieutenant Gus Morgan's SEALs were crouched, ready to slip over the side with the earmuff charges while Petty Officer Seth stayed with the inflatable. But there was still no sign of the bridge, even though Gus Morgan figured they must be there by now. It occurred to Morgan that in the dense fog they might have passed under one of the bridge's eighty-foot spans without realizing it, and he whispered to the knee-pad SEAL to check the GPS. The blue pencil light clicked on . . . and everything happened at once. There was the babble of excited voices somewhere up ahead, the bang of a flare gun, and the roar of an M60 machine gun, its one-in-four red tracer shooting out in the fog, whistling above the SEALs. The flare burst and in a breath-snatching moment the seven SEALs were starkly illuminated in the diaphanous light, drawing fire from a hundred yards either side of them on the bridge that was clearly visible beneath the flare—as were the figures of half a dozen dark militia uniforms—one of them containing Latrell, who was pouring fire down on the IBS. Seth took a full AK-47 burst in the chest, his wet suit exploding in a shower of black foam rubber and blood as he hit the water. Gus Morgan, grasping his handheld radio with one hand, shooting with the other, and the other five SEALs were now returning fire, their Heckler & Koch submachine guns spewing out a stream of 9mm Parabellum that immediately knocked a militia-man back from the rail, the man dropping his weapon, grasping his face, dead as he hit the bridge's steel-mat deck. Two other SEALs were hit and fell overboard.

"Get under the bridge!" Morgan shouted, his voice all but drowned out by the cacophony of the firefight, militiamen racing to the side of the bridge from a hundred yards in either direction, hostages hitting the deck for protection, militia hurling HE and phosphorus grenades, and catching the SEALs in a deadly cross fire. The remaining four, including Morgan, were already out of the boat and had dived under, heading toward the pylons, two of them with lines attached to the IBS, which, with one dead SEAL—Seth—aboard, was now drifting lazily after them. The current was with them, the tide beginning to ebb, militia spraying the water with

AK-47 fire in the dying flare light. There was another bang, and another flare burst into brilliance.

"Cease firing!" It was Nestar, livid with anger at his militia, who, in their excitement at discovering the SEALs, had, not surprisingly, concentrated on shooting at them and so failed to sink the half-submerged, bullet-riddled boat that now passed safely right beneath them under the bridge, its supply of inert earmuff charges intact, except for one pair scarred by ricochets off the water. "All right!" Nestar shouted. "Now go over the side and sink the fucking thing before they unload it. Then kill the bastards!"

The militiamen hesitated and a rush of clichés and platitudes surged through Nestar's mind—easier said than done, so near and yet so far—for the simple fact was that this was like having trapped someone in your basement: if you wanted to get him you had to go down, not knowing exactly where he was, but knowing that his weapons were ready to take you out the moment you appeared. And in this case there were four of them. Grenades? Fine, except first you had to lean over, a good way to have your arm shot off, and second you had to make sure you didn't hit any of the supporting structure, otherwise you'd blow *yourself* up or the grenade would plop and explode underwater. Then the worst-case scenario presented itself to Nestar. What if the four SEALs who'd escaped, joined perhaps by the two Nestar had seen fall overboard, went underwater and, trailing float pods to carry their equipment, swam to the other pylons closer to Desdemona Sands? They had over two miles of bridge to choose from.

Nestar was unaware that the two SEALs who'd been hit and fallen overboard were incapable of joining Gus Morgan and the other three. The two men had been fatally wounded and would eventually be sucked out by the withdrawing tide to the bar. The rest of his theory, however, was right on target, as he realized when, after a lot of wildly thrown militia grenades, acting as depth charges, had exploded under the bridge, he saw dead fish floating everywhere. In the same moment Nestar, who had been, bravely, the first militiaman to rush into the darkness between two carefully timed flares, his folded-stock AK-47 at the ready, also discovered that the SEALs were gone, their half-sunken, empty IBS tied forlornly to one of the pylons.

More than two hundred yards away, SEAL Lieutenant Gus Morgan, whispering into the VHF/FM radio's mouthpiece, was giving their GPS position as nearer the Washington State end of the bridge and requesting "assistance ASFUP"—as soon as fucking possible. Meanwhile they would *try* to rig the earmuffs.

CHAPTER FORTY-ONE

"GODDAMMIT!" FREEMAN EXPLODED. "I thought the SEALs had a good chance." But already his brain was racing at supersonic speed, his past experiences flashing before him, a computer searching for a possible solution. "Norton, I've got an idea. We'll have to use this strip here." He pointed to a spot a mile and a quarter south of Daggett Point near a navy radio mast. "I'll need Brentwood and Aussie . . . or is Aussie out with his leg?"

"It's a flesh wound. I can't see it stopping him."

"Huh . . . ?" said Freeman. "Well, pride's one thing, but being a liability is something else. If it's going to stop him moving fast, I don't want him along. I'll want nine others as well as Brentwood and Aussie. With me that makes twelve." The general sketched out his plan on the back of the map. Norton listened quietly, carefully erased the diagram afterward, and said, "General, you once told me that no matter what the consequences I was to tell you the truth—that is, as I see it."

"Shoot!" the general encouraged him.

"This is incredibly risky. . . ." He paused.

"And?" pressed Freeman.

"Sir, you're fit, but you're on the wrong side of fifty."

"You smart-mouthed bastard."

"*And* you're C-in-C Northern Theater Operations and now NWTO. I consider it irresponsible for you to risk your neck in this . . ." For the first time in weeks Norton was at a loss for words. "This—"

"This harebrained scheme—right?"

"Yes, sir."

"Very well, Colonel. Have you got a better idea for blowing that bridge . . . while they have hostages on it?"

"No."

Freeman slapped Norton on the shoulder. "But you're right about me, goddammit. I'm not as young as Brentwood, Aussie, and the rest of my troubleshooting team. I'll stay and coordinate an Eighty-second counterattack—assuming we blow the bridge. See if we can't start punching a few holes in the militia on both sides of the river. . . . Goddammit, I'd love to blow that bridge."

"It's your idea, General. If Brentwood, Aussie, and the ten others succeed, it'll be because of your tactical genius. Same as Patton beating Rommel's plan at Al-Guettar." Norton knew that the difference between sucking up and being reassuring was sometimes hard to discern. This was a case in point.

"Then," said Freeman, "seeing as it's my idea, they'd better not fuck it up. It's my reputation on the line."

"Yes, sir. I'll be sure to tell them."

"Helos," Norton told the team of twelve commandos, "can't be used even if there wasn't any fog, because of the noise. Might as well put up a neon sign saying, 'Here we come!' "

"So," said Aussie, "it's a night HALO?" He meant a high-altitude, low-opening drop. High enough that no one would hear the C-130.

"Yes," answered Norton. "General Freeman suggests you split up in two groups of six—Alfa, Bravo. Alfa to be led by Brentwood, Bravo by Salvini. And Salvini, you take Aussie."

Salvini, a native of Brooklyn and longtime buddy of Brentwood and Aussie Lewis, looked surprised. Aussie was normally the choice for a squad leader, even though the commandos, all with British SAS and U.S. Delta training behind them, operated as equals on the missions. Norton acknowledged the slight departure in procedure. "Problem is Aussie's leg," he explained.

"It's fine," said Aussie. "Hell, if I thought I'd be a fuckin' burden I wouldn't't've fucking volunteered."

"You'd volunteer for anything, Aussie," Norton told him genially. "Anything with action."

"No, he wouldn't," Salvini joked. "There must be women on the bridge!"

Norton smiled, but he was serious. "You're walking okay now, Aussie. But what if you have to make a dash for it?"

"I told you it's fine. But I've no objection to this fuckin' dago leading Bravo."

"Shit on you, too," riposted Salvini.

"You're welcome."

"All right, then," said Norton. "I'm not going to interfere anymore with how you're going to organize it. You'll be flying out of Portland. Do I have to emphasize how this bridge is the linchpin of the militia's offensive?"

"No, you don't," Aussie chimed in. "We get the drift."

"Questions?" asked Norton.

"How many hostages?" asked David Brentwood.

"Dozens," Norton answered worriedly. "Including women and children. They've obviously rounded them up from Astoria on this side of the river and from the Seaview–Long Beach area on the northern side. The militia is claiming they're not hostages but civilians under 'militia protection.' *Refugees.*"

"Christ!" said Aussie. "I knew that fuckin' creep Laser, Nestar, or whatever he's called had women and kids on YB, but I didn't know they had 'em on the Astoria."

Norton shrugged. "Copycat tactics. They saw it work on YB. Why not the Big Bridge?"

"Bastards!"

"Couldn't put it better myself," said Norton. "And don't ask me how you're going to handle it. I haven't got a clue."

"The general got any ideas?" David Brentwood asked, as he streaked the last of his camouflage paint on his face.

"Only the order he gave General Trevor. Clear the bridge. In your case, it's 'blow the bridge.' "

"You sure the SEALs have bought it?" asked Brentwood.

"We have to assume so."

"What's General Trevor say?" put in Salvini.

Norton shifted uneasily and looked about at the twelve men. "This is strictly off the record." He paused. "General Trevor is on the edge, fellas. Freeman, for all his toughness, hasn't kicked Trevor back to Washington because he doesn't think Trevor could handle the humiliation of the loss of command. The old man's afraid he'd do a Mike Boorda." They all remembered Mike Boorda. *Newsweek* had said they were looking into the time when Chief of Naval Operations Admiral Boorda wore a decoration he wasn't entitled to. He'd stopped wearing the two Vs two years before, but they were gunning for him anyway. It turned out to be the nudge that pushed Boorda over the edge. Trevor was already the target of the media for ordering the Airborne squad to fire into Nestar's civilian hostages.

"What's the matter with those media pricks?" Aussie exclaimed. "Freeman's already taken the hit for it—said it was *his* order to clear the fuckin' bridge."

"I know," agreed Norton. "But Trevor feels he's equally, if not *more*, responsible for actually giving the order to the troops. The old man's trying to protect him as much as possible. That's why he's kept Trevor here, nominally in charge of the Eighty-second."

Brentwood was watching Aussie, Salvini, and the rest. Maybe Aussie's outrage at the media was an expression of all the men's fears about engaging a target with women and children involved. Confirming Norton's suspicion, a member of Brentwood's Alfa squad, Morse, asked Freeman's aide, "Well, what the hell are we supposed to do if we see hostages?"

"I don't know, gentlemen," Norton replied. "I don't know what to tell you." He paused. "Anyone want out?"

One man stepped forward and looked uneasily at the

rest of his comrades. "Sorry, guys, I . . . I don't think I could handle kids. . . ."

Another man, his black face contrasting with the whites of his eyes, his NVD—night-vision device— hanging from around his neck, moved out of the group and addressed Norton. "Colonel. I reckon it's the same for me. The kid thing bothers me."

"Bothers all of us, mate," said Aussie, not meaning to put pressure on his comrade.

Norton was alarmed. Two out already and—

"Might not be any kids on the bridge," he proffered. "I mean we can't tell from here through the damn fog and mist. Even our NVDs can't tell us which is a woman or a child. If a teenage boy or girl was there, it'd be impossible to ID with any certainty." Norton stopped. Who was he to tell other men to throw themselves into harm's way, trying to hit a landing zone no more than seventeen feet wide, and never mind the horror of maybe having to fire against women and children? He shook hands with the two men who had withdrawn. "I respect your decision." He waited for the men to leave. In the distance he could hear another outbreak of small-arms fire. He turned to Brentwood, Aussie Lewis, and Salvini. "Can you do it with ten of you? I could put out another call for—"

Aussie Lewis was unusually quiet.

"Well," said Brentwood, "we can try."

Norton felt a knot in his gut. Normally the response from Freeman's specially chosen commandos was "Can do," "No problem," or some such testimony of their enormous self-confidence. Brentwood's equivocation was as uncharacteristic as it was alarming to the general's aide.

"One more thing," Norton went on, hoping it would encourage the commandos. "General Freeman's ordered the Washington side mined by air to discourage any militia counterattack from that side. The Astoria end is within effective range of our 155 howitzers here on the south bank."

"We'll give it a go," cut in Aussie, looking about at his compadres. "Right, gang?"

"Why don't you shut the fuck up?" came a voice from Alfa.

There was an awkward silence as they made their way to the C-130 Hercules on the landing strip.

As the C-130 Hercules carrying Brentwood and Salvini's Alfa and Bravo squads, ten men in all, headed out to sea, climbing as fast as its four screaming turbo-props would allow, Aussie Lewis asked the air-force pilot, "Are you fuckers CARP"—Computerized Airborne Release Point flying—"qualified?" At this same moment Gus Morgan and the three other SEALs under the fog-swallowed bridge were laboring to set up the earmuffs.

Voices could be heard shouting on the river as a flotilla of two dozen or more militia boats, everything from trawlers to dinghies, headed out toward the four-mile-long bridge. For the first twenty minutes there was nothing but confusion, radios squawking and people shouting, trying to get some kind of sensible search pattern going and to avoid colliding with one another, the rowboats, some with small outboards, staying fairly close inshore for fear of getting caught in the tide and sucked out into the bar.

Nestar, detailing the hostage watch to Latrell and some other up-country militia, wanted to tell everybody to shut up. It was difficult enough to hear anything with the sporadic sounds of battle, mainly from the Astoria side of the bridge, without having to contend with this Tower of Babel on the river. Nestar sent out a message for the trawlers—about eight of them—to split the search up into half-mile segments so as to cover the four miles of spans, and also put out an urgent request for any scuba divers in the militia. With water-conducted sound traveling four to six times as fast as in air, a few divers under the bridge might be able to pick up any SEAL activity around the pylons.

It was a vain hope, for the fact of the matter was that there was so much subsurface noise clutter from the trawlers and outboards that if the remaining four SEALs were making any sounds as they attached the earmuff charges and the concomitant long underwater lengths of primacord between the plastique charges, the searchers' engines drowned them out. Also, Nestar knew that to see the magnum-champagne-bottle shapes of any charges, the searchers, even if there was no fog, even if it was in daylight, would have to actually go right under the bridge. Now it would be all but impossible without using spotlights from the trawlers and other assorted search boats.

At Freeman's HQ the message Norton sent to Marte Price—that Mant was believed to have been killed in action—had yielded precisely the kind of surge in radio traffic that Freeman had predicted. Freeman's signals platoon immediately vectored the signals. "General, it's dollars to doughnuts that he's here." It was a point ninety miles east and only thirty miles from the Columbia.

Gus Morgan hadn't had time to think of the three men he'd lost in the initial encounter with Nestar's militia. He and his surviving team of three were too busy earmuffing the eight adhesive, eighteen-inch-long, eight-inch-diameter, nine-pound shaped charges to four bridge supports.

Suddenly a beam of light struck out in the fog, its sharply delineated outline sweeping north to south along the section of the bridge above the Desdemona Sands where the SEALs were working on the last of the detonating cord linkups. Gus Morgan froze next to the pylon he was working on, only his fins moving to maintain his position in the increasing, seaward current. The light was coming from about a hundred yards away. Morgan waited till the sound of the trawler abated, then, in a whisper, gave the call sign on his PRC-624. He told Freeman's HQ to abort the HALO op since it now looked as if the SEALs could pull it off themselves, that he'd set the timer and would escape with the current to a point on the riverbank closer to the bar. After that they'd stay hidden until the weather cleared and it was safe for FEDFOR to send in a helo for pickup and—

The searchlight swept back. The trawler had stopped its engine—one of the SEALs in the beam. Dead center. He dived. There was shouting—a hail of automatic fire flicking up the water—more shouting.

Morgan's message at HQ was received with the crackle of the automatic fire in the background. Norton could hear the militia shouting. "Will we tell Alfa, Bravo to abort?" he asked General Trevor, Freeman having taken off only minutes earlier with a team of thirty, "loaded for bear," as Freeman had put it, hunting for Mant.

"We can't abort," said Trevor glumly, indicating Alfa and Bravo's position on the COMPS, computer situation screen. "They've already jumped."

"Shit!" It was the first time in the war that the usually urbane Norton had used such an expletive.

When, like the nine men before him, Aussie stepped off the Hercules ramp into the black void at thirty thousand feet, steering himself in free fall, he felt the rush of adrenaline that always surged through him during a HALO jump. Through his fourth-generation night-vision goggles he could see the cloudy green world below as well as monitoring the altimeter on his wrist as he sped at two hundred feet per second toward the bridge, using the white blossom of the trawler's spotlight against the green background as an aiming point. He had done mission HALO jumps before, and like so many other sky-jumpers who used the more steerable twenty-eight-foot flat parachutes, he had landed on the bull's-eye of a tennis-court-size target. But he had never jumped over such a wide river and he had no desire, after two minutes' free fall and a short five-hundred-foot chute drop, to find himself suddenly immersed in ice-cold water with his full load of special weapons dragging him down.

The weapons had been carefully selected. With the problem of hostages in mind, the ten commandos of Alfa and Bravo—all veterans of the "shooting houses" at the U.S. Delta Force training area in Fort Bragg, North Carolina, and the British Special Air Service's "killing house" in Hereford—were treating this as essentially a hostage rescue mission, emphasizing all the split-second timing involved in identifying hostage from terrorist—in this case from the militia—and taking immediate action. The technique of instantaneously reading facial and body language at first baffled many recruits, but they soon learned to recognize the subtle differences in the stances of hostage taker and prisoner. Commandos also had to recognize the hostage taker who tried to blend in with the hostages. And they had to do all this in a split second.

Aussie Lewis and the others had also spent hundreds of hours learning the techniques of rapid IR—in-room—fire. One of the commandos' favorite weapons for such close-quarter ops was the Special Forces black steel Heckler & Koch MK-23 .45-caliber handgun equipped with noise suppressor and laser-beam aimer. The .45 might not be as fast as others, but when it hit someone, the hydraulic shock knocked them down, even if, like the commandos, they were wearing bulletproof Kevlar vests. And even if the bullet hit unprotected flesh, it wouldn't pass right through, endangering a hostage behind them.

As well as this quiet .45 he had strapped to his right side, Aussie was sporting a stock-folded UQS—ultra-quiet—MGSG machine-gun shotgun. It was an eight-round ventilated barrel shield MK-I Remington, each of its waterproofed rounds packed with nine-00 buckshot .33-caliber lead balls. With no escaping gases—due to the piston-driven Silent Shotgun Cartridges, such gases creating the normal roar we associate with the shotgun—all that would be heard if Aussie fired would be the click of the firing pin, all eight rounds firing in less than two seconds. As a backup sidearm weapon Aussie also packed a Smith & Wesson fourteen-round Mark-22 Hush Puppy, an "underwater-capable" 9mm handgun. With a plastic-gut silencer, the Puppy would be quiet for up to a twenty-two-round engagement. After that it wouldn't be so quiet due to the degradation of the quarter-inch plastic wafers in the can-shaped noise suppressor.

Aussie was anticipating that a firefight, if any occurred, would be over long before that. The trick would be to land smack on the target now rushing up at him from ten thousand feet below where, despite the cold fog and sea mist, the night-vision outline of the four-mile-long bridge was discernible because the wood, steel, and concrete of the bridge had retained daytime heat longer than the surface of the water. And now, at three thousand feet, what Aussie Lewis, like Brentwood, Salvini, and the other seven members of Alfa and Bravo, could see was a long, white line—the bridge—like a blurred silk ribbon stretching across the night-vision green expanse that was the fogbound river.

The trawler's spotlight had been shot out by Gus Morgan's Heckler & Koch MP5K, the tinkle of its broken glass when hit by the burst of 9mm Parabellum all but lost in the increasing ferocity of the ad hoc militia fleet's attack on the SEALs. With the spotlight gone, the white dashes of tracer that Aussie saw being emitted from beneath the bridge served as pointers to the white ribbon that was the bridge section above Desdemona Sands.

By now Brentwood and two of his five-man Alfa squad, one of them carrying the squad's disposable anti-tank Arpac missile and tube, had landed two hundred yards from the flickering light show that was the militia boats attacking the SEALs' position. The other two men of Alfa were set upon when they practically landed atop a squad of militia racing toward the light show. They were shot and clubbed to death. Brentwood and his two surviving squad members were returning fire so effectively that the militia quickly scattered, going down on the bridge's deck, several seeking protection by the one-and-a-half-foot-wide pedestrian walkway on either side. The fire from the three men of Alfa was so deadly, however, that after initially returning fire, the scattered militia squad, leaving five of their comrades dead on the deck, quickly retreated, shooting wildly and ineffectually as they did so.

Aussie had pulled his cord at five hundred feet, felt the short, sharp jerk from the twenty-eight-foot modified flat as it flared, pulled the right steering toggles on the chute for a tight right-hand spiral, and touched down with balletlike deftness and precision onto the bridge. He, Salvini, and the three others of Bravo squad, unlike Alfa on the south side, had come down just fifty yards north of the light show.

The unexpected appearance of the commandos, dim figures in the fog, on either side of the SEALs' section, had momentarily panicked the militia who, abandoning their hostages in their haste, attempted to prevent what they thought was a new Airborne invasion—which it was, but not in the numbers they thought.

Glimpsing two militia helmets suddenly appearing about fifteen feet to his left, Aussie pulled the trigger of the Remington shotgun. There was a click and suddenly the men flew back against the rail as if punched by some enormous, but invisible, fist, the helmet of one man clattering to the steel-meshed deck, the other man's helmet oozing with flesh and bone.

Apart from the noise of the helmet hitting the deck, there was no sound in Aussie's immediate area and he hoped the silent shotgun would buy him valuable seconds as he, now joined by three others, including Salvini, from Bravo, moved quickly on their Vibram-soled boots toward the light show, which had now resumed after having abated temporarily when the trawler's spotlight was taken out. More boats could be heard if not seen, joining in, one stupidly coming *up*river from the west toward the bridge while all the others were on the eastern side of the bridge. The lone boat soon returned to port, however, as it took several hits from militia M-16 fire that had missed Gus Morgan and his three SEALs and passed right on under the bridge.

By the time Aussie Lewis, Salvini, and the two others from Bravo made their way to the section of bridge below which were Gus Morgan and the other three SEALs, Nestar, on the southern, Astoria side, and Latrell, on the northern side, had recovered from their initial shock. Regrouping, Nestar with fifty militia and

Latrell with an almost equal number, were advancing from either end, with the two groups of four commandos each moving to meet one another, back to back, sandwiched between the two groups of militia.

Hearing the militia approaching from either side of them, both Salvini and Brentwood, not yet having met up with one another, knew it was a situation made for blue-on-blue. Aussie slipped the shotgun into its Velcro holster, taking out his Heckler & Koch Special Forces .45. Alfa and Bravo heard a loud, distinctive bang, then another, and went down on the deck before either of the flares burst, unlike the shadowy figures of the militia no more than fifty yards away and closing. Brentwood's group, seeing what looked like some of the militia stopping, confused, were tempted to take advantage of the situation but held their fire in case there were hostages as well. Instead, they used a grenade launcher to lob three "whiz-bangs" calculated to stun but not wound. The flash of these grenades seemed to revive the dying, flickering light of the parachute flares, and the shadowy figures could be seen reeling, Brentwood's group up and running, one of the three firing another two stun grenades, driving the militia back.

North of the SEALs section, Salvini, hearing Alfa's stun grenades, rushed Latrell's militia, some of whom, though dazed, managed to get off a few wild bursts, bringing one of Salvini's men down, leaving only Salvini, Aussie, and one other commando in Bravo, the missing man having swung into the side of the bridge at head height. Knocked unconscious, he had dropped into the water with his full pack and drowned.

With both Alfa and Bravo moving toward the eighty-foot-long section of the bridge that the SEALs were earmuffing, a group of about seventeen militiamen, who had mortally wounded two SEALs earlier, found themselves halfway between the three- and four-man commando groups about ten yards each side of them. The militia under Nestar quickly split up into two groups, one facing Alfa to the south, the other group firing on Salvini's three-man Bravo team coming from the north, Nestar gambling on the hope that the commandos, fearing blue-on-blue, would be inhibited from firing at the militia for fear of hitting one another. He was wrong, and here the superb marksmanship of Freeman's commandos argued, by way of well-aimed bursts and superior physical conditioning, the Gulf War American adage that quality beats quantity, the first bursts from Alfa's foursome taking out five of eight militiamen while Bravo took out four of the seven confronting it. The Bravo commando on Salvini's left went limp, a burst of wild M-16 fire hitting him, the bullets ripping into him at the neck above the flap of his Kevlar jacket. Salvini was still firing, shifting his aim slightly left, killing the militiaman.

Having seen that there were no hostages, Aussie, slipping out the Remington, holding it slightly above deck level, pointing downward so as not to hit Alfa, pulled the trigger and the remaining seven rounds of nine .33-caliber lead balls went off in under two seconds. It was as if some giant broom had swept the bridge. There were no more militia, at least none standing, a couple, including Nestar, fatigues shredded, writhing in pain, the acrid stench of cordite captured by the fog. When the five remaining commandos of Alfa and Bravo met at the carnage, Salvini, furious at the loss of three of his group and recognizing Nestar, pulled out his 9mm and, holding his left hand as a shield against splattered brains, shot the militiaman point-blank.

"Alfa Bravo!" It was a shout from Gus Morgan. "You above us!"

"Roger!" shouted Aussie. "You all set?"

"One piling to go. We need cover—" Suddenly a fusillade of intense firing broke out east of the bridge as militiamen aboard the boats opened up anew, most of them having held their fire when they'd heard their fellow militia closing with the FEDFOR commandos.

"Go for it!" yelled Brentwood, and the five commandos returned a curtain of fire at the flashes in the fog.

There was a scream not more than twenty yards away, and ever so faintly Aussie saw the dim outline of a trawler through his night-vision goggles. "Gimme that fuckin' Arpac!"

One of Alfa's three commandos—maybe it was Brentwood, he couldn't remember—handed him the squad's short, French-made antitank missile. Less than ten inches long, the Arpac, one of Aussie's favorite weapons, was so compact it weighed only three pounds, its shaped charge capable of penetrating ten inches of armor plate. Aussie flicked up the circular peep sight, brought the Arpac to his shoulder, aimed, and fired.

A wisp of smoke rose up as the propellant shot out of the six-nozzled rocket motor, no bigger than a soup can, that kicked the shaped charge up to eighty-two yards a second. There was a terrific orange explosion—the trawler's fuel tank—and black figures, some on fire, began dropping over the side of the stricken vessel, one falling from atop the mast into an inferno of burning oil and flotsam.

At that moment Freeman was approaching the magnificent spectacle of Mount St. Helen's, its once-towering cone now a lava-blasted crater, rising to meet the dawn. When it had blown in the spring of 1980 with a force greater than eighteen thousand Hiroshima A-bombs, the landslide of ice, rock, and snow had shot down the north face at over a hundred and ninety miles an hour, taking out a hundred and fifty square miles of forest in seconds and spewing up a dense pillar of gases, ash, and rock to a height of fifteen miles. The plume clouded the sun, so much ash that motorists had to turn on headlights at midday, and so much mud deposited over Washington and Oregon that it raised the level of one river more than sixty feet and clogged the Columbia River's main shipping channels. But now, in the pale wash of dawn, the snow-covered monolith was calm as four flare-popping Apache gunships protected the four big Chinook helos, bearing Freeman and his force of a hundred Airborne to an area just over two miles east of the crater off Ape Canyon. Here lava flows had bored through the earth then cooled to form long, winding, tubelike caves, Ape Cave, two and a half miles in length, being the longest in the United States. The spot that interested Freeman, however, was the precise point of triangulation where the radio beams had intersected after Norton's false report that General Mant was dead had gone out.

"No Stingers as yet," said the Airborne's Lieutenant Gene Tyre, he of the outstanding counterattack against the militia on the heights of Fort Canby.

"And there won't be," Freemen commented. "They're sitting in a bombproof lava den down there. They're going to give away their position so long as they're confident we don't know where they are."

The Chinook was descending, also popping sucker flares. No way was Freeman going to repeat the tragic mistake of War Creek should the militia suddenly lose their nerve at playing possum. As the Chinooks landed in a clearing north of Muddy River and south of Pumic Butte, dark green shrubs that had grown through the previously devastated terrain turned a lighter green as the new day stole upon the valley, a gunship's rotors bisecting the sun, and elk bounding over fireweed-sprouting logs that had been scythed by the St. Helen's blast. "Goddamn weeds are like the militia," Freeman opined as he stepped out into a brilliant carpet of pink monkey flowers and purplish-blue lupines, his men securing a perimeter around the LZ.

"How come?" Tyre asked Freeman. "Weeds and militia?"

"They get stomped out one place and pop up somewhere else." He called over to the signals officer. "You got the POT?" He meant point of triangulation.

"One of those three caves." The caves were about fifty yards apart, each entrance around ten feet wide.

"Which one, dammit?"

"Jesus!" the signals officer complained to his sergeant under his breath. "What the fuck's he want? The exact fuckin' stone where they have the fuckin' radio?"

"Well," said the sergeant, "he's gonna be the first one in. Guess he'd like to know."

"Which one?" Freeman repeated impatiently, unclipping his 7-shaped flashlight with his left hand, his right holding his personal *unquiet* Winchester 1200 loaded with three 00-buckshot 12-gauge combat load cartridges and two cartridges, each packed with twenty fléchettes, the latter a cluster of fluted steel darts that increased the killing range of the weapon from 60 to 360 yards. The signals officer checked the vectors again and pointed to an opening about ten feet in diameter in the rock face twenty yards away. "Closest we can figure it, General, it's the one." Freeman detailed nine men, including Gene Tyre, to follow him and moved off to the cave, the remaining Airborne guarding the LZ and ready for instant dispatch anywhere Freeman wanted them.

The first thing Freeman noticed upon entering the lava-tube cave was the revolting stink of carrion. He adjusted his NV goggles, already thinking ahead, wondering how deep this cave would go and whether, like Ape Cave, it had an exit as well as an escape route—*if* this was the cave.

Freeman was moving cautiously on point, leading the section of nine Airborne, potential firing cones dictated by their position in the line. The first man, Tyre, would cover Freeman's left flank, the next man Tyre's right flank, and so on down the staggered line so that no one was in danger of shooting the man in front of him. The stench of carrion, perhaps an elk carcass, increased, almost causing Tyre to gag and convincing him that no one in their right mind would have selected this cave as their hideaway. To Freeman, however, the sickly stink was a very good reason why Mant's staff might have selected it for their temporary HQ.

Despite his night-vision goggles, Freeman couldn't see the proverbial light at the end of the lava tunnel, only a jumble of rocks where the tube turned left before coming back on a straight course. He moved slowly, cautiously, for he'd been in pitch-dark places like this before as a tunnel rat, perhaps the highest-ranking tunnel rat ever to go down into the vast networks of the Viet Cong's tunnel complex at Cu Chi and elsewhere in 'Nam. Any turn was immediately suspect, and before he negotiated this one he knelt on one knee, signaling the nine-man squad to do likewise. He listened, the only noise he could hear his own breathing and that of young Tyre and the squad members immediately behind. Everyone was eager to get Mant, to finish it, but Freeman knew from 'Nam that impatience in tunnels came at a high cost and he wasn't about to rush it, carefully examining a pile of fist-sized spill of rocks near the turn.

That's when he saw the Elsie, a small, cone-shaped mine, propped innocuously between two flat rocks on the floor of the cave directly in front of him, enough power in it to take off your foot, genitals, or both. Freeman pointed to it and every man tapped the man behind him to make sure he had seen it, the last man, his head already throbbing from an NVG-caused headache, now feeling much worse with the foul air and the knowledge that the militia had mined the tunnel. It was a slow, agonizing business, moving through mines, but there was no other way.

Having difficulties of their own, the militia battalion under Lucky McBride, which Mant had ordered to reinforce the Washington State end of the Astoria Bridge so as to bolster Latrell and Company's force, discovered they would first have to negotiate a hillside of air-dropped FEDFOR submunitions—another name for air-dropped mines. Because of the recent rain, the mines had sunk, penetrating surface soil and becoming all but invisible.

In the cave Freeman walked around the Elsie, checked the next stretch of tunnel—when would the damn thing end?—and led his men forward. Strangely, in his anxiety, which he never allowed his men to see, his one comforting thought was the unlikelihood of discovering a punji pit—sharp excrement-tipped sticks placed in a pit below floor level—a favorite VC trick. The hard lava floor would not easily lend itself to excavation. The cave now began to dip slightly and—

It had come to a sudden end. At first Freeman refused to believe it. It had to be a fake door. It wasn't—it was solid lava. This wasn't the cave. It was the kind of thing that would never make the news reports, not if Freeman had anything to do with it. They'd all learned their lesson from 'Nam; you could see it in the way the press was kept in line during the Gulf War. Just as no one heard of the screwups in some of the tank companies, or saw the close-up views of thousands of Iraqis being buried alive by dozer tanks or the near-miss blue-on-blues, believing everything had been a nice clean push-button video war, so no one would hear that the legendary Freeman had wasted his time looking for his opposite number in a dead-end cave.

The general didn't say a word when he led Tyre and the others out. He didn't have to—his eyes said it all as he glowered at the hapless signals officer, who feverishly rechecked the GPS and radio intercept vectors.

"Ah, then, it has to be that one, sir," he said, pointing over to his right. "Yes, sir, I'd say it had to be that one."

Silently Freeman walked toward the second cave, eyes alert, knowing that if Mant had had a dummy cave mined with the Elsie, he sure as hell was going to mine his HQ. It took a minute or two for the men to readjust to the infrared. Again, the inside of the cave was really the inside of a lava tube. However, the glassy sheen of this cave's floor was littered with the flat, cow-patty-sized rocks of the kind that had been used in the last cave to hold up the Elsie. It meant they had to move more slowly than before. Even so, five minutes later they were well into the cave when Freeman saw a sharp turn ahead and thought, An ideal place for a booby trap. As it turned out, there wasn't any. Too obvious.

Young Gene Tyre wasn't going to tell anyone, but ever since entering the cave he had developed a tic in his left eyelid. Jesus Christ, he'd rather lead three counterattacks on the militia at Fort Canby Park than go poking through a goddamn cave, night-vision goggles notwithstanding. Gave him the creeps. Suddenly he was hit, something wet and furry, a frantic flapping of wings. "What the—" He peed himself in fright.

"Quiet!" hissed Freeman. "Only a bat."

Only a bat, thought Tyre. Jesus Christ, so why did it

have to fly into *his* face and not the general's? Now there were shrieks and a frantic deafening sound as clouds of bats erupted from the cave. It shook the whole patrol, including Freeman, not that he was going to let on. "C'mon," he said quietly, even though he knew that any surprise he might have hoped for against Mant was now long gone. After the left curve in the tunnel, the lava obviously having flowed out and around a huge granite rock, the lava tube divided in a Y, Freeman tapped Tyre and, via his NVGs, indicated that he would take the left fork with four men, leaving the one on the right to Tyre and the remaining four Airborne.

Two minutes later there was an ear-jarring explosion, Freeman's patrol hearing it resound through the rock. It had come from the right-hand branch of the tubular Y, a cloud of acrid smoke issuing from the cave's mouth, one of Tyre's patrol staggering out, clothes shredded and bloodied, his face blackened with soot, looking like part of an old vaudeville comedy act. But there was nothing comical about what had happened. Why, no one knew, but Tyre had missed seeing the trip wire, probably too busy looking ahead for more Elsies, and perhaps the wire had been "nuggeted," pulled through black boot polish to hide any sheen. According to the badly wounded Airborne soldier, the only survivor who'd made it out, the wire had detonated a "deuce," two claymores, one on either side of the cave but not directly opposite one another. The result, as the bodies of three "ground round" dead Airborne testified, was catastrophic, the hundreds of ball bearings at point-blank range screaming across the ten-foot-diameter lava tube that formed the cave cutting down every man in their way save two, virtually wiping out the patrol.

The Airborne major in charge of the helo force outside, around the LZ, radioed through what he knew about the incident to Freeman, who, despite using the earpiece from his Walkman-sized belt radio, had difficulty understanding the major over the static.

Young Tyre had made a mistake and the general knew that there was nothing he could do. He heard a helo taking off, no doubt rushing the two injured to Portland. Freeman would have to leave it up to the major at the LZ to figure out what to do after removing the dead, or what was left of them. Besides, while Freeman had no way of proving it, he felt in his gut that this time he was in the right cave, that the militia's supreme commander, the religious zealot who believed himself to be on the right hand of God, was nearby. And Freeman knew that if he could capture Mant and blow the bridge, the one-two punch would undo the militia. But after what had happened to Tyre, his patrol was undeniably spooked, proceeding at a snail's pace into the darkness, the last man in file experiencing the worst tension headache of his life but afraid to cop out for fear the others would think him a coward.

CHAPTER FORTY-TWO

OF ALL THE Washington State militiamen who were now serving on the Astoria front, none had been as uncommunicative as Charlie Ames. The other men in the platoon of misfits put together by Colonel Vance for "special duties" admired Ames. "Special duties" was a euphemism of Vance's. What it really meant was that there were some men who either couldn't or wouldn't be part of a team, men who were loners either by disposition or circumstances. In Ames's case it had been the federals' shooting of his wife and young Luke and Rebecca that had finally severed him from society. His conversation, if you could call it that, was now confined to monosyllabic grunts, signifying assent or rejection of any suggestion made to him. "Quite frankly," Colonel Vance, the militia's unofficial propaganda chief, told Mant's chief of staff, Somers, "Ames is a pain in the neck. He won't take direction. He goes off with that ugly damn rifle of his and his dog, Blue. Doesn't come back for hours. Won't tell anyone where he's going, where he's been. When he holds out his hand, it means he's out of ammo. Takes an MRE with him, not that he looks like he's eating much. Skinny as a rake."

"It's his life," Somers told Vance.

"Not now it isn't. He's a member of the militia. And besides, he's an important symbol. Should do what he's damn well told, like the rest of us."

"You tried it? Telling him, I mean."

"He knows the score."

"That's not what I asked you. Have you given him a direct order?"

Vance exhaled heavily. "No. He isn't the type you order to do anything. Least not now. He's a dangerous son-of-a-bitch. That's what he is."

"Leave him be, Colonel. If it wasn't for him we wouldn't have had a *cause célèbre*. It helped our cause. Besides, who's he dangerous to? The federals, right? Leave him be." Somers paused. "You don't like him because he won't fit in. Remember, a lot of our guys joined the militia because they don't fit in, don't like the federals telling them what to do. Besides, the federals murdered his whole family. He's got a right to be moody. He won't do any harm. Don't get your ego caught up in this, Colonel. He's a free spirit."

Vance didn't like being spoken to like that. "Free spirit" sounded like someone from California.

In California, Red Adair's legendary oil-well fighters had more than they could handle with the maelstrom that used to be Bakersfield, a forest of wind-fanned flames continuing to plume wildly hundreds of feet into the air, the clouds of thick, curling black smoke stinking up and heating the already polluted air. Normally this would have required flights to be rerouted for hundreds of square miles to and from Los Angeles. But there were no flights—militia threats ruled the air.

Ironically the way to put out the fires was the way they had begun, by exploding them, with the not-so-minor difference that the firefighters had to get close enough to place the charges, starting from the periphery, slowly advancing behind metal-asbestos shields, thousands of gallons of water coming from all directions to prevent the men from spontaneously combusting in the savage heat of the inferno.

It didn't help that local militia units, in support of their "brothers in the line," were taking potshots at the firemen, causing Bakersfield police to run interference for the fire brigades now converging from all over. This was a tragic mistake, for the absence of firefighters from other townships meant that brushfires started by red-hot ash from Bakersfield couldn't be dealt with and home owners in the outlying counties were left to their own devices. And the absence of policemen—who were off protecting the firefighters—meant outbreaks of widespread looting. The disorder encouraged every criminal element to vent his or her spleen, from south Los Angeles to Bakersfield. In San Francisco a militia-provoked attack against homosexuals rapidly degenerated into a bloody melee spreading throughout the downtown area, two of the five murder victims having been impaled rectally on militia bayonets, then strung up, dangling from the old city's iron fretwork.

CHAPTER FORTY-THREE

THERE WAS STILL firing on the Astoria Bridge in the sun-tinged fog, but it had abated, and Aussie Lewis, Brentwood, Salvini, and the other two commandos from Freeman's force guessed, correctly, that the militia was about to undertake some new stratagem to prevent the SEALs, beneath the commandos, from blowing up the bridge. The fog was still so thick that visibility was no more than ten feet, but the five commandos were under no illusion, knowing that the sun, unless it clouded over, would soon start to burn off the fog and sea mist and then their cover would vanish.

"How long do we have?" Aussie asked SEAL Lieutenant Gus Morgan.

"I've got ampules for thirty, fifteen, and ten minutes," answered Morgan, meaning the acid-in-glass delay fuses he would break to set off the earmuff charges. It was a deadly gamble. The shorter the fuse, the better chance they had of blowing the bridge before the militia could rush and overwhelm them and cut the primacord—but the shorter the fuse, the less time they'd have to get clear of the bridge.

"Where's Freeman's Airborne?" put in Salvini.

"Lost in the fucking fog," said Aussie, who then turned to David Brentwood. "Thought they were supposed to take heat off of us while we blow this fucker?"

"Fog wasn't supposed to be a problem," Salvini added. "They've got NVGs—same as us."

"Yeah," said one of the four remaining SEALs left out of the original seven. "Trouble is, Airborne isn't as tough as we are."

"Yeah, right!" said Aussie, slipping another two cartridges into his shotgun and addressing no one in particular. "I say we use a thirty-minute ampule. By that time the Airborne might have arrived an' hit the bastards in the rear."

"Salvini?" asked Brentwood.

"This a fucking seminar?" Salvini retorted. "I dunno. Leave it to Morgan. He's the fucking bang man."

Gus Morgan checked his watch-cum-underwater-pressure-gauge. "Way things have been goin' I'd say fifteen minutes—max."

"All right," Brentwood said irritably, pulling one of his Mae West vest straps out of the way. "Fifteen it is. Aussie, you and—"

They heard the sound of an engine moving through the fog. "Salvini," Brentwood continued, "you and Morgan with me facing the south end. You other three, two under Aussie's command, take the northern approach."

Despite his leg dragging, or because of it, Aussie was already moving north of the earmuff span, not wasting any time; Brentwood, Salvini, and Morgan headed south, each three-member team quickly swallowed by the fog, which offered protection and concealment but rendered the impending Airborne drop more difficult.

Given the thousands of men involved on both sides of the war, many from the Astoria Pocket itself, it was surprising that not more opposing family members and/or friends found themselves involved in the same action. As yet, however, Major William McBride, who, along with Sergeant Nye, had worked his way out of the tidal flat and estuary grass toward the northern end of the AB, was unaware of his brother's presence in the same area.

This was about to change, and with it the whole shape and direction of the war, but Lucky McBride had no way of knowing that his brother, William, was part of an ad hoc "wedging" force of a hundred or so men Trevor had quickly thrown together from scattered elements of the Airborne on orders from Freeman.

This wedge company had now managed to insert itself between the militia force, which included Latrell, on the northern end of the bridge, and Freeman's mile-long, semicircular, two-hundred-yard-deep strip of submunition mines, which lay directly in front of Lucky McBride's thousand-man force. Because of this moat of mines, Lucky McBride's second in command, Lieutenant Hartz, though as brave as any of the pro-Nazi faction that he headed, cautioned Lucky, who had lost over a dozen men already in trying to negotiate a way around the minefield, to postpone his drive for the bridge until the fog lifted and they could see if there was a way to navigate around the seemingly impenetrable minefield.

"We can't wait," Lucky told him. "Longer we wait, the more time we give FEDFOR to blow the bridge—cut us off completely from our forces in Astoria. Besides, if we hang around till the fog clears—*if* it clears—we'll have Freeman's air cover pounce on us now that we're in more clearly recognizable groups." Lucky paused, then gave a nod as if he'd solved the puzzle. "We'll go *through* the minefield."

"*Through* it?" Hartz protested. "In that tall grass? We'd need detectors, identification ribbons, and—"

"All we need," said Lucky, "is a platoon of men with bayonets to probe the grass. Divide them into three groups. Then we can take three paths through it."

"Maybe," said Hartz. "But the way they dropped them . . ." Hartz's old German accent kicked in during moments of stress. ". . . They dropped them all, how do you say, higgledy-piggledy? *Ja?* I mean the way through the field will be crazy paths, this way. It will have to be very clearly marked and—"

"Don't sweat it," Lucky McBride cut in. "You get a platoon of guys up here and we'll start probing. If we work fast we should be across the goddamn field in no time."

"But we will have to be careful marking—"

"*I'll* mark them, don't worry. You get those guys probing *now*." Lucky allowed himself a smile. Last thing Freeman would expect is for someone to go right through the minefield, and the fog would be a perfect cover.

While Hartz quickly and efficiently organized the bayonet squads to start probing through the grass, Lucky McBride gave what was thought to be a very strange order by those, mostly Oregonians, who had not known of his exploits in training the Washington State militia. He ordered an armored militia pickup truck crew to ransack the nearest drugstore in militia-held territory for a half a dozen cans of shaving cream.

CHAPTER FORTY-FOUR

THE NEXT TURN in the lava cave revealed an anomaly in the long tubular shape, a kind of antechamber about twenty feet wide, as if the molten lava, after having followed a steady course, had suddenly built up then gushed to produce this room, and beyond, a bigger, or main, chamber about fifty feet across. Leading out of these two telescoped chambers was a series of passageways, six in all, where the lava had resumed its permeation of the earth. Some of the passageways looked as if they might be fairly short cul-de-sacs running only a few yards into the darkness. Logic suggested that each of the five men, including Freeman, pick an opening and investigate, but Freeman's intuition went against splitting up an already small force, the NVGs of no help in the absence of any ambient light.

The Remington in his left hand, Freeman opened a pouch in his vest load, extracted a Bic lighter, and signaled the other four to watch the openings to the various passageways. He flicked the lighter and saw its yellow flame as a white scar through the night-vision goggles. A steady scar. He tried the next two passageways with the same result, then, proceeding into the fourth in the same way, he flicked the lighter again and saw the flame quivering, fluttering left and right. An air current.

Retracing his steps and using Special Forces armsqueeze signals, Freeman signaled the other four members of his patrol to gather about the entrance to this passageway while he "Bic'd" the remaining three holes, discovering all three to be dead ends. But look, he asked himself, if this *is* a militia HQ, why aren't there any guards so far? and answered himself just as quickly. Because they'd need some ambient light and would give themselves away immediately to anyone, like Freeman's patrol, wearing NVGs. Which meant only one thing in this high-tech age—that if and when he came upon Mant's HQ, it would be all of a sudden. He had no sooner come to this conclusion than, taking the next step in his Special Forces slow-march-slide, which normally looked ridiculous, the top of his foot felt a slight touch— some impedimenta ahead? Bringing his foot back, he went into a slow kneel in the six-foot-wide tunnel, again one hand holding the Remington 1200, the fingers of his right hand passing gently through the darkness, as if feeling for a naked Marte Price, his hand instead touching a taut trip wire. Another reason why he couldn't expect sentries, at least not—

A *whoop! whoop!* alarm sounded, the auto-theft kind, and there was a blaze of light twenty feet down the tunnel, blinding his NVGs. Freeman fired at it, twice falling backward, away from the trip wire. There was a tinkling sound, a scream, oaths behind. The light went out, a door slammed shut, and Freeman felt a burning sensation in his right foot, where he'd accidentally shot himself, a pellet passing through the thick leather, ripping open a toe. From the sitting position he kept firing, the roar of the shotgun, fléchettes buzzing, deafening in the tunnel, followed by the choking rattle of one of his patrol's AK-47s, its bullets tattooing what Freeman knew must be a door, a couple of shots ricocheting off the diamond-hard surface of the tunnel, the sulfurous reek of gunpowder filling the blackness. "Smoke!" Freeman yelled, and as a patrol member pulled the pin, tossing a smoke grenade ahead, he quickly reloaded the Remington with two slug shots designed to stop the Orient Express, the specially hardened sabot-held lead capable of passing right through an automobile at over a hundred yards. At fifteen feet the slugs, shrieking out from their polyethylene sabot, smashed into the door, knocking it right off its hinges, smoke immediately rushing in, several militia figures seen running, panic-stricken, away from the Airborne.

"We've surprised 'em!" Freeman yelled. "Pressure!"

"*We* surprised *them*," muttered the tail-end Charlie, a nineteen-year-old from New Jersey, his headache now making him feel like someone was bashing his skull with a sledgehammer. He was unable to focus properly in the NVGs, a stunningly beautiful and shimmering green arcing above his left eye, an unmistakable sign of migraine. He *had* to sit down—all there was to it. Freeman, cutting the trip wire, charged forward, fired two more slug shells, heard an ungodly cry—his slugs had smashed a militiaman's spine—and as the general dove to one side, reloading with fléchette cartridges, the three Airborne overtook him and kept up the pursuit. There was a burp of an AK-47 from the fleeing militia, and the first Airborne trooper, dead, crashed to the lava floor.

"Second platoon forward!" Freeman yelled, completing his reload. It did the trick. The dozen militia officers and men, on hearing him yell "platoon," assumed there were at least another thirty Airborne on their trail and kept moving fast toward an emergency exit twenty yards ahead around and up from a dogleg turn. The two

remaining Airborne now rejoined by Freeman, his shotgun reloaded, ran past the bodies of two militiamen
sprawled on the floor in a wider part of the tunnel that
had obviously been the radio command center.

"More smoke!" Freeman called out.

After Freeman and the two Airborne had passed, one
of the militia bodies stirred. Still somewhat stunned, he
picked up his fallen WWII helmet and a foot-long cylin-
drical map case that he'd held close to his body, and
began to feel his way along the tunnel, away from what
he thought was Freeman's platoon.

The Airborne soldier with the migraine, sitting down,
his aching head pressed against the blessedly cool lava
wall of the tunnel, saw the militiaman, a white blur,
through his NVGs from twenty feet away and fired a
burst from his M-16 that flung the man hard against the
wall, the map case rolling noisily a few feet away.

At the top of the militia's exit, a vertical four-foot-
diameter shaft that ran for fourteen feet like a natural
periscope up from the main tunnel, Airborne troops
who'd seen smoke venting from it were ready to nab the
militia. The first man out, Colonel Vance, realizing the
trap, yelled a warning before he was felled by a rifle butt
to the gut, and the remaining militamen began a frantic
shuffling back down the escape hatch, one tumbling on
another, cursing.

"Give it up!" shouted Freeman, waiting with the other
two Airborne clustered near the bottom of the lava
chimney that was like a rough-hewn control room in a
submarine, but where the militia could neither see them
nor get a clear shot down the shaft.

As the first militaman dropped down he immediately
raised his hands, sunlight now streaming down the
smoke-curling shaft. "There's only three of 'em!" he
shouted in a tone of outraged surprise. It was this warning

that cost his comrades their lives, for on hearing that there were only three federals at the bottom of the would-be escape shaft, they decided to fight. With no clear idea in the sun-bright smoke who had fired first in the confined space, the Airborne couldn't take a chance, firing down at point-blank range into the cluster of shadowy figures crowding the bottom of the lava chimney, cutting down the militia before they could find their feet, Freeman's shotgun firing from behind the militia until it was emptied. The Airborne troops to his left were killed by a militiaman's knife that had gone in above the neck flap of the Kevlar and Freeman felt warm and wet, a metallic taste in his mouth as blood from someone splattered him.

Then there was silence, the swirling white smoke still venting up the escape chimney, a deep, otherworldly moaning from the pile of bodies writhing at the base.

"You all right, General?" asked the major.

"Yes," hollered Freeman. "Get some medics down here. Quickly!"

"Yes, sir."

Freeman and the remaining Airborne waited until a team of four medics descended with stick flares and started working on the wounded, Freeman then going topside.

A medic saw the general's right boot shredded and bloody.

"Prick wasn't there," said Freeman, grimacing, sitting down on grass that was still wet with the morning dew, the numbness from the shock of being hit now starting to fade and pain replacing it. "Cunning bastard's holed up somewhere else. We were on a wild-goose—Jesus!" A corpsman was cutting off his boot. The general was embarrassed that he'd reacted to the pain. "Sorry, son— go ahead. Didn't mean to—"

"General!" There was some excitement over by the top of the militia's escape hatch, several Airborne struggling to get a grip on a body bag. "Over here!" Picking up the twelve-gauge and checking that the safety was off, Freeman used the weapon as a walking stick and hobbled on over, the pain from the severed toe excruciating, and him knowing before he got there what he'd find.

The corpse in the body bag was Mant, his map case coming up after him, along with the migraine-stricken nineteen-year-old from New Jersey, everybody whooping it up, patting New Jersey on the back, New Jersey telling them to shut the fuck up, the racket piercing his head, for Christ's sake, like fucking hot needles. He felt so ill he threw up, right there, as he later would tell his mom, "right in front of the general," but he'd won the Silver Star. They couldn't give him anything less, not after taking out Mant and getting the AUP—all unit position—maps of the militia's entire Columbia/Snake River line. And all because of a damn headache. God worked in mysterious ways, His wonders to perform.

Militia Colonel Vance was in great pain, experiencing a pleurisylike stab every time he breathed in, fléchettes having penetrated the right side of his chest. They'd left no visible marks, like fine needles passing through a wicker basket, but were inside him nevertheless, the only evidence of them X rays that would be taken later. But he and the two other wounded militia—the other nine, including Mant, dead—still had hope. If the militia battalion under Lucky McBride could swarm the bridge and hold it, the Astoria Pocket—bad country for Freeman's armor—would be theirs and they would have an enormous bargaining chip with the federals. "Isn't over," Vance told the federal medic, "till the fat lady sings."

"Shut up!" the corpsman told him, and gave him a shot of morphine. "You killed one of my buddies in that fuckin' cave."

CHAPTER FORTY-FIVE

THERE WERE TEN minutes to go and on the bridge, SEAL Lieutenant Morgan was cold, the sweat from his climb up the truss supports onto the bridge having cooled in the fog. Lying down near part of the wooden pedestrian beam that separated the roadway from the eighteen-inch pedestrian walkway he, Brentwood, and Salvini, who made up this three-man team, could hear the sound of a slow-moving vehicle. Whatever it was, it was creeping behind them, but they tried to pay it no mind, as Aussie and the two other remaining Special Forces commandos would have to attend to it, Brentwood's team responsible only for the approach from the southern, Astoria, end.

Aussie was taking a chance, lying facedown nearby, a militia helmet taken from one of the dead upside down beside him as if it had been his. If they, however many there were on the as-yet-unseen vehicle, gave him a burst it would all be over, unless the burst hit his Kevlar vest. But the militia truck, its grader blade high for protection, rolled slowly by in the fog, its occupants clearly not wanting to pinpoint their position with any premature or unnecessary shooting.

Aussie, his wax, rather than standard-issue foam-rubber earplugs in for protection, knew that the only advantage he and the other two Special Forces personnel had was that the militia didn't know how many federals were on the span. Under his right thigh, his hand gripped a flash-bang, its pin out, his hand holding down its lever, a fragmentation bomb alongside it packed tightly with serrated weak-link razor wire designed to throw out a shower of hot steel.

He glimpsed the oncoming grader pickup truck looking ominous in the fog and hugging the center line, then passing him. He saw a phalanx of rifles and AK-47s—at least a dozen—sticking out. He waited till it was another six feet from him and lobbed the flash-bang into the truck. He didn't look at the purplish-white flash but immediately it went off, thumping his eardrums despite the earplugs and lighting up the fog. Then he tossed the fragmentation grenade, wreaking further havoc in the back of the pickup. Aussie was now on his feet, firing the ultraquiet shotgun. Eight clicks in under five seconds, the force of the pellets at fifteen feet blowing militiamen out of the truck like so many ninepins, the last cartridge firing fléchettes, their buzzing telling Aussie the rotary mag was empty.

A figure armed with a Kalashnikov appeared running down the off side of the truck. Aussie drew his H&K .45-caliber handgun. He saw his red laser dot on the militiaman's chest and fired twice. The shooter's helmet flew off and Aussie saw it was a woman. He fired again and she was down, her wild burst of AK-47 fire tattooing the bridge's railing behind him.

As militiamen in the Revolutionary War had outshot the British, the Special Forces now outshot the militia, a militiaman's training, no matter how good, being nowhere as intensive and demanding as that of Delta Force, SEALs, or SAS. Aussie, his leg hurting where the Steri-Strips had been placed over his wound, limped over to the mess of bloodied bodies and limbs, smelled a pungent odor of urine, excrement, and cordite, yanked open the driver's door, pulled the dead driver out, and tried to start the engine, intending to park the truck sideways across the bridge as a roadblock. The engine coughed but wouldn't start. "Don't have time for a fucking tune-up!" Aussie murmured, yelling out now. "Hey, Bravo, up here!" As the other two men came running through the fog, Aussie looked at his watch. "Four minutes to go!" he told them. "Over the side and pull your tits!" He meant the Mae West flotation vests.

"You comin'?" the other two asked him.

"I'll be along in a jiff."

"Fuck you!" said one of the two Bravo men. "You stay, we stay."

"You puss nut," Aussie retorted. "Do as I fuckin' say."

"Fuck you!"

"Puss nuts!" Aussie answered affectionately. "Well, at least get under the fuckin' truck so when that fuckin' slab blows, the shit won't come down on you."

As they scrambled under the truck they heard a pop, then saw the fog toward the northern end of the bridge pulsating green with what had to be a fifteen-second parachute flare.

"It's a go signal," said one of Aussie's two comrades.

"One guess," said the other.

"I wouldn't have a clue," joked Aussie, who, despite the fact that he knew these might be the final moments of his life, felt honored to be with such men. He reloaded the shotgun and for once wished it wasn't a quiet weapon but would make as much noise as possible in what he was certain would be a coming rush of militiamen.

* * *

Under Lucky McBride's hurried instruction, the three teams of bayonet probers were almost through the two-hundred-yard-deep minefield that lay between their battalion and Major William McBride's Airborne wedge.

Tossing a shaving-cream can to each of the two men he had designated markers along with himself, Lucky McBride knew that the last fifty feet or so would probably have to be probed and marked under fire. The curtain of thick fog was starting to burn off. True to his nickname he was lucky again in that the fog-shrouded FEDFOR wedge that he knew was ahead of him hadn't yet caught on to his ballsy ploy of going straight through the minefield where they would least expect him.

As Lucky McBride and the two other markers advanced, spraying big dabs of white shaving cream to mark three winding foot-wide safe trails through the field, General Douglas Freeman was en route to the Astoria front by fast Apache gunship, sitting in what would normally be the WO or weapons officer's seat in the nose.

At first, after coming out of the cave, he'd refused a pain shot, not because he was determined to be super-macho in front of his men but because—something he had told only his late wife and not even Attorney General Sheila Courtland—he was irrationally afraid of needles, as Admiral Halsey had been. When he first joined the army and was lined up to get his shots and the orderly touched him with the swab of alcohol, he felt his arm go ice-cold and fainted. Without saying a word, the orderly unbuckled and pulled down the young recruit's pants, and *"bam!"* as a friend had told him, "right in the ass." But he'd relented at the cave because the pain was so severe he found he wasn't able to focus on the job at hand. Now, though, he was focused, the morphine giving him a high, as he instructed the pilot to pop sucker flares and get as low as he could. The pilot dropped the Apache to a hundred feet over the northern end of the bridge, flying purely by instrument radar and infrared goggles.

"Can't see a goddamn thing," the general complained. "Go lower!"

"Jesus Christ!"

"What was that?"

"Nothing, General. Goin' down—Jesus!—takin' fire, General!"

"You poppin' flares?"

"Roger."

"Good." Now Freeman, unable to make contact with Major McBride's wedge because of static, glimpsed, through a swirling layer of diaphanous cloud, several men squirting something on the grass. "What the. . . ?" And at that moment Freeman was about to add to his legend, taking the magic from Lucky McBride. Perhaps no other man could have done it. Or perhaps they could have if they'd been given time, but time was something that Freeman, C-in-C FEDFOR, NTO, and NWTO didn't have. What allowed him to outthink Lucky McBride was his prodigious memory and justly celebrated attention to detail. In the computer that was his memory, Freeman, like Rommel and Patton before him, had filed away every conceivable bit of information about his enemies, the men he might meet in the field. He was ready. He knew of Lucky McBride's famous minefield technique with shaving cream, in turn borrowed from Schwarzkopf. And so it was that, though he didn't know who exactly was below him in the fog other than that they were militia, when he spotted the cotton-ball-like dabs against the green grass, he immediately knew what was up. "You see those little blobs of white?" he asked the pilot.

"Yes."

"They're pathways through our minefield. I want you

to go low, sweep back and forth over this area—a hundred yards either way. Go!"

"Yes, General."

As the Apache swept low, the militia not firing for fear of giving away their exact position to the FEDFOR wedge ahead, the fierce wind of the helo's prop wash blew the dabs of shaving cream every which way, dotting the entire minefield with splotches of white. Within moments the curving safety paths through the minefield were history, and now Freeman was working them over with the chain gun, its red tracer seen by William McBride's FEDFOR. The latter now quickly regrouped from the flanks of the minefield into the center of Major William McBride's defensive area and began pouring a deadly cross fire into the minefield where Lucky McBride's troops were stranded, unable to move, frozen in fear. Several mines had already blown, killing and maiming impatient and panic-stricken militiamen, in turn sending panic through the remainder of the battalion, most of whom, except for those already trapped inside the minefield, quickly withdrew north of the river. Only someone who has been in a minefield can comprehend the full extent of the terror experienced by those militia who had started to cross the minefield only to have their safe passages suddenly disappear in a confusing blur of puffy white splotches. They could only move and die . . . or surrender. Only a handful, Lucky McBride leading them, had actually made it through the minefield, and most of these were immediately cut down by Major William McBride's wedge.

Abruptly the earth moved—a rumbling, some thinking it was a quake. The bridge had blown.

Despite the obvious conclusion—that the militia was now decisively cut in two, that they had lost the battle—some militiamen, particularly those on the northern end, refused to bow to the inevitable and threw themselves against the FEDFOR's wedge. It was crazy or heroic, depending on your point of view, and it claimed the life of federal Randy Nye, whose militia brother, Jim, also participated in the action. It would haunt Jim Nye for the rest of his life. As he slowly descended into alcoholism he endlessly asked himself if it had been his bullet that had felled his brother. He would never know the answer.

Major William McBride's experience was perhaps even more dramatic, and one of only a few cases on record—though certainly there could have been more. During the war he came face-to-face with his own brother in battle. The fog had been clearing, but not fast enough for Major William McBride to be positive that it was his brother he'd seen amid the squad of militia, their nerves at the breaking point, who exited the minefield and were bravely, if futilely, attacking the wedge even as the Airborne's second wave of paratroopers were descending—this time on the right LZ. Suddenly Lucky McBride saw a federal firing. At the same moment William McBride saw a militiaman firing. In a split-second shock of recognition, Lucky saw his brother and his brother saw him . . . but the mutual realization was a nanosecond too late. Lucky's aim had been better. It was as simple and terrible as that.

When a FEDFOR sergeant noticed the militiaman bent over the fallen major, his hand at Major McBride's throat—Lucky McBride was feeling for the carotid pulse—he fired, and missed. Lucky McBride's response was to sit back and weep. He wished with all his heart that the federal had killed him. Instead, he now joined the ranks of the war's POWs, to be exchanged in the coming weeks after the militia's formal surrender, though in fact thousands slipped back into the hills and civilian life, reburying their caches of arms along with their hopes until the next time.

It was a strange dawn on and around the mighty river and its tributaries, normal things assuming grotesque shapes, the fog, though lifting, blurring what were usually easily recognizable features, wreathing them in shrouds that kept changing in the alternating battle between sun, sea mist, and fog. One of the more unexpected sights off Old Youngs Bay Bridge that day—reminiscent perhaps of the Frenchman who suddenly appeared with champagne and flutes to welcome astonished Allied soldiers on the beaches of Normandy during D day—was the shadowy shape of a dinghy, barely moving on the calm surface of the bay. Its lone occupant, either foolhardy or simply contemptuous of the battle that had been raging for hours about the river, sat huddled against the chill, rod fishing, his back turned to the bridge.

General Trevor, now in command of all militia surrender south of the bridge but still acutely depressed, lowered the binoculars through which he'd been looking at the river, sighed, and called over to his aide.

"Sir?"

Trevor handed the major a sealed, buff-colored DOD envelope. "If anything should happen to me, I'd like you to make sure this gets to my wife."

Surprised, the major took the letter from the general. "This thing's over, General. Or damn near. Bridge is blown, our second-drop guys are comin' in. Pretty soon we'll be in mop-up mode."

Trevor was only half listening, again looking through his binoculars at Youngs Bay and beyond. "Perhaps the fat lady," he said, "hasn't sung yet."

The major nodded accommodatingly. "You see any fat

lady, General?" he asked in a weak attempt to cajole Trevor out of his moroseness.

Trevor lowered the binoculars again, squinted hard as a burst of sunlight momentarily suffused the mist with a golden light. Without looking at him, the general passed the major the binoculars and began to walk, the major behind him.

"No," Trevor told him, turning. "I need to be alone."

"Yes, sir."

Alarmed, the major didn't know what to do. The general wasn't himself—not since he'd given the order to—

Jesus, he thought, maybe the general was going to shoot himself, but then the major noticed that Trevor didn't have his side holster on. He calmed down but resolved to keep an eye on his boss. Now Trevor could have been mistaken for a tourist from the relaxed way he walked, or rather ambled, along the bridge, stopping only once by the brownish stains where the hostages—the children—had fallen. Walking on, he made his way, hands behind his back, a man finally at peace with himself. He went over to the rail and gazed down on the calm, cobalt-blue water, the bay littered with a surprising amount of debris from the fighting, some of it, he could see, bumping up against the side of the fisherman's—or rather the fisherwoman's—boat about a hundred yards off, her broad summer hat casting a shadow on the water now that the fog had almost completely lifted.

The general, leaning on the rail, hands folded, seemed to be waiting for someone to join him.

The major shoved his submachine-gun strap out of the way and brought up the binoculars to survey the bay. He saw that the fisherwoman was bending down in the boat, sitting up again a moment later with another rod that was partly obscured by her billowing dress but that looked much heavier and shorter. By the time the major realized what was going on, the sniper had fired and Trevor's head was flung back, his body dropping to the deck, his face hitting the cement, expelling his denture.

The major's machine gun was chattering, chopping up the boat and killing Ames, who had, finally, taken his revenge against the child killer.

CHAPTER FORTY-SIX

ACCORDING TO NORTON'S verbal report to Freeman, the other networks were "highly pissed off" that CNN had gotten an exclusive interview with "Lucky" McBride and that it was handled by a reporter, Marte Price, who had *willfully* defied Freeman's ban on members of the press "going into the battle zone near War Creek." Freeman figured Marte Price had deserved the exclusive in return for the trick in which he had used her to spread the then-false rumor of Mant's death, and so he handled this information uncharacteristically, saying, "No comment," and managed to get away with it, because for now at least, he was a winner, a public hero, for being brave enough to go in and, in the words of a *New York Times* editorial, "reassert a central tenet of the Republic, namely, that no American is above the law."

All over the world the hot question on the Internet was whether the skinhead Hearn, alias Rock, would survive for what was already being billed as the trial of the century. It wasn't a question that was bothering Aussie at the moment, however, as he, Brentwood, and Salvini enjoyed two weeks of R&R at Fort Derussy in Hawaii, Aussie assigning marks—from one to ten—to every woman who passed them on Waikiki Beach. David Brentwood was in a more pensive mood, recalling a conversation he'd had sometime before with two federal agents at Pateros, one an FBI agent, Tracy somebody, and a BATF agent called Tony Beck about what would happen to the captured militiamen like this so-called Lucky McBride. The two agents had told him that someday the militias would probably hit back. And hit hard.

"Hey, Aussie?"

"Yeah?" Aussie, his shades on, was watching a blonde that rated an eight-point-five, possibly a nine.

"You think the militias'll retaliate?"

"Is water wet?"

Another blonde walked by. Aussie took off the shades and nodded approvingly. She was a definite ten. Right now he didn't want to think of what might happen if the militias all around the country decided to strike back. Right now he was enjoying himself, the smell of rum and coconut oil in the air, his leg mending nicely, warm in the tropical sun.

IAN SLATER
Don't miss one explosive novel!
Find out which Ian Slater
blockbuster you need.

WWIII
In the Pacific, Russian-made bombers come
in low. In Europe, Russian infantry divisions
strike aircraft and tanks begin to move. All
are pointed toward the Fulda Gap. And World
War III begins....

WWIII:
RAGE OF BATTLE
From beneath the North Atlantic to across the
Korean peninsula, thousands of troops are
massing and war is raging everywhere,
deploying the most stunning armaments ever
seen on any battlefield.

WWIII:
WORLD IN FLAMES
NATO armored divisions have escaped near
defeat in the Russian-ringed North German
Plain. The once formidable Russian assault
falters and NATO forces struggle to end this
worldwide conflagration.

WWIII:
ARCTIC FRONT
In the worst Siberian winter in twenty years,
blizzards are wreaking havoc with U.S. cover,
and it is up to the unorthodox U.S. General
Freeman to hold this arctic front.

WWIII:
WARSHOT
General Cheng is massing divisions on the Manchurian border while Siberia's Marshal Yesov readies his army on the western flank. If successful, this offensive will drive the American-led U.N. force into the sea.

WWIII:
ASIAN FRONT
At Manzhouli, near the border of China, Siberia, and Mongolia, the Chinese launch their charge into the woods. It's all-out war, and only the brave and ruthless will survive.

WWIII:
FORCE OF ARMS
Four sleek Tomahawk cruise missiles are headed for Beijing. It is Armageddon in Asia.

WWIII:
SOUTH CHINA SEA
On the South China Sea an oil rig erupts in flames as AK-47 tracer rounds stitch the night and men die in pools of blood. From Japan to Malaysia, the Pacific Rim is ablaze in a hell called WWIII.

**The World War III series
by Ian Slater
Published by Fawcett Books.
Available in bookstores everywhere.**